Cover design: Jennifer Quinlan
Internal design: Deborah Bradseth

Published by Gallica Press

This is a work of fiction and a product of the author's imagination. Characters and events are either wholly fictitious or, in the case of historic
people and incidents, are used fictitiously. Similarities to real persons,
living or dead, are coincidental and not intended by the author.

The Proposal/Margaret Porter
ISBN 978-0-9907420-9-8

Front cover: *Portrait of Elizabeth Johnson,* c.1780 (oil on canvas), Reyn-
olds, Sir Joshua (1723-92) / Private Collection / Photo © Philip Mould
Ltd, London / Bridgeman Images

Also by Margaret Evans Porter

The Islanders Series
Kissing a Stranger
The Seducer
Improper Advances

Novellas
The Apple Blossom Bower
The Love Spoon

THE PROPOSAL

By

Margaret Evans Porter

GALLICA PRESS

CHAPTER 1

Believe me, noble lord, I am a stranger here in Gloucestershire.
These high wild hills and rough uneven ways
Draws out our miles and makes them wearisome.

~William Shakespeare

January 1797

Drumming her fingers on the window sill, Sophie Pinnock surveyed the busy inn yard scene.

A farmer wearing a smock unloaded milk cans from his cart. A servant girl used a stick to drive a gaggle of noisy geese toward a water trough. The hostler and a post-boy harnessed a pair of horses to the chaise that would carry Sophie on the final leg of her journey. Although she was fully ready to depart, her traveling companion had not appeared. She couldn't leave without him.

His failure to join her for breakfast could mean he was still sulking after last night's quarrel. Riding in a closed carriage with an angry gentleman for a further twenty miles was a dismal prospect, but she must endure it. Sophie's impending interview with the Earl of Bevington marked a new direction in her professional journey. Before today, each prospective client had been a prospective victim. The years of deception had taken their toll, and she was eager to put the dishonesty of the past behind her.

The clock on the wall struck the hour of nine. Moving away from the window, she paced the length of the cramped parlor. Her trailing skirts swept the floor, gathering dust, but she didn't care.

Where was he, what was keeping him?

Another ten minutes ticked away before her partner in fraud entered the room. A gentleman of medium height, he wore his coppery hair in a short, smart crop. His dour expression warned Sophie that he hadn't slept off his ill-temper, and his blue eyes bored into her accusingly.

Spying the portfolio under his arm, she breathed a small sigh of relief. While tossing and fretting the night away, she'd wondered if he might be spiteful enough to destroy its precious contents.

He placed it on the table and set his valise on the floor next to Sophie's *baheur*, the small leather bound trunk she'd brought to England as a bride.

"You look most fetching in green." His harshness sharpened the Scots burr. "It suits your hair and eyes."

"Compliments will gain you nothing, Fingal Moncrieff." She thrust her hand into the pocket tied beneath her skirt and felt for her silver card case, embossed with roses and engraved with her initials. She removed their trade card and held it up. "Remember, Pinnock and Moncrieff is a business partnership.

It will never be anything more." Satisfied that she'd made her point, she returned the card to the case and slid it back into the pocket-hole.

"But I've waited so long already. Your husband died over two years ago."

Did he suppose it had slipped her mind? Losing Tobias had been the one great tragedy of her life.

He seized her hand. "You're but twenty, too young a lass for this endless mourning."

Young she might be, and often lonely, but she preferred widowhood to becoming Mrs. Moncrieff. Her marriage had been based on mutual affection, dependence, and respect. The man standing before her inspired none of those feelings.

"I've discussed my intentions with the Pinnocks. They consent to the match."

"*Naturellement,*" said Sophie bitterly. "My brother-in-law wants the partnership kept intact until his son finishes his schooling and apprenticeship. It's part of their plot to wrest control of the firm from me."

"I could prevent that. As your husband, I'd look out for your interests." He inched closer, until he was much too close for comfort. "Say yes. Don't be so stubborn, Sophia."

No one but Tobias had ever called her by that name.

"You know it's for the best." Moist lips nuzzled her neck. He placed his hand upon her breast.

"*Sécours dé grace!*" she cried in annoyance, wrenching herself out of his embrace. "How many times must I repeat it until you understand? I told you yesterday—last evening— and I tell you now, I cannot be your wife." When he reached for her again, she darted to the opposite side of the table.

"Sophia—"

Picking up one of the rock-hard breakfast rolls, she flung it at his rusty head. "I never gave you permission to be so familiar!"

Furiously he smashed his fist upon the wood, rattling the crockery and cutlery. "Why will you not be reasonable? My expertise as an architect, coupled with your artistic talents, could make us the premier landscape designers in Britain."

"Us?" Sophie repeated incredulously. "If we married, you'd carry on pretending all my sketches were your own, exactly as you've done since the day Tobias died."

"You didn't object."

"I was grieving, and you took advantage of that. You swore it was a temporary measure, and I believed you. You were hoaxing me, as you've hoaxed all our clients."

"With your assistance."

Voicing the suspicion that had nagged her all morning, she said, "When you received Lord Bevington's letter you promised this commission would be all mine, that in future I'd receive full credit for my drawings. You never meant it, did you?"

Clenching his jaw, he retorted, "Now you'll never know."

"What does that mean?"

"If you won't wed me, there's no point taking on new business together. I'm resigning from the partnership." To underscore his statement, he picked up his valise.

Amazement deprived Sophie of both her command of the English language and her native patois—until he snatched up the portfolio. "Leave that. Those designs are mine. *I* created every one of them."

"Nobody knows that but you and me. They bear my signature," he reminded her.

Her heart thudded against her breastbone as she followed him out of the room and down the rickety staircase. *Bouon Dgieu,* she prayed, don't let him take the drawings. This punishment was too severe for the necessary sin of deceiving their clients. None had suffered from it, only herself.

Moncrieff, reaching the front door of the inn, he paused on the threshold and spun around to face her. "I'll ask you once more. Will you—"

"Nou-fait! Never!"

"Then our attorneys will decide which of us should keep these designs. In the meantime, they'll remain with me. After all, you've got copies of the Blue Books."

She watched him cross the inn yard, stepping around the farmer's cart and scattering the geese. As soon as he climbed into the chaise the postilion spurred and whipped his horses. They trotted off at a fast clip, hooves cutting up the mud and making it fly.

Overwhelmed, Sophie dropped onto the hall bench. This catastrophe far exceeded the many smaller disasters that had plagued her since arriving at the Royal Oak.

She'd been drawn to this inn by a notation Tobias had penciled in his well-worn gazetteer, linking it to King Charles II. All her life Sophie had heard legends about the merry monarch, for he'd taken refuge on her island early in his exile from England. But the peppery Scotsman cared nothing for its historic associations and had spoiled her pleasure with his persistent proposals of marriage and his quarrelsome ways.

Now he'd taken her portfolio, and with it a significant portion of her past. Enclosed between its stiff boards was artwork that represented untold hours of painstaking labor. Her design projects were an important connection to her late husband, her greatest solace in the aftermath of his death.

Her initial horror at being deserted—and robbed—was subsiding. No time to sit about and bemoan Moncrieff's treachery. She needed to act, and swiftly.

Hurrying out to the yard, she found the hostler and carter shifting the last of the milk cans. "Have you another chaise for hire?" she asked the hostler breathlessly.

"Nay, lady. Your gentleman has taken the only one."

"He's no gentleman," she contradicted. "And he'll never be mine!" Striving to be heard over his guffaw, she insisted, "I must reach Bevington Castle as soon as possible."

"That's near twenty mile from 'ere."

Said the owner of the cart, in a marked West Country accent, "It's not far off the Bristol road. I'll be traveling that way, ma'am, if it suits you to ride with me."

She could have kissed his leathery cheek. "It does," she assured him before rushing back to the inn to collect her belongings.

A heavy cart pulled by a single shire horse wasn't likely to win a race with a chaise and pair. But Sophie's driver, a man of few words, boasted that he knew the way as well as any post-boy.

"If not better," he added.

"How much farther to the castle?" she asked when he diverted from the principal road. She worried that the narrow, twisting lanes confused him as much as they did her.

"Naught but two mile more. Don't fret, I'll have you there afore yon clouds open up."

The fog occasionally parted to reveal ragged hills, rocky

vales, and remote cottages. But it was thick enough to obscure the distant view of the Severn River and the Welsh hills so glowingly described by the guidebook in Sophie's *baheur.*

Whether or not she reached the castle before Fingal Moncrieff, she intended to transform this apparent defeat into victory. By convincing the earl to hire her as his landscape gardener, she'd bring her lengthy and uncomfortable charade to its desired end. But could she manage it without showing samples of her work? The collection of Blue Books was at her house in Chiswick, too far away to be of use.

Clinging to the side of the cart as the wheels bumped over the ruts, Sophie recalled the more comfortable journeys she'd known during the years as her husband's willing and enthusiastic assistant. With Tobias she'd traveled the country inspecting grand estates and modest suburban villas, taking detailed notes and making sketches. When preparing his designs, he'd sought her advice. And every time one of their collaborations, elegantly bound in indigo leather, was presented to a client, her sense of achievement had matched his.

She understood why he hadn't publicly acknowledged her innovations, and she hadn't wanted him to. Her reward came in those private moments when he praised her for being as clever as she was comely. Unlike his junior partner Moncrieff, he'd never displayed any jealousy of her talent. Quite the contrary, he had nurtured it—purchasing the most expensive materials for her to work with, encouraging her to spend hours at the easel.

Despite the fact that statuesque, azure-eyed blondes were all the rage in artistic circles, not short, auburn-haired females like herself, she'd been his favorite model. Their artistic life had been as rewarding as their domestic one—but both had been tragically brief. In the second year of marriage, they had learned about his illness.

As Tobias's health failed, his dependence on others increased. He relied on his partner to maintain contact with clients, and relinquished all design work to his wife. Whenever Sophie had watched his trembling hand scrawl *Tobias Pinnock* at the bottom of her sketches, she'd felt a sharp but fleeting prick of remorse.

Devotion to a dying husband had deafened her to the cry of her conscience. But Fingal Moncrieff, as ruthless as he was ambitious, had never deserved her cooperation.

The final mile of her journey was uneventful, apart from a near-mishap with a sheep reckless enough to push its way through a gap in the hedge. Sophie's farmer was as good as his word—no sooner had they passed through the quiet village of Bevington than the swirling mist transformed itself into the chilling, driving rain typical of January. He set her down near the church, too cautious to attempt the steep and slippery drive leading up to the castle.

"A gurt big pile, that," he commented. With a cluck and a light slap of the reins, he urged his horse to walk on.

To Sophie's eyes it looked like a larger version of Gorey Castle in Jersey and was built from a similarly reddish stone. Studying that daunting expanse of crenellated walls and towers, she wondered what sort of man occupied this fortress.

In the course of her travels she'd encountered several marquesses, three dukes, and on one memorable occasion, a royal princess—and every one outranked an earl. She had no cause for nervousness, she need but summon that calm confidence Tobias had always displayed when calling on prospective employers. But he'd been famous, his services in high demand. She lacked a reputation as landscape designer because she'd always used her talents to bolster her husband's. And Moncrieff's.

The memory of his betrayal roused her courage. She shifted the *baheur* to her hip and brushed at the straw clinging to her green pelisse, assuring herself that this Lord Bevington was about to become the first of her many satisfied clients.

She followed the long avenue of oaks to a plain stone archway similar in shape to the Norman ones common on her island. Farther on she passed beneath the breezeway of an inner gatehouse, and came to a spacious, stone-paved court.

Where was the entrance? Perplexed by so many projecting towers with arched doors, Sophie halted. At last she settled on a wooden, nail-studded portal framed by a clinging vine.

At her approach, it swung open with a squeal of hinges. A young man stepped out, urging her forward with a welcoming smile. His complexion was exotically dark and his hair quite damp—he, too had been rained upon.

"How may I serve, senhora?"

Handing over her trade card, she explained that she'd come at Lord Bevington's request.

"I tell him right away. Follow me, *por favor*—I take your box. *O carregador*, the carrier, he deliver these today," the foreigner informed her as they stepped around the collection of wooden crates cluttering the vestibule. "Senhorio worry his fine chairs and tables for the large drawing room take harm by coming so far in bad weather."

Sophie spied the legend *Ince and Mayhew* stamped on a large canvas-wrapped object. The earl had ordered his new furniture from the most fashionable and expensive of London's cabinet-makers.

"Has Mr. Moncrieff arrived yet?"

"Mon Creeve?" The young man shook his head. "No, senhora."

Her hopes for a successful interview soared. If her rival was lost somewhere in the wilds of Gloucestershire, she had a better chance of winning this commission for herself.

The servant led her through a great hall with a high ceiling supported by vaulted timbers, cathedral-like windows, and a stone fireplace at the far end. Beyond an arched opening lay a wooden staircase of unmistakable antiquity.

He ushered her up the stairs to a chamber decorated with tapestries and a worn Turkish rug. "I go find senhorio and leave you here in morning room—even though is now afternoon," he said, his parting grin showing his fine white teeth.

Although thankful to be indoors, she regretted the lack of a fire. Her limbs ached with cold. Five years in England, and still she was unaccustomed to winter's chill.

To warm herself she walked up and down the length of the room. She craned her neck to read the words inscribed on the painted wooden ceiling, and was surprised to recognize them as Norman French, from which her own Jèrriais language had evolved. She examined the allegorical scenes depicted in the wall hangings. Pausing before a mirror, she discovered that the raindrops had imprinted a haphazard pattern of dark spots on her pelisse. The sleek black feathers tucked into her bonnet sagged with damp.

Masculine tones from the corridor sent her to a more strategic position at the window. She stared intently down at the landscape requiring improvement, and her optimism ebbed at the sight of terraced walks and walled gardens. Three little bridges spanned a long central canal, and beyond stood a two-story structure with large windows overlooking the gardens.

Closing her eyes to shut out the view, she pressed her forehead against one cold, diamond-shaped pane.

Nânnîn, she thought. No. Not again. Not here, too.

"A dismal prospect, isn't it?"

Sophie turned away from the fearsome vista. She'd imagined a much older, less attractive earl—this man couldn't be more than thirty and was outrageously handsome. His hair was black and waving, his eyes quite blue. He towered above her, and his figure was as well-formed as it was tall. Staring up at him in mute amazement, she couldn't remember if she was supposed to extend her hand or curtsy to a man of title.

"What has Luis done with the gentleman?"

"There is no gentleman," she blurted.

"Oh? I've been corresponding with someone called Fingal Moncrieff, and that can't possibly be you."

"Mr. Moncrieff recently resigned." She preferred not to reveal quite how recently.

He frowned down at the card he was holding. "And what of Mr. Pinnock?"

Her breath caught in her throat, then emerged as a sigh. "My husband died two years ago."

"Pray accept my belated condolences." It was a perfunctory civility, and to her ear devoid of true sympathy. Again he glanced at her card. "Did you come all the way from Chiswick to announce that the firm of Pinnock and Moncrieff is no more? A letter would have sufficed."

Head high, her shoulders squared, Sophie announced, "I am a landscape gardener myself. My husband trained me—I was his apprentice. His assistant, really."

The earl's sharply suspicious stare was a dagger slicing

through her confidence. Sophie was tempted to claim sole responsibility for the many well-known designs attributed to Tobias in the months before his death, but she couldn't bring herself to betray him.

Choosing instead to sacrifice Fingal Moncrieff, she continued, "My partner—my *former* partner—takes credit for the plans I've produced since my husband's death. I'll not trouble you with the details except to say that when Mr. Moncrieff represented himself to you as a landscape artist, he did so falsely. He is merely an architect."

"I have no great need of him," he responded with a careless shrug. "All the top men have been 'round to look the place over. Humphry Repton. Samuel Lapidge. William Emes. John Webb. Some other chap, his name escapes me."

"Adam Mickle?"

The earl's dark head moved up and down.

She seized upon the valuable clue about the type of design he wanted. All the gentlemen he'd named were noted for their highly picturesque landscapes.

"You must not be altogether satisfied," she ventured, "or you wouldn't have sent for Pinnock and Moncrieff. After conferring with your lordship and touring the grounds, I shall devise a landscape in the most modern style. You'll receive watercolor drawings and other renderings, with a list of suitable shrubs and trees. All of which will be bound into a blue leather cover with Bevington Castle and your title stamped on the front. In gold letters."

"I've already received a Red Book from Repton."

"Who poached that idea from my husband." Modifying her acid tone, Sophie went on, "Mr. Repton has an instructive style. I say nothing against it. But I doubt he presented you with more than a few pretty aquatints. I can supply the more detailed information required by a clerk of the works."

Displeasure had deepened the crease between his inky brows. "This debate is quite unnecessary."

"Because I'm a female?" She scarcely recognized the strained voice as her own.

"I intend to make extensive alterations. I also expect the person I employ to supervise the entire project. You cannot abandon your children for weeks on end."

"I haven't any children."

He looked down his nose at her for some time, then moved purposefully to the door and called for his servant.

Sophie rained silent *malédictions* upon the head of that *vilain* Fingal Moncrieff. If she could show her portfolio, the earl wouldn't be turning her away with such disheartening abruptness.

"Luis, this lady will take tea before she goes. Tell Mr. Searle that I'll join him in the library as soon as I'm able."

And she called upon *lé dgiâbl'ye*—the devil—to punish this cold-hearted wretch of an earl for refusing to accept that her skill was equal to Humphry Repton's. He lacked the common courtesy, and the fairness, to consider her credentials or her merits. She was a woman, so he was offering her a cup of tea she didn't even want instead of the employment she so desperately desired.

The Countess of Bevington would surely have been a more sympathetic listener, for noblewomen had the leisure to study horticulture and often had strong opinions about the arrangement of their gardens. But it hardly mattered, for this proud and lordly fellow would never permit his wife's interference.

Lord Bevington's great height made her self-conscious about her lack of inches. Tipping back her head, she reminded him of his promise to reimburse her travel expenses.

"Yes, of course," he agreed, with a haste that told her he'd pay any amount just to be rid of her. "Tell Luis what you want, and he'll get cash from the strongbox. I must go now, Madam. Another visitor waits."

Sophie was determined to make her escape before Moncrieff arrived, wanting no witness to her humiliation. She retrieved her *baheur* from the chair where she'd left it and rushed out of the morning room. At the foot of the great staircase she nearly collided with the earl's swarthy manservant.

"Is for you, senhora," he said, holding up his tray. "Tea and cakes."

"I cannot stay."

"But you are wanting to see gardens, is why you come. I take you out, is no raining now." He placed the tray on a hall table shrouded in white cloth.

Reluctantly Sophie went with him across the courtyard and through the shadowed breezeway. Halfway between the gatehouse and the outer arch was a set of stone steps leading to the uppermost terrace. The grassy path was strewn with damp leaves; dead stalks littered the unkempt borders on either side. Here and there Sophie spied small green shoots of the earliest blooming bulbs, bravely struggling to rise from the debris.

"Your little trunk safe here." Luis placed her *baheur* on a step. After pointing out the way to the walled gardens farther down, he excused himself to fetch her money.

Sophie was tempted to flee before he came back. But curiosity won out over her eagerness to depart.

Another set of steps descended to a lower terrace paved

in stone and edged with lavender. A favorite of hers, so she brazenly plucked a silver-green sprig and inhaled the familiar, soothing scent.

Farther down she found a rectangular lawn enclosed by a tall, unruly hedge on one side and an ivied wall on the other. A long tunnel of mature laburnums, their naked branches trained over an arbor, brought her to the first of the three walled sections she'd viewed from the morning room window. There was a shrubbery walk with large and misshapen clumps of yew—neglected topiaries.

She followed a paved walk along the waterway to an adjacent garden planted with shrub roses and climbers. Bare, thorny canes rambled along the stone walls or clung to supporting trellises. The French influence was very strong here. In summer, she thought, this would be a bower of blossoms as depicted in paintings by Fragonard and Boucher.

A dun-colored dog was frantically digging in a border. She must scent a mole or vole, for the many burrows and breaks in the ragged lawn indicated their presence. A lean and leggy female, she had a head shaped like a greyhound's and the rougher coat of a herding breed.

"For shame," Sophie scolded.

The animal looked up.

When it raced over to greet her, she stroked the pointed, dirt-crusted muzzle. "On my island we would call you *un tchian mêlé*. A mongrel."

Her explorations took her next to a series of intricate knot gardens, the patterns nearly ruined from lack of attention. As she strolled the circular paths, her new friend trotted over to the canal to lap the murky water. Creeping under the open porch of the viewing pavilion, Sophie peered through a grimy window at an empty bathing pool within.

With the dog bounding and prancing at her heels she retraced her steps. Luis was waiting for her in the shrubbery walk.

"Are no gardeners employed at Bevington?" she asked him. "Judging from their growth, these yews haven't been trimmed for two years or more."

"Since senhorio come to live in England, he spend money for inside castle only. His sister, Senhora Fonseca, say is no reason to keep up gardens being soon destroyed. All here is to be made different." Shaking his head, he added mournfully, "I wish it not."

"That is the way of things," she told him, concealing her own regret.

"In England, *sim*. Would not happen in Portugal, my country."

"Nor in mine."

In Uncle Edouard's Anneville Manor garden, the subject of her earliest sketches and watercolors, her childhood love of flowering plants had flourished. Even in her youth she'd admired formal landscaping, nowadays criticized as unnatural and undesirable.

Let someone else destroy this gem of the antique style, she thought bleakly. It was not a task she would relish.

"You are not *inglês*?" Luis asked as they ascended the terrace steps, the mongrel charging ahead of them.

"By marriage only." She was too weary and heartsick to offer a detailed explanation of Jersey's singular status as an independent possession of the British crown.

"Your *esposo,* he let you travel without him?"

"I'm a widow," she explained. "Does Lady Bevington

approve of the earl's plan to alter the grounds?"

"Is no senhoria." When they reached the outer gate, Luis handed over a fistful of banknotes.

"You're very kind," said Sophie.

The sweetness of his smile cheered her a little when he said, "*De nada.* Stay," he commanded, his hand curling upon the dog's collar. "She no want you to go away." He bent down to murmur in the animal's ear, "Perhaps senhora come back to us one day."

But Sophie had no desire to return. Bevington Castle was a sad and gloomy place, and without flower gardens it would be far worse.

Retreating down the avenue of ancient, stately oaks, she mourned their inevitable demise. Humphry Repton would surely fell the lot of them.

⟡

Cassian Carysfort watched the tiny figure in green grow ever smaller. When it vanished over the crest of his sloping drive, he turned around to find his friend and tenant, Andrew Searle, sprawled upon a burgundy leather armchair.

"The lady must've been quite a charmer, Cass. If I'd known you were going to ignore me, I wouldn't have tramped across your deer park—in a driving rain, I might add—to call upon you."

"You didn't come to see me," Cass retorted. "You wanted to borrow one of my books."

The library was one of the few rooms that the late Lord Bevington had maintained in a style befitting his rank. Cass had made no changes here, apart from giving orders that the vast collection of calf-bound volumes be taken down from the shelves and dusted. He hadn't yet decided whether to remove the portrait of his predecessor, an overdressed chap in a curly wig who gazed serenely upon a young gardener planting a rose tree.

"A beauteous unprotected widow," his friend continued, "seeking your patronage. If you made no attempt to ravish her, you're a disgrace to your title."

With a laugh, he said, "I don't dispute that. I'm naught but an upstart earl, whose claim to all these dignities was so remote that it took more than a year for the lawyers to prove me the rightful heir."

Andrew ran ink-stained fingers through his shaggy, honey-brown locks. "Never did I guess when we were Bristol schoolboys that someday you'd live at Bevington Castle."

"Neither did I," Cass admitted. "But I don't live here yet."

Luis materialized in the doorway. "*Excelência,* is a gentleman here to see you. Senhor Mon Creeve."

"Moncrieff?"

The servant nodded vigorously.

Lifting his brows, Cass murmured, "An unexpected development. Yes, I'll receive him."

The gentleman whose abilities the Widow Pinnock had disparaged was singularly unimpressive. His bow lacked polish, and his Scots brogue was thicker than the fog outside when he said, "Lord Bevington, I pray my lack of punctuality hasn't offended you. I was misled by an unreliable postilion."

"I didn't specify an hour for our meeting, merely the day. Mr. Moncrieff, I present to you Andrew Searle, a poet of increasing repute." And decreasing sobriety, added Cass silently, troubled by his old schoolmate's bloodshot eyes and droopy lids.

The Scotsman nodded. "Honored, sir. Now then, my lord, I have here examples of my completed works. Shall I lay them out for your examination?"

"By all means."

Moncrieff opened his portfolio and spread several sheets across the desktop. "My designs for the Marquess of Gillingham's seat at Evensloe. In order to add picturesque features to the landscape, we chose to—that is, I personally advised him to eliminate the parterres and fill in the empty space with earth and turf. I also suggested planting these well-spaced trees in the near distance. His lordship was vastly pleased with the result."

Cass nodded absently.

According to the Widow Pinnock, Moncrieff had resigned from the firm. Presumably he'd traveled here to compete against her for the commission. A risky stratagem indeed, if the lady was the artist responsible for all these excellent drawings. He'd brought an endless supply, and Cass had ample time to look them over during his visitor's long-winded presentation.

"This is my plan for the grounds of Sir Antony Conway's Italianate villa near Roehampton. At my recommendation, firs and cedars were grouped to resemble the views painted by Claude of Lorrain."

"The designs bear your signature," he observed. "What contribution did your partner make?"

Moncrieff flushed. "I'm solely responsible for all designs. The late Mr. Pinnock," he said stiffly, "was merely a figurehead, whose taste and methods I oftentimes questioned." Abruptly gathering up several pictures, he uncovered a watercolor of a flower-filled border.

Cass picked it up. Drawn by a female hand—blunt, businesslike Moncrieff couldn't possibly be capable of such fine, delicate brushwork. The initials at the bottom confirmed his impression. Pointing at them, he asked, "Have you an apprentice, Mr. Moncrieff?"

"That sketch belongs in a different file." The Scotsman tugged at the picture so forcefully that it tore.

Definitely not his creation, thought Cass.

Moncrieff offered an architectural rendering in exchange, and said a shade too heartily, "You'll want to see this Temple of Adonis I created for Mr. Hamish Renfrew of Aberdeen."

"Exemplary. Now, sir, let me show you this." Cass opened a desk drawer and removed a thin, rectangular volume bound in red leather. "Humphry Repton produced this plan. Can you devise a better one?"

While Moncrieff paged through the Red Book, Cass exchanged glances with Andrew, who seemed puzzled by his cavalier treatment of the landscape gardener.

"Mr. Repton," said Moncrieff reverently, "is a master. He prudently elects to fell the avenue of oaks, as any man of taste would do. I cannot argue with his choice to demolish the antiquated walled gardens and replace the canal with a meandering stream. Yet I believe my own firm will serve your lordship far better."

"Your firm," Cass repeated. "I understand your partner has died. Will the enterprise continue to bear his name?"

"Not for long. As soon as his widow becomes my wife, I shall make the necessary change."

Marriage? The lady had not only testified to a rift, she'd made clear her disdain for Mr. Moncrieff. Recalling her earnestness, the hint of vulnerability about her mouth, and the steady gaze of her fine brown eyes, Cass chose not to believe anything this man told him.

Andrew Searle's sleepy voice called him out of his reverie. "Cass, didn't you say the vicar was expecting you on the half-hour?"

The words were no sooner out than the long-case clock in the corner chimed a single long note.

"Quite right," he said, rewarding his shamelessly untruthful friend with a smile. "Mr. Moncrieff, I regret I cannot review your past triumphs more thoroughly. If you leave your card, I'll inform you as soon as I've made my decision."

"I neglected to bring any cards with me. But I have many more drawings. I would most gladly return later in the day. Or even tomorrow."

"I'm off to London in the morning." It was no lie.

Unlike Mrs. Pinnock, Fingal Moncrieff accepted his dismissal without argument or demands for money. He gathered up the sketches and replaced them in the portfolio. With another bow, even stiffer than his first, he exited the library.

"I do believe," Cass commented to his friend, "that I'm now acquainted with every garden designer in the land. I've gazed at enough pictures to fill a gallery. But I'll be damned if I can say which one of these fellows is most capable of satisfying me."

"If it's satisfaction you crave, look to the lady."

Cass shook his head, in no mood to be teased.

He remembered the little widow's boast that she was more capable than any of the gentlemen he'd summoned to his castle. His inability to banish her lively image from his mind—hair the color of warmest mahogany, almond-shaped brown eyes, a complexion like a lily, rose-petal lips—didn't mean he wanted her for his landscape gardener. And he refused to be swayed into a foolish decision by the fact that she was, undeniably, by far the most attractive of the many applicants for the position.

CHAPTER 2

But elegance, chief grace the garden shows,
And most attractive, is the fair result
Of thought, the creature of a polished mind.

~ William Cowper

$\mathcal{C}$ass wondered how soon he could wrest himself from Balthasar Prowdie's feeble clutch. When handed a paper to sign, he scrawled his name in haste with the quill, and watched impatiently as the old man replaced it in an elongated black tin document box marked *Bevington*.

Closing the lid, the elderly solicitor quavered, "Now that our business is done, I'd be honored if your lordship stayed to share my dinner."

Civility—and pity—forced Cass to accept the invitation. Poor old Prowdie lived alone above his Arundel Street chambers. His clients, every one of them a fossil, were expiring daily.

A doddering manservant, even more aged and infirm than his master, waited at table. After sampling the dishes that made up the first course, Cass discovered that his host was no epicure. He struggled with a single slice of tough beef, a pudding as tasteless as the bag in which it had been boiled, and a wine of middling quality. The attorney's dull and pedantic conversation in no way compensated for the unpalatable meal.

Eventually the butler shuffled out of the room, leaving behind a bowl of fruit long past its prime. Mr. Prowdie reached for an orange with a hand that was no less yellowed and wrinkled than those parchments he'd reviewed with Cass before dinner.

"Have I told your lordship about the late Lord Bevington's attempt to interest me in gardening?"

Cass steeled himself for another boring tale about the stranger whose property and title he now possessed. "Not that I recall."

"His effort was wasted, for I'm a city-bred man. But my good wife, when she lived, had a fondness for flowers. Every day she sent a servant to Covent Garden market to buy up great bunches of 'em. They always made me sneeze." Hunching forward, the lawyer fixed rheumy eyes upon him. "What become of that Welshman, d'you know?"

"What Welshman would that be, sir?"

"Lord Bevington's gardener. Emrys Jones was the name. Occupied a cottage *ornée* somewhere on the grounds and may still, for aught I know."

"There's a new tenant now," Cass reminded him, "my friend Mr. Searle. I've never heard of this man Jones. But I visit the castle infrequently."

"You surely recall from reading his lordship's will that Jones received a generous annuity and a dwelling in the village. A reward for services quite unrelated to weeding the borders and filling 'em with plants. I'll not go into the particulars except to say that the relations between Lord Bevington and this Welshman were, in a word, peculiar. They were discreet, but I've no doubt whatever that their intimacy was the sort which all men most abhor, a gross offense against nature. If not for that stain upon the earl's honor, I might have esteemed him greatly."

So old Bevington had been a molly. Cass had wondered about his predecessor's prolonged bachelorhood and lack of an heir. If Prowdie, sitting here in London, had guessed the shameful secret, the castle servants and the village folk probably knew it also. Yet none had given Cass any cause to suspect the truth.

When the solicitor continued his droning reminiscences about the late earl, Cass's thoughts shifted from the subject of the Welsh gardener to his own search for a landscape designer. He was annoyed that the firm of Pinnock and Moncrieff was in disarray; it had a reputation for reliability and innovation. On his way into town yesterday, Cass had very nearly halted at Chiswick to find out if the pretty widow and her brusque Scotsman had patched up their differences.

After draining the last bitter drop of wine from his glass, he declared, "I've imposed upon your hospitality too long, sir."

"Must you go so soon?" Prowdie asked mournfully. "I have a bottle of port."

Cass barely repressed a shudder. The wine still tortured his tongue, raising doubts about whatever else lay in his host's cellar. His family associations and his years in Portugal made him extremely particular about port. "If I didn't have to leave London tonight—but I really must be on my way. My sister expects me tomorrow, and she's the sort to worry over any delay."

"Determined to hide yourself away in Gloucestershire, aren't you? Ah, well, the last earl was much the same." The attorney shook his bewigged head in disapproval. "But he had much to fear from living in the world. You do not."

Cass could have refuted that assumption but preferred not to.

Within minutes he was hurrying through the falling snow toward the Strand, where his carriage waited. The Bevington coat of arms had been painted on the door so recently that the colors glistened: a quartered heraldic shield of gold and sable, supported by a pair of stags with collars of roses encircling their necks.

The driver, warming his hands over a street vendor's brazier, popped one last chestnut into his mouth and sauntered over to the coach. Still chewing, he reported, "I walked your lordship's horses up and down till their hooves nearly dropped off."

"You didn't tire them out, I trust. I mean to go as far as the Red Lion at Henley tonight. What's become of Luis?"

"I s'pose he wandered 'cross the way to water the side of a building."

Moving to the rear of the vehicle to check that his portmanteau was securely strapped on, Cass noticed three shadowy figures standing just beyond the street lamp. One wore a low-crowned hat, its round brim pulled down to hide his face. The second, a tall individual in livery, held a struggling Luis Costa by the arm and brandished a cudgel.

"Release him!" Cass commanded.

The man in the hat stepped into the light, saying, "Ah, Carysfort, here at last." An ugly scar puckered his right cheek.

Observing his handiwork, Cass could still picture the blood

seeping from the fresh wound, the shattered bone visible beneath the torn flesh. He remembered the blustery dawn when he'd stood on Hounslow Heath, a smoking pistol at his side, uncertain whether Sir Michael Tait would live or die.

"But I ought to call you Bevington now," said the baronet. "Be not alarmed, I come in peace."

"Your companion carries a truncheon."

"Merely a precaution. There are footpads about."

"That's why my coachman is armed," said Cass as a warning. "Luis, on the other hand, is not so bloodthirsty and poses no threat to you."

"Let him go," Tait barked.

The Portuguese youth hurried to his side. "I sorry, senhorio," he panted. "They take me when I walk away from *coche*."

"You've done nothing wrong," Cass assured Luis. "It's all a misunderstanding."

In fact, this was something far more sinister but he couldn't be sure exactly what. He knew only that the meeting hadn't occurred by chance. Advising Luis to wait for him inside the vehicle, he turned to the baronet and asked, in a voice sharpened by mistrust, "How did you find out I was in London?"

"I spotted you walking along Bond Street this afternoon. Your appearance has changed very little these seven years. I'm hardly surprised by your failure to recognize me. My divorce was a greater scandal than our duel, and both left me a wreck of a man."

Cass remembered when Sir Michael Tait's eyes had flashed with arrogance, and his body had been firm and muscular. Shocked though he was by his enemy's thin, wasted frame and damaged face, he had no sympathy to spare. "I don't give a damn about your misfortunes. You brought them on yourself."

"What of Cecelia, is she so heartless?"

Rage boiled, spilling over. He lunged at Tait, thrusting him backward against the iron lamppost. The footman took a step forward and waved his stick, but Cass ignored him. "You aren't fit to speak my sister's name," he growled. "And you'll leave her alone. Let her mourn her husband in peace."

"Husband?"

"She married within months of our arrival in Lisbon." Cass took perverse pleasure in the baronet's dismay.

"I didn't know. I've had no news of her since you dragged her away to share your exile. Where is she now?"

"That's no concern of yours."

"I must see her."

"Trust me, you won't."

"I feared you'd be unreasonable," said Tait bitterly, reaching into his coat pocket. "You always were. I've written a letter. Will you take it to her, wherever she is? When she learns what agonies I've suffered—"

"Hand it over and be quick about it. My horses have already stood too long in the night air and the snow."

The letter was thick and heavy. It felt like a hot coal in his gloved hand.

Cass turned and went back to his carriage. He didn't hesitate to expose his back to his adversary; with so many witnesses, Tait wouldn't dare slip a knife between his shoulder blades.

He climbed inside and sat down. Luis was still rubbing his arm. When Cass asked if he'd been badly hurt, he shook his head in vigorous denial.

"Tell me exactly what happened."

"I go to stretch my legs. Those men, they come up to ask questions—where the earl is staying, do he bring his sister? I no give answers. I speak only the Portuguese, senhorio, just as you tell me to."

"*Muito bem.*" As the carriage rolled along the broad thoroughfare towards Charing Cross, Cass leaned his head against the leather seat.

Although Sir Michael Tait had proved dangerous in the past, he'd detected no real menace in him tonight. Had their battle truly ended on dueling ground?

He ran his thumb across the disk of red wax that sealed the letter. There was no writing on the outside to identify the intended recipient. "Luis, lower the window."

When the valet had carried out his impetuous command, Cass pitched the baronet's unopened missive into the icy street like the scrap of rubbish that it was.

Sophie touched a tiny star-shaped flower, leaning forward to breathe in the sweet, heady fragrance of the hyacinth. For weeks she'd watched the bulb as its roots descended and the leaves grew and the stalk rose ever higher. Now it was in full bloom, pink and highly perfumed, a much-needed glimpse of spring in the midst of winter.

She untied the loose knot of her fichu and peeled it from her shoulders. Her ash-colored gown was made of wool, and the oil lamp on her work table put out as much heat as it did light. After making a minor adjustment to the specimen in the hyacinth glass, she picked up her paintbrush and gently dragged it across her drawing paper to deepen the green of the stem.

Botanical illustrations were less profitable than landscape

designs, but she could complete one in a matter of hours. In the peace and privacy of her own home. Without interference from a male partner.

The slamming of the front door and the thump of the bolt being secured shattered Sophie's concentration.

"Men!" sputtered her housekeeper, drawing the curtains. "They cannot do a thing without making a stir. If you mean to sit up much longer, ma'am, I'll nudge the coals."

Briefly squeezing her eyes shut, Sophie answered, "I'll soon be done. You and William can go to bed now."

"Aye, and so should you," said the motherly woman before leaving the parlor.

One more leaf, Sophie encouraged herself. She pressed the tip of her brush against the green chip in her paint box.

At last she finished, and with a defiant flourish signed her own initials beside her completed watercolor. Never again would Fingal Moncrieff falsely claim her artistry.

Lack of employment had turned the blustering Scottish lion as meek as a Highland lamb. He'd called upon her yesterday, ostensibly to beg pardon for his behavior in Cirencester. His ulterior purpose had been to dissuade her from severing the partnership. She smiled, recalling how shocked he'd been by her decision to carry on without him. She'd derived considerable pleasure from pointing out that she wouldn't be the first widow to take over the management of her late husband's business. Had he ever, she'd inquired, counted the number of distilleries and printing presses and theatrical companies headed by a female proprietor?

For two years she'd lived quietly at the Chiswick villa she'd inherited from Tobias, producing plans for her associate to sign and present to clients. The time had come to prove that she, not Fingal Moncrieff, had absorbed the Pinnock genius and was the master's rightful successor.

When she finished washing out her brushes in a saucer of water, she closed them away in the shagreen paint box Tobias had given her, with handle and lock and hinges of gleaming silver. She wiped her hands on a cloth, then pressed her fingers against her throbbing temples and rubbed hard. At last she rose from her chair—slowly and stiffly, for she'd scarcely moved in the past hour.

Before she extinguished the lamp she heard the unmistakable sound of horseshoes and carriage wheels churning the gravel drive. Moments later there was a rap on the door.

By the time she reached the entrance hall, both Redmonds had emerged from their room, Mary in her nightgown and stocking feet, a shawl draped about her stout person, and a barefooted William in his long shirt, chamber-stick in hand.

He peered suspiciously through one of the sidelights framing the door. "Who goes there?"

"Bevington."

Sophie drew a sharp, surprised breath.

"Shall I warn him off, ma'am?"

"That's not necessary." Meeting Mary's astonished stare, she explained hastily, "He comes on business. You may both return to your room."

"We'll not slumber till we know he's gone," William grumbled. "Come along, woman." Hooking his wife's arm in his, he led her back down the corridor.

Sophie slipped the bolt and opened the door to find the earl's imposing figure looming tall in the darkness, draped in a gray garrick overcoat with gold buttons as big and bright as guinea coins.

"I had the devil's own time finding this place."

No apology for disturbing her so late!

Her temper flickered, then blazed high and hot when he strode past her, his long coat billowing behind him. Without being invited, he took it off and casually tossed it onto an upholstered hall bench. Fighting the urge to order him off the premises, she led him to her parlor.

Prowling the perimeter of the room, he reminded her of a great black panther she'd once seen at an exhibition. She detected a tenseness in him and he looked as if he would erupt into violence if crossed.

He paused before the oil portrait of Tobias. "Your famous husband? I imagined him to be an older man."

"He died at thirty-two." She went back to tidying her drawing table, intentionally repaying his rudeness in kind.

While he continued his exploratory circuit, she hoped he was noticing that her Chippendale chairs and settee were in the best taste, covered in rose damask to complement the dominant hue of the Persian rug. A gilt-framed chimney glass filled the space above the mantel, and landscape paintings in the style of Claude of Lorrain decorated the walls.

His long stride brought him to her table. "What project is this?"

She passed him her watercolor of the hyacinth. "It's still damp," she cautioned.

While he studied it, she was able to study him. Her artist's eye traced the chiseled lines of his face, moving downward from the broad brow to his lean jaw, ever so slightly shaded with a growth of beard. He had pleasingly sculpted cheekbones and his nose was perfectly straight. What a magnificent model he would make, she thought, provided he could sit still long enough for his likeness to be taken.

"You do have a gift, Madam."

"I had an excellent master. When I began to study drawing, flowers were the subjects most readily available. My Uncle Edouard Nicolle, Seigneur of Anneville, is a keen gardener and renowned as a plantsman."

"You're French?"

"I spent my entire life, save the past five years, on Jersey," she clarified. "Mr. Pinnock came to the island one summer at my uncle's invitation. I painted the horticultural specimens he collected during his visit."

"And he added you to his collection." He regarded her in brooding silence before saying, "I am English-born myself, but for many years I lived abroad."

"In Portugal. Your manservant told me."

His tone was guarded when he asked, "Did he reveal anything else about my family?"

"Not that I recall. Is Luis the keeper of your darkest secrets?"

"He is my valet, Mrs. Pinnock." He glanced again at the drawing and muttered inscrutably, "Just as I suspected, it was your cipher. What does the first initial signify?"

"So-*phie,*" she answered, giving the proper inflection. "My husband always called me Sophia."

"Unusual. It's generally the other way 'round."

She bristled at his designating Tobias as odd; her objection to having her name Anglicized had faded long ago. "You've not descended upon Chiswick at this late hour to discuss botanical illustration," she hazarded, taking back her watercolor. "Why *are* you here?"

"To resume the interview begun several days ago. After you left Bevington, Mr. Moncrieff put in an appearance." He narrowed his eyes. "That surprises you?"

"He neglected to mention it."

"You remain partners?"

"*Nânnîn.*" With a smile, she added, "I'm no longer afflicted by the Scottish curse."

"I see." After a pause, he asked, "Do you keep any port? I rather fancy a glass."

"My servants have retired for the night," she said pointedly. "I'll have to fetch it myself." She lifted the lamp from her table.

Reaching out to take it, he said, "Allow me."

Sophie proceeded to the dining room, and the belatedly chivalrous earl followed close behind with the light. Going to the rosewood cellaret, she knelt down. "Lower, please," she instructed, turning the tasseled key in the lock. She opened the door and felt about for the cut-glass decanter and a glass, then placed them on the sideboard.

Her hand quivered as she withdrew the stopper. His nearness made her feel twitchy—and wary. She trusted this arrogant nobleman even less than she liked him, which was to say not at all. And she regretted discarding her fichu, for her low neckline exposed entirely too much of her chest.

They returned to the parlor. Sophie's visitor took his wineglass to the settee. Too uneasy to sit, she drifted over to the fireplace. Lifting the top of a porcelain potpourri vase on the mantel, she raked her fingers through the dried petals of last summer's roses.

After his first sip Lord Bevington commented, "A quality vintage." Amusement softened his voice—and his expression—when he said, "You wish I'd go away, don't you?"

Bearing in mind that this exasperatingly perceptive man was still a prospective client, she composed a careful reply. "I hope

I haven't given that impression, my lord. I'm unaccustomed to receiving evening guests. Certainly not aristocratic ones."

"You needn't assign so much value to my title. I was born a commoner."

His revelation startled her. If any man had been born to command, she thought, it was the one lounging on her settee.

"What's more, my background is mercantile. My mother's relatives owned plantations in the West Indies, and the Carysforts of Bristol were active in the Portuguese wine trade. My sister and I received many painful lessons in class distinctions while being educated at English boarding schools."

He was forcing her to revise her opinion of him. She had difficulty imagining him as a schoolboy, much less one who'd been tormented about his humble origins.

"A few months after I came age," he went on, staring at the twisted stem of the wine glass, "our parents died of a tropical fever. My first independent act was to rescue my sister from her academy in Bath and take her to London. Wealth opened many doors to us, but we were too closely associated with trade to be welcomed into the upper echelons. The lack of invitations to fashionable balls and routs troubled me very little, but Cecelia suffered enormously. Females are more sensitive about their social status. Or lack of it."

Sophie confirmed this with a nod. When she'd arrived in England as the bride of a professional man, she'd learned that merchants and tradesmen were not treated as respectfully as in Jersey. Her Nicolle pride had occasionally been stung by the condescension of a highborn client, or his wife.

"After receiving numerous slights during that unhappy year, my sister and I deserted soggy London for sunny Lisbon. She found herself a husband there, a gentleman from Sintra."

He did not strike her as a confiding sort of man, and she wondered why he'd chosen to reveal so much of his history. She didn't flatter herself that he wanted her to like him. Perhaps he meant merely to allay her antagonism.

"Why," she asked, "did you return to England if neither you nor your sister care for it?"

"Because I inherited—quite by accident and most unexpectedly—the earldom and the estate entailed upon it. Old Lord Bevington was the last twig from a branch of Carysforts ennobled many centuries ago. The direct male line died with him. An army of lawyers traced the family pedigree all the way back to the seventeen hundreds and determined that I was the rightful heir to his property and title."

"What a stroke of good fortune," Sophie marveled.

His lips curled derisively. "It wasn't till I arrived in Gloucestershire to claim my birthright that I discovered the great trick fate has played. My tenants at Bevington graze cattle and make cheese, and the rents are low compared to more productive farming districts. My castle is a drafty ruin. Because my predecessor contributed no money to its upkeep or embellishment, I've spent the better part of a year making it habitable. For my sister's comfort, I was obliged to purchase a town house in Clifton, near Bristol Hotwells. Her physician believes a regular dose of the mineral waters will benefit her."

If only, thought Sophie, the doctors had been able to prescribe a cure for Tobias. But no medicine yet known could strengthen a failing heart.

"Having now spent a fortune refurbishing the interior of my castle, I am eager to improve its setting."

At last he'd touched upon the topic that most concerned Sophie. Her pulses raced in anticipation, even as she warned herself not to hope.

"Mrs. Pinnock, the position of landscape gardener remains open. If you still wish to be considered a candidate, you'd better show me those Blue Books of yours."

She crossed to the glass-fronted mahogany bookcase displaying the entire collection. Determined to impress him with the designs she'd produced herself, she gathered up the most recent editions and carried them to the settee.

"Not every client chooses to follow my recommendations," she acknowledged when he opened the first book.

"Sit down beside me, and explain what I'm looking at."

Sophie perched on the edge of the cushion, keeping her back straight to prevent him seeing more of her bosom than her gown already revealed. "That's my plan for Bastwick House in Shropshire. Unlike Bevington, it sits low in a valley. As you can see, it's an ancient dwelling and well suited to the picturesque style. If you turn to the last page but one, you'll see more clearly where the larger oaks were removed to open up the view. The final sketch depicts the vista to the west, framed by the remaining oaks and chestnuts."

"Was this your notion?"

"Yes, my lord."

She'd agonized about sacrificing so many mature trees, until Fingal Moncrieff had reminded her that if she didn't, Repton certainly would—and pocket a sizable fee for doing so.

"There used to be a shrubbery walk to the rear of the house," she continued, "not unlike the one at Bevington, though it wasn't walled and had no canal running through it. I replaced the evergreens with a lawn."

He reached for the next Blue Book. "Alderbury Lodge."

"The owner commissioned a Gothic tower and wanted advice on new plantings. Exotics, mostly."

Evidently unmoved by the Alderbury Lodge plans, he took up another set. "Mainwaring Park. A Palladian mansion. What did you do here?"

"Parterres," she intoned, wishing she could forget them. "Terraces. On the south side of the house. I eliminated them."

The degradations committed at Mainwaring Park would forever haunt her. Those exquisite parterres had been lovingly tended by generations of Mainwarings. The present baronet, infected with the improving disease, had decreed that they must go, so Sophie had obliged him. And Moncrieff had taken all the credit.

"I've seen enough of these," the earl stated in his unequivocal fashion. "Now let me look at your garden."

"My garden?"

"How else am I to judge your skill? I have no intention of visiting all these places you've shown me."

"But it's nearly midnight," she protested. "And snow is falling."

"Not any longer." He climbed to his feet. "If you're too ashamed of your own grounds to let me tour them, I'll be on my way."

"Wait." She couldn't resist his challenge. "I'll need my cloak. And a lantern."

Marveling at her obedience to the persuasions of a madman, she left him to retrieve her scarlet cloak from its peg by the kitchen door. A relic from her girlhood, it was shabby from frequent exposure to foul weather.

❧

During the widow's absence Cass resumed his study of Tobias Pinnock's portrait. An ordinary man, unremarkable in face and form. Yet he'd won the hand—and presumably the heart—of that hardheaded little Jerseywoman.

Amazingly, this impromptu eleventh hour visit to Chiswick had stopped him from brooding about his encounter with Sir Michael Tait, and he was no longer tortured by his gnawing suspicion about why Luis had been accosted. Now all the thoughts and questions careening in his mind centered on Sophie Pinnock.

She returned with a lantern, cloaked in a garment that made her look even smaller and more dainty.

"We'll go out this way," she announced, lifting a damask curtain to reveal a set of French doors.

He followed her out to a broad terrace. The cool night air was invigorating, and carried a fresh scent. "Flowers in January?" he asked, pointing to a classical urn. Peeping through the light snow cover was a plant bearing large white blossoms.

"*Helleborus.* Commonly called the Christmas Rose." She held the lantern high as she led him along a stone-paved walkway. "Do you mean to inspect my kitchen garden?" she demanded, her voice as tart as unripe fruit.

"I want to see everything," he replied.

She heaved an impatient sigh before turning down a pathway veering sharply to the right.

"This long border provides flowers for cutting," she said with an expansive gesture that opened her cloak and briefly revealed her compact, lushly rounded figure. "In summer these bricks are scarcely visible behind the foliage, the plants grow so thickly here. My roses are dormant now, but you can see how high they climbed last year. I grow a few modern specimens, but I do love this dear old-fashioned *Rosa mundi* best of all." She held the light up to the brambles to show the ice-glazed hips.

They passed through a gate into a tidy kitchen plot with rows of glass frames protecting the most tender plants from the winter chill, and a hothouse in the corner where produce could be forced. Espaliered apple and pear trees grew all around the wall, leafless skeletons outlined by the clinging snow.

"Come April they'll be in full bloom. And from summer into autumn I'll have a fine selection of cherries, nectarines, and apricots."

Continuing her tour, she took Cass to a spacious, grassy area sheltered by mature cedars. Life-sized statues, ghostly in their whiteness, formed a graceful semi-circle. Yew hedging concealed the pedestal of each, giving the impression that each god or goddess was floating in space. A powdering of snow frosted the neatly clipped evergreens.

"Was this your husband's design?"

The lady laughed softly. Fondly. The first genuine sound of mirth he'd heard from her, and it rang out in the chilled air like music.

"Tobias was too busy making landscapes for other people. What you see here resulted from *my* planning, and the work was done at my direction. From time to time, I even dirtied my own hands. I was the one who visited Mrs. Coade's stoneworks to choose the classical figures. They aren't genuine marble."

Cass surprised himself by being utterly charmed by her grove. Simpler than the plans depicted in the Blue Books and yet more formal, it testified to the versatility of its creator.

She was still smiling reminiscently when she said, "Come,

my lord, if you wish to view the willow walk." In her haste she nearly slipped on a patch of ice.

"Careful." The cautionary word slipped out involuntarily—he repeated it so often to Cecelia and the child.

With her rapid progress across the lawn the lantern light grew dimmer, enticing him to a stand of willows with arching, whip-like branches that dipped down to the river's edge.

"My favorite retreat in summer," she confided, indicating a rustic seat perfectly sized for two. "On bright days I come here to sketch the view. Or if I'm feeling idle, to watch the boats drift past. And I often bring bread scraps for the swans nesting on the other side."

As the black waters of the Thames lapped at the reeds along the riverbank, Cass studied the pale oval of her face.

This unworldly little creature fascinated him. First and foremost, because of her singular beauty. But he also appreciated her rare ability to see beyond the folds and flatness of the land and search out the possibilities hidden there. Not only did she understand the mysteries of nature, she shaped and molded it at will. She was blessed with taste and talent, and possibly a touch of genius.

The candle stub in her lantern flickered and suddenly died.

"Mrs. Pinnock. I—you—" He was unsure how to phrase his desires.

She looked around, her almond-shaped eyes as dark and fathomless as the river itself. "What is it, Lord Bevington?"

"I want you to re-create the Bevington Castle grounds," he said, more abruptly than he'd intended. "To make all the necessary drawings and provide plant lists. You shall hire the labor and supervise the alterations. From start to finish, however long it may take."

"*Ma fé,* here is a sudden change," she murmured. "At our last meeting you scorned my competence and turned me away from your door."

"An error of judgment which I pray you'll overlook."

"You're choosing me over the illustrious Humphry Repton? And Emes, and Mickle—and the other *gentlemen* you interviewed?"

"A pack of bores. I covet my own copy of your Blue Book, with 'Earl of Bevington' stamped in gold on the cover, exactly as you promised. You've seen what remains of the castle gardens. Surely such decay and neglect inspired you to make a change?"

She shuddered beneath her cloak, as if shaking off a hurtful memory.

From a distance, a bell tolled twelve times. Cass waited for the last chime to fade before saying, "You must turn Bevington into a masterpiece of the modern landscape style. Tear down the crumbling stone walls, rip out that old-fashioned shrubbery walk and all those scraggly roses. The canal can go as well, and that gloomy avenue of trees along the drive."

She shook her head. "You move too fast, my lord. I haven't accepted the position."

"Why so hesitant? A few days ago you were courting my patronage."

Gazing over the water, she said, "You're certain to be a demanding client. I've had them before."

"I'm not concerned with the process, only the result," he assured her. "On my honor, when we lived in Sintra I never once dealt with those who cared for our pleasure grounds. I left that to Cecelia."

"You had a garden in Portugal? What was it like?"

"A miniature Versailles. Endless parterres with fountains, finicky little plots hedged with box. There was an orange grove, too, and more fig trees than you've ever seen in your life."

He had an extraordinary desire to take her there. The warm southern sunshine would melt her cool reserve. She'd have no need for that woolen cloak, she could wear wispy gowns of white muslin that would flatter her coloring. And her curves.

But instead of whisking her away to a sunnier clime, he must lure her to his gloomy castle in Gloucestershire.

"As I said the other day, I'd want you to stay at Bevington. I'll not be there to interfere, for I won't take up residence until midsummer, at the earliest. Should you wish to return here on occasion, my traveling carriage would be at your disposal. As for your fee—what say you to a guinea per day, to complete my Blue Book? And double that amount while the alterations are in progress."

"Your lordship is generous. Nonetheless, I need time to consider." Lifting her dark head, she told him serenely, "I cannot think clearly after midnight."

"But—"

"Lord Bevington, I've treated you with greater courtesy than you did me when I traveled across the country at your whim. For the better part of an hour you've had my undivided attention. I served you a glass of vintage port and let you look at my designs. You have explored my gardens. So you will not, I trust, be cross if I leave you and return to the house. The hour is late, and I was quite weary before you arrived."

Dismissed—by a pert young slip of a widow!

"I'll not keep you from your rest a moment longer," he told her coldly. "Goodnight, Madam."

Striding across the snow-frosted lawn, he tried to believe he'd be better off without her. And he failed.

This second, more substantive interview had convinced him beyond any doubt that Sophie Pinnock was brilliantly capable. Her tiny white hand, with deft strokes of the paintbrush, could turn her visions into works of art. She had enhanced the beauty of the surrounding terrain and imposed order upon it. He would not be content until she had done exactly the same at Bevington Castle.

Chapter 3

Where'er you tread, the blushing flowers shall rise,
And all things flourish where you turn your eyes.

~Alexander Pope

"You must've been thinking t'always snows or rains 'ere at Bevington, ma'am," said the maidservant who shared Sophie's quarters. "But at long last the sun's come out to welcome you." She placed a squat china teapot on the gate-leg table.

"This is February, after all." Now that the showers had ended, Sophie could be philosophical about them.

An assurance of fine weather, she thought wryly, had not been included in the earl's lavish offer. She'd been promised only that tempting guinea per day and her room and board. In return, according to the legal document her attorney brother-in-law had drawn up, she must produce "Designs for a Modern Landscape, bound in Blue Leather," and afterwards "Supervise the Labor necessary to implement the said Designs." And, taking her employer at his word, she reserved the authority to hire the contractor and workers she deemed most capable of executing her plans.

Lord Bevington had promptly signed and sealed and returned the papers to her legal representative. At that point, all communication from him had ceased.

Not only had her journey to Gloucestershire been hindered by mud and delays, upon her arrival she received blank stares from his lordship's servants. Fortunately Mr. Andrew Searle had emerged from the book room to support her claim of being the earl's landscape gardener, whereupon she'd been shown to her gatehouse lodging.

By the end of that first trying day at the castle, Sophie's grievances against its master had eclipsed her satisfaction in gaining him as a client. His long silence, rather than assuring her of the autonomy he'd promised her, signaled all too clearly his disinterest in her activities, and her welfare.

Surveying her airy sitting room, she acknowledged that her accommodations gave her no cause for complaint. The surrounding walls were paneled with honeyed oak carved in a linen-fold pattern, and plasterwork decorated the low ceiling. Frayed and faded needlepoint covered the pair of old-fashioned armchairs flanking the stone fireplace, but they were comfortable enough.

On opposite sides of the long, narrow room were broad diamond-paned casements. One framed a view of the outer gate and the long, oak-lined drive beyond; the other looked out on the inner courtyard and the many arched doorways to the castle keep and towers. While waiting out the wet spell, Sophie had often curled up on the cushioned window benches to watch the comings and goings of carriers delivering goods and the artisans working feverishly to improve the earl's residence.

"So you'll be going out this morning?" asked Nan Parham, bringing her a plate of food.

Sophie had quickly developed a taste for the sharp, rich cheese produced in the district, typically served to her melted on toast. Eagerly placing her napkin on her lap, she answered, "I want to continue exploring the grounds, and I am eager to speak with the gardeners."

"Mr. Wilkins tends the kitchen gardens only. With the new earl soon coming to live 'ere, he and his son are busier than ever."

Sophie frowned, recalling her only encounter with the dour kitchen gardener. A simple request that he pot up some auriculas produced the same incomprehension she might have expected had she addressed him in Jèrriais. First he'd muttered that he hadn't been told to take orders from her, then grudgingly admitted he wasn't used to messing about with flowers.

"'Tweren't always so," Nan continued, wagging her curly golden head. "The old earl had Mr. Jones to look after his grounds. For at least twenty year he lived in that prettified cottage on t'other side of the wood."

Sophie looked up from her plate. "Is he still alive?"

"Aye, and has a little a house in the village. Keeps to himself nowadays."

"Did his age prevent him from working? Was he too infirm?"

"Last time I saw him he looked much as he ever did. I'd reckon him to be me da's age." In answer to an inquiring glance, Nan said succinctly, "Forty-odd years."

"I should meet this Mr. Jones."

"Likely you'll find him by the church. Sexton lets him

putter about the burying ground, trimming back the ivy and suchlike."

With twenty years' experience behind him, Sophie mused, Mr. Jones must be a master of his trade. Moreover, he'd know the names and types of roses that had been planted here in years past. Perhaps he could even tell her where she'd find the missing key to the pavilion. These questions, and so many others, constantly plagued her.

She sorely missed her own well-regulated household and tidy gardens. Refilling her teacup, she imagined her dear, devoted Mary in the kitchen, polishing the copper pots until they gleamed, and William in his hothouse, sowing seeds in wooden trays.

Fighting homesickness, she reminded herself of her salary, and the prestige she expected to gain from this commission. Of how restless she'd been before coming here. This change of scene was as necessary to her well-being as having a complex and consuming project to fill her days. At Bevington she could work independently, without interference from the perfidious Moncrieff.

"Your egg, ma'am." Nan set the porcelain cup before her.

Sophie's spoon slipped from her grasp and fell to the floor. "*Zut,*" she grumbled, picking it up.

"Drop a spoon and love comes soon," Nan quoted merrily on her way out.

The rhyme echoed in Sophie's mind throughout her solitary meal, and later when she climbed the stone stair spiraling up to her bedchamber. The joy of loving, in her experience, had been eclipsed by the pain of losing the beloved one. She changed her slippers for a pair of sturdy half-boots, and settled her scarlet cloak upon her shoulders.

Her pensive gaze fell upon the heavy Jacobean bedstead. Because she'd never shared it with Tobias, she didn't feel his absence as keenly as in their bed at home. The flower-embroidered counterpane, a wedding gift from her Tante Douce, had never been used and thus harbored no tragic associations.

Following Nan's directions, she searched for the well-worn path the castle servants used to reach the church or village. Lying just beyond the outer archway, it wound down the slope of a hill to a pair of neatly shaved yews marking a side entrance to the burial ground. A rusty-breasted robin fluttered down to the ground and poked at the damp turf with the point of its beak.

"You must be that female the new earl sent for to improve his grounds."

Sophie looked away from the bird and saw a wiry man pushing a one-wheeled barrow around the side of the church.

"Are you Mr. Jones, who worked in the castle gardens?"

Slowly he nodded. His features were bony, his face all sharp angles, and he had long graying hair pulled severely back in a queue.

"Your services are sorely missed," she told him frankly. "The hedges want clipping. The grassy walks haven't been rolled. As far as I can tell, no one has bothered to propagate annuals for planting out this spring."

"'Tis the proper time for it," he commented, selecting a hoe.

She reached down to pinch off a leaf from the low bush growing beside a stone marker. "Rosemary in a graveyard?"

"In Wales we use it to mark the graves of older people, for it signifies remembrance." He trilled his r's and l's, and there was a faint underlying sibilance to his speech. Indicating a smaller stone close by, he said, "Here, where an infant is buried, violets will bloom. And for the children lying over there, I planted primroses and daffodils."

"What a charming custom." She studied the many headstones, some cracked with age and covered in lichen, others starkly new and pristine. Only one was left unadorned; it occupied a lonely corner far from the rest.

Curious, she walked over to the gray slab to read its inscription. *"Here lie the bones of Frances Charlotte. Born a Virgin, died a Harlot."* Looking to Mr. Jones, she asked, "Who was this lady?"

"The last earl's mother, a notorious adulteress. Or so claimed her lord, who composed the verses himself. He refused to have her interred inside the church with the rest of the Carysforts. Legend says he murdered her, though 'twas never proved."

"Poor Frances Charlotte," Sophie sympathized. "You should plant something for her, too. *Rosa mundi*, with its pale petals stained with red, would suit a lady of dubious virtue. Whatever her sins, she doesn't deserve so bare a grave."

"Soft-hearted," he muttered.

Or had he called her soft-headed? She was confused by his odd, unfamiliar accent. "Mr. Jones, would you consider returning to your former position?"

His sparse brows shifted downwards in a frown. "Why should you want me to? There'll not be any gardening work left ere long. Not after you've dug up all my earl's treasures, and also mine, and cast them onto the rubbish heap."

"Nânnîn! Oh, no," she protested, sensitive to the pain she read in his strange, pale eyes. "I wouldn't discard them, I couldn't. I'd give the plants away, to you or anyone who wanted cuttings or divisions. I've a particular fondness for

roses—indeed, I'm quite desperate to know which ones have been planted. Before they bloom I shall probably have to move them."

"You'll find a variety of the damasks and gallicas and albas."

"Can you make up a list for me?"

"I suppose."

Sophie sensed his reluctance to assist her. She watched him flex his thin, dirt-caked fingers—his hands were delicate, almost womanly, with wrists as slender and fine-boned as her own.

"My work is hampered by more than a lack of information," she continued. "I'm distracted by the neglect I see everywhere. I want the herbaceous borders tidied and the dead leaves cleaned out of the canal. The flowering shrubs haven't been pruned. I can't do it all myself—indeed, I shouldn't make the attempt, that isn't what Lord Bevington pays me for. If you fail me, Mr. Jones, I must hire a person who knows even less than I do about which specimens are worth saving."

"Why must any of them be lost?" he wondered. He took up a hoe and hacked at the brambles encroaching upon Frances Charlotte's grave site. "The shrubbery and the canal walk were created a century ago. The laburnum arch and rose bower have been maturing these two decades. What manner of man is this new earl, who sees no beauty in what already exists?"

"I know not." It was a question she had often asked herself, about Lord Bevington and many a previous client.

"I've had but one master, may his soul rest with God. I want no other."

Clearly he intended their conversation to end there.

Sophie, wise in the ways of his kind, knew exactly how

to phrase her appeal. "There can't be enough work in this churchyard to keep you busy day in, day out. How much have you to do, after you've planted a rose bush for the harlot countess? Yews and box want clipping but once or twice a year, and ivy is easily kept in bounds. Besides that, your talent and experience are wasted here. You're a master gardener, not a groundskeeper."

"Aye," he admitted gruffly. "There's truth in that."

At least he hadn't refused her outright. "If you decide you want to work at the castle again," she told him, "come to me. I lodge in the gatehouse."

Before she turned to go he said, "When the village folk began talking of his lordship's lady landscape gardener, I never imagined she'd be a mere lass."

If he ever worked with her, she thought wickedly, he'd quickly discover how strong-minded—and demanding—a mere lass could be.

Emrys Jones wasn't what she'd expected either. He was intelligent and well-spoken, and not a bit deferential. Proud, too. Even though he'd been intrigued by her request for help, he hadn't immediately agreed to it. He didn't conceal his disdain for her assigned task, but seemed resigned to the inevitability of change. And he was a dedicated worker, otherwise he wouldn't have taken on the unpaid job of churchyard caretaker.

Trusting that he'd soon give her the answer she hoped for, Sophie spent the remainder of the day neatening the terrace gardens. With a pair of secateurs borrowed from the otherwise unhelpful Wilkins, she clipped away the dead stalks of the perennials. The sun warmed her back as she bent over to trim the lavender borders.

Her fragrant task was so absorbing that until Andrew Searle

spoke, she didn't even notice that he'd sat down on one of the stone steps to watch her.

Lord Bevington's tenant seldom emerged from his cottage beyond the chestnut grove, designated *the Wildernesse* on an old estate map. According to the chatty Nan, he was composing a lengthy poem and remained in seclusion for days at a time.

"I beg you to excuse my yawns, Mrs. Pinnock. I was awake all night scribbling, and slept the morning away. You've been more industrious, I see. But shouldn't you be sketching?"

"I can't begin till I've studied more of the illustrated books in his lordship's library. I draw inspiration from prints of buildings similar in style to Bevington."

His green eyes swept across the battlements and looming towers. "In my opinion the castle is sufficiently picturesque as it is. I can't fathom why Cass needs to be rid of those quaint knot gardens and the long arbor and all the rest of it."

Striving to keep her voice neutral, Sophie said, "Those were his instructions." Tenderly she brushed damp leaves away from the budding white crocuses.

"My own preference is for the romantic," the gentleman volunteered in his languid fashion. "Enclosed gardens are so ideally suited to dalliance. One can only wonder how many lovers have sought the privacy of the shrubbery walk, or used the pavilion for their assignations."

Sophie laughed. "You ought to be writing novels, Mr. Searle, not poetry."

He looked capable of neither. In the shabby coat and faded breeches, his hair mussed and his eyes pink from lack of sleep, he resembled an exhausted, overworked farmer.

"But many of my poems do tell a story—my style is narrative. Would you like to hear one?"

Without waiting for a reply, he embarked upon a recitation. In a slow and rhythmic cadence, he told the tale of a humble lady whose misplaced love for a nobleman resulted in heartbreak, a curse, death, and revenge. Sophie was able to clearly envision each character, the windswept moor where the heroine roamed with her false lover, the mossy sepulcher in which she was entombed, the velvet-hung bedchamber she haunted on the baron's wedding night. Searle's carefully modulated voice brought the scenes to vivid life, with such chilling effect that by the poem's conclusion she felt cold and shivery.

"What is the title?" she asked when he finished.

"'The Blackened Betrothal.' I hope you found it pleasing."

"I've never heard anything like it," she said frankly. "I shouldn't like to read it alone, late at night. However did you think up such a tragedy? Is it based upon a local legend?"

Andrew shook his head, his shaggy, golden brown locks whipping about his face. "I dreamed part of it, the rest I made up. I write such pieces to make young ladies shudder, and receive a pittance for them. I prefer more serious compositions. Lately I published a philosophical essay on the nature of mankind, an examination of our inbred reluctance to embrace a more complete freedom." With a shrug, he added, "My notions are considered radical, and I have difficulty promoting them."

Sophie cultivated a few radical notions of her own, and since coming to Bevington Castle they had flourished.

For the past half-century landscape gardeners had professed to study the "genius of the place" before making improvements. A false claim, in Sophie's estimation. Rather, they laid down arbitrary rules and codified their pet principles so they could impose their visions—and sometimes the client's—upon a mature landscape.

Why, she wondered, must so many glorious gardens be altered to conform to a single prevailing style?

The decay of the Bevington pleasure grounds inspired her to repair them, not replace them with an artful—and by definition counterfeit—representation of an Italian painting. This was no proper place for jagged boulders and non-native conifers strategically positioned around a grotto and a cascade.

These walls and towers dated from the Middle Ages, their crenellations and oriel windows had been added during the Renaissance, and the gardens had taken their present form in the age of the Stuarts. Each era was notable for man's attempts, through architecture and landscaping, to create order in a sadly disordered world.

The result was a beauty well worth preserving.

Intruding upon her reverie, the poet commented, "You look like someone preparing to set out on a holy crusade, or on the verge of fomenting revolution."

"I'm no crusader. Nor a revolutionary." Regretfully she added, "Not by my actions. Only in my head and heart."

"Ah, that's how we all begin," he informed her sagely, before he ambled off.

She must be careful not to speak so frankly. Andrew Searle was a close friend—possibly a confidant—of the earl. She could only hope he was too self-absorbed to ever ask exactly what sort of mutiny she contemplated.

Fifteen miles separated Summit House, Cassian Carysfort's Clifton residence, and his estate at Bevington. Invariably he covered that distance on horseback, taking a circuitous route through Thornbury, Rockhampton, and Stone—villages whose grim names belied their charms. The weather, remarkably bright and mild for mid-February, had prompted him to travel to the castle and assess the progress of the workers. He was accompanied by his lurcher bitch, valiantly keeping pace with Saladin, his coal-black thoroughbred.

Along the winding, hedge-lined lanes he met more than one farmer's cart bound for the Tuesday market at Berkeley. The respectful cap-tugging and bows indicated that he was recognized by the people of the district and roused a welcome sense of belonging.

When he came upon a shepherd whose large flock blocked his way, Cass was forced to go down an unfamiliar track. Narrow and rutted, it turned out to be a more direct route than the one he'd formerly relied on. And every bit as scenic, with splendid vistas of the Welsh hills on the other side of the Severn Estuary.

Nearly a year as lord of Bevington, he mocked himself, and still he was learning his way around the countryside. He regretted having so few opportunities to explore it. In Portugal he'd been free to pursue his own interests, but here in England he dared not drop his guard over his sister. Or the child.

He spent nearly every morning at the New Pump Room, bored but uncomplaining while Cecelia took her daily dose of water from the Hot Wells. He accompanied her to the Clifton shops and purchased whatever trifle she fancied. He made certain that she rested in the afternoon. Their dinner was a long and dismayingly formal meal, a Portuguese habit Cecelia refused to discard. In the evening she took up her needlework and listened to him read aloud from a novel, or entertained him by playing on the pianoforte while he glanced at his

Bristol newspaper.

Cecelia's love for Daniel had always been a complex, curious thing. Since coming to England she'd seemed more detached than ever, leaving him to the care of his plump Portuguese nursemaid and Luis Costa. As a result, he was sometimes more fluent in the servants' language than English. A lively, healthy lad, he was less capricious than his parent and had a quicker wit, and would soon be old enough for a tutor. With his ward's future education in mind, Cass had offered the tenancy of the cottage *ornée* to his learned friend Drew Searle.

Wealthy enough to please herself in choosing a husband, at present Cecelia showed no greater interest in matrimony than Cass himself. She held herself aloof from the gentlemen she met, with the possible exception of the poet. Drew visited Bristol regularly to deliver verses to his printer, and each time he called at Summit House. He'd even presented Cecelia with a bound edition of his published essay, greatly to Cass's amusement, for he doubted she understood a word of it. He hadn't bothered to speculate on the significance, if any, of their relationship, but he was confident that Drew posed no threat to his sister's fragile peace of mind.

But someone else did. Hands clenching the reins, he considered Sir Michael Tait. Divorced from his wife, mired in scandal, the scarred baronet would be the worst possible match for a female as sensitive to public disapproval as Cecelia. And that was without taking into account the disastrous events that had caused the duel.

He entered the Vale of Bevington, populated by herds of cows and their keepers, and his spirits soared at the sight of his castle looming on the horizon. The sudden surge of possessiveness was as novel as it was startling. High time he felt an attachment to the place—within months he'd be living there. And he trusted that those walls of rose-hued stone were thick and sturdy enough to make his troubled sister feel safe and secure.

Cass handed Saladin over to the young groom raking dung in the stable yard. As his first order of business, he decided, he'd review the Widow Pinnock's designs for his new landscape. He strolled to the gatehouse, commanding Echo to wait for him under the breezeway, where she was perfectly content to nose out interesting scents.

"Mrs. Pinnock isn't 'ere," an aproned maidservant declared as she admitted him to a sunny parlor. "She spends most fair days out in the gardens, sketching and weeding and chatting with Mr. Searle."

"Oh?" Cass directed his attention to a pair of watercolors hanging on either side of the fireplace. One depicted the Pinnock villa in Chiswick and the other, he assumed, was her uncle's manor house in Jersey. "Does she seem satisfied with her living arrangements?" he asked the bright-haired girl.

"Aye, my lord. She's a quiet, pleasant lady to work for, easy to please and not at all demanding."

None of his Clifton servants would say the same about Cecelia.

"I've a notion Mrs. Pinnock might feel a bit lonely," she confided, "but she never says so. If you ask me, Mr. Searle would gladly keep her company. He often stops by of an evening just when she's about to sit down at table, but she always makes me send him away."

That Drew would establish a friendship with Mrs. Pinnock was an outcome Cass hadn't previously considered.

Continuing his explorations, he wandered from the parlor

into the small adjoining room, furnished with a table and chair. The tall, south-facing window provided abundant light and overlooked a corner of the terrace walks. A selection of leather bound volumes occupied the window ledge—he hadn't realized there were so many books devoted to gardening and the theory of landscapes. He studied some of the title pages: *Planting and Rural Ornament* by William Marshall, and *The Florist's Directory, or a Treatise on the Culture of Flowers* by James Maddock. Propped on a tiny easel was an oval miniature of Tobias Pinnock painted on ivory, another of the personal belongings that had accompanied the widow to Bevington. Cass recognized the Argand lamp and shagreen-covered paint box from his visit to her home in Chiswick.

Spying a familiar book, Cass picked up the bound copy of Andrew Searle's essay on the freedoms of man. In a rare display of virtue, he repressed his urge to look inside and see if the author had written a revealing inscription on the flyleaf.

Here was proof of an intimate friendship, he thought with displeasure, possibly of a flirtation. He hoped Drew wasn't distracting the widow from her duties.

With a sense of foreboding, Cass went in search of her. He passed through the long laburnum arch. The appearance of the shrubbery walk, he noted, had improved since his last visit. He peered behind each neatly shorn topiary, while the lurcher dashed ahead of him along the broad alley of oddly-shaped evergreens.

In the rose garden a gray-haired man perched atop a ladder leaning against one wall, his hands protected by thick leather gauntlets. Deftly he sheared away thorny branches and tossed them down to the ground.

Echo froze. The tawny fur at the back of her neck stood on

end as she delivered her most menacing growl.

"Pray keep your dog close," the gardener called out. "The earth in these borders is fresh-tilled for seed, and mustn't be trampled."

"Where might I find Mrs. Pinnock?" Cass asked the proprietary stranger, who had a strong Welsh accent.

"Somewhere hereabouts. In the wilderness, mayhap."

Wilderness? Unwilling to admit his ignorance, Cass retreated toward the shrubbery walk.

"T'other direction, sir," the man corrected him. "There's a gate behind the pavilion."

"Come along, Echo!" Cass called sharply.

Colorful crocus blooms brightened the knot gardens, not as unkempt and shaggy as he remembered, and the canal was no longer fouled by the leaves and twigs that had made it so unsightly. Going to the rear of the ornamental building, he found a gate with intricately wrought iron bars separating the formal gardens from the deer park.

And there was Sophie Pinnock, adrift in a sea of white snowdrops, clutching a bouquet of them.

Echo gave an impatient yelp. As soon as Cass opened the gate she raced toward the lady, who laughed and twirled about, enticing his dog to dance with her. Echo capered blissfully, bowing and leaping, and when her new friend ended their brief game her long tail drooped.

"Here, you must have one of these." Sophie Pinnock waded up to Cass and inserted a blossom into the lapel of his riding coat. A faint flush tinted her cheeks, and her dark eyes shone with delight. "Have you ever seen a more glorious display?"

Enchanting, Cass agreed, focused on her lovely face. Swayed by pure impulse, he bent his head to kiss her rosy, smiling mouth and found it as smooth and soft as the petals of her flowers.

Letting them fall, she twined her arms around his neck. *"Oh, las,"* she breathed. And then she returned his kiss.

Deeply shocked and supremely flattered by her provocative response, Cass grew bolder. One hand splayed itself across her fluttering ribcage, just below the swell of her breast. The other roved up her arm to her neck, slipping under the wool gown and pushing the strap of her shift away from her shoulder to caress her heated skin.

She gave a faint gasp, not of alarm but of delight. He continued kissing her, ravenously, wondering how he would ever be able to stop and hoping he would never have to.

Her pliant body suddenly tensed. *"Ma fé,"* she cried, "what have I done?" She ripped herself from his embrace and sank to the ground.

The dog, sensing a human's need of comfort, stretched out on the grass beside her.

"I cannot imagine what came over me. Or what you must be thinking."

Cass was thinking that the little widow was remarkably adept at love-play, but thought it best not to say so.

He bent to gather up the scattered snowdrops. Lightly, with feigned carelessness, he asked, "Don't you know what day this is? The Feast of St. Valentine, when any man bold enough may kiss a fair maid."

"You are no ordinary man," she protested. "You're the Earl of Bevington. And I'm not a maid. I cannot excuse what just happened, except to say that I—" She glanced down at the flowers he'd returned to her, long black lashes shielding her eyes. "Well, you see, it has been a very long time since . . ."

As her head drooped, a lock of red-brown hair slipped down to cover one flaming cheek. "So long."

His pulses stilled when he heard that wistful, haunting phrase.

Studying the tiny fingers curled around the bouquet, he saw a gold signet ring. A man's piece, cut down to fit. A keepsake of someone dear to her.

While he'd held her to his heart, passionately kissing her, and receiving her kisses, she had been remembering the husband she'd lost. In that moment of comprehension, a bitter and wholly irrational jealousy was born. And with it, a desire so intense that he wondered how long he could bear to let it go unslaked.

Someday he would hold Sophie Pinnock in his arms again. Next time, he vowed, she would yearn and sigh for him and no one else, living or dead.

CHAPTER 4

His spacious garden made to yield to none,
Was compass'd round with walls of solid stone.

~Alexander Pope

*P*lacing her ringed hand on Echo's head, Sophie Pinnock asked, "What breed is she?"

"None—or more accurately, many. Echo is a lurcher, which is to say a combination. A smattering of collie, a soupcon of greyhound. Bred for speed and endurance, and particularly skilled at chasing rabbits Her mother was a poacher's dog seized by my gamekeeper Parham. He granted me pick of the litter."

With an entrancingly lopsided smile, she murmured, "I hope she's discreet and will say nothing about what she just witnessed."

Her jesting tone and renewed composure made Cass wonder if her senses had been roused as much as he'd believed.

"We must count ourselves fortunate," she continued evenly, "that Mr. Jones wasn't peering over the wall."

"The gray-headed fellow I saw clipping the rose bushes?"
She nodded.

A Welsh name, and a common one. "Not the gardener in my predecessor's time?"

"Oui-dgia," she confirmed, nodding. "Emrys Jones. Do you know him?"

"I've heard of him," he told her curtly. "And I don't want him working here."

Sophie scrambled to her feet. "What do you mean? I almost went down on my knees to him, he was so reluctant to return to Bevington."

"You should have left well enough alone."

She regarded him soberly. "Why, what is the matter?"

"He must be dismissed. At once."

"That's hardly an explanation."

"It must suffice."

With several vigorous shakes of her head, she muttered, "No, no, no, there's no cause for it. Your dislike of him seems quite—oh, what is the word? Arbitrary," she finished triumphantly.

"Not at all," Cass insisted, uncertain whether he could—or should—explain his reasons for getting rid of the Welshman. She'd been married and had experienced physical love. But he doubted she was aware that some men lusted after members of their same gender. He didn't care to enlighten her.

With a harshness born of discomfiture, he declared, "My reasons are no concern of yours, Mrs. Pinnock."

"Emrys Jones is a skilled gardener," she shot back. "He might disapprove of the alterations I intend to make, but he's a valuable source of information—and advice." She drew herself up to her full height. "I will not send him away, Lord Bevington."

"Not even at my command?"

"You have no power of command—in this instance. You signed a document granting me the authority to hire whomever I please. What's more, you gave your promise not to interfere."

Cass had no answer to that, for she'd hemmed him in with the truth. Studying her determined expression and the mutinous set of her mouth, he recognized her as the hardheaded little businesswoman. The avid creature he'd held in his arms, who allowed him to kiss and touch her, had vanished.

She had a habit of defying him, this female whose stubbornness flared at their every encounter. He didn't like it, wasn't accustomed to it. Passive Cecelia seldom questioned his decisions. Daniel, a mere child, was by definition obedient. His servants did his bidding dutifully, either from loyalty or else to obtain promotion and a higher wage.

He couldn't permit this vixen, however pretty and desirable and talented, to rule him. "Madam," he raged, "I do *not* tolerate disrespect from an employee."

"And I, Lord Bevington, cannot continue working for someone incapable of keeping his word."

Echo, roused by their angry voices, prowled restlessly between them, her ears flicking back and forth.

Cass feared he'd gone too far. If she resigned . . .

Faced with the prospect of losing her, his fury subsided. He must keep her at Bevington, even if it meant accepting the temporary employment of Emrys Jones.

But, he reminded himself, Sophie Pinnock's employment was equally temporary.

Preferring not to dwell on that oddly troubling fact, he said quietly, "I pride myself on never breaking a pledge, madam. Jones stays for as long as you have work for him here, but not a minute longer. I assume you've got finished designs for me to look over?"

"Preliminary ones only. And very few."

"I'll see them now."

Sophie barely had time to congratulate herself on her victory before she found herself back in the position of humble laborer. Their relationship had been strained from the outset, and was now adversely affected by his advances—and her reaction.

Oh, las, those kisses.

So long . . . .

Her own plaintive words lingered in her mind. *Not ever* would have been nearer the truth. No man had kissed her like that. Her susceptibility alarmed her as much as it must have amazed him. Walking back to the house with her silent and glowering employer, she wished she could forget the troubling contact. But every time she glanced up at his face, her gaze sought the very lips he'd used to such tantalizing effect. His expression was guarded, revealing nothing of his mood.

She had invited his kisses. In all innocence, quite unintentionally, but the harm was done. If she had any sense, she would pack up her things immediately and depart for Chiswick, where she wouldn't be plagued by this new and shameful longing. Her heart raced anew at the memory of being imprisoned by his arms. She'd felt so deliciously overwhelmed, so gloriously alive—so entirely female.

Tobias had been an affectionate man, seldom a passionate one. It was disturbing to find out now, after losing him, that perhaps they hadn't been as well-matched in that respect as she'd always supposed. She'd discovered a new sort of passion in a field of snowdrops, and now was conscious of her dangerous vulnerability.

At least, she consoled herself, she'd managed to overcome the earl's mysterious and unstated objection to Emrys Jones. Her experiences with Fingal Moncrieff had taught her the effectiveness of a logical argument backed by strong feelings. Her case had been helped by Lord Bevington's detachment. The process of garden planning didn't matter to him, he was interested solely in the result. While she couldn't make a habit of wrangling with her client, she fancied she could work her will upon him again, and win future concessions. Over time, perhaps, she might even manage to temper his misplaced enthusiasm for the picturesque style.

Although the terrace steps were broad enough for them to ascend side by side, the earl stepped back so she could walk up before him. Near the top he came to a sudden halt.

"Blast and damn!"

His outraged stare guided Sophie's eye to a carriage standing before the gatehouse. It had just arrived, for the footman was just now opening the door and unfolding the step. It was a splendid vehicle to have inspired the earl's critical response, varnished to a brilliant sheen and adorned with a painted crest.

Turning to Sophie, he said, "You're about to meet my sister Cecelia—Mrs. Fonseca—and her son Daniel. And here is Luis—you will remember him." He strode forward and greeted them in an over-hearty tone. "What brings you to Bevington so unexpectedly?" he asked the lady.

"The merest whim," she responded softly but audibly. "Need I give you a reason? For that is how you reply when I dare to question your actions, *meu irmao*—brother of mine."

Seldom had Sophie seen a pair of siblings so much alike— their resemblance was startling. Cecelia Fonseca's features were more delicate and her complexion paler than the earl's yet both had curling black hair and the same brilliantly blue eyes. Her extreme slimness gave her an air of ethereal elegance, and her height made Sophie even more regretful about her own lack of inches. And that modish traveling costume made a plain morning gown of gray kerseymere seem regrettably frumpish.

Examining the lady's son, Sophie received an instant impression of what her employer must have looked like in childhood. There was no sign of Daniel Fonseca's foreign parentage; in appearance he was entirely a Carysfort.

He gestured at her, chattering to his uncle in Portuguese. Sophie caught the words *"Menina bonita."*

"Don't point, Daniel, it's rude," chided his mother. "You must make an effort to speak English."

Said the earl, more gently, "The pretty young lady is Mrs. Pinnock. She's staying at the castle."

"Quanto tempo?" asked the child.

Sophie couldn't avoid his lordship's enigmatic stare. "For as long as she pleases." Shrugging, he said, "I confess my ignorance of the proper form for introductions. Cecelia, am I supposed to present Mrs. Pinnock to you, or the other way 'round?"

"Need we stand on ceremony? Mrs. Pinnock, my brother tells me that you shall make the Bevington gardens as fashionable and famous as we wish them to be." After rearranging the folds of her indigo velvet carriage dress, Cecelia tucked her hands back into her fur muff. "I'm eager to see the new furnishings from London, Cass. Shall we go inside?" Before they proceeded to the courtyard, she added to Sophie, "Daniel will not trouble you. Luis has instructions to keep him amused."

The manservant grinned. "To also keep him from tumbling into the canal. I careful of him always, Senhora, I leave him alone never."

"I know. *Estou muito contente,* Luis."

Fortunate woman, Sophie thought, admiring Cecelia's graceful progress through the gatehouse arch. Why shouldn't she be content? Beautiful and rich, with a living keepsake of the husband she'd lost.

In the early years of her marriage to Tobias, Sophie had longed to have a child. Initially she'd blamed herself for her failure to conceive, her only sadness until the greater tragedy had befallen her. When her husband's health had failed, his doctor had cautioned that physical exertion would severely damage his heart, an edict which destroyed Sophie's lingering hope that she would become a mother.

She was covetously regarding young Daniel when Andrew Searle came up the terrace steps.

"Sturdy little chap, isn't he?"

For the first time since coming to Bevington, Sophie welcomed the poet's company. The earl's coolness after their heated dispute about Emrys Jones, and his sister's casually dismissive air forced her to seek an ally.

"Have you encountered his mother, the beauteous Cecelia?"

"Just now. An accurate description."

Shrugging, he said, "A pity she isn't more clever and less dependent upon her brother. Cass spoils her, and I daresay Fonseca did the same. I get the impression he was quite a bit older than she. Daniel, was your papa an elderly gentleman?"

The boy hung back, so Luis answered for him. "He a *bebé* when Senhor Fonseca die, he no remember *nada.*" He took his charge's hand.

Sophie smiled and asked, "What sort of games do you like to play, Daniel?"

He gazed up at her solemnly. "*Tio* tosses the ball to me."

"In the Portuguese, *tio* mean uncle," Luis translated.

Sophie asked, "Can you find a ball, Luis?"

"Servant boys are sometimes playing the cricket," he told her cheerfully. "I borrow from them." Off he went, ever eager to please.

Daniel showed concern at being abandoned.

"I also have a *tio*," Sophie confided. "Like yours, he has a grand house surrounded by gardens. I was fond of visiting him. Don't you like to come here, to the castle?"

He nodded shyly.

She asked Andrew Searle if he knew any children's tales.

"None that I recall," he admitted. "Shall I invent one?"

"Even better," she approved. "Daniel, when Luis returns I shall teach you a game I played when I was your age. And afterwards we'll go up to my parlor for tea and toast, and Mr. Searle will tell us a story. Would you like that?"

"*Sim,*" said Daniel softly. Then, with greater confidence, "Yes."

The dog came up from behind to lick his ear and he began to laugh. Ignoring the adults, he focused his whole attention on Echo.

"You like children," commented Andrew under his breath. "Yet you haven't any."

Attempting a smile, she answered, "I used to dream, but it wasn't meant to be."

"You're young yet. Many a lonely bachelor seeks a wife."

This conversation was veering too close to the personal to

suit Sophie. "One cannot tell what the future may bring," she said carefully. "But I'm satisfied with my life as it is now." Solitary and quiet and sometimes rather dull, she thought, but much less so here at Bevington.

The servant's return ended their dialogue. Luis had located a ball, and they all went to the flat stretch of turf commonly called the bowling green. Sophie gave instructions for the version of catch-ball she'd played as a child on Jersey.

"The person tossing the ball into the air calls out the name of the player for whom it is intended. If that person catches the ball before it touches ground, he gains a point and can call and toss to another. But if he fails to catch it, he loses a point. Shall we begin?"

Naming Daniel first, she threw the leather ball in a low arc so he could easily reach it. The little face beneath the thatch of dark curls was solemn no more, and his bright blue eyes sparkled with pleasure.

Their noisy play attracted the notice of Emrys Jones, still tending the roses on the opposite side of the stone wall. Sophie waved when she saw him atop his ladder, spying on their game. Not until he inclined his long head in response did she recall Lord Bevington's violent reaction at hearing his name.

"Senhora," cried Luis, "I call out, but you miss the ball!"

Her preoccupation had cost her a point.

The small drawing room opened onto a balcony from which Cass watched the foursome down on the green. He studied one of the moving figures more intently than the rest.

Thinking back over the times he'd been with Sophie

Pinnock, he couldn't picture her at rest. At their first meeting, she'd paced up and down the morning room in a flutter of disappointment over his abrupt refusal to hire her. During his late-night visit to her Chiswick villa she'd led him through her gardens, darting in and out of shadows with her lantern. Earlier today she'd romped with Echo in a wilderness of snowdrops, laughing and skipping about.

But in his arms—ah, there she'd been still, except for the rapid beat of her heart and the heave of her chest as she gasped her pleasure.

His fingers curled tensely on the iron balustrade.

His valet, his close friend, his nephew—also his dog—inspired her smiles. He could only rouse her defiance and raise the specter of a dead husband.

She ran across the grass to catch the ball Daniel had hurled in her direction, but it flew past her outflung arm and soared over the garden wall.

Cass saw Emrys Jones scramble down his ladder. Moments later he climbed back up, showing the ball. He then tossed it down to Luis, who laughed at whatever comment he'd made.

Luis Costa was a remarkably attractive youth, with considerable personal charm. Even Cass was aware of it, and he had a lively appreciation of—and appetite for—females in general and Sophie Pinnock in particular. He would not let a confirmed pederast prey upon his valet. Or the child.

"Meu irmao?"

His sister's plaintive voice called him back inside. Out of weariness or boredom, she'd settled on one of the yellow damask chairs surrounding a card table. Unlike the energetic Sophie, Cecelia was happiest when lounging.

"The arrangements here please me very well," she

commented, surveying her surroundings. "This room will always seem hopelessly antiquated to me, but no one could possibly imagine in what disarray we found it a year ago."

"Because I followed your guidance when selecting the furniture," he reminded her, "all the credit goes to you."

"I'm trying desperately to convince myself that living here won't be so bad. Though I confess, I'll miss the shops."

"My dear Cecelia, what can be left for you to purchase? You've single-handedly depleted the entire stock of every milliner, mantua-maker, and modiste in Clifton."

"Unfair!" she cried.

"Take comfort from the likelihood that on Sunday mornings you'll be the grandest lady in Bevington church. Our neighbors and tenants will study your bonnets and gowns as a guide to local fashion."

Cecelia made a face. "With such a fate as that hanging over my head, I may well choose to remain at Summit House. In Clifton I've discovered the delights of anonymity."

He moved to the door. "Continue your tour of the house, if you wish. I must see to a matter of business."

He went back outdoors, down the terrace steps, through the tunnel of laburnums to the green. The shaggy turf beneath his feet belonged to him, yet he felt like an intruder when he joined the lively party. His arrival brought a swift end to their game.

Daniel's cheeks were flushed like ripe apples and dimpled by a broad grin. Luis idly tossed and caught the ball, his dark brow furrowed in concentration. Andrew Searle looked more alert than usual, doubtless because Sophie had gravitated to his side. She hastily smoothed back wisps of russet hair slipping from her chignon, unaware that Cass much preferred her in an imperfect state.

"Warm enough, Daniel?" he inquired. "Luis, take him to the kitchen, I'm sure he'd be glad of some food and drink after his exertions."

The lady stepped forward. Her eyes were flinty, no longer molten as they'd been in the aftermath of his fiery kisses. "I invited him to my rooms," she said. "Mr. Searle is going to tell us a story."

Hoping to soften and to please her, Cass suggested she order refreshments from his kitchens.

"This is my party," she responded with quiet dignity, "and I won't trouble your lordship's staff. I've taught Nan Parham to make apples wrapped in pastry—*bourdelots*—as well as any Jerseywoman. And she's certainly capable of brewing tea." Andrew and Daniel and Luis were already making their way to the terrace steps when she added, belatedly, "Does your lordship care to join us?"

His need to protect those in his care warred with his earnest wish to placate Sophie Pinnock. He would have accepted her unenthusiastic invitation if he hadn't desired a private conference with Emrys Jones. "Not today."

Again he'd offended her, this time with his swift refusal of her hospitality. The excessive formality of her curtsy and the rigid set of her shoulders as she followed her guests to the gatehouse told him that he'd erred in refusing her hospitality.

Frustrated, he kicked at a tuft of grass with the toe of his riding boot. Looking around, he found the Welshman peering down from the ladder.

"Come here to me, Jones," he commanded. "I want to speak with you."

The silvered head vanished behind the broken, stone-

THE PROPOSAL ～ 75

capped ledge.

Cass waited impatiently until the gardener emerged from the long arbor of laburnums, carrying that deadly-looking pair of shears.

"My lord?"

Cass was uncertain how to begin. Never before had he informed an employee that he would not tolerate the practice of perversions. "You've lived at Bevington a long time, I understand."

"Twenty year."

"Before that you lived in Wales?"

"I was steward to a landowner across the Severn. My master had a need to reduce his staff, and he recommended me to the Earl of Bevington."

Surprised, Cass said, "I thought you came here as a laborer."

"Nay, my lord. I kept the accounts and oversaw all expenditures till his lordship passed away. No one e'er remembers that," he commented bitterly.

"Why, then, did you become a gardener?"

The ghost of a smile flickered across the narrow, pointed face. "Gardening was a pleasure, I ne'er expected it to be my profession. I was impertinent enough to offer advice to his lordship. In time he enlisted me to maintain these grounds."

Cass recalled the portrait hanging in the library. It depicted the late earl, wearing a wig of frothy white curls and a gaudy satin coat, observing a man planting a rose tree—Emrys Jones.

"According to Mr. Prowdie, the solicitor, you inherited a house in the village and receive an annuity. You appear to want nothing. Yet you now work for Mrs. Pinnock."

"We have an understanding," Jones explained. "She misliked the untidiness all 'round, and needed to know what was planted where. I don't accept wages." He nodded in the direction of the walled gardens. "I set many of yon roses in the ground, and I'll tend them till they're moved. Does your lordship object?"

Those gray eyes pierced like the pointed blades of his shears. "Not unless you do something objectionable," said Cass. "In the weeks before I take up residence, my servant Luis will be spending time at Bevington. He has numerous duties to perform. I would not want him to be—" He searched for a word.

"Distracted?"

"Harassed," he stated firmly. "Do you understand my meaning?"

"I keep to the gardens, my lord. Your young foreigner is a household servant. We aren't likely to meet. Is there anyone else I must not harass?" Hostility hardened the gardener's voice.

Damned Welshman, Cass thought. "I trust I've made my point," he said loftily. "Return to your task."

Emrys Jones retreated down the arbor, his head bowed and his figure shadowed.

Cass congratulated himself on delivering a discreet but unmistakable warning. A carefully chosen euphemism and the deed was done. Thankfully, he need never discuss the man's sexual inclinations with Sophie Pinnock. As soon as she had converted the formal landscape to a more natural one, the gardener would go away again.

And so would she.

✃

The carriage rocked and swayed, and Cecelia moaned at every jolt.

"Better than traveling across Portugal," Cass commented.

"Hardly," she gasped, holding onto the leather strap.

He peered through the window to assure himself that Saladin behaved, for Luis was in the saddle with Daniel perched in front of him.

"You used to be an entertaining companion during a journey," his sister commented. "Since we left the castle you've barely uttered a word. You haven't even asked my opinion of your lady landscape gardener. Your account of her was misleading. I imagined her to be widow of more advanced years, plain and sedate."

"I believe her age is close to yours. But I never said she was plain."

"Andrew Searle is obviously smitten."

Cass jerked his head away from the glass pane. "What makes you think so?"

"Feminine intuition," she said on a superior note. "And the way he hovered so attentively." Oblivious to his grim face, she prattled on, "It's no wonder, she's quite lovely. She'd be stunning if she were better dressed. Perhaps I should encourage her to order a few new gowns, to enhance her allure. It would be a most suitable match."

"Suitable in what way?"

Cecelia waved a languid hand. "Andrew Searle hasn't any relations, and very few friends. Mrs. Pinnock's husband died, and her family is far away on some island. She has money of her own and a house, and he's virtually penniless. However, now I think on it, there does appear to be an impediment."

Cass lowered his eyes and studied the stag head carved into

his signet ring.

"Aren't you curious to know what threatens to keep this promising couple apart? Or perhaps I should say *who.*"

"I can't imagine."

"Meu irmao. My oh-so-interested and frightfully jealous brother," she teased. "For he, too, has fallen under the spell of the captivating little widow."

Cass forced a careless laugh, spoiling its effect by saying too emphatically, "Sophie Pinnock may have as many flirts as she wants, marry whomever she pleases. I don't care, as long as she produces a superior landscape plan."

His sister's knowing smile indicated that she didn't credit a word of his assertion. Much to his dismay, Cass hadn't believed it either.

CHAPTER 5

High on a hill with beauteous structures spread
Delightful Clifton rears its rural head,
And looks with pleasure on the vales below,
Where towns are planted and where rivers flow.

~William Heard

*F*ormerly his purest pleasure, composing verses had become a disheartening form of drudgery to Andrew Searle. For the better part of a month he'd labored over a poem, artfully re-phrasing the philosophies of his published essay. After laboriously completing the first section, he found that his words flowed more slowly each day.

Struggling to summon an appropriately poetic vision from the recesses of his fevered brain, he stroked one flushed cheek with the tip of his quill.

Nothing.

His free hand shot out to grip the handle of a tankard. One more swallow—no harm in that. He lifted the vessel to his lips. The wine was faintly bitter, augmented with laudanum.

A sharp rap sounded on the windowpane. He looked over and saw Sophie Pinnock—she smiled and nodded at him, the hood of her red cloak forming a cowl about her face.

A scarlet nun. There might be a poem in that image, thought Andrew, going to open the cottage door.

"You're wandering this wood at an early hour," he greeted her, his spirits rising at the sight of her bright eyes.

"Not so early as you think, sir—it's well past noon. Did you forget to wind your timepiece again?"

Their friendship had prospered, and she was already familiar with his habits and quirks, and even a few of his failings. Admiring the effect of a yellow daffodil pinned to her breast, he observed, "Your flower is a welcome sight on this blustery day."

"Emrys Jones gave it me, a token of St. David's Day."

"Be glad he didn't give you a smelly leek." Could it really be the first day of March? He'd expected to be finished with his poem by now.

"He's in a rare good mood, because his countrymen vanquished the French invaders. The Welsh are a fierce race indeed! You've heard the exciting news from Fishguard?"

"They talk of little else in the Bevington Arms taproom." Recalling that Sophie had neatened his disordered rooms on a previous occasion, Andrew wasn't about to let her escape. "Will you come in?"

"Not today. I stopped to ask if you wanted to join in my ramble."

"Tempting. But I've set myself the task of finishing six lines of poetry by nightfall."

"Mr. Searle, you do your health no good by sitting hunched over your papers all day. This fresh air will benefit you, I'm sure."

"This *cold* air." He gazed pointedly at the overhanging branches, whipping about in a violent gust.

"On my island we say, *'Quant Mars veint coume un agné, i s'en va coume un touoré.'* When March comes in like a lamb, it goes out like a bull. I prefer rough weather early instead of late, when it can harm tender plants."

He struck his chest with his palm. "This tender plant dislikes rough weather at any time of the month."

"You should come along with me," she said coaxingly. "My maid Nan, whose father is gamekeeper here, tells me there's a doe with twin fawns somewhere in this wood. I'd so like to see them, wouldn't you?"

Andrew hadn't the will to decline. If exercise inhibited the effect of the opiate, he could take another dose when he returned. Besides, he wanted as much of Sophie Pinnock's company as she would grant him. The quiet isolation he'd experienced at Bevington was less conducive to writing than he'd imagined, and the solitary hours depressed his spirits. The village blacksmith's daughter, who adequately satisfied his carnal desires, was no companion in any real sense, merely a convenience. Ready enough for a vigorous session of rumpy-pumpy, but out of bed she irritated him with her uncouth accent and slatternly appearance.

Unaccustomed to physical exertion, Andrew quickly wearied of walking. As they followed the deer track winding through the woodland, he was conscious of his deep, heavy breathing and dampening brow. His scarlet-cloaked companion moved briskly and effortlessly, pausing only to point to the nuthatches trilling to one another atop the lofty trees. With a whispering flash of gray wings, they darted from trunk to trunk in search of food. Sophie soon strayed from the path, and bent down to exclaim over a patch of precocious wood violets.

"I don't know how you can bear to keep indoors all day," she declared when she rejoined him. "With so many gardening tasks, and the endless marvels to discover here in the woods, I've made very little progress with his lordship's designs." Her hood fell back, revealing a pair of flushed cheeks.

"What a child of nature you are," he commented.

"*Oh, las,* you must mean I've got leaves caught in my hair. Or has my cloak dragged in the mud again?" She looked down to check.

"You look splendid to me, Sophie. Do you object to my calling you by your name? I feel as though we're comrades."

"Are we?" She seemed surprised. "But you, sir, are a poet and an author. I must treat you with the same respect I'd show your illustrious friends Mr. Coleridge and Mr. Wordsworth. If I ever met them."

"I can assure you they would be charmed by you. As I am."

She resumed her swift march to the heart of the wood, leaving Andrew to wonder if he'd forced a premature intimacy. He knew next to nothing about female expectations. This one had given the impression of being approachable, but perhaps he'd misinterpreted her warmth of manner and high spirits.

Cass Carysfort, whose amorous career had been a long and spectacular one, could no doubt tell him how to proceed. Even in their schooldays, his best mate had been devoted to the fair sex. Andrew couldn't remember a time when Cass had lacked a sweetheart. He hadn't shared the details of his most recent exploits but undoubtedly there was a mistress somewhere, one whose identity he preferred to keep to himself.

"Senhor Searle!"

Luis Costa was loping after them, hat in hand.

"Where senhora is?"

"Here," Sophie replied, stepping out from behind a broad oak tree. At the sight of her employer's Portuguese valet, she felt a curious mixture of anticipation and dismay. Had the earl returned to Bevington?

"Senhora." The servant's heels came together and he bent low from the waist in a polished bow.

She smiled at the formality, so incongruous in this wilderness setting.

"You return with me."

"To the castle?"

"Where senhorio live—in Clifton. You travel there today. Is his command."

His high and mighty lordship had slyly avoided a confrontation—and a debate—by sending his servant to give the order. *Zut,* but he was a wily *dêmon!* "Can you tell me *why* I've been summoned, or how long I can expect to be away?"

Luis shook his head. "He say to Senhora Fonseca you staying in blue bedchamber. Is very fine." With one of his gleaming smiles, he added, "And he send his carriage. Most comfortable for you."

Said Andrew Searle, "Strong inducements, indeed. It seems I must bid you farewell."

No one cared whether it suited her convenience to go to Clifton. Nettled, Sophie said, "I've no choice, then, if everything is arranged. Mr. Searle, I look forward to resuming our ramble as soon as the earl allows me to return. Whenever that may be," she concluded waspishly.

Living with Tobias Pinnock, working as his assistant, she'd grown accustomed to traveling at short notice. By the time she returned to the gatehouse, she'd made a mental selection of clothing she intended to take with her.

Nan Parham's bemused reaction to the abrupt summons reinforced Sophie's annoyance.

"Whatever can the new earl be wanting, so sudden-like?" the girl wondered, voicing the very question that nagged at her mistress. She said darkly, "He may be a lord, and handsome as he can stare, but he hadn't ought to treat you so harsh. Why, you're a proper lady."

Sophie interrupted this show of support by telling Nan which garments she wanted packed into her *baheur*. Then she sat down to write out a list of instructions for Emrys Jones. At her behest he'd potted up a variety of favorite plants—double wallflowers and sweet williams and campanulas—and the seedlings required regular attention. He was ready to sow the hardy annual flowers in the borders, and needed to know about her preference for larkspur, oriental mallow, and nasturtiums. At the bottom of the page she added a pithy reminder that he hadn't yet provided a list of the rose bushes. How cross it would make him!

"Carry this note to Mr. Jones, please," she said, holding it out to Luis. "He's working in the knot gardens."

As he took the paper, his face wore an uncharacteristic frown. "I glad to do anything senhora ask. Only—senhorio, he warn me no go near Senhor Shones."

Sophie was unsure how to answer this puzzling statement, for she had no right to contradict the earl's instructions to his servant. But Luis apparently decided that her wish superseded his master's, and with an acquiescent bow he hurried off to fulfill her request.

By the time he reappeared, she had changed into her green

traveling habit and finished her preparations.

"Is what you wear first time you come to Bevington," he commented. "Color of—of *musgo*. Plant covering damp places, like growing velvet."

"Moss," said Sophie as she stood before a mirror, carefully setting her bonnet on her head. "Did you find Mr. Jones?"

He nodded, his countenance quite pensive. "This *jardineiro*, I no think he like me. After he take letter, he turn and walk away fast." After lifting her box to his shoulder, Luis shook his head. "*Ai, ai, ai,* am forgetting! Senhorio, *ele disse-me*— he tell me is something you are needing. Say he want you bring—" He wrinkled his brow. "I cannot remember words. In my language, *matériais de desenhos.*"

"Designs?" But of course, she thought, the earl intended to review her drawings. Her sense of impending doom increased tenfold.

Not that she was wholly unprepared. But she'd produced several rough sketches only, none that could pass for a proper landscape plan. Each time she settled down to work, she invariably made a detailed drawing of the existing scenery. Shoving page after page between the stiff boards of her portfolio, she was appalled to see how many studies she'd made of the castle towers—the terrace walks—the pavilion— the canal.

If her unrefined proposal for a new landscape failed to impress her employer, she might well find herself on the very next coach bound for Chiswick. Surprisingly, that distressed her. At first Bevington Castle had seemed as unfriendly as its master. Had she become attached to the place?

She tied the broad ribbons of the portfolio and tucked it under her arm. Resigning herself to whatever unpleasantness fate held in store, she made her way down the spiral stairway.

The Portuguese servant's assurances about the comfort of the earl's carriage had not prepared her for its luxurious appointments. The seats were upholstered in leather and were remarkably well sprung; the glass windows on either side were equipped with folding screens that could be lowered to shut out errant beams of sunlight. Pinned to the interior's silken lining was a flower holder containing a nosegay of daffodils.

"Is all right to pick for you?" said Luis, climbing in after her. "Are so many here."

Indeed there were, and she'd miss gazing down upon their golden glory from her lofty gatehouse chambers. She regretted having to leave them, and wished she knew whether it was only for a few days, or forever.

Sophie spied a milestone at the edge of a hedgerow, and realized she and her chatty escort were but five miles out of Bristol. In his broken but comprehensible English, Luis had entertained her with tales of his family and his native village in Portugal.

"How did you become Lord Bevington's valet?" Sophie wondered.

"Senhor Carys-fort," Luis corrected her. "He no was senhorio when I meet him. *Aconteceu há seis anos*—seven year ago it happen. He stop in Colares one day to let horses rest and drink, and see my sister Ines by the fountain. Promise he give her money and clothes, take her away with him to live at his *palácio* at Sintra. He want her for—because of her—she have such—" He cupped his hands over his chest to illustrate breasts.

"Oh."

Sophie's days as a blushing virgin were long past, and she was seldom shocked by any man's behavior. The former Mr. Carysfort was ruled by his desires—that much she already knew. There was absolutely no reason why his servant's revelation should make her feel so wretched.

"Ines agree to be—I do not know the word," he concluded, shaking his head.

Sophie could think of several, but had no desire to expand his vocabulary.

Eh bien, she thought. Luis Costa's bosomy sibling had been Cassian Carysfort's mistress. Hardly surprising—beneath that hard, uncompromising exterior he was a passionate man, as she'd discovered on one unforgettable occasion among the snowdrops. Having experienced the power and persuasiveness of his kisses, she could understand how masterfully he'd overcome the girl's scruples—assuming that she'd had any. Possibly the parents had insisted that she make the most of a good opportunity. Portuguese peasants might have no qualms about handing over an attractive daughter to a man of wealth and power, in the hope of gaining by it.

"One day, when I carry message from *familia* to *palácio,* he say do I want to be servant, he offer to pay me well like Ines. I happy to work for him and Senhora Fonseca." Luis exhibited pride rather than shame over his sister's surrender of her virtue, from which he had benefitted greatly. But his smile faded when he said, "I no like leaving Portugal. One day I go back there, see my home again."

"Did Ines not come to England?"

Shaking his head, he replied, "Senhor send her home to Colares long before. Much money he give her. She and *esposo* have two boys now."

The eldest, Sophie gathered, had been sired by Cassian Carysfort. That was the way these affairs ended, whether in Portugal or in England: the girl, falling pregnant, was paid handsomely enough to attract a husband in her village. Ines was hardly an object of pity—unless her pride or her heart had been bruised by her abductor's brusque dismissal. And even if he'd bestowed a small fortune upon her, still she had suffered the stigma of raising his child where its bastardy would be common knowledge.

This troubling revelation about her employer made Sophie wonder about his other mistresses. Had there been many of them, did he have one now? Her curiosity would go unsatisfied—encouraging a servant to gossip about his master was contemptible, and she couldn't take advantage of Luis Costa's confiding nature.

Sooner than she expected the toll road brought them to Clifton, a peaceful hilltop village scattered across furzy downland. Rows of pale stone townhouses overlooked busy Bristol and the deep gorge the River Avon had carved into the landscape. Sophie noticed that fully half of one long crescent was merely a facade, its roofless structures pitted with holes where sash windows ought to have been.

"Because of French war," Luis explained, "no money for finishing houses or making more. Builders and carpenters not working now, and must set man-traps to keep away *ladraos*—thiefs."

They proceeded up a steep incline to a triangular common grazed by sheep. The postilion pulled up his horses in front of a large stone-built residence in the Palladian style.

"Is called Summit House. Senhorio has finest view in

Clifton, *é verdade!*"

The house was indeed impressive, Sophie acknowledged grudgingly. Older in style than the plain-fronted terraces stretching along the green, it was partly hidden from the road by a low wall and had a front lawn unrelieved by plantings or ornaments. Half a dozen steps ascended to the entrance, where a pair of slender columns supported a triangular pediment above the front door.

She followed Luis inside, and found herself in a broad hall that extended the entire length of the house, lit by great chandeliers placed at intervals. Standing beneath one of them was her employer. Sophie tensed as he moved forward.

"Mrs. Pinnock, here you are at last. I'm very pleased to see you again."

A greeting more gracious than she'd ever received from him, accompanied by a winning smile. Even so, her nerves remained on edge. "Good day, my lord," she answered coolly. "Am I to learn why you so urgently demanded that I come to you?"

"Not demanded. Requested."

"You should be more careful in the wording of your *requests*. And perhaps you might communicate more clearly your reasons."

When he lunged at her, she almost expected him to box her ears for impertinence.

"Come with me." Gripping her arm, he towed her down the long hall to the door at the far end and led her out onto an elevated landing. There was a plunging double stairway, and he forced her to go down, hurrying her to the bottom.

Sloping away from the house was a wasteland with a few stunted, windswept trees and jutting boulders. Because the property dropped off sharply at a cliff edge, it offered an unobstructed view of the rooftops and conical glassworks of Bristol, as well as the woodland on the opposite side of the ragged gorge.

"What is your opinion?" he asked.

She drew a deep breath. "Magnificent."

"Not the distant prospect. I want to know what you think of the nearer landscape."

She regarded him uncertainly. "What do you mean, what 'landscape?'"

"Ah, precisely," he said, with a vigorous nod. "You, madam, shall tame this wilderness. The man who built this house had no money left over to complete whatever vision he may have had for his grounds, and subsequent owners left it in its natural state. I have no vision whatsoever and am vastly weary of Cecelia's complaints. We depend upon you to perform your magic here."

"What about my work at the castle?"

"For the time being, you must concentrate all your efforts here at Summit House."

Sophie felt she ought to refuse on principle, in protest. Only she didn't want to. Her fingers curled, as if gripping the pencil and sketchpad she craved. This undeveloped terrain, unlike the well-established gardens at Bevington, presented an ideal opportunity for creating a picturesque landscape to complement the elegant Palladian house.

"You must have some sort of plan in mind." She prayed he wasn't contrary enough to insist upon a formal garden here, where it was least wanted.

"My sister and I will be guided by your judgment, Mrs. Pinnock."

His response pleased her so much that she wasn't discomfited by his warm tone and even warmer smile. Treading the rocky, uneven ground, she said, "But I haven't got the necessary paper, or pencils. No pen or ink, or watercolor paints to mix and work with."

"Why ever not? I instructed you—rather, I *requested* that you bring your drawing materials with you. Did Luis neglect to tell you?"

"I misunderstood. He didn't know the English word, and I had difficulty translating his Portuguese. I thought you meant to examine my completed sketches. Those I've brought with me."

"Never mind. He can go back to the castle for all that you require. I'll order fresh horses put to the carriage."

"Sécours dé grace!" she cried.

Cass stared, wondering what the devil he done to annoy her.

"You can't make him travel so far a second time in a day. It wasn't his fault that I failed to interpret your wishes correctly."

"As you say, madam," he said, feigning meekness. "He can go tomorrow, or even the day after."

Much to his own astonishment, Cass liked being dictated to by this tart, straightforward little woman, whose brown eyes sparkled so delightfully.

Manfully, and with great difficulty, he'd tried to forget about Sophie Pinnock during the fortnight since their momentous encounter at Bevington. And despite his tendency to dwell upon her lovely face and lively personality, he'd almost been persuaded that it was a ridiculous infatuation and would likely be of short duration. The novelty she represented, he'd persuaded himself, would soon subside. Besides, he reasoned,

Drew was also interested and had possibly developed more serious intentions. For the sake of a long friendship, he would stifle his interest in a flirtation.

Life was complicated enough. Not only was he concerned about Cecelia's fragile state of mind and health, there was also the chance that Sir Michael Tait might make a nuisance of himself. Such considerations prevented him from pursuing any female just now, however appealing she might be.

These good intentions were undermined by his sister, who had immediately detected his burning jealousy of Searle. Even more surprising for a lady so self-absorbed, she had correctly identified the cause. And Cecelia had even suggested a way to separate the poet and the lady landscape designer. Mrs. Pinnock's expertise, she declared, would be extremely valuable here at Summit House. After a token but feeble show of resistance to her scheme, Cass had dispatched his valet to Bevington with orders to bring back the very person he was trying to put out of his mind.

She was pacing well ahead of him now, lines of concentration etched into her white brow. Murmured phrases spilled from her lips—not French, but that similar patois peculiar to the Isle of Jersey.

"Clusters of native conifers there and cedars just here, *p't-être*." Her hands moved constantly, illustrating. "Wild dog roses scrambling down the hillside, ivy made to ramble across these great rocks. A serpentine path of crushed pale stone, *absolument*, to harmonize with the color of the house."

She was going about this business far too quickly. Cass, determined to keep her near him for as long as he could, broke in upon her flights of fancy. "You needn't decide all at once. After the long drive you must want tea, and time to rest before coming down to dinner."

"Coming down? *Nânnîn,* I prefer a tray in my room."

"Cecelia won't hear of it. She regards you as our guest, the first we've had since coming here to live. I warn you, she still follows the Portuguese custom of formal dining, and arrays herself in finery even when we are but two at table."

"In that case I beg to be excused. None of my gowns would be suitable."

He smiled. "My dear Mrs. Pinnock, a beautiful lady is a pleasure to behold no matter how simple her attire."

Her expression was disapproving. "Lord Bevington, I would be much obliged if you'd refrain from making personal remarks. Our association must continue to be—to be—"

"Businesslike?" Her flushed cheeks indicated that her thoughts had already strayed from garden-making. Very likely she had also remembered their last meeting, and the heated kisses she'd bestowed as well as received.

With a single compliment he had made a breach in that damnably frustrating reserve of hers. This was, he congratulated himself, a promising start to what he trusted would be a protracted and highly stimulating alliance.

CHAPTER 6

She yet more pure, sweet, straight and fair,
Than gardens, woods, meads, meadows, rivers are.

~Andrew Marvell

The dining room reeked of money and superior taste. Nile green damask curtained the tall windows, and an Aubusson rug with pastel hues covered the floor. Mr. Sheraton's London workshop had produced the long parquet table and its matching chairs, and the elegant mahogany sideboard. A giltwood-framed mirror and a variety of tasteful paintings adorned the walls.

A beautiful room for beautiful people, thought Sophie. Despite the frothy neck ruffle and blue silk bow at her breast, she felt woefully underdressed in her muslin gown. The brother and sister were exquisitely turned out: he in starched cravat and black evening coat, she in bronze silk with a topaz necklace and dangling eardrops.

Sophie lifted a forkful of fish to her mouth, listening to the pair converse in their light, well-bred voices. There was, she perceived, no depth to their exchanges. They talked at each other, and confined themselves to trifles. Did her presence inhibit them, or were they more conscious of their liveried footmen?

Mrs. Fonseca caroled on about her latest purchases. Lord Bevington alluded to the financial crisis that roiled the nation yet appeared not to be adversely affected by it. They were so rich, marveled Sophie, that rampant bank failures and a currency shortage didn't concern them in the least. The lady saw no reason to curtail her daily visits to the Clifton shops. The gentleman had just decreed that his garden designer might order as many plants as she pleased without counting the cost. The recent invasion scare and the French landing in Wales hadn't unsettled the Carysforts' rarified existence.

The meal dragged on. Even though Sophie had been warned, yet she was amazed by the number and variety of courses—and with each, another bottle of wine. A bowl of soup and a breast of chicken in the privacy of her room would have suited her far better than the platters of meat and fish spread out before her and the tureens brimming with rich sauces. At home she seldom ate elaborately prepared dishes, and since her husband's death she'd continued eating the simple, healthful fare she had provided during his illness.

The presence of the little boy Daniel might have enlivened the meal, but he'd been tucked into his bed hours ago. With a smile at her hostess, she said, "I was pleased to renew my acquaintance with your son, Mrs. Fonseca."

"If he makes a nuisance of himself, you must be sure to inform his *criada,* Maria."

"I can't imagine he will. He doesn't seem at all naughty to me."

Mrs. Fonseca wore a pained expression. The earl smiled broadly.

"Daniel," he explained, "has a habit of wandering off. We permit him to play on the green only if Luis or Maria accompanies him. But at the castle he'll be able to roam to his heart's content."

Cecelia looked surprised. "I'm not sure it's wise to grant him too much freedom."

"What harm can befall him at Bevington?"

With a delicate, pale hand, she picked up her knife and pushed at the food on her plate. "He might tumble into the canal. Or meet with some accident in the stables. And those dense woods—what if he got lost in them? So many poor, beggarly people live in the countryside, he could be stolen away."

"Be easy, Cecelia. Luis is vigilant enough to prevent such mishaps. The time for mollycoddling the boy is past. Let him get as dirty as he pleases and make mischief. As I did," he added with a grin.

"You were incorrigible, and I can't conceive of a worse example of conduct for my son."

Clearly Daniel's upbringing was a sensitive topic, and Cecelia Fonseca had a highly developed protective instinct—having lost a husband, she was desperate to ensure her little boy's safety. Love and fear, Sophie had discovered during her own marriage, were never very far apart.

The arrival of the fruit and cheese signaled that her ordeal was nearly over. The strain of socializing with a client was new to her, for whenever she and Tobias had been called in for a country house consultation they'd stayed at a nearby inn. No patron, until now, had offered her more than a glass of ratafia and a biscuit. She didn't approve of such intimacy with her employers—far better to maintain a proper distance.

"Step into the drawing room, Mrs. Pinnock," Cecelia invited, effectively preventing Sophie's intended flight to the blue bedchamber. "I've been trying out a new piece of music, and want to show off my progress. You must join us, *meu irmao*—I'll not have you sitting here alone with your port."

They removed to a chamber across the hall, even more ornately ornamented with a rococo plasterwork ceiling and sculptured marble chimneypiece. The mongrel dog lay stretched out before the hearth. At her master's approach she thumped her long tail in greeting and lifted her head from the carpet.

The earl guided Sophie to the settee, seating her near the fire, and chose for himself an armchair directly across from her. The soothing notes of a sonata and the warmth of hissing coals soon coaxed her into a state of relaxation. While studying her surroundings, she studiously avoided the gentleman's gaze. This oppressive luxury did not please her as well as the comforts of her own parlor at Chiswick, or Bevington's antique grandeur. If this were her house, she'd choose this east-facing room for dining and use the west-facing one as a parlor, to take advantage of the afternoon light.

The earl stared at her. She lowered her eyelashes, wondering what he'd think about her brazen re-arrangement of his fashionable furniture.

"Well done, Cecelia," he commented when his sister finished her piece.

Widowhood, thought Sophie, was the only trait she shared with her willowy, impeccably dressed, and musically gifted hostess. "I wish I could play so beautifully," she said. "I learned to play when I was a girl, but I liked sketching far better."

"And I can scarcely draw a straight line," Cecelia answered. She leaned forward to blow out the candles in the holders affixed to her instrument. With light and graceful steps, she made her way across the room. "I hope you won't mind, *meu irmao*, if I retire early tonight."

"Are you feeling unwell?"

Cecelia's thin shoulders lifted in a shrug. "Ever so slightly fatigued. Your pardon, Mrs. Pinnock, for deserting you on your first evening. I'm afraid Cass has a habit of hiding behind *the Bristol Gazette* or Mr. Farley's *Journal*. But you're not his sister, so perhaps he will be more attentive." With a vague smile, she glided out of the drawing room.

Sophie hastened to say, "I shan't keep you from your papers, my lord. It is time I also went upstairs."

He prevented her from following his sister with a sharp, "Not yet. Please stay." More mildly he added, "I'm eager to view your designs for my new landscape at Bevington." Crossing to the door, he stuck his head into the hall. "Edward, fetch Mrs. Pinnock's portfolio from her chamber." He directed a questioning glance at Sophie. "Would you care for tea? Cecelia has a standing order for a tray to be sent in at eleven, but we can have it sooner."

She declined the offer, hoping to escape him as soon as possible. After the footman delivered her portfolio and promptly vanished, the earl moved a candelabrum from the mantel shelf to a low table.

"I'll spread the drawings out on the floor." His foot gently prodded the dog's flank. "Up you go, my girl, I need that place."

Echo rose and stretched, then leaped onto the settee and curled up next to Sophie.

"I'm afraid," said his lordship, with false gravity, "you've become entangled in a conspiracy. I grant Echo the privilege of lying there after Cecelia goes up to bed. In the morning a parlor maid brushes any fur off the cushion and she turns it over every week. My sister is none the wiser."

Leaving the mongrel in full possession of the settee, Sophie joined him on the floor and opened her portfolio. Bleakly she stared at a detailed watercolor of the terrace walk before sorting through the contents. When she found what she wanted, she said apologetically, "These are preliminary sketches."

The landscape depicted in the black ink and sepia wash design was rough and wildly picturesque. Thickly planted roses and ivy concealed the retaining walls of the terraces. Italianate statues and classical urns decorated the bowling green. The laburnums were missing and as was the shrubbery walk, with only a few bushy remnants of evergreen left behind to fill the space. She'd removed the wall of the rose bower and had taken away the arbors. The antique knot gardens had vanished, giving way to an unobstructed carpet of grass. A serpentine river meandered past the pavilion—a support for more creeping vines—toward the deer park and a sham ruin.

If Emrys Jones ever sees this plan, thought Sophie, he'll never speak to me again.

Lord Bevington examined each drawing closely, and reviewed them yet again before giving his opinion. "A drastic alteration."

"For the most part I did what you asked," she defended herself. "I tried to."

"I'm not dissatisfied, Soph—Mrs. Pinnock. Quite the contrary."

She was sorry to hear it, because now he would expect her

to implement the plan. A major re-structuring of the grounds would take at least a year, if not two. And during that time, he would require her to return to Bevington Castle.

"It will be a lengthy process," she warned. "And costly. An engineer must re-direct the flow of the water. Laborers are needed to take down walls, and masons must construct the ruin from the stones. As for gardeners, it will take an army of them to position all the plantings."

"Yes, of course," he said absently. He looked over her study of the golden daffodils and colorful crocuses growing along the upper terrace. "A charming picture. There's liveliness in this that the others lack."

His discernment startled her. Painting the castle gardens in their present state had inspired her to greater feats of artistry than creating the new plans. "Your designs will look prettier after they are finished in watercolors and bound in your Blue Book," she assured him.

As they both reached for the drawing of the spring bulbs, his fingers brushed against the back of her hand—deliberately, she was certain. He hovered so close that her shoulder was grazing his shirt sleeve—when had he removed his coat? To her dismay, she discovered that her full white skirt had billowed across his long legs.

The candlelight made his black hair glisten. His thick lashes cast dark shadows, like strokes from a charcoal pencil, across his cheekbones. He turned his head. His mouth was only inches away, temptingly close. She felt faint and flushed. She had difficulty breathing—swallowing.

All that wine at dinner—she was tipsy, that's why her mind was so muddled. And he'd been drinking, too. She didn't trust him, and trusted herself even less. *Oh, las,* if he put his arms around her now, she would disgrace herself again. His ardent gaze was already melting her resistance.

"Sophie," he said softly, turning her name into a caress.

Unable or unwilling to save herself, she swayed toward him.

Her hot blood was abruptly chilled by a long, low moan.

Abruptly they drew apart. Then they shared a shaky laugh, for the noise had come from Echo, slumbering soundly on her cushion.

"*Ma fé,* it must be late," she said, her voice strangled by shame. Nervously she twisted the ring encircling her finger—Tobias's signet. The earl saw her doing it.

"Yes," he answered, his tone subdued. "After traveling some fifteen miles and enduring a long evening you've earned your rest. And you'll need it, for I predict that Cecelia will invite you to accompany her to the New Hot Well tomorrow morning." His hand closed firmly on Sophie's forearm as she gathered up her artwork. "Leave them. Not just the Bevington plans—all your drawings."

An argument would only serve to prolong her agony. "Of course."

"I wish you a good night, Mrs. Pinnock."

Pausing in the doorway, she turned back to say, "*Bouonne niet* to you also, Lord Bevington."

Why, she wondered, did his return to formality make her feel so forlorn?

Sifting through a drawer in search of a pen-wiper, Andrew Searle unexpectedly found a shilling. Delighted to learn that he wasn't completely destitute, he decided to visit his friend and fellow poet Samuel Coleridge. This piece of silver, together with his meager collection of copper coins, would adequately fund a journey to Somerset—provided he didn't stop at Bristol and allow himself to be tempted by the booksellers' wares.

High time he took a holiday from writing, he told himself while searching the untidy cottage for his sturdiest shoes. He thrust his shaving gear and some clothes into a battered valise and pocketed his purse. Armed with his trusty and well-traveled walking stick, he set out for Nether Stowey.

He followed the Severn Estuary to the mouth of the Avon, arriving some time after the last ferry departed. He slept in a hay-barn that night, like a vagabond, and caught the first boat the following morning. During his crossing, he offered tuppence to the driver of a milk wagon to carry him to an Axbridge inn. There he hired a horse for the rest of the way, intending to return it in two days.

Sam Coleridge occupied a thatched cottage at the farthest end of Lime Street, but the glowing descriptions in his letters didn't prepare Andrew for the muddy lane, or his small and derelict dwelling. The happy couple and their lodger had just sat down to dinner when Andrew knocked at their door. Their greetings were surprised but perfectly cordial and welcoming. Another place was set at the rickety table, and he shared their meal of parsnips and boiled pudding.

"It gladdens my heart to see you," said the poet when Andrew apologized for his unexpected arrival. "Sara and Charles will confirm that I've been feeling rather low."

"Sam is always better for having company," his wife commented.

"He has me," Charles Lloyd declared, apparently slighted by her comment.

Mrs. Coleridge pressed her lips together as if trying to withhold a retort. All eyes returned to their plates, and Andrew sensed a heightened tension in the cramped dining room.

The former Sara Fricker, whom he remembered as quite pretty and amiable, had lost some of her bloom during the year and a half since her marriage. Her slight acquaintance with the unpredictable and eccentric poet had resulted in a long and rocky engagement. Apparently they had settled into a cozy partnership, though perhaps not as perfect a one as her idealistic spouse had envisioned. She listened with rare patience to Sam's dreamy oratory, cheered him as best she could during his bouts of depression, and was an attentive mother to their infant son Hartley. She alone was practical and capable enough to deal with the common concerns of life: money, food, clothing.

"If our venture in rural self-sufficiency fails," said Sam morosely, "we needn't go far to seek shelter. This hovel, you see, lies conveniently near the local poorhouse."

The sparsely furnished house was overrun with mice whose scurrying kept Andrew awake much of the night. Sam, so concerned about the welfare of animals that he ate meat but once a week, couldn't bring himself to kill them.

The establishment's sole servant was a moony girl with a weak chest, ill-suited to hard labor. Sara Coleridge, therefore, was constantly harried and overworked. Her ambitious husband lacked any agricultural experience and was unaccustomed to tending a garden and orchard. Their student lodger was, in Andrew's estimation, no fit companion for a melancholy poet. Even worse, Charles Lloyd suffered from uncontrollable fits of frenzy. But because he also represented the couple's chief source of income, they were reluctant to send him back to his family. And they were in sore need of companionship, for the villagers suspected them of being radicals and Jacobins—rightly so—and they were shunned.

Sam, mired in apathy and dejection, isolated from the familiar bustle of Bristol, resorted to regular doses of laudanum.

"What a favor you did me by recommending it," he said one afternoon while they struggled together to prepare the ground for a row of cabbages. "I wouldn't have survived my illness last autumn without those twenty-five heavenly drops every four hours."

Always interested in the drug's effect on others, Andrew asked, "What's the most you've taken at once?"

"Upwards of seventy drops. And you?"

"Two or three teaspoons. My teaspoon measures exactly one hundred drops. But my tolerance exceeds yours because I've used the drug far longer."

Seven years, he reflected, since Cass Carysfort had educated him in the use of opiates. He'd been slaving away as a journalist in London, writing for the gutter press, and Cass had been caught up in the social whirl. Laudanum had rendered their very different worlds appear less bleak, it had sustained their confidence and lifted their spirits. Many a night they'd met at Andrew's lodgings and dosed themselves into a transitory sense of cheerfulness. Although his memories of that period in London were hazy, in his diary he'd faithfully recorded their experimentations in the weeks before Cass's inexplicable flight to Portugal. It would be interesting to review his account when he returned to Bevington.

Resuming his inquiry, he asked, "Have you done a great deal of writing since coming here to live?"

Shrugging, Sam replied, "I compose very little. I absolutely hate composition. At present I'm editing verses for a new edition of *Poems on Various Subjects*—by myself and others—for Joseph Cottle's press in Bristol. I shall continue using the laudanum, for it alone induces the dream-like state that inspires my best poetry."

"Lately my own muse has slumbered," Andrew admitted. "Every attempt to rouse her has failed. Without the laudanum I'd get nothing written at all. I came here in hopes that a change of scene might refresh and inspire me."

"Writing is a hopeless profession," declared Coleridge gloomily. "Friends become carping critics and counsel you to alter your verses to conform to their opinion. Have I told you of Charles Lamb's comments about my *Destiny of Nations?* They don't bear repeating. What's more, he mislikes my choice of refuge. 'Remember,' he says, 'you're not in Arcadia when you are in the West of England.'"

"A Londoner," Andrew muttered. "What does he know?"

"The only encouragement I've received of late comes from that fellow Wordsworth. You met him in Bristol shortly before my marriage." Impatiently, Sam shoved at the dark fringe tumbling over his brow. "Nowadays my penury forces me to write reviews of ridiculous novels. I'm sick to death of reading about castles and dungeons and horrors."

Andrew resolved never to show his friend "The Blackened Betrothal," the story ballad he'd once recited to Sophie Pinnock, or any of his similar efforts.

Sam pursed his full, plummy lips disdainfully. "And yet my latest scribblings make as little sense to me as they did to

Lamb. There's a great work swelling in my mind, I'm sure of it. I'm haunted by images of a rolling sea, and sails that refuse to billow in a calm. And a bird—a large, strange bird."

Andrew cast a pitying glance at the wild-eyed, shock-haired fellow wielding the hoe. He transferred his gaze to his hostess, seated on a nearby stump with young Hartley balanced on her knee. In a counterpoint to her spouse's anguished recital of woe, Sara was singing like a nightingale as she pinned their son's baby cloth.

Sam paused in his work. "My advice, friend, is to accept the position as tutor to Lord Bevington's nephew. You'll be happier for it, and better compensated than any poet. With an earl's patronage, you could do very well for yourself. Open a school, mold young minds."

"That's your ambition, not mine." He would continue his writing, whatever else he might decide to do.

Andrew departed Nether Stowey with four fresh poems in his pocket, all devoted to domestic subjects. Despite their tribulations, Sam and Sara had forged a strong marital bond, one that he greatly envied. A solitary existence, he now believed, had stifled his creativity. He needed a woman of his own. He couldn't go on fending for himself, or begging favors from his friend Cass. A wife, moneyed and efficient, would cater to all his wants. The prospect of sleeping beside a warm female body, eating regular meals, and living in a servant-run household exerted a strong appeal.

Retracing his route in the direction of Bristol, his thoughts centered on the marriageable females he knew.

That sluttish girl in Bevington village had a flair for bed-sport, but was illiterate, dirty, and hadn't a penny to her name. A female without funds was no use to him.

Cecelia Fonseca, the opposite of his lowborn mistress, was too rich and beautiful for a humble poet—even one whose work she professed to admire. Seven years ago he'd adored her from afar, tortured by her indifference. In the throes of despair he'd written dozens of sonnets and had sought solace in liquor and opium. But her long absence from England had aided his recovery. She was no longer the exquisite butterfly for whom he'd sighed. Foreign living and marriage and motherhood had matured her, dimming her luster.

His thoughts turned to Sophie Pinnock. Attractive, but not dauntingly so. Sensible and serene. Past the age of romantical fantasies but still of child-bearing years. After dandling the infant Hartley on his knee a few times, Andrew rather thought he'd like having sons. An artist, and an artist's widow, she wouldn't be troubled by his devotion to his work. Most necessary of all, she had both money and property.

Andrew assumed she'd be eager to stop traveling the country in the service of clients. Though he expected her to abandon the designing of landscapes after remarriage, he couldn't imagine her leading an idle life. Upon reflection, he decided that she could give drawing lessons, receiving pupils while at the same time producing and rearing his children.

He prided himself on being too rational and experienced to fall prey to a female again, but by the time he reached the city he was quite desperate to see Sophie Pinnock again. Summit House was only a bit out of his way, and in any case Cass was sure to offer him a bed for the night.

Wearily he trudged up the steep streets leading to the heights of Clifton, partly obscured by fog. His leg muscles rebelled during the ascent of Sion Hill, but he forced himself to keep going. Charming Sophie waited for him at the top. He could see the pale stone house—nearly there.

"Senhor Searle!" the Portuguese servant greeted him at the door. "You have walked from castle?"

"Somerset," Andrew panted. "I need to see—I was hoping—I say, would you tell Mrs. Pinnock I'm here?"

"Senhora gone away. She take Daniel and senhorio's dog to the Durdham Down."

A ramble across the downs—so like her! Exhaustion, unfortunately, prevented him from chasing her down. "Lord Bevington is here, I trust."

"Senhorio go after them an hour ago and no has returned."

Andrew's optimism was rapidly waning, and frustration sharpened his voice. "And Mrs. Fonseca, is she at home to visitors?"

"Resting, as she always do in afternoon. I no allowed to disturb her. But I tell her you stop, senhor."

He'd never much liked Luis, ceaselessly grinning and nattering on in broken English. Now Andrew heartily wished him at the devil, damned foreign upstart that he was. But his own dependence on Carysfort goodwill prevented him from forcing his way in.

He lacked the strength to tramp the fifteen miles of road to Bevington; he would have to hire a horse in the village. Before starting back down the hill, he saw a group of men at work behind the house. Most were armed with shovels, others were raking gravel. Their presence explained the summons that had removed Sophie Pinnock from Bevington.

Cass never ceased to find ways to spend that fortune of his, Andrew observed sourly. Improve this, alter that. Well, he'd better make good use of the lady's services while they were still available to him. It wouldn't be long before she retired from her profession, changed her name from Pinnock to Searle, and began devoting all her time and her full attention to her new husband.

CHAPTER 7

The morning rose that untouch'd stands
Arm'd with her briers, how sweet she smells!

~Sir Robert Ayton

Cass's attempts to improve his foundering relationship with his lady landscape gardener were thwarted not only by her devotion to her work, but also by his sister's incessant demands. For two full weeks Sophie Pinnock was a constant but elusive presence in his household. Her mornings were claimed by Cecelia, pitifully starved for female companionship and conversation, who insisted that Sophie attend her routine visits to the Pump Room and the endless shopping forays that Cass found so dull. During the remainder of the day Sophie consulted with the contractor and supervised the crew of laborers leveling and re-shaping the grounds. In the evening, her attention again turned to Cecelia.

The opportunity he'd sought came one morning at breakfast, when she asked Cass whether she might use his carriage to visit a nurseryman's establishment on Durdham Down. Eager to get her alone, he volunteered to drive her there himself in his new phaeton.

"Nânnîn," she protested firmly, "I couldn't impose."

"But I'd already planned an outing," he replied. "A pair of bay horses is being brought round for me to try, and this excursion of yours will permit me to study their faults and merits." When she failed to answer, he added, "You can depend on me to get you there and back in perfect safety, Mrs. Pinnock. I'm an experienced driver."

Cecelia readily supported his assertion, saying, "It's true. When he stayed with our Carysfort cousins in Oporto, he won a gold cup at a competition. He's just as clever about boats—he even sailed up the coast of Portugal in his yacht." With a reminiscent smile, she said to her brother, "You were so amazed when you returned from your voyage and found that Daniel had learned to walk during your absence."

"And quite cross to have missed those first steps."

When he assisted Sophie into his phaeton, she commented, "A sailor, and a charioteer—your lordship's accomplishments are more numerous than I supposed. What other talents have you neglected to mention?"

"I daresay they'll reveal themselves in due course," he responded. "Are you comfortable?"

"Oui-dgia."

The body of his expensive and highly fashionable acquisition was painted bottle green and bore a thick coat of varnish; the seat, covered in cordovan leather, had a graceful curving back. The bay horses were every bit as handsome as the carriage. But their habits were unfamiliar, and he concentrated on his driving as they neared a treacherously uneven stretch of Gallows Acre Lane.

His pretty passenger spread a broadsheet upon her lap, a catalogue of plants offered for sale at the nursery gardens. Now that her sketches for his new landscape were complete and the workers had shifted earth and rock, her busy little mind was consumed with Latin names and habits of growth and prices.

"I'll be disappointed if Miller and Sweet cannot supply me with Madagascar periwinkle," she said, eyes fixed on the page before her. "The white flowers will look especially fine by moonlight."

"Cecelia is most unlikely to be wandering outdoors after the moon is up."

Smiling, Sophie looked over at him. "I'm making a garden so splendid that she'll be tempted to use it at all hours."

"If she doesn't, I shall," he vowed. A moonlit landscape was the perfect place to carry out the seduction of its fair creator.

"I intend to provide your sister with plants she knew when living at Sintra. Portugal quince, dwarf Portugal laurel, white Portugal broom. If they can be had," she added, returning her attention to her list. "There are other possibilities. This red Roman honeysuckle might provide a welcome note of color. But olives are rather dear at two shillings and sixpence, and so tender. However, if planted in tubs, they could be kept in the hothouse over the winter."

"I didn't know about any plans for a hothouse."

"Eventually one of the laundry rooms will be converted," she said sunnily. "Parts of the lead roof can be replaced with glass to let in more light, and a stove is already in place. Mrs. Fonseca and I were discussing it just last night. Didn't you hear us?"

Cass had been looking rather than listening, imagining how she would look lying in his bed. Pale, bare limbs caressed by firelight, hair streaming across the pillows . . . .

He sighed.

Her forefinger slid down the page. "Lombardy poplars, six feet tall, fifteen shillings the hundred. I need but twenty-five, which allows for a few failures. I wonder if I can get the lot for three shillings?"

"Will there be roses?" Cass asked, knowing her fondness for them.

Once more he summoned up his favorite image of her. Stripped of her gown and petticoats, her mahogany tresses unbound and disheveled by his foreplay, she reclined on his great fourposter. He showered her with handfuls of wine-red rose petals, an exquisite counterpoint to her alabaster skin, before drawing her tenderly into his arms . . . .

Her calm voice called him back from his dream. "Several sorts of roses. I've already ascertained Mrs. Fonseca's color preferences, my lord, I need to know yours as well. If you've got any."

"Red ones," he said firmly. "The deepest, darkest red. Like burgundy wine. Isn't there one like that?"

"You must be thinking of the Velvet rose. It has a semi-double and a double form."

"When does it bloom?"

"June. Usually by Midsummer Day."

So long a time to wait. But, Cass consoled himself, anticipation would make the realization of his fantasy all the richer.

"It's quite an ancient rose, listed in Gerard's *Herball*. I'd expect to find it in a garden as old as the one at Bevington. But I won't know if you've got one—or more—till Emrys Jones completes that inventory I've requested. I'm hoping for my own favorite, *Rosa mundi*. I've a weakness for striped and mottled roses," she confided. "Tobias didn't much care for them."

Cass was quick to assure her, "I consider striped roses quite the most interesting, myself. By all means plant some at Summit House. And at Bevington also, if they are lacking."

She beamed upon him, cheeks pink and eyes glowing. He felt an ache in his chest as he gazed back at her. So lovely—so unattainable. For if he attempted a simple, harmless kiss, she would turn away from him. And toy with that damned ring she wore, the relic of the man whose name she always spoke so reverently.

Driven to action by an attack of jealousy, Cass flicked the whip at the glossy rumps of his bays and the phaeton picked up speed. Glancing over at Sophie, he saw no evidence of alarm. One hand secured the broadsheet on her knee, the other gripped the low side of the carriage for support, but still she smiled.

"You don't mind going so swiftly?"

"Not at all, my lord." On a laugh, she added, "You assured me you were trustworthy, so I've little fear of being tumbled into the hedge!"

"Have done with all these 'my lords'," he pleaded. "Let us be Cass and Sophie, if only for this one day. Is that so much to ask?"

"It would be most improper."

"I don't see why. I was born a commoner. And I haven't a scrap of lordliness about me."

"Nevertheless, you're my employer." Her face brimmed with mischief when she asked, "Would you be satisfied if I simply called you 'Mr. Carysfort' rather than 'Lord Bevington'?"

"No, damn it, I wouldn't!"

"Mind your language. My lord," she added wickedly.

"You, madam, are by far the stubbornest creature I've ever encountered."

"So I've been told, and always by men. My brother, my uncle, my husband." She paused reflectively. "Fingal Moncrieff, too."

"Whatever became of your Scotsman?"

"He wasn't *my* Scotsman," she said direly.

"He wanted to be, didn't he? When he came to Bevington for his interview, he declared his honorable intentions."

"Vilain," she spat. "He felt no affection for me, not a jot. He courted me because he was ambitious and meant to rise in the world by using me. I was so very lonely and bereft that he thought I'd want him."

"But you didn't."

"The match was perfectly suitable and quite convenient, *dé vrai*. But our business partnership was so contentious that a marital one had no appeal for me. He's a competent architect," she admitted, "and by now must have found employment."

Cass slowed his horses for the approach to the toll booth. On the other side, at the edge of Durdham Down, lay the nursery. Miller and Sweet, having outgrown their former premises at St. Michael's Hill, had transferred their flourishing nursery business to a more rural location. Across its many acres stood row upon row of trees and shrubs, as well as a succession of glass-paned houses where fruit and flowers were forced for the Bristol market.

Sophie, clearly in her element, scrambled down from the carriage unassisted. She rushed towards the offices, halting just long enough to say, "I fear I shall try your patience mightily, my lord—I could spend hours here."

"I don't mind if you do," said Cass generously. "The bays are in the care of the nurseryman's son, and he offered to walk them for me if we're delayed."

John Sweet, the proprietor's elder son, led them through the grounds. His evident respect for the Pinnock name didn't prevent him from patronizing Sophie, until she began pelting him with questions that were specific and indicative of a comprehensive knowledge of horticulture. Cass enjoyed watching her march down each narrow alley of saplings, tapping her chin in a distracted manner as adorable as it was deceptive.

Consulting the catalogue, she informed Mr. Sweet that she required a selection of forest trees. "Beech, Scotch fir, larch—as mature as possible."

"Beech is priced at eight pence for a ten foot specimen, madam, and larch are six pence for eight feet. I regret that our Scotch firs are but three feet in height, but you can have them for a mere sixteen shillings the hundred."

"I want only a quarter that many," said Sophie, "for a quarter the cost. Have you weeping ash?"

"Indeed, madam. Right this way."

"And Lombardy poplars. I must see them also."

Cass followed behind them, admiring the gentle sway of Sophie's hips as she embarked upon an earnest discussion about cedars of Lebanon. After placing an impressive order for trees, she insisted on seeing the display of ornamental shrubs and subsequently crossed rhododendrons, flowering almonds, and bush laburnums from her list. Surveying the Portugal laurels with satisfaction, she requested a dozen. Her only disappointment was the unavailability of Portugal quince.

With a mournful sigh, she said, *"Tchi pitchi.* Pity."

"You might seek it t'other side of Bristol, madam, at Lauder's nurseries on Lawrence Hill."

Sophie turned to Cass. "Do you know where that is?"

"I'm Bristol born and bred," he reminded her. "I could find my way wearing a blindfold."

She inquired about the packing procedure for her purchases and settled on a time for their delivery. Her steps were light and bouncing, almost childlike, when at last she and Cass made their way back to the phaeton.

"*Eh bien,*" she cried, "the Earl of Bevington is going to have the grandest garden in all the West Country! People will come from afar to admire it." Her tiny gloved hand pawed at his forearm. "You must remember to tell everyone that I made it for you, my lord."

"Perhaps I will, perhaps I won't," he teased. "The odds in your favor would be vastly improved if you'd call me Cass. Or even Cassian."

"*Zut,* but you are persistent. *Têtouongne,* as we say on my island."

Her inflection indicated that it was not a complimentary term. "What does that mean?"

"Pigheaded."

"I was less specific when I called you stubborn." Bending his head close to hers, he said, "Very well, then. I am a Gloucestershire pig. And you're a little Jersey cow, with great brown eyes."

She jerked her hand away as if flames had risen from his sleeve to scorch her. "*Dé vrai.* It is true, so beware my sharp horns!"

During their cross country drive to Lawrence Hill, and throughout Sophie's consultation with Mr. Lauder, Cass was preoccupied with the problem of convincing her of his affection. It was imperative that he begin his campaign before she went back to Bevington, which she would do after planting that forest she'd bought for him today.

With a flash of inspiration, he decided upon a detour. If she couldn't see beyond his title, he must show her who he'd been long before becoming Earl of Bevington.

"Do you mind delaying our return to Summit House?" he asked, as his high-stepping horses bore the phaeton away from the nursery gardens.

"What's the time?" she asked, folding up the catalogue Mr. Lauder had provided.

"I can't take my hands from the reins to get my timepiece. You'll have to reach into my waistcoat pocket yourself."

A moment later he felt her fingers moving under his coat, searching for the chain. His spine tingled at the contact. When she leaned in closer to study the face of his watch, he breathed in her lavender scent.

"Past two already! Mrs. Fonseca invited me to go with her to the New Hot Well, but she'll have gone by now."

It took all the willpower Cass possessed to keep from taking advantage of her proximity. The strategic placement of one wheel in a rut would send her sprawling across his lap. But he'd set his hopes higher than a furtive cuddle.

He guided the horses into the heart of his city, to the old market cross and the remnants of the ancient wall, and the twisting lanes familiar to him from his earliest youth. He showed Sophie the docks where the Carysfort ships were unloaded, the warehouses in which the barrels of port and sherry were stacked and stored. If this descendant of Seigneurs of Jersey looked askance upon his family's mercantile background, she was considerate enough not to comment.

"Perhaps you'll allow me to make a few purchases of my own," he said. "I warn you, my sort of shopping won't amuse you as much as buying plants or helping my sister choose her bonnet trimmings. Redcliffe Street, as you see, is populated with wine and brandy merchants."

He went directly to Merchant Fry's, where he received a familiar but respectful greeting from the lad who tended the customers' horses and carriages. As Cass escorted Sophie into the shop, she remarked that he must visit it often.

"Yes, certainly, my lord," said the delighted proprietor, when he announced his desire to stock Bevington Castle's depleted cellars. "It is well that you make the selections yourself, being so particular in your tastes. Step into my office, for I'm sure the lady will be more comfortable there."

Cass and Sophie accompanied him to a smaller room with chairs for his most illustrious clients. "Can I tempt you to try my wares?" he asked brightly. "I've an excellent sherry here. Twenty-five pounds the dozen," he added, beaming at Cass.

After pouring out two samples, he sat down behind his desk to study a ledger. "Let me review your lordship's account. Beginning with the ports—you were satisfied with the Old Lisbon?" Cass nodded, and he went on, "I need hardly ask whether you care to lay in a supply of Carysfort Vintage Red. Every sip a reminder of the Douro Valley—the birthplace of port."

To Sophie Cass explained, "A generation ago, the wines of northern Portugal were deemed harsh and heavy and undrinkable, for our British palates inclined towards the lighter clarets from France. The Portuguese trade suffered greatly until the makers began following the example of the Abbot of

Lemago, and fortified their product with *aguardenta,* a type of brandy. That step interrupted the fermentation, producing a sweeter, richer wine. There are also tawny ports, mellowed by a longer aging in wood."

"Speaking of wood, my lord, at the Customs House I heard about a shipment of Madeira due to arrive soon. Shall I put you down for several barrels?"

Cass also put himself down for other varieties on offer. "Some Italian wines, of course—the Aliatico. Of the French, I fancy first growth claret, a burgundy, some champagne—"

"White or red?"

"White. Also, a quality hock. My sister favors Rhenish wines."

"Very good, my lord. And when will you take delivery?"

He considered before replying, "The middle of May, let us say. Send everything by water, up the Severn to the landing place at Parham Pill." Turning to Sophie, he said, "This sherry is worth having, wouldn't you say?"

"I'm not enough of a connoisseur to venture an opinion of its quality," she answered. "But I like it well."

"Send two dozen bottles round to Summit House," Cass instructed Mr. Fry.

"Excellent, my lord," said the wine merchant, his eyes twinkling his pleasure at Sophie's response and the resulting purchase. "And should you think of anything else you require—rum, or geneva, or cognac—I know my colleague Mr. Ireland will be only too happy to oblige."

"I'll save those for another day," said Cass.

His business concluded, he reclaimed his carriage.

"I must say," said Sophie as they drove down Redcliffe Hill, "I'm appalled by the cost. In Jersey we wouldn't pay more than twenty-five shillings, in our own currency, for a dozen bottles of port. And our wine houses sell thirteen bottles to the dozen. All our goods come duty-free, and thus more cheaply."

"If ever I lose my fortune, I shall go there to live," said Cass. "I believe I could survive quite happily in poverty, as long as I needn't give up fine wines."

He crossed over the bridge again, driving Sophie past St. Peter's, where his maternal grandparents had wed, and a nearby hospital his family had supported with generous donations. He showed her the Theatre Royal before cutting over to Queen's Square to point out his Grandfather Carysfort's house.

"My parents exchanged their vows in the front parlor," he explained, "and immediately afterwards set sail for the West Indies. Each brought a fortune to the marriage. Father hoped to return to England one day and purchase a country estate. I'm not certain Mother shared his dream. Whenever she spent time here she missed her island, its warmth and sunshine. Neither of them could possibly have imagined their son would one day inherit an earldom and a great castle."

Cass prodded the horses forward with a gentle stroke of the whip. He proceeded around the square and negotiated a sharp turn, exiting to the west. Across the drawbridge spanning the River Froom lay College Green, and beyond it Park Street, where he halted before a building with a brick front and stone dressings.

"My uncle's house. I was born here, in an upstairs bedroom, when my parents were visiting Bristol. They lingered for nearly four years. They were so fearful about taking me to an island plagued by heat and fevers that they left me behind, in damp England and a town rife with consumption. Some years later they returned, and Cecelia was born. Not in this house, for by then my uncle had acquired his country place."

"And your parents sailed away again, without either of their children."

"Exactly. They made two more Atlantic crossings, the last one shortly after I left university. Then they sailed back to the island and never returned. There was an outbreak of fever, and both succumbed."

"I'm so sorry."

"I remember them well, and was more attached to them than Cecelia, who was so young when they died. She regarded our aunt and uncle as her parents. Quite rich, but a generation removed from active participation in trade, therefore my sister has no real understanding of where money comes from, or its value. A lifetime of being pampered has made her a trifle self-centered, but she has a good heart," he said staunchly.

"What happened to your family's West Indies property? Do you own it still?"

"Despite my reservations about owning and working slaves, I did consider living there. But all accounts of plantation life make it sound like an outer circle of hell—intense heat, unremitting labor, regular crop failures, the threat of hurricanes. That wouldn't have suited Cecelia, so I sold everything to my mother's brother. We went to Portugal instead."

"How did you know you'd like it any better?"

"I can't remember."

"You must have had a reason for going."

"Cecelia's poor health. And we had cousins there."

Though her questions revealed a flattering interest in his past, they were devilishly inconvenient. For Cass newer forgot the necessity of concealing the real motive for the hasty move to Portugal, even from someone as discreet and benign as Sophie.

"You lived abroad long enough for your sister to marry and have a child and lose a husband. And then you brought her back, even though she didn't care to live in England again."

"She told you that?" When she bobbed her head, he said, "It must have been raining. Like our mother, she misses sunshine, and those hot, lazy afternoons we knew in Sintra."

"What do you miss most?"

He looked down at her. "Difficult to say. I can't decide whether it's the Portuguese wines—or the women."

He'd hoped to pique her with his provocative reply, and was disappointed when she calmly resumed her study of the nursery catalogue.

Discontent marred what had been, up to that moment, a most enjoyable outing. Sophie, perverse and unyielding creature, apparently derived more pleasure from her horticultural pursuits than from his company. But he wouldn't let this latest blow to his pride deter his efforts to entice her into a flirtation—if not more.

In their determination to show off their city, the Carysforts insisted on taking Sophie to the original Hotwell House on the Bristol side of the Avon Gorge near St. Vincent's Rock. This was a sacrificial gesture by Cecelia, who preferred the gentility of the newer spa in Clifton, and Sophie was reluctant to refuse so unselfish an invitation. Although she preferred to pass the morning at Summit House, where the men were planting the new trees and shrubs, she obediently arrayed herself in her whitest and most fashionable morning gown and took her place in the earl's town carriage.

Cecelia Fonseca was a riddle Sophie despaired of solving. There was no doubt that she dearly loved her little boy, yet she consigned him to the care of servants and was only remotely involved in his daily routine. Her late husband rarely surfaced in her infrequent reminiscences about the years she and her brother had spent abroad. Her impetuous kindnesses were contrasted by intermittent spells of aloofness, and she had a disconcerting habit of retreating upstairs to her rooms whenever Sophie felt there was a chance of their becoming closer.

Her attempts to know the sister better were less successful than the brother's concentrated effort to befriend her.

As a result of living in the earl's house and touring the Bristol environs on a daily basis, she felt more at ease in his company. Nevertheless, she didn't consider their warmer relationship a lasting one. As his employee, she was too vulnerable to let down her guard completely. Her inability to overlook what had transpired in the field of snowdrops—and the emotions the episode stirred up—troubled her. The tale Luis had imparted about Ines, the Portuguese mistress, was still fresh enough in her mind to make her wary. Judging from the way Lord Bevington deflected even the most innocent questions about his lengthy residence in Portugal, he had other unsavory secrets.

"You ought to drink the water," said Cecelia when they arrived at the Pump Room. "It's warm, with a mild and pleasant flavor, and does me a world of good."

Laughing, the earl said, "Mrs. Pinnock is in splendid health. I vow I've never seen a finer complexion."

His sister went on, "I remember how busy and elegant this place seemed to me when I was a girl. There were musicians playing, and weekly breakfasts and balls in the Long Room."

"The high season won't begin till May, Cecelia. That's why you find it so slow."

She shrugged. "The clientele won't improve. Lords and ladies used to flock here, but now all I see are down-at-heel merchants and hopeless consumptives."

With a playful smile at their escort, Sophie observed, "There's one lord here."

"I doubt that even my exalted presence can bring the Hotwell back into vogue," he replied. "For me, the mineral spring is the lesser of its advantages. I prefer strolling along the parade and watching the ships pass up and down the Avon. And the view of the gorge is magnificent. Come, Mrs. Pinnock, you're too lively to remain indoors with a pack of invalids. Allow me to show you these marvels while Cecelia takes her daily dose."

"Yes, do go with him, Sophie. When I'm finished here I shall go directly to the Colonnade, where the shops are. You can meet me there."

Sophie promenaded with her patron up and down the formal tree-lined walk. The scenery was indeed majestic, and she wished her style of drawing was bold enough to capture it.

"Watercolors would never do it justice," she declared, "although black ink and a sepia wash might serve. If only I'd had more practice painting in oils, what a picture I could make! I've often had the same thought at Bevington. I can accurately render the castle's architecture and the unique color of the stone, but lack the dramatic flair necessary for expressing its—its essence."

"Your sketches of the Bevington gardens are exquisite," he

told her.

She was silenced by the recollection that soon she must return to his castle to complete her unfinished work. The employment contract stipulated that she produce a picturesque landscape similar to the one she was making at Summit House, but on a far grander scale. The elimination of Bevington's magnificently historic garden was a burdensome, soul-destroying assignment.

At times—and this was one—she was tempted to tell the earl about her reluctance to carry out his wishes. But that would anger him, and she couldn't bear the indignity of being sacked by her very first client.

Deep down, she knew that expressing her true feelings to this man would be far easier than confiding in Tobias, whose fragile heart would have been shattered by the confession she hadn't dared make.

Her husband had risen to fame by eradicating old gardens to make way for new. Wifely devotion had compelled Sophie to assist his efforts. Throughout their marriage she served him faithfully as partner, carefully concealing her private prejudice against every project they had undertaken. She'd let him die believing—falsely—that she shared his philosophies of garden design. The guilt of that crucial deception would forever haunt her.

Her association with her employer could be refreshingly uncomplicated if he hadn't spoiled it by kissing her. Their every encounter was colored, to some extent, by her expectation that he would try it again. And if she let him, her scruples would dictate her resignation. He would then bring in someone else—most likely Repton—to carry out his alterations.

Oh, las, but he was temptation personified! Vital and strong, a masterpiece of flesh and blood and bone. His physique could be the model for heroic statues, and his handsome face the pattern for pictures of Greek and Roman gods. And if her instinctive and tumultuous awareness of his magnificence was a betrayal of her dead husband, there was nothing she could do about it. But to reveal to him what she'd never even told Tobias—*impossibl'ye!*

"Sophie, is anything the matter?"

"Nânnîn," she lied feebly.

"Perhaps we should go back to the pump room for a glass of that miraculous water."

Forcing herself to smile, she shook her head. "Might we explore the Colonnade? I've just remembered that I need a length of lace to freshen a gown."

The curving breezeway was connected to the Pump Room and housed ground level shops with living quarters and lodgings above. Sophie separated from the earl long enough to make her purchase. She exited with her parcel and found him leaning against one of the tall white columns.

"Come here," he said, "and hold out your hand. I bought a present for you."

When she did as he commanded, he placed a tiny object in her open palm. A gold ring, set with a single, sparkling gem.

"A souvenir of your visit to the Hotwell. The stone is a crystal, mined locally. We call them Bristol diamonds."

"It is very like a real one," she marveled. "You are most kind, my lord—"

"Cass," he interrupted. "Or even Cassian. No one calls me that, but if you chose to I'd be delighted."

"Cassian," she said gently, as a means of softening her rebuff, "I cannot accept your gift."

His hand joined with hers, forcing her fingers to close over the ring. "Keep it, Sophie. I don't insist that you wear it."

His diffidence was a facade. In his eyes she read his hope that she would.

Even though their hands were gloved, the contact caused her heart to skip several beats. Why did she always respond to his touch, his smiles—his kisses? And why, she wondered, must he add to the complexities of her situation by making her like him too well?

"I am your employee," she said. Her statement hadn't come out as the firm refusal she'd intended, but a regretful one.

Cass read the confusion in the fine brown eyes turned up to him. "You never fail to point that out. As a justification of your dislike of me, or out of a general aversion to persons who hold authority?"

"I don't dislike you," she contradicted. "And your authority over me is limited by the contract."

Because his need for her was more than a physical yearning, Cass didn't fully understand it. He shrank from analyzing his tumultuous emotions, or even acknowledging his uneasy suspicion of the cause. He simply knew that when she was absent, he missed her. If she frowned at him, he longed to make her smile. Her laughter enchanted him, her gravity tore at his heart. Surely ordinary, uncomplicated lust hadn't turned him so moony, and increasingly desperate for assurances that she cared for him, even a little. That she regarded him as something more than the man who was paying her to design landscapes.

Barely containing his frustration, he continued, "You're not my servant, Sophie. If I wish to converse with you—which I greatly enjoy—or admire your drawings, or even give you a ring, what's the harm?"

"That depends on your motive."

The only way he could ever gain access to that tantalizing body was through her stubborn mind. He must try to reason with her.

"I am a man. Not a saint, but certainly not an ogre. You're a beautiful, intelligent, and highly desirable woman, living in my household. And I do desire you."

He waited for the storm to break, certain that she would rage or run away, or worse.

Her lush lips parted, but she made no sound at all.

"Did you think me lost?" trilled Cecelia.

His sister was coming. Before turning to meet her, he saw Sophie slip the ring into her reticule to hide it.

"I fell into the clutches of a stupid, tiresome female who for some reason thought I was interested in her aches and pains."

"Softly, Cecelia," Cass warned, "else you'll be overheard."

A party of visitors was advancing, two wizened old ladies and a young man with a halting gait. Sophie stepped out of the way but Cecelia stood rooted to the ground, her body rigid and tense as she stared at the threesome. Her immobility forced them to form a single file, for the passage was narrow.

"My pardon, ma'am," said the fellow, as he limped past her.

Her hand clutched her throat. She whirled around to stare after him, unaware that her brother had hastened to her side. Murmuring distractedly and gesturing at the man, she collapsed against him.

Sophie rushed forward to lend support, placing her arm around the slender waist. Cecelia's body went completely limp. With a hiss of crushed silk and lace, she collapsed on the ground, unconscious.

CHAPTER 8

Few self-supported flowers endure the wind uninjured....

~William Cowper

*C*ass, hovering over his sister's prostrate form, raised her head and shoulders from the paving stones. "Cecelia, Cecelia," he said urgently, desperate to rouse her.

"What shall I do?" asked Sophie, admirably controlled.

"Smelling salts." He slipped the embroidered silk purse from the slack wrist and handed it over. After digging about inside, she passed him the tiny silver-chased vinaigrette. He held it beneath Cecelia's nostrils until they twitched. Her effigy-like figure tensed, then it stirred.

Gasping, she rocked her head back and forth to escape the acrid, unpleasant odor. Her eyes opened, and her lips parted for a moan. "I saw him, Cass. He found us!"

"You're mistaken," he soothed her. In her confusion and fear, she was forgetting the necessity of silence. "Can you sit up?"

"Where has he gone?"

"You mustn't worry," he insisted. "A strong resemblance, I grant you, but the man you fear looks very different now. I know, I met him in London."

Cecelia stared at him. "When?"

"Two months ago."

"You should have told me."

"I knew it would alarm you, and for no good purpose. Come now, make an effort to rise—we mustn't attract attention." She let him help her up, and Sophie stepped forward to take offer additional support. "Stay with her," said Cass, "while I find the coachman. Cecelia, quiet yourself. Sophie will lead you over to that bench, and you must wait for me there. I'll be but a few minutes."

As he left, he heard his sister say wonderingly, "How odd that he should call you Sophie. He never does."

Cass hastened to the carriageway to explain the situation to his driver before entering the Hotwell House to purchase a glass of water from the pretty female dispensing it from the pump. He scanned the depressing assembly of the aged and infirm, seeking the man responsible for Cecelia's panic.

Despite his limping gait, he carried himself well. Cass judged the fellow to be in his early twenties, and related to the pair of elderly women. His build was very like Sir Michael Tait's had been seven years ago, and his facial features were remarkably like those of the baronet—before the duel.

Discovering a stranger's name was a simple business. The Master of Ceremonies maintained a subscription book, listing regular customers who paid their twenty-six shillings a month for entrance to the spa.

Cass was grateful for Sophie's placid acceptance of his sister's listless explanation of her swoon. Her composure, both at the height of the crisis and during the homeward drive, was particularly impressive, and she aided his efforts to distract the brooding Cecelia. But as they vied to engage his sister's interest, he was unable to judge her response to his declaration of desire. She appeared unmoved, offering calm, collected answers to his queries about her island.

"What sort of social life did you lead? Are there public assemblies, as we have here and at Bath?"

"Seldom," she answered. "Only one St. Helier hotel has rooms large enough for dancing. Our Jersey roads are so rough that my family seldom troubled to make the journey from Anneville."

"Your uncle, as a member the island aristocracy, must have provided entertainments," Cass prompted.

"Not on the same scale as an English lord. A few of our seigneurs are rather grand, but not Uncle Edouard. He manages his own estate, tills his gardens, and brings in his crop. Any tourist to the island who shares his horticultural interests invariably calls at Anneville Manor. That's how I happened to meet my—how I met Mr. Pinnock."

Cecelia turned her head from the window. "Really?"

Cass had heard quite enough about Sophie's sudden romance with the Englishman. He forestalled another account of their whirlwind courtship by saying, "Your uncle must be responsible for your affinity for gardens."

"He and my aunt were childless, and I was their only niece. I often stayed at their home, and after my father's death they persuaded my mother to let me live with them for long intervals. I grew up in two worlds. At the manor house I spoke English or French, and had drawing lessons, and was presented to distinguished men. When I was at the farm with

Méthe and my brothers, I spoke common Jèrriais, and kept house and milked the cows."

"How many brothers?" Cecelia asked.

"Three, all older. And every one of them a *cotchin*—a rascal. They mocked my airs and graces."

Cass commented, "I'll wager you were the sort of sister who bent them to your will."

"And how they teased me for my managing ways. We had such fun together! They took me to the fairs at Lessay and Guibray, and every Good Friday we had our picnic at the seaside. Our circle of friends was large, and we were related to most of them. As we say on the island, everyone is a cousin."

Once more, Cecelia joined in. "Are your brothers married?"

"Only the eldest. Philippe will succeed Uncle Edouard as Seigneur of Anneville, so he was regarded as a great catch by the girls from landed families. But none had a chance after his fancy lighted on a wealthy shipowner's daughter. They have two children now. Brelade engaged himself to a French *emigrée* whose lack of a dowry troubles Méthe. According to Tante Douce, who fills her letters with family gossip, Tanmin is courting a neighbor who promises to make a fine dairywoman. He's ready to settle down to farming himself. The upheaval in France has hampered trade."

"One always hears that Jersey's soil is rich and her climate mild. Farming, I gather, is a common occupation."

"But we have many seafarers as well," Sophie elaborated, "for no one on Jersey lives more than a few miles from the water. The sons of landholders often become sailors or fisherman, or seek a career in the Navy. Uncle Edouard offered to purchase commissions for my brothers, but they didn't care to go out of the island."

"And what about you?" Cass asked, curious to know how willingly she'd left her home.

"I always assumed I'd stay at Anneville," she admitted, her gaze alighting on an unfinished crescent of houses. "Even though I never expected to wed an Englishman, I don't regret coming to live in this country. I was slow to learn English ways—after I lost Tobias, I did fall back into my Jersiaise habits. My family expected me to return, but I couldn't leave my dear house, or my lovely garden. Someday I'll pay them a visit, but I doubt they can persuade me to remain. I've changed just enough that I fit in quite comfortably here in England."

She fits especially well into my particular corner of England, Cass acknowledged. If Cecelia hadn't intruded upon us, would she have accepted me as her lover?

"Cass," said his sister upon entering Summit House, "may I have a word with you before my nap?"

Torn between his duty to poor Cecelia and his eagerness to resume his highly-charged conversation with Sophie, he accompanied them up the staircase. On the middle landing he detained Sophie by taking her hand.

He removed her snug kid glove. She blushed and tried to stop him—he might have been stripping off her gown, she looked so shocked. After pressing his lips to each of her tiny fingers he pulled her gently forward so he could savor those plummy lips.

She shrank from him, backing against the wall. "Go to your sister, my lord. She needs you."

She rushed up the remaining steps hurriedly and he followed. Before she could withdraw to her blue bedchamber, he asked in a low voice, "And when shall I come to you?"

"Nou-fait," she whispered. "Never." Tears glittered among

her thick black eyelashes.

She slipped inside the room and closed the door in his face, shutting off his protest.

He had been completely honest and open with her, no concealment of his true feelings.

I should have kissed her, he told himself on his way to Cecelia's suite. She likes being kissed.

Time to abandon the reasonable approach for a physical one, he decided. Her professed reluctance stemmed from surprise than rather than unwillingness, he was sure of it.

His sister had collapsed on a French rococo chaise longue. The instant he closed the door behind him, she wailed, "I knew no good would come of visiting Hotwell House! Why did I let you persuade me? That man—the very image of—of—" She paused.

"Of Sir Michael Tait," he said, completing her unspoken identification.

"And while I'm recovering from *that* shock, you admit that you met him when you in London!"

"It's no wonder you're distressed," he said quietly. "I've more unpleasant news for you. According to the Master of Ceremonies, the young man we saw was Captain Roderick Tait. The younger brother."

"Roddy? Impossible, he's a schoolboy."

"Seven years is long enough for him to grow into a soldier. I discovered he was wounded in France and received his discharge. The old aunts took him in and are caring for him during his recuperation."

"His resemblance to his brother is astonishing."

"You wouldn't think so if you'd seen the baronet lately," he told her reluctantly. "His appearance is greatly altered."

He refrained from describing the scarred face, lest he arouse misguided sympathy for their hated enemy.

"Is it possible Sir Michael is also in Bristol? Or Clifton?"

"Every week I scan the list of new subscribers published in the paper. His name hasn't appeared."

"You missed the Captain's."

"Only because it hasn't yet been printed."

Cecelia's trembling fingers mangled her handkerchief. "Oh, what shall we do? He might also come here."

"Perhaps," Cass conceded, "if he learns our whereabouts. It was not by chance that our paths crossed in London. He insisted that I deliver a letter to you. I destroyed it."

Climbing to her feet, she said, "I won't see him."

"You needn't. I promised to keep you safe, didn't I?"

She clasped her arms around his neck. "You must be so weary of my clinging. I'd be lost without you."

Gently he patted her back. "I'm here, Cecelia. And will be—for as long as you have need of me."

She sighed. "I'm not so selfish—or blind—that I don't realize your dilemma."

"Which one?" he muttered.

"I'll wager my best taffeta bonnet that you find me and my troubles quite inconvenient just now. I may be dense, but I've noticed how entranced you are by that pretty, love-starved Mrs. Pinnock. Every night you sit by her on the parlor sofa, pretending to admire her sketches while you peer down the front of her gown. You've driven her to every nursery garden in and out of Bristol. Just today I saw you holding her hand in the Colonnade. And," she concluded triumphantly, "I heard you call her Sophie."

"Your powers of observation," he said in a wry voice, "are

exceptional indeed."

"Your interest in Sophie Pinnock isn't wholly due to her artistry. I'm hurt, I confess, by your reticence. We've always shared our dreams and sorrows. How else could we have survived so much?"

"How could I tell you, when I hadn't even spoken to her of my—my feelings? I'd just begun when you came upon us in the Colonnade."

"I can't imagine you need to speak at all, you give yourself away whenever she's near. Unworldly she may be, but she must know by now you mean to have her for your mistress. I guessed, and I'm not half as clever as she is."

"You don't mean to talk me out of it, I hope."

Cecelia smiled. *"Meu irmao,* I know your history with women. Your little widow won't be your first conquest, and I'll be much surprised if she turns out to be your last. If I must accept her into our household, so be it. In fact, I'll do everything in my power to help you win her. One of us deserves a taste of happiness." Frowning, she wandered over to her window. "But there's one thing you mustn't expect of me. I will not— cannot—no, *dare* not make her my confidante."

"We can trust her. I'd stake my life on it."

"That may be. But no good can come of opening up our past to Sophie Pinnock," she declared. "If she knew our secrets, she would despise us both. You'd lose your *amante,* and I a pleasant companion."

Cass hated to think his sister might be right.

Seven years ago, he'd lived recklessly, stupidly, seeking out the prettiest whores in London and consuming far too much liquor and laudanum. Maddened by his anger at another and hatred of himself, he'd committed a crime. Afterwards, he'd done other terrible, unspeakable deeds.

From the day he'd returned to England, he had tried to be a better man. He was beginning to believe that Sophie, a priceless gift bestowed by the most generous of fates, was a reward for his reformation.

Her love still belonged to her husband. Knowing his unworthiness, he would not attempt to win her heart. But he wanted her companionship, and not merely because he sought relief for his pent-up passion. He was unattached. Sophie's status as widow freed her from society's stricter rules about sexual conduct. There no reason they couldn't be together, and be happy. Provided he kept quiet about his past.

"Each time she questions me about Portugal," Cecelia went on, "or shows curiosity about how I met Fonseca, I'm so uncomfortable I can't give sensible replies. Luis is danger enough to my peace of mind, he gabbles on and on without thinking."

"I've warned him repeatedly to be careful in what he says. As far as I know, he has been."

"And now these Taits have suddenly appeared in Bristol," she concluded morosely. "My poor nerves will never be the same."

Cass sat down on one of her cushiony armchairs. "There is a remedy: a swift and strategic retreat before the enemy advances farther into our territory. It's time we left Clifton and removed to Bevington."

"So soon? Before the summer?"

"Immediately."

She considered his plan. "I suppose we've no other choice. But I'll need several days to make ready."

"No matter. As long as you remain here at Summit House, you

needn't worry about running into Captain Roddy or his aunts. I'll hasten to the castle this afternoon and forewarn the staff. Luis will go with me, he knows how to organize everything to your liking. And I'll take Daniel. In a few days I'll be back to fetch you. Sophie also—her work here is nearly done."

The neatness of the arrangement pleased him.

In a few days he would collect his mistress-to-be and sweep her off to his castle, and they could begin their affair in a romantically secluded and pastoral setting.

He felt certain that his courtship would swiftly reach its desire conclusion. Despite an apparent setback, he had cause to congratulate himself. At long last Sophie had addressed him by name. When he'd stated his intentions, she hadn't slapped him or fallen into a faint. And, he thought jubilantly, she still possessed the ring he'd given her.

"Para que é isso, senhora?" Daniel Fonseca pointed at the small wooden object in Sophie's hand.

"Inglês," Luis chided him from the bottom step of the stone stairway. *"Repita, menino."*

"What is that for, Missus Pinnock?"

"This is a dibber," she explained, permitting him to examine her instrument. "It pokes little holes in the ground for planting. Would you like to try?" When he knelt down at her side, she showed him how to use it. "Take these seeds and place one in each of the holes. Yes, that's right. Cover them with soil—perfection! What a talented assistant he is," she told Luis.

"Claro," he replied with a nod, running his hand across

Echo's ribcage. "He like to be—how to say? Opposite of clean. Maria always scolding about it, but I say he only is little boy and need to play. In *palácio* at Sintra, even when he very little, we often catch him climbing in fountain. Once he hide in stable loft for three hours. *Ai,* but senhora was distressed!"

"I can well believe it," said Sophie. Cecelia Fonseca regularly demonstrated her tendency to succumb to emotion.

Delegating her duties to Daniel, Sophie studied the landscape. The near-completion of her assignment provided an uplifting sense of accomplishment.

Half of the new trees and shrubs were in place, arranged in artful groups. Tobias had taught her the technique of making a fresh planting appear natural, and she believed the result would have pleased him. The canes of wild dog roses obtained from the downs now dangled over the cliff edge as she'd envisioned. Strategically positioned clumps of upright cedars framed the view of the gorge, and those elusive Portugal laurels bordered the new path of crushed stone.

"More seeds, *por favor,*" pleaded Daniel, tugging at her skirts with a grubby hand.

Smiling at his eagerness, she offered him the entire packet marked *mirabilis jalapa: Marvel of Peru.*

The door opened above on the landing and the earl stepped out. He'd changed his town clothes for riding dress, Sophie noted. He was going away, and she was relieved.

He leaned over the balustrade to call down to his servant, "Luis, I'm off to Bevington, so you must pack my gear— yours, too. If we depart within the hour, we can make the castle before sundown."

"*Sim,* senhorio. I come at once."

Daniel dropped the seed packet and dashed up the steps

after Luis. "Take me, Tio, take me!" he cried, flinging himself at his uncle.

The earl lifted him high in the air. Much to Sophie's amazement, he said indulgently, "Tell Maria to get out your trunk and start filling it with clothes. And not the best ones, either."

"Is Echo coming with us?"

"Not today," Cass replied. "We'll leave her here to guard your mother and Mrs. Pinnock." After Luis and the boy went into the house, he made his way down the stone steps.

Sophie was glad of her menial garb. Her long pinafore of brown holland cloth was plain and unalluring, and at the moment she preferred to be both. "Will Mrs. Fonseca let Daniel go away with you?" she asked coolly.

"He'll be out of her sight for only a few days, and during that time Luis and Maria will keep him out of harm's way."

"As they did when you lived in Sintra, and he hid himself in the stable?"

His dark brows slanted downward, forming a vertical crease. "Luis told you about that?" Accepting her silence as affirmation, he said firmly, "Nothing of the kind will happen while Daniel is in my care. Keep Cecelia cheerful, should she pine for us. She looks upon you as a friend—and she needs one."

"How long must you be away?"

"Oh, you'll see me again before the week is out. Will your work be finished by then?"

"I expect so, since you won't be around to dist—" She interrupted herself.

"Distract you? Is that what I've been doing?" He sounded vastly pleased with himself.

"The longer I stay in Gloucestershire," she continued, "the

greater the expense for you. I receive a guinea each day, and that's no small sum. I should think you'd be impatient for a return on your investment."

"Indeed I am. More impatient than you seem to realize."

With a fond smile and a few words, he'd revived her shame about what had passed between them at the Hotwells. And afterwards on the staircase, when he'd tried to kiss her. And outside her room, where he'd made it quite plain that he intended to lie with her.

The lingering glances . . . the occasional brush of his hand against hers . . . the light in his eyes when he greeted her at breakfast . . . his habit of sitting so close to her in the evenings when he reviewed her sketches . . . . All were the techniques of a practiced seducer.

He had a talent for shrewdly assessing his victims and using their vulnerabilities to his advantage. By promising money to Ines, the Portuguese peasant, he'd lured her to his bed. Experience must have taught him how vulnerable a lonely widow could be when confronted by a barrage of soft looks, kind words, fleeting caresses—and heated kisses.

She watched him survey his grounds, but his satisfied smile failed to lighten her resentment.

"When you resume your work at Bevington, you must bear with my distracting presence. I'm taking up residence at the castle earlier than I'd originally planned. The purpose of today's journey is to make the final household arrangements on my sister's behalf. You and I, in future, will spend a great deal of time together. I hope you're as glad of that as I am."

So there would be no reprieve after all—not from his attentions, or from the hateful task he expected her to perform. Time had strengthened her misgivings about altering the landscape at Bevington. Here was her chance to state her objections and save herself from the turmoil and heartache that lay ahead.

"Sophie," he said, with excruciating tenderness, "don't look so dismayed. I promise not to rush you. If I did, neither of us would be satisfied."

She wanted to believe he referred to the changes she must make to his gardens, but it was useless.

"Don't be afraid of me. All I've done is express how very much I want you."

"And what you want to make me," she said angrily. "Your *contchubinne.* Did you truly believe I would accept such a proposition?"

"Won't you? Think how wonderful it will be when you and I are—"

"There will never be such a time," she broke in. "A more intimate relationship is not possible. Do not, I beg you, mention it again."

He came closer. "You've no cause to feel insulted."

"If you think that, you have no understanding of a woman's feelings."

"I never claimed to. But I do understand certain things about you."

He framed her face with his hands and kissed her. And her body's instantaneous response confirmed his assertion. Her heart leaped about in her breast as though it had never been bruised. Her mind, so prejudiced against him, proved most unreliable when he pressed his hips against her suggestively, and she had trouble remembering why she should make him stop.

Her struggle to detach herself made him hold her even more tightly. He looked down at her with vivid blue eyes. "Say you will be mine."

"I cannot." She was unable to continue, he'd kissed her into a state of breathlessness.

"And I can't accept that as a final answer. When we next meet, I hope you will consent to be mine, in every possible way. We will find great joy together—I swear it."

His fingers traced her cheekbone in silent farewell. Slowly he turned and climbed the stairway, pausing once to look back at her before entering his house.

Desperate to relieve her agitation, Sophie trod the meandering path of her making which ended at the cliff. Never would she be swayed by the gallantries of the handsome, insistent, and breathtakingly desirable Earl of Bevington. Capitulation could only lead to *d'sastre*. Becoming his mistress—*impossibl'ye!*

A virile lover he would undoubtedly be. But any pleasure she might derive from the liaison would be overshadowed by the loss of her reputation. His passion had proved short-lived in the past, as Luis Costa's sister could attest. He was too volatile, unlikely to remain faithful to any woman for very long before moving on to the next. She would be discarded, paid off, sent back to Chiswick and an existence that would seem more solitary and unfulfilling than ever before.

More chilling than any of these considerations, the one that strengthened her resolve to guard herself, was an overpowering reluctance to dishonor her dead husband. She'd been faithful to Tobias while he lived and so she would continue to be, even though he was lying in St. Nicolas's churchyard in Chiswick. The marriage vow that she'd made in the distant past, when life had been so simple, would ordain her behavior now, in this complicated present.

CHAPTER 9

Sometimes occasion brings to light
Our friend's defect long hid from sight.

~William Cowper

With Luis riding Saladin, Maria sitting outside on the coachman's box, and Daniel gazing silently at the scenery, Cass was free to concentrate on Sophie Pinnock. His conscience had stirred after a long sleep, and gnawed at him.

In the early stages of their acquaintance he'd shared a few basic facts about his life, solely to ingratiate himself. Lately, in an effort to make her like him, he'd discussed his family background and his upbringing. Today, eager to advance her seduction, he had revealed his desire for her.

Now he wished to confess everything. And couldn't.

He considered the events that had occurred from the time he'd liberated Cecelia from her ladies' academy and taken her to live with him in London. Not even Drew Searle, Cecelia's admirer and Cass's companion in excess, had been privy to their many sufferings. The brief yet crucial foray into society—the hysterics and quarrels, public snubs and private humiliations—had ended with a duel, drastically altering the direction of their lives.

"Prepare to die," he said, and drew the remaining weapon from the case his second held out to him. Tait, the challenged party, had chosen first.

"Are you here to avenge your honor, Carysfort, or to commit a murder?" the baronet asked.

"To make certain that justice is done." Cass welcomed the heavy, deadly feel of his loaded pistol. It gave him the power to redress all wrongs.

He was no true gentleman. Ostensibly he was here to defend his honor, but he'd been thrust onto this desolate heath by a searing and most ungentlemanly desire for revenge. If all went as Cass intended, the services of that surgeon waiting in the carriage would not be wanted.

Regardless of the outcome, his plans were unalterable. Whether or not he killed the baronet, he and Cecelia were sailing for Lisbon today. If he was killed, she would go alone.

"Gentlemen," said Tait's second, "you are certain that there's no possibility of reconciliation?"

"Let's get on with it," Tait muttered.

Cass and his adversary marched their ten paces, turned, and waited for the signal to fire.

The white handkerchief, weighted by a pebble, was flung. As it fell, two successive pistol shots shattered the silence of the dawn.

Both duelists survived, but each had been permanently damaged. Tait's scar was the more visible. Outwardly Cass appeared unscathed yet his wounds, hidden within his mind and heart and soul, gave him no peace.

Opium and Michael Tait had been his downfall. He accepted full responsibility for everything that had preceded and resulted from that early morning exchange of fire with the baronet. And for the remainder of his time on earth, he would strive to make amends to Cecelia.

Resting his head against the seat-back, he returned to the problem of Sophie, that pattern-card of frankness.

Judging from the scraps of information she'd supplied, her husband had been a good sort, honest and trustworthy and everything else that was admirable. Cass had no hope of ravishing the paragon's devoted widow if he confessed to a period of debauchery and inebriation that had culminated in a murderous encounter on Hounslow Heath. For once he would be guided by Cecelia, and confess nothing about their past.

He craved Sophie's respect no less than he prized her lovely face, but he also lusted for her sweet body. His mind dwelled upon all those tantalizing curves—her gently rounded cheek and chin, the swelling breasts and flaring hips. Her hidden parts must be similarly delectable. He dreamed constantly of the day—no, the night—when she would let him peel away her clothes and examine her thighs and calves and ankles.

"Tio Cass?"

He opened his eyes.

"Will we be there soon?" For the first time Daniel showed signs of restlessness, drumming his heels against the bench.

"Fairly soon. Come sit here," he invited.

The child scrambled down from his place and climbed up

beside him. Out of habit he curled his arm around Daniel's shoulder, pulling him close.

"Tio?"

"Mmm."

"Why doesn't Mama ever hold me? You do. And Maria and Luis. Even Senhora—*Missus* Pinnock hugs me sometimes. But not my mother."

At a loss, Cass struggled to find an answer. Much to his sorrow, his sister's obsessive devotion to the boy and constant concern for his safety rarely translated into maternal behavior. He couldn't possibly clarify Cecelia's inability to express her affection, for Daniel was far too young to make sense of the explanation.

"I remember to speak *inglês* always now, except with Luis and Maria, just as Mama wishes. But still she doesn't love me."

The pensive declaration prompted Cass to say, "You're mistaken, Daniel. She loves you very much, more than anyone or anything in all the world. Late at night, after you've fallen asleep, she slips into your room and watches over you."

"Réalmente?"

"I've seen her," he confirmed. "If you kept awake long enough, so would you."

"Padre watches me," announced Daniel. "From up in heaven. He pushes away the clouds and looks down. Once I caught him doing it."

Cass supposed that Maria, her head stuffed with Catholic superstitions, had encouraged this belief. "And what does your father look like?"

"Like a man."

Amused by the comprehensive simplicity of this reply, Cass

said, "Well, if you catch him spying on you again, be sure to point him out. I'd like to see him myself."

The boy did resemble his sire—beneath the youthful roundness of his face Cass could trace the familiar lines of nose and jaw. Fortunately for everyone, he was even more like Cecelia. As a child her complexion had been just as pink and healthy, her mouth had curled upward instead of down, and her blue eyes had shone in innocent joy.

Daniel's stomach rumbled loudly. Giggling, he placed his hand over his belly.

"Hungry, are you?"

"Sim." The child nodded vigorously. "And thirsty. Are we almost there?"

"Not quite. This is Alveston village. If you like, we can stop at the Ship. I'd be glad of a tankard myself."

Situated on the busy Bristol-Gloucester route, the inn was a flurry of activity on this bright spring day. After Luis had downed his drink, Cass ordered him to ride to the castle ahead of the carriage.

The weather was warm and mild, so Cass chose to sip his ale outdoors. Daniel, seated on an inn yard bench with Maria, tucked into a meat pie and a slice of currant cake. The yard was bustling: hostlers and grooms harnessed horses to departing vehicles and watered the animals whose masters dined within.

"Ho, there, Nib!" shouted an aproned waiter, hanging out of an upper window. "Dr. Jenner is leaving. Make haste to fetch his horse!"

Within minutes a soberly dressed gentleman briskly exited the inn. In his late forties, he had a broad forehead, a masterful nose, and a smiling mouth.

Cass rose. "Dr. Edward Jenner?"

The man paused and turned. "I am he. Lord Bevington, isn't it? Forgive my failure to notice you. My mind was still running on Medical Society affairs—we just concluded a lively discussion of *angina pectoris.* Our meetings last many hours—after presenting scholarly or scientific papers, we share a formal dinner. But with my dear wife expecting to lie in at any time now, I must forgo our evening festivities and ride home to Berkeley."

"I'll not detain you longer than a moment or two. A timely encounter."

"Your lordship isn't ill?"

"Thankfully, no. It's my sister, Mrs. Fonseca. Presently she's in the care of a Clifton doctor, but I need someone reliable in the Bevington neighborhood."

"I should be delighted to wait upon you both. I'm honored to name other members of the local nobility among my clients—Lord Berkeley and his lady, and Lord Ducie's family at Tortworth Court. I travel in all weathers and my fees are reasonable."

Cass was impressed by such confidence, exactly what he sought in a physician.

Dr. Jenner expressed curiosity about his sister's symptoms. "Is she troubled with palpitations in the chest?"

"No."

"We can rule out a heart complaint. Are her cheeks flushed, and does she often appear short of breath?"

"Not that I've ever noticed."

"She isn't consumptive, then. Appetite good?"

Cass shrugged. "No worse or better than usual. She's never been a hearty eater."

"Tremors in her limbs or extremities?"

He shook his head emphatically.

"Sleeplessness?"

"When she's dejected or overly excited."

The doctor's graying brows were naturally set high, and they rose still higher. "Interesting. Her disposition is a nervous one?"

"Decidedly so."

"Ah. Well, I'm more than willing to attend her, my lord, but I must warn you that I haven't any cure for a bad set of nerves. In such cases I can only advise fresh country air, plenty of exercise, and wholesome food." With a glance at Daniel, he asked, "Your son looks to be a sturdy lad."

"Nephew—my sister's child. His health, unlike hers, is excellent."

"Six or seven years old, I'm guessing. Last summer I successfully inoculated a lad of his age against the smallpox. I've devised a new method and am most eager to repeat the trial. But if Mrs. Fonseca is the anxious sort, she won't favor a procedure that can only be considered experimental, despite its great promise."

"It's a dangerous operation?" asked Cass.

"Oh, no. I'd infect the boy with cowpox. It's a mild strain that apparently makes our local dairymaids immune to the more virulent forms of pox. At most your nephew would suffer a slight fever for a day or two, and during that time I'd keep him under close observation. The recovery is swifter than with the old variolation treatment, which I underwent as a child."

"I, too," said Cass. "Daniel was born in Portugal, and hasn't been inoculated yet. I'll raise the issue with my sister, if you think it wants doing."

"Trouble is, we haven't any cowpox cases in the district now, so I've no means of extracting lymph from an infected person. But I or my nephew Henry, who assists in my practice, can variolate young Daniel in the usual way, if that's his mother's preference. Ah, here's my horse, saddled and ready." Dr. Jenner took the hand Cass extended and gave it a firm shake. "A pleasure, my lord. You should know, our countryside buzzes about your lady landscape gardener, and all the changes to be made at Bevington Castle."

The reference to Sophie made Cass smile.

"I'm a keen gardener myself, and take a most particular interest in her progress. I've devised a secluded little grotto of my own behind my house in Berkeley, where I vaccinated young Jamie Phipps last summer."

With a cheery smile, he climbed upon his horse.

Daniel, his appetite satisfied, was content to play simple games with Cass during the rest of the journey to Bevington. He counted black sheep on either side of the road, and by the time the novelty wore off the carriage reached the castle drive. It passed beneath the outer arch and swung around to the stone-paved stable yard.

Cass climbed out first and helped the child negotiate the folding steps. "From this day onward, Daniel, Bevington is your home."

"Forever and ever?" asked the child.

"Until you become a man," said Cass. "Remember how you picked out your own little room in the tower many months ago? Luis will have a fire going, to make it bright and cozy."

Maria extended her hand to the boy, and he took it, murmuring excitedly in Portuguese as she led him away.

For the rest of that day and part of the next, Cass roamed

his vast domain, working his way from top to bottom. In the many corridors, colorful strips of carpet covered the ancient stones or wooden floorboards. The thousands of diamond-shaped windowpanes were at long last cleared of dust and grime. In the picture gallery, a coat of light paint provided a contrasting background for collection of dark landscape paintings. A glittering chandelier of Waterford crystal floated above the new mahogany dining table. The tapestry hangings in the morning room, great hall, and small drawing room had been cleaned. Floral wallpaper freshened Cecelia's chosen bedchamber, decorated to her taste with chintz draperies and furniture upholstered in petit-point.

While touring his refurbished rooms, Cass didn't picture his sister in them. No, Sophie was the person he imagined seated on the elegant giltwood sofa in the long drawing room, and studying the portraits in great hall, and poring over the books in the library. In the morning room, he could see her standing at the tall casements, looking down upon the gardens—exactly as she'd been doing the first time he laid eyes upon her.

He wanted to share his castle with her. Sophie, he was sure, could learn to love its oddities and beauties in a way Cecelia never would.

A whim carried him to her quaint, old-fashioned parlor in the gatehouse. Prey to a desire to see the room in which she'd slept—and would again after her return—he climbed the spiral stairway. Her oak bedstead was a plainer version of his, and the other furnishings appeared to be well-made, if a trifle ordinary. She should have better ones, he decided.

He was intrigued by a wood-paneled door set into an arch in the wall. Because it lacked a handle, he was unable to discover where it led.

Mentally he reviewed the layout of the castle. Very likely this uppermost room of the gatehouse adjoined his suite. And if he could locate the key—

Before he'd completed the thought, he was hurrying out of Sophie's bedchamber, down the steps, into the courtyard.

He located his housekeeper in her sitting room and told her he'd found a door that wouldn't open.

"D'you mean that low wooden one at the back of your lordship's dressing room?"

"The very one. Have you got the key?"

Mrs. Harvey waddled over to an array of hooks protruding from the wall, each holding a key-ring. "It'll be here. Upper floor, the master's chambers—'twill be with this set. All of 'em brass, save this gurt iron one. That's surely the one you need."

Thanking her, he slipped the key off the ring and carried it away with him.

What could be more perfect, he thought in exultation, than a door connecting his rooms and Sophie's?

His Jacobean bedstead, with carved posts as thick as tree trunks, looked a great deal more inviting now that it had a goose down mattress and plump pillows. As for those needlework hangings—he wasn't sure he liked them, but at least they were nicer than the old moth-eaten ones.

He passed into the narrow, closet-like space fitted up with a shaving mirror and a bureau and a wardrobe. The arched door was at the far end, its wood whitewashed to blend with the pale stone of the wall. He slipped the iron key into the crude metal lock and turned it.

A feminine shriek curtailed his explorations.

A blonde girl in mobcap and apron clutched a rag to her

bosom. "Lord Bevington!" she cried.

At a loss, he stared back at her.

"I'm Nan—Parham. Mrs. Pinnock's waiting woman," she explained, bobbing a curtsy.

Now he remembered. "Right. Of course."

"Your lordship's valet told me she was coming back 'ere soon, so I come up to do the dusting," she told him, her eyes wide.

"Carry on," he said, embarrassed to be caught intruding. "I needed to know where this passage led. Now that I do, I shall leave you to finish your work."

Retreating to his dressing room, he shut the door and leaned against it.

Would the housemaid tell Sophie what he'd done? He preferred to inform her about his discovery himself. Examining the key, he wondered what he should do with it. Best to keep it close, he thought, and hid it in the uppermost drawer of the chest.

With a dreamy smile, Andrew Searle looked away from the brilliant blue kingfisher fluttering up from the woodland stream. "And how," he drawled, "is the estimable Mrs. Pinnock getting on?"

"She has improved the grounds of Summit House," Cass reported. "My sister is most pleased."

"Her lively presence is much missed here at Bevington. I trust you'll bring her back."

Cass eyed his friend with suspicion as they strolled toward the cottage *ornée*. Why should Drew miss Sophie? "When she does return, she'll be busy with the task I hired her to perform," he warned. "She won't be at leisure to amuse you."

"Poor girl, you work her so hard. She must regard you as a slave-driver." After a pause, Andrew said, "Sorry for that slip—I know you dislike reminders of your plantation origins. Step inside, old fellow, there's a matter we must discuss."

The cottage looked as though a tempest had struck it. Heaps of clothing and piles of books and stacks of filthy dishes covered every surface. Andrew collapsed onto a chair by the table where he ate and also worked, judging from the bread crumbs and papers everywhere.

"Sit, please. I can't converse sensibly with you looming over me." When Cass complied, he continued, "I've been considering that tutorial position you offered when I first came to Bevington."

"Oh," said Cass in relief. He'd prepared himself for an awkward and one-sided discussion, with Drew rhapsodizing about Sophie. "You've decided to accept?"

"Regretfully, I must decline to take on your nephew as pupil. I've formed an alternate plan for my future."

"I'm sorry to hear that. What is it?"

The poet shook his shaggy head. "I cannot be more specific, not yet. But my future endeavors require that I settle nearer London. My mind has been dulled by rural living."

Cass pierced him with a sharp, suspicious glance. Rural living, he wondered, or too much laudanum?

"Don't be surprised if I'm soon begging for assistance. It would be a temporary loan."

"You won't have to beg," Cass said. He'd pay any price if it endured Drew's departure before Sophie's return. "When do you leave this cottage?"

"Not immediately. I'll notify you as soon as my arrangements are finalized. If I hadn't drunk up the last of my wine, we could raise a glass to toast my prospects. I'm afraid this is the best I can offer."

Cass recoiled when his friend brandished a blue glass vial.

"Come now, there's no harm in it. Quite the opposite, it has the power to smooth away the worries denting your brow and place a smile on your face. That's what you used to tell me. Remember?"

Laudanum. Cass recalled the despair that had driven him to use the drug, but the agonies he'd suffered in freeing himself of its grip had been far worse. "It doesn't agree with me," he insisted.

With an air of superiority, Drew commented, "What a stodgy chap you've become."

"I'm more careful now," he said grimly. Seven years ago his insobriety had cost him dearly, and nowadays he had so much more to lose.

"One day," his friend declared blithely, "I shall write a treatise on the blessed powers of opium. After I attain my heart's desire, it will be my first—and greatest—composition."

"You should abandon the habit," Cass responded. "Every dose steals more of your energy and drains you of ambition. Trust me, I know."

Andrew took a defiant sip from his bottle. "My friend Sam Coleridge would laugh to hear you talk so. In his experience— and mine—the drug inspires greater things. If I showed you my most recent verses, you'd see how very wrong you are. I'll make clean copies and bring them to the castle tonight."

"Not tonight," Cass protested. "I've rent books and tenant lists to study before I leave for Clifton in the morning."

The poet accompanied him to the door. "You're not miffed?"

Cass placed a hand on his friend's thin shoulder and said soberly, "I've looked out for you since we were schoolboys together. That's one habit I'm happy to retain."

Making his way through the deer park, he reflected on Drew's persistent interest in Sophie. Nothing she'd ever said or done indicated that it was reciprocated. His only real rival, it seemed, was the late Tobias Pinnock.

He tried to think of some service he could perform that would please her. She wanted a rose list from Emrys Jones, he recalled. By getting it, he might obtain a rich reward.

He located the Welshman in the rose garden, kneeling in the dirt and pulling weeds along the edge of the wall. Two bright spots of color showed in his pale cheeks when he learned that Cass expected him to produce the desired item on the spot.

"I'm aware of Mrs. Pinnock's request," he said impatiently. "She'll have her list."

"She's asked you for it repeatedly. What prevents your compliance?" Cass received no answer. "You may be here at her invitation, but the gardens are mine. If you expect to stay on, you'd best summon up more respect than you've shown heretofore."

"I've told your lordship, Mrs. Pinnock is the only one who can dismiss me. I receive no pay," the man reminded him, "so I'm beholden to no one."

As obdurate as the lady he worked for, thought Cass, and every bit as impertinent.

"Have you any other message for me, my lord?"

He did not, although he had a personal need of information. "I want to know whether a particular specimen, grows here. It has petals the color of wine. A Velvet rose, Mrs. Pinnock called it."

"Aye, and many. The plants sucker freely, they spread themselves about."

"Show me."

Jones led him around the enclosure, pointing out each of the tall, twiggy shrubs growing against the wall and a few others that clung to the arbors. Young leaves were springing up along the canes.

"If left undisturbed, you'll have flowers afore July. But if they're moved, they mightn't bloom at all this year."

"Leave them where they are," Cass commanded. Determined to scatter those wine-red petals over Sophie's naked white body, he must preserve them.

"Isn't that for Mrs. Pinnock to say?"

"Neither you nor she will do anything here that hasn't been sanctioned by me. Is that clear?"

"Perfectly, my lord," said the Welshman, glaring into the distance.

Cass turned his head and spied Luis Costa picking the variegated tulips growing in the border.

Holding up his bouquet, he called out, "Beautiful flowers, so many colors! You teach me names, Senhor Shones?"

"He's far too busy to bother with you," Cass rebuked him. "And you have much to do yourself. Come away now."

The youth's shoulders slumped, but he answered obediently, "*Sim,* senhorio."

"Have I not warned you," said Cass furiously, as they crossed the springy turf, "to keep well away from that man? I brought you here to prepare the house for Senhora Fonseca, she depends on you to arrange things for her. But I cannot leave you behind if you defy me."

"I no defy," Luis promised.

Not only was Cass cross with Luis. The stubborn Welshman had annoyed him. Drew's persistent use of opium frustrated him. He was plagued by his own failings, past and present. And he feared that if Sophie Pinnock ever discovered the bitter truth, he'd have no use for those velvety rose petals.

All these pent-up feelings exploded in the direction of his valet, whom he bullied into a state of distress.

"I sorry for making senhorio angry. I keep away from Senhor Shones."

"See that you do. And for the love of God, Luis, keep quiet about Portugal. You could do great harm by talking too much."

"*Sim, sim.* I no want to hurt Senhora Fonseca and Daniel."

"Then be careful what you say, and to whom you say it."

Luis lifted his dark head, and eyes that were dark pools of conviction. "I have sweared it, on souls of my ancestors. And I wish to die, senhorio, before ever I break my vow to you."

CHAPTER 10

Improvement, the idol of the age,
Is fed with many a victim. Lo! he comes,
The omnipotent magician...

~William Cowper

Sophie pressed a hand into the small of her back and rubbed the ache she felt there. She'd been sticking brown and shriveled anemone corms in the ground, a late planting to extend the summer display. By the time they bloomed, in a rainbow of colors, the Carysforts would be permanently settled at Bevington, miles away from their lovely town house and its improved setting. But as a gardener she must consider not only this year, but all the ones to follow.

She dropped her well-used dibber into the large pocket of her brown pinafore, where it joined bits of string, empty seed packets, and a round white pebble. Giving in to weariness, she lowered her weary body onto the bottom step where Luis Costa and young Daniel had often sat to watch her work. Over the past two days she had missed their interested questions as she'd gone about her tasks.

Echo's inquisitive nose discovered the freshly tilled soil, prompting Sophie to call out, *"Nânnîn!* If you *dare* dig up those anemones—" She didn't state what the punishment would be, for her sharp cry had been enough of a deterrent.

The culprit cocked her head, and her ears lifted. With a piercing yelp, she raced around the side of the house. She soon pranced back into view bounding beside her master.

His face lit up when he saw Sophie, his smile sent her spirits soaring to the skies. Until she recalled why she should distrust it.

"Here you are, just as I left you. No, don't take off your pinny, you look so industrious."

Dismayed by the dark splotches all over his breeches, she responded, *"Ma fé,* what have you been doing? You have dirt on your—" Her astonished gaze fell upon his firm thighs and calves. "On your garments."

"I know."

He held out his hands and she took them. She breathed in the mingled scents of sandalwood shaving soap and leather saddlery.

"I bring good tidings. Yesterday I talked to that man Jones. This morning, too."

"You brought my rose list?" she asked eagerly.

"I'm afraid I haven't. But I committed certain information to memory. *Rosa mundi* grows in the castle grounds, just as you hoped. Jones says it has striped petals of carmine and white, or palest pink."

"Yes, I know—it's my favorite." Delighted by his new enthusiasm, she made no attempt to unclasp their hands. "What else?"

"Alba semi plena," he enunciated carefully.

"The fabled White Rose of York," she interrupted. He stood so close that the hard buttons of his riding coat pressed against her bosom. "Go on."

"And Velvet roses. I saw them myself—leaf buds have begun sprouting. I told the Welshman he mustn't move them until after they've bloomed."

A strong gust of wind whipped her pinafore like a sail, and trifled with his hair. Impatiently he plowed his fingers through the black curls in an effort to restore order, disarranging them far more than the breeze had done.

"I found a florilegium in the castle library. The Velvet rose is a form of *Rosa gallica,* with masses of petals, the deepest red imaginable."

Why he should be so intensely interested in that particular variety, Sophie couldn't imagine. His conversion from indifferent client to fellow rose-fancier was as endearing as it was perplexing.

She asked, "Did you dirty yourself grubbing about in the rose beds with Mr. Jones?"

"Before I left Bevington, Daniel insisted on one last game of rough-and-tumble. As you see, my compliance cost me dearly. I'll have to discard these breeches, unless you think they can be salvaged."

"My servant Mary cleans her husband's dirty leathers with soft soap and a flannel," Sophie recalled. "Doesn't your valet have a trick of his own?"

His mouth compressed into a taut, flat line. "I expect so."

The blue eyes had narrowed until they were slits, and he glowered as he hadn't done for quite a long time. Sophie wondered what Luis had done to displease him. Seeking to restore his good mood, she reported that his sister had recovered from her indisposition.

"But she hasn't yet left the house, not even to visit the Pump Room. She isn't idle, though. She has picked out the clothes and other possessions she wants transferred to the castle. Her trunks are stacked in the upper corridor."

"Not for long. The carrier fetches them tomorrow, and we'll depart the following morning. I trust you'll also be ready to travel?"

"At a moment's notice," she responded promptly.

"Excellent."

After he went up the stairs and into the house, she realized that he hadn't alluded to the shameful proposition he'd made on the day of his departure.

The earl's return put an end to the increasingly frantic scurrying of the harassed servants. Unlike his sister, an impetuous and disorganized manager, he issued commands calmly and clearly. Cherished ornaments were stripped from the tabletops and mantel shelves, wrapped in brown paper and placed in sturdy packing crates, each identified with a letter inscribed in black chalk. The furnishings disappeared beneath the pale holland cloth that would guard them from the ravages of dust and sunlight. Tradesmen's bills arrived hourly and were settled on the spot.

The next morning, Lord Bevington spent an hour closeted in his study with a pair of lawyers, one old and one young. In his absence, his sister fluttered about the house distractedly, dodging the footmen and maids and brushing off Sophie's attempts to calm her. With the arrival of the carrier's wagon, chaos reigned once more. Echo signified her disapproval of the proceedings with flattened ears and drooping tail. Lying down in the middle of the entrance hall, she ignored all attempts to shift her.

As the solicitors passed her on their way out she growled at them ferociously, until silenced by her master and ordered outside.

Marching over to Cecelia, the earl said, "You're wearing yourself out, for no good reason. Did the footboy fetch your daily dose of well-water from the Pump Room?"

"I suppose so," she said absent-mindedly. "I haven't drunk it yet."

"Do so now, otherwise you'll forget. And please, let these good people go about their business undisturbed. Return to your room and read your novel, or lie down."

"But the carrier has just come, and I must—" Her head swiveled to follow a manservant's progress. "Treat that box with especial care, Edward."

"Yes, madam."

"You're supposed to call him Bitton," Cass reminded her, "we've promoted him from footman to butler."

"I know," she said wearily, "but my mind is all a muddle. You're right, *meu irmao,* I ought to rest." She drifted up the staircase, supporting herself with the handrail.

Trusting his staff to transfer the trunks and boxes from the hall to the wagon outside, he turned to Sophie. "Come into my study—but mind you don't trip over the stacks of books."

Sophie stepped carefully around the obstacles as she entered his private retreat. The room had already lost much of its character, for the glass-fronted cabinets no longer held his collection of mementos from other lands, and the usual array of wine and brandy decanters was missing.

He cleared away the newssheets cluttering an armchair and

encouraged her to sit.

"Can't I help you with your books?"

"If you don't mind, I'd be grateful. This lot is ready to be wrapped and crated."

They worked together in companionable silence. He roamed from bookcase to bookcase, selecting volumes and dusting each leather cover with a rag before he surrendered it to Sophie. By studying the title pages she educated herself about his primary interests—agriculture, foreign travel— and discovered that he read French as well as Portuguese. He preferred plays to poetry, and the absence of any classical texts told her that he'd given up the Greeks and Romans after his schooldays. Many of his books were antiquated, printed in old-fashioned type on rough, thick paper. Others were so new that their pages hadn't even been cut.

"Here's one you'll like," he said, presenting her with an octavo edition. *"Bacon's Essays.* Didn't he write one about gardening?"

She nodded. "I haven't read it for a long while, but I remember the opening sentence. 'God almighty first planted a garden—and indeed, it is the purest of human pleasures.'"

When she reached for a sheet of newspaper to wrap around it, he told her to keep it separate from the rest. "It's yours now."

"What if you should want it?"

"I daresay I'll find a copy in the castle library. Perhaps you'll value this little book more than the ring I gave you."

The ring.

Sophie's first impulse had been to return it, lest she be compromised by keeping it. But sufficient time had passed that she could regard it as harmless, and she hated to give up her only souvenir of her visit to the Hotwells. Examining the book of essays, Sophie remembered that Andrew Searle had presented her with a copy of his philosophical treatise, a far more personal gift than this. But he hadn't expected her to become his mistress, either.

Their cozy comradeship ended abruptly when Edward Bitton announced the arrival of two gentlemen callers.

"Waiting on the doorstep, my lord—no room for them in the hall." He handed over a pair of cards.

Cass's brows darted upward as he read the inscription aloud. *"H. Repton, Landscape Gardener. Hare Street, near Romford, Essex."*

Sophie's head jerked up. *"Sapresti!"*

When he surrendered the card to her, she glared at the familiar scene engraved upon it, a landscape of woodland and water. Two male figures—the great man and an assistant—posed before a surveying instrument, observing a party of laborers wielding axes and pushing wheelbarrows.

"And this," he said, handing over the second card, "belongs to your former associate."

"Fingal Moncrieff? *Bouon Dgieu,* why would they come here? Together?"

"By all means let's find out," said Cass, nodding at his servant.

The most famous garden-maker in the land strode confidently into the library and removed his round-brimmed hat, bowing low. His hairline receded almost to the middle of his skull; the powdered locks were cropped short at the sides and pulled tightly back in a queue.

"Lord Bevington, my apologies for intruding at this inconvenient time. And Mrs. Pinnock is here as well!" He nodded in Sophie's direction. "Madam, as always it is a pleasure to meet you."

"The pleasure is mutual, sir." Jumped-up haberdasher, she fumed, bestowing a false smile upon him.

Her husband had been amused by her disdain for his professional rival. Tobias had regarded Repton as a clever practitioner, working hard to fill the void created by the death of the great Capability Brown. But in Sophie's opinion he was no great artist, nor a master of horticulture.

"We stopped at Bevington Castle yesterday," he was telling the earl, "and your groundskeeper said we'd find you at Clifton. By happy coincidence I was on my way to Blaise to call upon my client Mr. Scandrett, who is altering a hillside cottage on his property in accordance with my Red Book recommendation. Moncrieff, my architectural assistant, is just the man for the job."

"Mr. Moncrieff and I have met," said Cass thinly.

The Scotsman insinuated himself into the conversation, commenting, "Before Mr. Repton invited me to join his practice."

"Quite so," Cass agreed. "At that time you were trying to impress me by claiming another artist's designs as your own. I hope you gained your present position more honestly."

"Mr. Repton," said Sophie hastily, "is fortunate to gain such a talented associate." Moncrieff's flashing eyes and ruddy cheeks warned her that he was losing his fragile control over his temper.

A vindictive man, he might choose to retaliate with a fatal dose of the truth. She shrank from acknowledging their past conspiracies, and couldn't bear for her employer—or his—to learn that she'd engaged in dishonest practices. Too many patrons possessed Blue Books attributed to Tobias Pinnock but which were in reality Sophie's creations. She couldn't let her former partner wreck her chances of establishing a respectable trade under her own name. Or worse, impeach Tobias Pinnock's lasting reputation for integrity in the presence of his most illustrious and influential competitor.

Smiling at Repton, she added, "Had you solicited my recommendation, sir, I would have given it wholeheartedly. Mr. Moncrieff is worthy of your trust."

The architect's flush receded, but his manner was stiff when he said, "I thank you, madam. How astonished I was when that fellow Jones informed us that you alone will be responsible for improving the landscape at Bevington."

Impossible to improve upon perfection, she thought.

"Mrs. Pinnock has done wondrous things here at Summit House," said the earl. "I am vastly pleased with what she's accomplished, and I invite you to tour my fine new landscape."

His compliment failed to gladden Sophie. She was horrified by the prospect of hearing Humphry Repton pass judgment on her handiwork. But there was no escaping the ordeal, for Lord Bevington intended to show off his grounds.

The splendid view across the Avon was the first thing to excite Repton's admiration. "The drama of the gorge is sublime," he enthused. "And in the distance, hanging woods and outcroppings of rock—magnificent!"

Fingal Moncrieff bobbed his carroty head, but added nothing to the great man's raptures.

"The arrangement of boulders and trees in the foreground is most appropriate," Repton continued. "I, too, would have planted conifers, their vertical lines provide a most desirable contrast to the rectilinear shape of the house, with its classically Palladian structure." Rather than addressing Sophie, he directed his remarks to her employer. "The positioning of these pines and cedars, and their maturity, gives the impression that they've grown here for many years. Yet they must have been planted quite recently."

"Within the past fortnight," Cass confirmed.

"Astonishing." Deigning at last to notice Sophie, Repton said, "I am curious to know, Mrs. Pinnock, how you achieved such naturalness."

Did he seriously expect her to impart her secret? It was a simple but effective one: she'd selected the largest available specimens and planted them closer than the recommended distance so their branches would touch each other, as in a forest. She had covered the bare ground underneath with mosses and ferns, knowing they would thrive in the damp shade. She did not merely imitate natural scenery—guided by nature itself, she'd recreated it.

"It's a trick I learned from my husband," she said, but offered no details.

"He instructed you to use so many evergreens?"

"That is my own choice. Conifers provide foliage in winter months, when deciduous trees are bare."

"You include a great many flowering shrubs, I see."

"Even the most modern landscape benefits from color and fragrance."

Said Fingal Moncrieff dourly, "'Twould not be a Pinnock design without floral displays."

Sophie glared at him. A great debate had raged during their uneasy partnership, and she knew he disapproved of her methods. "Flowers are lovely to look upon. They lift the spirits. They perfume the air. They can be cut and taken indoors. They can be dried for potpourri or distilled to make fragrant water. I'm too practical a gardener not to consider the utility of the plants I choose."

Focusing his round eyes upon her, Humphry Repton said ponderously, "Madam, you must always consider the primary rule of landscape gardening—to impress upon the viewer the importance of the landowner. Our clients come to us because they desire to be in the forefront of fashion."

"And you, sir, care too little for the function of pleasure grounds. They are meant to be used and lived in and enjoyed."

Clearly nettled by her criticism, he answered quickly, "Yes, yes, that is also important. Certainly it is."

Having won this concession from him, she was emboldened to point out, "Yet your parks, like those of Capability Brown, are dominated by extensive grassland—vast green fields with a few clumps of trees. You both have replaced too many gardens of old-fashioned, highly scented flowers that delight our senses of sight and smell. As for the ornamental water features you recommend—*ma fé,* I cannot understand why you chose a winding serpentine river over a canal."

"Straight lines are not natural," he decreed.

"Nature must rule," Moncrieff added. "Artifice should never intrude."

"Oh? What is more intrusive than felling a formal alley of trees that has stood for a century? Or replacing native varieties with exotics? Consider Mr. Beckford of Fonthill— he planted one hundred thousand specimens last year, few of them English. For some unfathomable reason he is creating an Alpine forest on the chalky hills of Wiltshire. There is nothing natural about that! Or desirable," she concluded pithily.

"Sophia," Moncrieff intoned, "remember to whom you speak."

Disregarding the Scotsman, she resumed her attack upon Repton. "You wreak havoc everywhere you go, sir. You advise your fashion-conscious patrons to knock down their garden walls and ancient woodlands. But unless they live on for fifty years or more they won't see their new landscapes reach the peak of perfection. By then you'll have gone out of fashion yourself. How does it feel to know that future designers will regard your style as antiquated, and be called upon to 'improve' your undulating parks and remove your stylistic embellishments?"

"Madam, you followed the tenets of modern landscaping here at Summit House."

"I destroyed nothing," she defended herself. "Have you never once regretted sacrificing so many historic Tudor and Jacobean gardens to satisfy your patrons' desire to be fashionable?"

"I admire beauty in any form," Repton acknowledged. "The human mind has an inborn appreciation of order and symmetry, it is true. In your case, Mrs. Pinnock, it appears to be overly developed."

"Why must we always reduce existing gardens to something inferior, why can we not preserve what is already there?" She studied the faces of her listeners. Repton was skeptical, Moncrieff frowned, and the earl was—

The earl!

He'd kept silent so long that she'd forgotten him. All this time she'd spoken her mind freely, never realizing that she was repudiating all the high-flown theories she had tossed about when showing him her Bevington sketches. She'd made clear—in front of witnesses—her personal distaste for the task he was paying her a fortune to perform. *Bêtasse,* she mocked herself. Oh, what a great fool she was! Such recklessness would be rewarded with dismissal.

Her two male rivals coveted her Bevington project. They were transparent in their desire to steal her noble client. And she'd made it so very easy for them.

"My lord," said Repton silkily, "I am amazed that you would consult a reactionary—indeed, a revolutionary. Perhaps this explains why your planned alterations at Bevington Castle proceed so slowly."

Sophie's employer came forward to stand at her side. "I insisted that Mrs. Pinnock leave her work there in order to supervise the changes my sister and I wanted here. I assure you, she has produced a splendid set of plans for the castle grounds."

His steadfast defense intensified Sophie's mortification.

The castle's flowery borders and shaded shrubbery walks and overgrown rose bower meant far more to her now than the prestige she'd sought two months ago. And she couldn't even save them by resigning. Repton and Moncrieff would fall all over themselves to take her place and gleefully tear down walls and uproot the plants they considered uninteresting.

While Lord Bevington was seeing his visitors off the premises, Sophie wandered to the edge of the cliff. Drearily she stared out over the view that had so excited Repton.

Everything had gone wrong. If she didn't extricate herself from this impossible and hopeless situation, it would only worsen. She should consider her reputation, her private one and her professional one, and the dangers to both.

For a long time she stood there, meditating on her mistakes and pondering methods of repairing the damage.

When the earl returned, she held her position. She was

reluctant to face him, fearing that he could sabotage her newly formed decision with a single smile.

"I believed I knew you rather well, Sophie," he said, in that deep, rich voice. "But when you attacked Repton, you surprised me."

She stared at the rugged vista without seeing it, saying dully, "I should have known better. Two against one—I stood no chance against them."

A firm, insistent hand on her shoulder compelled her to turn around. His blue eyes shone down at her from a great height. "My brave Sophie."

The impact of his kiss caught her off guard. Her emotions were running high, her resistance was at low ebb. She tried to swim against the rising tide of desire, but it washed over her, choking her. It dragged her down to the depths before relentlessly pitching her onto an unfamiliar shore.

She clutched at him like a drowning victim, parting her lips for his life-giving breath. Was he her salvation? Or had he called forth this tempest in order to destroy her?

"Nânnîn. No, you can—" Again his lips claimed her, interrupting her protest. "Cannot do—this. Not now."

He rubbed his cheek against hers. "Is it so terrible?"

"Intolerable," she managed to say and took a backward step. "Lord Bevington, I resign my position."

Her announcement had a profound effect. His black head jerked up and his eyebrows swept downward. "You're bound by a contract—at your insistence, not mine."

"I'm asking to be released from it. Don't make this more difficult than it need be."

"Damn it, Sophie, what a vexing creature you are!"

"I'm abandoning my career as a landscape gardener."

"To do what? I can't imagine you as a lady of leisure."

She put a greater distance between them. "I shall seek employment as a botanical artist."

"By all means, if that's what you prefer. You'll find a multitude of plants at Bevington to inspire you. I've got enough of them growing there to fill vast volumes of illustrations."

"I'm returning to Chiswick," she insisted. "To be near Mr. Curtis, the printer—he purchases my pictures, and often pays me to color the finished engravings. He has a display garden himself, in the Fulham Road. The subscription fee is two guineas, but he grants me free entry." Aware that she was rambling, she concluded, "Besides, I have my own garden. I've neglected it too long."

"And what of mine?"

"Naturally I shall finish your plans. After that, any contractor can carry out the work. I'll be happy to suggest some names."

"I don't want anyone else. You will supervise the alterations yourself. Your contract stipulates it." He shook his head at her. "One skirmish with Repton, and you surrender. This isn't like you."

"Not a surrender, *pon du tout*. I view this as retirement." Lifting her chin, she explained, "In my own mind, I've attained the pinnacle of success. For just under an hour the most highly respected of all landscape gardeners regarded me as a successful rival—and accused me of being a threat to our profession. What was it he called me? A reactionary. A revolutionary."

"His opinion be damned, and to hell with him."

"I've labored in his shadow long enough to know it doesn't suit me," Sophie declared. "I was terribly unhappy in my partnership with Fingal Moncrieff. When he stole my portfolio I fought back the only way I could, by setting up as a competitor—to him, and to Repton and Mickle and Emes and the rest of their kind. I'm satisfied with my achievements, insignificant though they may seem to others. I've completed the project here at Summit House, and you declare yourself satisfied. Rest assured, the final watercolors and planting recommendations for Bevington will be presented to you wrapped in blue leather binding as agreed."

He regarded her silently for some time before saying, "You want me to believe Humphry Repton's visit is the reason for your resignation. I suspect it has more to do with what passed between us before I left for Bevington."

She forced herself to meet his piercing stare. "Yes, that also contributed to my decision. Stop smiling at me like that," she chided. "It will do you no good."

"You always smile back so prettily I never guessed it was distasteful to you."

"It is. I hate being preyed upon. And if I continue plying my trade, it won't be long before I must fend off some other aristocratic patron."

"Is that all I am to you, a *patron?* After ogling you and touching you and stealing kisses at every opportunity?"

"That's all you can ever be," she answered. "I have been a wife, Cassian. I am now a widow. I do not aspire to be anything more."

"You are also the woman I want. I need you, Sophie."

"Stop, please," she begged him. "You tear me up inside by saying such things. This is a sad end to our association—but end it must."

Cass was determined to keep her at Bevington. His great

house needed a mistress. So did he.

There would be no permanence to their relationship, he reminded himself. He was falling in love with a woman whose prior experience of love made her incapable of reciprocating. A grand passion could not be one-sided. She'd leave him eventually.

The prospect was like a slash across his heart.

Coveting this enigma that only one other man had possessed, he re-evaluated his strategy—not objectively, but from her unique perspective. Sophie came from a good family, her uncle was Seigneur of Anneville. She'd been wed to a man both respectable and respected. Taking these facts into consideration, Cass could see why she was so affronted by pursuit by a libidinous earl. She knew her own worth. And he was rapidly discovering it.

What would her answer be, he wondered, if he suggested a more honorable alliance?

Marriage had never been an option during his previous entanglements with Englishwomen. Those who had shared his bed had belonged to an unsuitable class, and his encounters with them had been brief. In Portugal, his most enduring liaison had been with a married noblewoman, and its chief purpose had been to alleviate boredom.

Don't be a fool, he warned himself.

Sophie would never commit herself wholeheartedly to another man—not unless he possessed all the excellent qualities of Tobias Pinnock, and perhaps not even then. Better to take whatever he could get, and be satisfied.

He advanced purposefully, trapping her between two large boulders and the cliff edge. "I won't let you go, Sophie."

"You have no power to stop me," she said defiantly.

Each gazed fiercely back at the other.

Their long, intent regard was broken by a frantic voice calling, "Lord Bevington! Missus Pinnock!"

A young woman hurtled toward them, her feet scattering the fresh-laid gravel.

"Isn't she one of the castle servants?"

"Nan Parham," said Sophie, troubled by her maid's reddened eyes and blotched cheeks.

His voice was taut with dread as he asked, "What's the matter, girl? Has Daniel suffered an accident?"

"Nay, he's hearty enough, but so downcast because of what's happened. 'Tis your lordship's valet, the foreigner. He's gone missing. No one's seen him for two days." Nan paused to fill her lungs with air. "That Portugee woman, Maria, come to me this morning. I could 'ardly understand her—she was weeping into her shawl, and every other word was gibberish or else a groan. She kept making a cross over herself, the way the papists do."

"Why?" Cass prompted.

"She says he's dead." Her eyes welled with tears.

Dread inched down Sophie's spine. *"Nânnîn. Such a thing isn't possible."*

"She took me to his room, I saw his bed myself—'tweren't mussed, or slept on. His clothes were in the wardrobe, folded up so neat-like. We even found his valise," she added sorrowfully, bowing her head.

"That's insufficient proof that Maria's fears are true," said Cass. "She's a good woman, but far from clever—or rational. She builds up every minor catastrophe into a crisis."

"Did you come so far on foot, Nan?"

"Nay, ma'am, I rode 'ere on the stagecoach. Maria said his

lordship needed to know, and she paid the fare. 'Tweren't no inside places, so I sat high up on the roof."

Said Sophie in sympathy, "I can imagine how uncomfortable that must have been. I'll take you to a quiet place where you can sit down with a cup of tea."

"Wait," said Cass.

Sophie, already leading the travel-weary Nan towards the house, looked back at him.

"Here's a chance to prove your famous boast that you can be ready to leave at a moment's notice. We depart for the castle immediately—you and Cecelia and me. Nan, you're coming with us, but this time you shall sit inside the carriage."

The girl mumbled her thanks for his generosity.

"There must be a logical explanation," he added. "Luis wouldn't run away, certainly not when I've saddled him with so many household responsibilities."

"It seems unlikely," Sophie acknowledged. "He wouldn't risk angering you."

"Are you implying that he's afraid of me?"

The question startled her. "His devotion to you and Mrs. Fonseca is remarkable. And he's so fond of Daniel." She'd tried to quell his obvious concerns, yet his face was more somber than before.

"I shouldn't be at all surprised to find that he has returned, safe and sound, by the time we reach Bevington."

If only he'd smiled at her, Sophie might have been comforted by his hopeful prophecy.

CHAPTER 11

*And of all love's joyful flame
I the bud and blossom am.*

~Giles Fletcher

Springtime was the season most closely associated with poetry. So why, wondered Andrew Searle, was composition as unsatisfying now as it had been in winter's darkest depths? Seated on the stump of a felled oak, surrounded by nature, he struggled to recapture his lost enthusiasm for his art.

Looking to love for inspiration, he came up empty. The awkward and thus far woefully ineffective courtship he'd begun should inspire fine and touching verses. But he hadn't created anything worthwhile.

Sophie Pinnock's impending departure from Bevington was a harsh blow to his dream of making her his wife. If he attempted a passionate appeal, flinging his arms around her and declaring his undying devotion, she would surely think he'd lost his wits. Gestures of that sort were for men more heroic than he. He preferred a reasonable approach and required time to organize his disordered thoughts into coherent persuasions. He was studying the diary he'd kept seven years ago in London, when he'd been a poorly paid journalist. During the height of his infatuation with Cecelia Carysfort, he'd written a number of sonnets detailing her beauty and charms. Simple and effective, and after several minor deletions and amendments—altering references to hair and eye color—he would present them to Sophie.

He thumbed through the entries. Page after page detailed his wild exploits with Cass. Together they had frequented brothels and bagnios in the Covent Garden district. They had visited the roughest and most dangerous taverns of Seven Dials, drinking and exchanging rude jests with the regulars. As dawn broke over the vast city, they had slunk back to their very different worlds—Cass to an elegant terrace house in Marylebone, Andrew to his dismal one-room lodging near Blackfriars Bridge.

Arriving at a familiar and significant passage, he read every word.

Last night Cass produced a vial of Bristol glass, assuring me that its contents would soothe my pangs and heartburnings. (Knowing not that his sister is the cause.) Laudanum, he declared, is the remedy for his sufferings. What they might be I cannot guess, blessed as he is with his handsome phiz—a quick mind—the roguish charm that endears him to the fair sex—abundant wealth—rich and influential friends.

At his urging, I swallowed the dose. Laudanum's power over my mind is not easily described. Vapors of calmness suffused my hitherto busy brain, a sense

of lassitude stole over my corpus. A wondrous sensa-
tion, indeed. Alas, my funds are too limited to allow
frequent indulgence. But Cass is a generous friend, he
offers to supply the miraculous substance whenever I
may desire it.

Reviewing this account of his introduction to the drug, he acknowledged that the fateful vial had altered the direction of his life. Repeatedly he turned the leaves of his journal, each filled with enthusiastic and rapturous descriptions of the dreams and visions induced by the opiate. Andrew alternately smiled and frowned over his writings. Unaided, his recollections of that period were vague.

At first his use of laudanum had been conservative. Cass had been the one to consume it lavishly and recklessly, desperate to escape a gnawing problem that he refused to discuss. But eventually he'd ceased taking it altogether, swearing never again to seek solace from what he referred to as a wickedly intoxicating fluid.

"For God's sake, man, return to earth."

Andrew looked up from his book.

His friend stood before him—vigorous, healthy, liberated from their shared vice.

"I hope I don't interrupt your work."

Shaking his head, Andrew answered, "I was re-living our London adventures."

"Are you as fervent a diarist now as you were then?"

"It is a habit. I could not stop if I wanted to."

"Another day without news of Luis," said Cass heavily. "The third since his disappearance. I begin to believe he's deserted me after all."

"Is it such a loss? I've never understood your fondness for that boy."

"A discreet and reliable servant is hard to come by. Were you conscious of anything unusual in his behavior lately? Did you ever observe him with a stranger?"

"No strangers hereabouts, to my knowledge. Twice on the same day I saw him with that Welsh gardener. At midday and again at dusk."

"Do you recall where they were?"

"The first time, under the laburnums. Jones was attaching the vines to the frame, and Luis stood by chattering at him. Later I noticed them strolling together among the roses. Darkness was falling."

"You're certain he was with Jones that night?"

Shrugging, Andrew replied, "I assumed so. But no, I'm not positive. You should ask the man."

"I doubt he would admit to it. When I wanted to know what he was doing at the time Luis disappeared, he claimed he was drawing up the list of rose specimens for Sophie Pinnock. Not that she wants it any longer." Cass kicked at the decaying leaves with the toe of his boot. "She leaves the castle as soon as she finishes making her own copy of my landscape design."

"How long will that take?"

"Judging from her diligence, I'd say she means to finish as quickly as she can. Am I such an ogre, is that why everyone is deserting me? You'd rather live near London. Luis took off without a word. Now Sophie returns to Chiswick. I wish—" Again he jabbed the ground with his foot. "I don't know what I wish."

Andrew mulled over this ambiguous remark, disliking its implications. Cass had the look of a man struggling to unburden himself.

He couldn't possibly be seriously involved with Sophie Pinnock. Oh, he might lust for her, but that wouldn't last— after the object of his desire removed herself from his orbit, his fancy would light upon another. He could have any woman in the world, just by producing that devilish smile and crooking his finger. Sophie was a simple, honorable woman, nothing like the flashy trollops Cass had consorted with in London.

"I've fallen in love, Drew."

He summoned a laugh, but there was no life in it. "You, Cass, in love?"

"My heart has spoken. Hers, it seems, lies buried in her husband's grave."

Andrew also assumed this to be the case and wasn't troubled in the least. With nothing more than mild affection to offer, he demanded nothing more in return. A hopeless passion wasn't for him, as he'd learned when he'd been dazzled by the rich and beautiful Cecelia Carysfort. For a time she had stirred his muse and fired his emotions—but he hadn't really known her. Sophie, such a steadying, calming influence, was becoming a friend. A source of support and companionship, she would cure his wretched aimlessness. With that busy little lady at his side, he could lead a better and more productive life.

His rival's evident distress relieved him. If the widow hadn't tumbled to Cass, with his good looks and title and great wealth, then there was a chance he could win her for himself.

"This is a most inconvenient time to embark upon romance," Cass continued. "Cecelia is down with one of her nervous attacks, and I'm struggling to manage the estate. I don't relish the prospect of traveling back and forth to Chiswick to court Sophie. But I cannot hold her here against her will, like a villain from one of your wild gothic poems."

Andrew narrowed his eyes. Was he being mocked?

"The one way I can keep her respect—assuming that I've got it—is by setting her free."

"You're agitated, you aren't making any sense," he declared. "You should take a glass of wine. Or," he added, increasingly conscious of his own needs, "a calming dram."

"No," said Cass emphatically. "Whatever frustrations lie ahead, I shall meet them. Never again will I disintegrate into that numb, ineffectual being I became under the influence of the drug you imbibe so freely. It destroyed my life, and Cecelia's, and—" He broke off. "What a damned fool I was. If Sophie ever learned of my weakness, how she would despise me."

Weak, indeed, thought Andrew disdainfully. Cass had dabbled but a few months only, he couldn't possibly comprehend the true power and effectiveness of opium and its extract.

His hand curled on the journal lying on his lap, a detailed record of the foul history Cass meant to conceal from his ladylove. A powerful weapon. Rather, he amended, it might have been if it hadn't also revealed every flaw in his own character.

"Go to London," Cecelia pleaded. "Find proof that Sir Michael abducted Luis."

"Is that what you believe?"

"Don't you?"

Cass studied his sister. Worry had taken its toll on her

slender frame, and her cheek was as white as the damask pillowcase on which it rested.

"I'm not sure. I've made inquiries, but none of the servants ever saw Tait here, and there's no report of his stopping in the village. This is a quiet hamlet, the presence of an unfamiliar gentleman in town garb would be noticed and commented on."

"He might have sent somebody else to do his dirty work. That would be more like him," she declared bitterly.

Cass recalled his encounter with the scarred baronet, whose brawny footman had raised a cudgel against Luis. Tait had already demonstrated his capacity for violence.

"Will you go?"

Cass nodded. "I've no other choice. With each passing day there's less likelihood that Luis will reappear as magically as he vanished. But you must promise to behave sensibly while I'm away. No more lying in bed all day or refusing your meals."

She managed a listless nod.

"And you must take more exercise, as Dr. Jenner recommends. Walk in the gardens, they are truly a sight to behold. Devote yourself to Daniel. He's so withdrawn, not himself at all. He clings to Maria, and won't go to bed unless Echo is allowed to sleep beside him. He wants comforting, Cecelia."

"What can I do?"

"Read to him. Teach him to play the pianoforte."

"He's too young to learn."

"You began your lessons at the same age," Cass reminded her.

"So I did." She heaved a plaintive sigh. "Our aunt instructed me."

"The boy misses Luis. He's attached to Sophie now, and

she's preparing to leave us."

"*Meu irmao,* you aren't letting your pretty widow slip away?"

Her question startled him. He'd supposed she was too worried about Luis and too fearful of Tait to consider his affairs. "She tendered her resignation. All that remains to be settled between us is her fee for services rendered."

"That is *not* all," she declared with more vigor than she had displayed in days. "I thought you offered her your protection."

"It was refused, in no uncertain terms."

"You might have told me!"

"My pride was wounded. But not, I think, as much as hers."

"I must say, I'm surprised," she told him.

"She's unlike any other woman whose favors I've courted, and I realized it too late. Trouble is, I've made such a muddle that I've no idea what to do."

"Don't be a simpleton, Cass. Let her know you care so deeply. Perhaps you'll discover she cares for you."

Heartened by this comment, he asked hopefully, "Has she said something to you?"

"No."

"That's encouraging," he said with heavy sarcasm. "She doesn't talk about me. She doesn't talk *to* me. We've scarce exchanged a dozen words since our journey from Clifton. She avoids me."

"That could be a good sign. If she were indifferent, she wouldn't be at such pains to keep away from you."

"Cold comfort."

He valued Sophie's companionship, he appreciated her wit, he was dazzled by her face and form. She was as intoxicating as opium, and even more addictive, for each small dose of her gave him a stronger craving.

But this stubbornly virtuous female, who would not have him as a lover, had given him no chance to reveal his aspiration to be something more.

Her husband.

It was possible—though far from certain—that he might, over time and after exhaustive persuasions, entice her to his bed. But he wouldn't delude himself that she would love him for stealing her precious honor. Only by offering matrimony could he demonstrate that he wasn't merely a selfish, opportunistic cad, wanting only to pounce on her and paw at her. It was the one way he could prove that his feelings were as strong and true as Tobias Pinnock's had been.

His secret ambition was not to be shared with anyone, not even his sister.

Making his way to the chamber door, he told her, "I'm off to the cellars. No," he said, in response to her raised eyebrows, "not to drown my sorrows, but to determine how many additional wine racks are needed. The shipment from Fry's is due to arrive in a few weeks' time."

He spent an agreeable half hour in the musty, dark vault. Stripped of coat and vest, he helped his butler shift a number of smaller casks from one side of the room to the other to make room for his recent acquisitions.

Nobleman he might be, but he wanted no majordomo in his household. He preferred this young Bristolian. Not only was Edward Bitton undaunted by the size of the establishment over which he presided, he had an aptitude for selecting wines.

"Your palate is remarkably acute," Cass praised him as they worked together.

"'Tis no great wonder, my lord," the young man replied.

"You might say my grandmother was in the wine trade. She worked as a cork cutter."

Wiping his hand on his breeches, Cass surveyed a set of wooden shelves. "The estate carpenter does a commendable job. It's time I had him take measurements for the new racks."

Said the butler, reviewing the notations in his cellar book, "There's great deal of wine here that wants drinking. The last earl laid down a quantity of the '88. And some of the cognacs have been sitting here since the War in the Americas." He rapped his knuckles lightly against one of the casks.

"No time like the present," Cass asserted. He ran his eye over the ledger. "My predecessor was partial to Bristol milk— my uncle's name for Spanish sherry. We were weaned on it, my sister and I. Pour out a glass for Mrs. Fonseca and carry it up to her bedchamber. And bring one to me. I'll be in the library."

"Yes, my lord."

Cass picked up his coat from a stool and flung it over his shoulder. "You can spend the rest of the day drawing off samples and rating them. Drink as freely as you please, you'll not be waiting at table tonight. I daresay I shall be the only one dining downstairs, and a footman can serve me."

Smiling broadly, Bitton said, "Thank you, my lord."

Cass wandered upstairs to his book-lined refuge, intending to select a guide to estate management to take along for his journey to town. He found Sophie standing behind the broad leather-topped desk, sorting and stacking papers—with Drew assisting her.

For once, his friend's hair was neatly combed and he wore the least shabby of his jackets. This was perhaps the only time in their long acquaintance, Cass realized with dismay, his own attire compared unfavorably with Drew's. Unfortunately, there was no way to remedy his loosened cravat and rumpled shirt.

Sophie glanced up briefly, commenting, "A few days ago you were covered in dirt, my lord, and now—sawdust? You and Daniel have been playing rough again."

Count on his sharp-eyed Sophie to notice. Carelessly he replied, "Country living has a detrimental effect on my appearance." He laid his coat across the back of his chair. "Were you waiting for me?"

Said his friend, "Mrs. Pinnock is putting your designs in the proper order for the printer. I've recommended Cottle of Bristol, who serves Coleridge and me so well."

"There," said Sophie, placing a title page on the top of the stack. "All is ready. I'm including detailed instructions about the materials and fonts to be used. Here's my sketch of the Bevington coat of arms for the cover. However, if your lordship prefers that I rely on the same firm responsible for all the other Pinnock Blue Books, I can carry them to London."

Favoring the option that would detain her, Cass said curtly, "My own book should be produced in Bristol. We must discuss financial arrangements—a subject that can be of no interest to you, Drew," he told his friend pointedly. No tactic was too foul if it earned him a few precious minutes alone with Sophie. Love, lust, longing—a potent combination.

He gritted his teeth when he saw how warmly she shook hands with the poet when thanking him for his advice about the printer. As he exited, Andrew narrowly avoided a collision with Bitton, arriving with the requested glass of sherry.

"Shall I fetch another for madam?" the butler inquired.

Cass looked to Sophie, but she shook her head. After dismissing the butler, he sat behind the desk. "Do you mind if I examine these?" he asked, indicating the papers she'd arranged so carefully.

"They belong to you."

He made a cursory study of the written descriptions, plant lists, and annotations to the printer about typesetting. Then he studied the accompanying artwork. Each scene was meticulously drawn in pen and ink, finished with a watercolor wash. The artist's technique was obvious, but Cass had an uneasy suspicion that she'd derived scant pleasure from her labors. He supposed the joy of creation had been dimmed by regret that someone else would bring her visions to life.

She hovered nearby, anxiously awaiting his opinion.

"You've definitely earned your fees," he told her.

Without a word she reached for her own copy and placed it in her portfolio.

He studied the gentle contours of her profile. Her milky skin seemed paler than usual. Or was it merely the contrast with the dark arching brows and thick lashes that veiled her eyes?

Impetuously he reached for her hand. It was cool and smooth, like marble. "Sophie, I'm bound for London tomorrow. To investigate Luis Costa's disappearance."

"The situation must be serious to take you so far," she responded gravely.

"I fear it may be."

How he wished he could share his and Cecelia's suspicion that Luis had been spirited away, that their enemy might now be privy to the full history of their long residence in Portugal. No matter how discreet and trustworthy the valet might be in the abstract, if treated brutally—by Sir Michael Tait or another person—he was unlikely to hold his tongue.

But by telling her the truth now, he would lose all hope of achieving the greatest desire of his heart.

"Luis often seemed homesick," Sophie said meditatively. "Whenever he talked of Sintra and Colares, he stopped himself. I think it distressed him to speak of the places that were dear to him. Perhaps he decided to go back to Portugal, and didn't say so because he didn't want to disappoint you."

"Not only would I have permitted him to return, if he wished it, I'd have paid him his back wages and covered the costs of the voyage."

"Don't vessels bound for Lisbon sail from Bristol? You should make inquiries among the shipping agents there, before traveling all the way to London."

"I dare not delay my journey any longer." He bounded up from the chair.

After chewing her lip uncertainly, she asked, "So we'll say our farewells now?"

"Unnecessary. You must stay here until I return."

"I'm sorry to disoblige you, my lord, but—"

"Just listen to me, Sophie. I don't speak as your patron, or as the Earl of Bevington. I stand here before you, an ordinary man with a most extraordinary affection for you."

"I will not stay. *Nânnîn-dgia!* How can I, when my work here is done? It isn't proper."

"Propriety be damned. I'm begging you. There's a reason—"

"I know it," she interrupted. "You mean to make me your *contchubinne,* and that I will never, ever be. I'm no ignorant Portuguese peasant, like Luis Costa's sister. I can't be bought, or swept off my feet by—"

"What the devil are you talking about?"

"You know." She chopped the air with her hand. "Ines. Luis told me how you lured his sister away from their village with an offer of money. She had large—she lived in your palace and was your— your—" A fiery flushed stained her cheekbones. "He used the Portuguese word, he didn't know the English one," she concluded lamely.

"In English, the word is wet-nurse. I paid Ines to suckle Daniel. Cecelia couldn't."

"Oh, las."

There was no mistaking the relief in that gusty sigh. "Why, Sophie, were you jealous?" His fingers followed the line of her jaw, probed the fullness of her lower lip.

She shoved his hand away. "Not a bit."

"Liar," he said, turning the word into a caress. "And I thought you honest and true, a very marvel of virtue."

"My virtue," she said breathlessly, "is what you seek to destroy."

"You jumped to the wrong conclusion. And not only about my association with Ines. My behavior has been crass at times, I admit, but my intentions are no longer dishonorable."

Her head tipped back and she stared up at him. Her dark eyes were blank.

He hadn't planned to make his declaration in his shirtsleeves. But he couldn't hold it back any longer, he ached to show her he wasn't the villain whose motive she mistrusted. If he parted from her without expressing his deepest desire, she would flee to her Chiswick house, a shrine to her late, lamented husband. He must not let her go, he could not bear to lose her.

Despite his great longing to hold her in his arms and whisper the words whirling in his brain, he stood stiffly. One hand balled itself into a fist, and he flattened the other on the desktop. He required the support, for he was quaking from head to foot.

When he could no longer bear the tense silence, he broke it by speaking from his heart.

"I want you to stay with me, Sophie, but not as my mistress. If you are willing, I prefer to have you for my wife."

CHAPTER 12

The rule is certaine, that Plants for want of Culture,
degenerate to be baser in the same Kinde; and sometimes
so far, as to change into another Kinde.

~Francis Bacon

The slanting rays of an afternoon sun showered gold over the gardens. The most pleasant and peaceful time of day, thought Sophie as her artist's eye feasted on the effect of sunlight shimmering on the canal. With her tasks complete, she could revel in solitude and idleness, leisurely contemplating the scene before her.

This was her birthday, although no one was aware of it. A new year, a fresh beginning—and the proper time to consider her future.

I prefer to have you for my wife.

Twenty-one today, and she'd received three offers of marriage from three men. First Tobias, when she was brimming with the optimism of extreme youth. Next, the annoying Fingal Moncrieff, as soon as her second year of mourning ended.

And lastly, the insistent, compelling, and utterly bewildering Earl of Bevington.

From the instant she met the man, she'd been acutely aware of his handsome face and splendid physique, although his arrogance had swiftly obliterated her favorable impressions. At the beginning of their association she hadn't guessed that her titled and wealthy employer would jolt her dormant emotions back to life, much less that she would be so moved by his kisses and embraces. The belief that his advances were a calculated attack upon her honor had strengthened her resistance.

The proposal changed everything.

Sophie bent over to gather a selection of wallflowers springing up along the terrace walk—white for moonlight, yellow for sunshine. Heartsease spilled out of the border and onto the path, and she was careful not to tread on the tiny tri-colored blossoms.

The loss of a husband had harrowed her soul. She had survived it, but in the aftermath had perceived the emptiness of her quiet life at Chiswick. Craving activity and an occupation, she'd accepted an offer of employment from a persuasive nobleman, never guessing that he would awaken her desire for so much more.

She snapped the stems of the gaudy, variegated tulips, adding them to her haphazard bouquet. The petals were fringed and boldly striped: crimson on white, yellow on blue, violet on pink.

Her flesh tingled at his touch, his warm glances heated her blood. In his arms, she melted. But the volatile earl did not, she fretted, inspire the same sweet tenderness she'd felt for her staid, dependable Tobias. Even so, her attraction to him was a powerful and disturbing one. She was torn, fearful that these turbulent new emotions might nullify her abiding affection for her departed spouse. He wanted to rush her into matrimony, without granting her sufficient time to discover for herself whether she cared for him enough to wed him. He was so impatient—he would demand an answer the moment he returned from London.

She paused beneath the arching laburnums to study the racemes hanging from each branch. In a few weeks they would burst into golden bloom. Would she be there to see?

Entering the topiary garden, she asked herself whether the castle had enchanted her, or its master. Both, she decided, for the man and this place were so intertwined that neither her heart nor her mind could separate them.

If she married him, she'd remain at Bevington—no great hardship, she felt very much at home now. Yet she was aware of a faint, lingering nostalgia for her Chiswick villa, and an unbroken attachment to the garden she had made there.

She emerged from a cluster of clipped yews and came to a sudden stop. *"Ma fé!"* she gasped, as a figure in ghostly white glided toward her.

"Forgive me for startling you," Cecelia apologized. "After so many indoor days, I grew restless. I've worn myself out, and there's no bench to be found. What glorious flowers!"

Sophie handed over her bouquet. "Take them. They'll brighten your chamber."

"But you chose them for yourself."

Smiling, she said, "I can gather more. *Dé vrai,* they belong to your brother and I'm sure he'd want you to have them."

Accepting the bouquet, Cecelia fell into step with Sophie. Time had fostered familiarity, but apart from both having been wed and widowed, their experiences were very different. And they had never openly confided in each other.

Now Sophie couldn't even raise the one subject that interested them equally—Cassian. She'd promised to maintain a circumspect silence until she informed him whether she would accept his proposal—or not—and the strain of shielding the secret from his sister made her uncomfortable.

Horticulture, she concluded, was the only safe topic. "Do you miss your garden in Sintra?" she asked.

The lovely face brightened. "Oh, yes."

"It must have been quite splendid. According to his lordship, it was formal in style."

"Grander than this, yes, and more open, with nicer walks— they were patterned on the Trianon gardens at Versailles. Our grounds were delightfully sunny."

"Perhaps they only seem so in retrospect," said Sophie.

"Oh, but I carried a parasol whenever I went out," Cecelia insisted.

"And did the palace belong to your brother, or your husband?"

"Cass purchased it outright from the Fonsecas, impoverished Portuguese nobility. They couldn't afford its upkeep."

Cecelia seldom mentioned Senhor Fonseca, whenever she did her decided neutrality gave no clue about her feelings for him. Nevertheless, Sophie had always assumed their match had been one of love, not of convenience. Now she wondered whether the gentleman had chosen the rich Miss Carysfort in order to maintain his familial connection to the property.

As they stepped into the rose garden, she asked, "Do you expect to marry again?"

"I'm quite certain that I shan't."

"Not even for your son's sake?"

"He has an attentive and careful guardian in my brother and needs no stepfather."

"But you might fall in love," she persisted.

Cecelia gave a mirthless laugh. "One mistake is enough for a lifetime."

She must be exceedingly tired, thought Sophie. Never before had she revealed so much, so succinctly.

"Yours, I gather, was a happy marriage. Fortunate creature."

"I was," she agreed. "When I met Tobias Pinnock I was young, dazzled by his fame. He never betrayed my trust, or made me regret our hasty marriage."

"Some couples are more blessed than others." Cecelia's chest rose and fell with her sigh.

"My devotion has outlived him," Sophie declared, "and so strong an attachment seems unlikely to occur again. It might not be fair to encourage a marriage-minded suitor. If I should ever have one," she hastened to add, belatedly recalling the need for concealment.

"At least you've encountered true affection—you'll recognize it when next you meet it. I was led astray by foolish dreams and false promises, and paid a very high price. I want no more of love and passion and all the nonsense we dreamed of as giddy young girls."

This summation of her romantic past surprised Sophie. Never had she known such a passionless female.

"All I crave now is perfect peace and seclusion."

"I can think of no more peaceful or secluded existence than yours."

Cecelia shook her head until her dark curls danced. "I cannot be easy in my mind, not even here. Not when I'm so constantly plagued by worry. I want Daniel always to be safe and well. I fear Luis has suffered some great harm. I wish he would return."

"He will."

For days Sophie had tried not to give in to the dread shared by the Carysforts. She couldn't understand their pessimism about their servant's disappearance—unless they possessed some crucial piece of information that they kept from her.

"And my brother—I'm concerned for him as well." Cecelia cast a sidelong glance at Sophie before speaking again. "He behaves so oddly. We used to share every thought and feeling, but not lately. Of course, I've been secretive myself. I'm tempted to tell you my plan for the future, Sophie, for I could use an ally."

"I dislike conspiracies," Sophie told her frankly.

"Cass, you see, regards the castle as his rightful home. I accept that he must live at Bevington, and we've agreed that Daniel will benefit from a country upbringing. But I preferred to remain at Summit House. When my son is old enough to go away to school, I shall return to Clifton. No matter whether Cass thinks I shouldn't."

"You fear he would prevent you?"

"He might, he's that protective. But if he took a wife—" There was a pregnant pause before Cecelia continued, "How I wish he'd marry, for then he might not oppose my wish to live on my own."

Sophie struggled with the concept of an independent Cecelia.

"I'm certain I could be more active—and useful—if I parted from Cass. He indulges me. And dictates to me." Smiling, Cecelia went on, "My lack of resistance doubtless contributes to his expectation of ruling others. The woman he marries would need to be very firm with him if she seeks to correct this fault."

Sophie bit down hard on her lip to hold back her enthusiastic agreement with this observation. How much did Cecelia know, or guess, about her brother's marital prospects?

Soberly, Cecelia went on, "I am ready to do as Cass has done, and reform myself. To follow the example set by the aunt who raised us. She was a good and generous woman, who allotted much of her time and our uncle's money to any number of charities—schools and foundations and relief societies. I'll always regret that I was too flighty to heed her teachings. I should have done. But I turned my back on stodgy, middle-class Bristol and ran off to London with Cass to live among the lords and ladies."

Sophie was pleased to find an unperceived depth to Cecelia's character. She'd unjustly catalogued the earl's sister as a spoiled, self-concerned female, condemned to boredom by an excess of leisure and money.

"Wouldn't this be an idea spot for a garden seat," observed Cecelia, indicating the broad niche halfway along the wall.

"Emrys Jones believes it was a hutch for fowls. Peacocks, most likely."

"In summer it will be pleasant to sit here and admire the rose arbors and the canal."

"*Oui-dgia.* But they are going to be removed," Sophie reminded her. "Tomorrow a builder comes from Gloucester to give me an estimate for labor costs."

"Since Cass went away you've been busier than ever. I feel his absence keenly—he's a managing sort of brother, but he knows exactly how to amuse me. Dine with me tonight, Sophie. I must take advantage of your companionship while I have it. You will be greatly missed when you leave Bevington."

Flattered, Sophie accepted her invitation.

Her suspicion that Cecelia would spend the evening talking about her brother turned out to be well-founded. Throughout dinner she listened to timely and illuminating reminiscences about his youth and education and favorite pursuits. While Cecelia was occupied with her needlework and Sophie sketched her doing so, she revealed even more of the earl's exploits. By the time she retired to her chamber, she no longer doubted that the earl's sister was promoting a match.

Lying in her bed, she resumed her consideration of Cassian Carysfort. When she sifted through the complexities of his character, she found much to admire.

He displayed a remarkable devotion to his sister and her child. His wife could expect similarly kind treatment.

Few wealthy gentlemen bothered to take on the management of a large estate personally, or showed so great an interest in local affairs. He paid his servants well and treated them humanely.

He was intelligent, his mind broadened by travel and books.

His dog adored him.

Oh, las, but he could be so disagreeable—how he tried her patience! Making demands, imposing his will. Even his sister was affected by it. Cecelia naively believed that the right woman could reform him. Sophie, possessing many more brothers and an uncle, had learned early that a man's general temperament could not be altered to suit. At best, his bad habits might be amended but never eradicated.

He had a most distressing appreciation for modern landscape gardens.

And despite his occasional bursts of candor, he harbored

secrets—probably unwholesome ones, to be so closely guarded. But Sophie resolved to judge him as the man she knew in the present, and to be swayed by speculations about what he'd done in the past.

The next morning she received a message from the builder, regretfully informing her that he must survey a site for another client and had to postpone their meeting until later in the week. Sophie only wished the interview could be delayed indefinitely. It signaled the next step in the improvement process, the dismantling of the gardens she'd valued at first glance and now dearly loved.

Her gatehouse rooms were littered with the various materials she'd used for the creation of the new design: maps, books, folios of engravings. With the help of her maidservant, she gathered them up and bore them back to the library.

"Do you s'pose his lordship will ever read all the books 'ere?" Nan wondered, scanning the tall mahogany cases.

Laughing, Sophie replied, "I trust he's too wise to make the attempt. It would take a lifetime."

After dismissing the maid, she replaced each volume where she'd found it. Most belonged on a single shelf, a treasure trove of castle lore—financial records compiled by the various Bevington stewards, a family history commissioned by a previous holder of the title, and other ephemera. She crammed a folded estate map between two unmarked folios. Reconsidering, she tried to dislodge it. It stuck, so she slid one of the large volumes from its place.

The folio she removed was heavier than she'd expected. As she struggled to hold it, a paper fluttered to the carpet. On retrieving it, her attention was caught by even lines of flowing script.

> *Bevington, November ye 16th, 1765. Rec'd from Jas. Wheeler of Gloucester, via Ebbersley's wagon and pack'd in matting:*
> *1 Le Roche Courbon dwarf Plum, 1s. 6d.*
> *3 Black Old Newington nectarine, ditto, Lilacs/syringa vulgaris (2 purple and 2 white), 6s.*

Sophie knew those lilacs. They marked the four corners of the rose garden. Until they bloomed she could only guess which were purple and which were white, but they were tall and vigorous, covered in green, satiny leaves.

She abandoned her original task and transferred both folios from their shelf to the desk. Inside the covers she found more papers. A complete set of architectural drawings for the pavilion. A collection of receipts from nurserymen in Gloucester and Bristol, with purchases itemized. A variety of letters, several addressed to the earl and some to Emrys Jones. One was penned by Lord Mountstuart, describing at length the improvements Capability Brown had made at Cardiff Castle for his father, Lord Bute. But despite the glowing recommendation, Lord Bevington had been disinclined to consult the great man, or was unable to afford him. Otherwise, there would be no gardens, but an open park with Brown's signature clumps of trees.

The second folio contained the oldest records. The most fascinating were stiff parchments covered with small, precise, and very ancient characters. Frowning with the effort, she deciphered a letter lacking its first page.

and in situ for the visite of his majestye the kynge, postes and rayles for the pleasaunce, also to be paynted green and white as seen at Nonsuch. Madam Bullen has shown her favour for peaches, may they be forward this season and in all readinesse. Bevington.

Henry the Eighth had visited the castle—and he'd brought Anne Boleyn! Sophie wondered whether the peaches had ripened in time for the royal visit. Too impatient to read through the many similar notes, she laid them aside—except for the one written in an ornate but legible hand.

Dearest wyffe,

Our Queen, all goodnesse and beauty, doth make good her promise to stop at Bevington during her progresse through the West Country with her favourite, Leicester. Before comynge to this Court I did order the carver to make two beestes in freestone, staggs collared with rose garlands. I desire each to be mounted upon a base and sett at the approach to ye bowlynge greene. And I charge you also to order from the clockmaker one bronzed sun-dyal, likewise to be sett upon a stone base among ye knottes of clipped rosemarie. Command for me the gardener neatly to tie up the woodbine and train young trees of appel and pere and chery. I do eagerly await the time when I may kysse you again, dear wyffe, more fayre to me than roses, violettes, and all other sweete flowers.

Not only had Henry and Anne come to Bevington—so had their daughter Elizabeth. Sophie longed to tell Cassian that the Virgin Queen had passed a night—or more—beneath his ancestral roof. She smiled as she re-read the lord's endearments to his lady, clear evidence that they had been a fond couple. What had become of their stone stags, and the bronze sundial?

She regarded the array of papers she'd stumbled upon, aware that the full history of the gardens was laid out before her. All plans for their improvement, major and minor, were documented, along with every plant purchase, and each gardener's name and wage.

As absorbing as this record was, the information was of no real use to her or anyone else. These fragile pages represented centuries of effort and expense and labor, resulting in a magnificent and venerable creation—destined to be destroyed.

With regret, she decided that the folios were a curiosity, nothing more, and returned them to their shelf.

Three days, and Cass had not located Sir Michael Tait. Three days of scouring London's streets in a relentless, driving rain and returning nightly to his comfortable but impersonal suite in Nerot's Hotel.

He intended to find his enemy, and soon, because he longed to return home. He missed Sophie's fresh face and bright smiles, his sister's music, and Daniel's piping questions.

Seven years ago, during his brief stint as Tait's crony, Cass had learned the man's habits and haunts. Before their divorce the baronet and his scandalous lady had occupied a grand house in St. James's Square. The property still belonged to Sir Michael but he'd leased it a family from Hampshire whose country-bred servants had no knowledge of the owner's whereabouts.

Cass attended a mid-week performance at the Royal Opera House. His seat in Fop's Alley afforded an excellent view of baronet's private box but to his regret it contained a party of over-dressed females. Like Tait's residence, his theatre seats were rented out.

While the ladies and gentlemen on the stage warbled their arias and duets, Cass could only think of Sophie. Did she care for this sort of entertainment? He tried to imagine her in this setting, swathed in satin with plumes rising up from her glossy hair, and couldn't. In his imagination she never wore opera dress and elbow-length kid gloves, she was always aproned in brown holland cloth, her little hands protected by gauntlets of thick leather.

He visited a gentlemen's club formerly frequented by Sir Michael. Vaguely he remembered yearning to belong to a select society in St. James's Street, where he might rub shoulders with dukes and ministers of state and wealthy bankers. Tait had often tantalized him with political gossip and other tales that circulated in White's exclusive gaming salon. The baronet continued to pay his annual fees but no longer asserted his membership rights. The club steward couldn't remember the last time he'd stopped by.

Cass was learning that Tait's interests, like his own, had altered over time.

Keeping a private opera box no longer appealed to him. Mingling with other aristocrats, or government officials, as his title permitted him to do, didn't interest him in the slightest. As an earl and the owner of a great estate, he could probably join any of the great clubs, but his desire to become a clubman had waned.

London was no use to him at all. Every dream for the future centered on his Gloucestershire castle, and the flower-loving lady he'd left there.

In desperation he broadened his search, though instinctively he knew that Sir Michael, if still in town, wouldn't stray far from St. James's. One afternoon, bored with his endless trudging about in the rain, he stepped into Hatchards bookshop in Piccadilly to read the newspapers.

He saw a clerk accept a set of music books from a printer's boy. Cecelia would be happy to get the latest popular tunes, for her appetite for new pieces was insatiable.

Cass consulted the young man, who told him apologetically, "None of this music is for the pianoforte. The selection we presently have available is for stringed instruments."

The man he sought was a violinist. Or used to be.

"I've a friend who would be interested in recent additions to your stock." This description of the baronet burned his tongue; Cass hadn't regarded him in that light for a very long time. "But perhaps you already supply music to Sir Michael Tait?"

The clerk replied, "Possibly. I can look at my ledger." He turned back several pages, his finger sliding slowly down each column. "Why yes, his name does appear—twice in the past six months. On one occasion we supplied him with a German songbook, and we also dispatched some Italian music to his house."

"You've got his direction there?"

The young man showed him the book, pointing to a house number in Cleveland Row, St. James's.

Cass purchased a ballad-sheet for his sister and left the shop.

A vehicle was waiting at the nearest hackney stand. Urging the driver to make haste, he gave the address and climbed inside.

The brick row house was narrow and small, squeezed between larger, more impressive ones. The door lacked a knocker, so Cass struck it with his ivory-handled swordstick. When no one responded he opened it for himself. The building was divided into separate lodgings. Which belonged to Tait?

He crossed from door to door, studying the engraved cards nailed to each one, when his answer cascaded down in a series of notes from a violin. He climbed the staircase, following the music to its source—an upper room at the back of the house.

The door was ajar. Peering through the gap, he saw an empty chair with mahogany ball and claw feet and curved armrests, and on the floor the fringed corner of a carpet.

The musician played on.

Cass stepped into the room.

Sir Michael Tait stood before a wooden music stand positioned near the window. His bow stilled in mid-stroke.

"Surprised to see me?" asked Cass.

Tait lowered his instrument. "Beyond description."

"You must have expected me, sooner or later." His gaze lingered on the disfiguring scar. "I'm here to rescue my valet."

The baronet's lips curled. "I don't know what you're talking about. Stop storming about, Carysfort—sorry, Bevington— and tell me why you've come. In terms that I can understand."

"Where's that henchman of yours? If I offer a large enough reward, I daresay he'll tell me what I need to know."

"If you refer to my footman James, he's at Oakes Court— my country property near Guildford." Carefully Tait laid his violin in its case. Reaching for a decanter of amber liquid, he asked, "A glass of cognac?"

Cass had no intention of accepting hospitality from his enemy. "Don't try to ingratiate yourself, this is not a formal call. Tell me what you've done with Luis Costa."

"The foreign youth? I've not laid eyes on him since I last saw you, whenever that was." The baronet stroked his cheek—the intact one—and said mildly, "I'm not sorry you've appeared, even if a false errand brings you. I've wondered why I never had an answer to the letter I sent to Cecelia."

"We'll leave her out of this discussion."

Tait sipped from his glass. "I was thinking about her just now. I always do when I play that piece—my part from the duet we used to perform together. Our last time was at that party my wife gave in St. James's Square. Seven years ago."

"The night sticks in my mind for quite a different reason. On that occasion I issued my challenge to you."

Tait winced. "Did Cecelia keep up her music? She was enormously talented—one of the few points my wife and I could agree upon. She's in England, isn't she?"

"Your wife? How should I know?"

"Your sister. Don't deny it—I've obtained proof."

Cass stiffened. "What do you mean, proof?" He regretted his words; it was a mistake to react.

"For a long while I assumed you'd left her behind in Portugal. But eventually I discovered that the pair of you returned to this country in February of last year, in the company of one bearing the name Daniel Fonseca."

Careful, careful, Cass warned himself. Say nothing, show no alarm.

"She married, you said. But you intimated that she's now widowed. Her name *is* Fonseca, is it not?"

"It's no business of yours," Cass stated firmly, searching

for a way to discover the informant's identity without being too obvious. "Did this report come from your brother? I understand he has returned from the wars."

"Who told you that?"

He shrugged. "My source, like yours, is anonymous."

The baronet strode forward, face taut with fury. "Damn your arrogance—and your mysteries! Leave me, Lord Bevington, and don't return unless you want a bullet through that cold, black heart of yours. I had my chance, seven years ago—and aimed my pistol at the sky to fire in the air. By doing so I acknowledged my fault. Your honor was preserved—you didn't have to wound me."

"What do you know about honor? If you had any understanding of the concept, you'd realize that while you live and breathe I'll never have complete satisfaction."

Cass reached into the open instrument case and lifted the violin from its velvet nest. His hand swept across its gleaming varnish, his fingertips plucked the strings. "I remember this well. Its associations are not the happiest for me." He raised it high above his head.

"Careful!" cried Tait. "For God's sake, man—it came from the Guarneri workshop!"

"Who informed you about my sister? Tell me!"

"Not unless you reveal her whereabouts."

His anger and frustration erupted with the sound of splintering wood. Repeatedly he slammed the violin against the jutting shelf of the mantelpiece until the severed body was held together only by the strings. Then he let it fall to the floor.

Tait stared down at his broken treasure. "You bastard."

Cass congratulated himself that his cruel vandalism was more effective than any words or threats.

Outside, the rain still streamed from the leaden skies. This time he didn't hail a hackney, he walked back to his hotel. A drenching couldn't possibly make him feel worse.

Tait had found out about Daniel, most likely from Luis Costa. He had dispatched his burly footman James to Oakes Court—where the hostage was being held? Tait had drawn a false connection between Daniel and Cecelia, but through sheer persistence he might uncover part of the truth. A man capable of kidnapping an innocent party was probably vindictive enough to make his discoveries public.

It was time, Cass decided, to expand his investigation. He disliked delaying his journey back to the castle but felt compelled to travel to Surrey instead.

Conjuring his sweet Sophie's image, he hoped she missed him. His abrupt marriage proposal had confused her, he knew. But had it pleased her?

She didn't love him. Wishing couldn't make it so. But he prayed that she cared just enough to stay with him. He needed her so very much—in his house, and in his bed, and yes, even in his gardens.

He intended to court her, tenderly and with great care. Eventually he would win her away from that sainted husband of hers. At her marriage to that most fortunate of men, she'd bestowed her body and her life upon him, vowing to be faithful through good and ill, until death came to part them.

Cass would be satisfied with nothing less.

CHAPTER 13

A flower was offered to me,
Such a flower as May never bore...

~William Blake

"Isn't this a Scotch rose?"

Emrys Jones made a cursory examination of the prickly cane Sophie was holding. "Aye. A pink one. And 'twill be among the first to bloom."

She scrawled the species name on her sketchpad and moved on to the next bush. "And this one, *de Meaux*, is a Provence rose?"

"The last to be planted here," the gardener informed her, "and mayhap the prettiest. At the height of bloom it's covered with miniature pink blossoms."

"I long to see it!" Tapping her chin with the pencil, she studied her notes. "My inventory is nearly complete. As for the half-dozen you're unable to identify, I can consult the purchase records I found. From their size and the thickness of the canes, I should think they're the oldest of all."

"This one has leaves in the gallica shape, but if it's got a proper name, I ne'er knew it. It might've been here as long as your *Rosa mundi*—hundreds of years, belike."

Sophie touched a bract of tender new foliage, a living connection to ancient history. She wanted to paint the plants exactly as they looked now, green with promise as they rambled along the stone wall and climbed up the arbors.

"Now you'll have no more thought for roses," muttered the Welshman, tying an errant branch to the trellis.

"Why ever not?"

"Here comes his lordship."

Sophie whirled around. Seven long days of yearning for him, of wondering whether or not she could become his countess. Self-consciously she smoothed her chignon, vaguely aware that Emrys Jones had slung his hoe over one bony shoulder and was rapidly exiting the garden. She had eyes only for the tall, broad-shouldered figure crossing the lawn.

How weary he looked, and startlingly pale. The deep lines etched into his brow told of failure and disappointment.

"You couldn't find Luis."

With a doleful shake of his head, he answered, "It appears to be a lost cause."

Terribly concerned by his appearance, Sophie asked if he was ill.

"I've a headache. And I feel like my body has been stretched on a rack and flailed with a stick. Those blasted rains cut deep furrows into the roads, and for the better part of two days I've been bumping over them. Just beyond Guildford my carriage met with a mishap, and I had to wait for a repair to the coach wheel."

"Guildford? We thought you'd been in London all this time."

He gazed silently down at her for a moment, his face grave. "I came up empty in both places. It is difficult to accept, but I may never learn what became of Luis. I pray you're right, that he did board a ship bound for Portugal."

"Wherever he may be, he's safe and well. I expect you'll receive a letter from him soon, explaining everything."

"My optimistic Sophie," he said softly, gratefully. "Tell me, are you truly mine?"

She used her sketchbook to shield her uncertain heart. "I've considered all that you said to me before you went away."

"And?"

She hesitated, still tottering on the brink of certainty and not quite prepared for the plunge.

"May I know my fate?" he asked gently.

"*Dé vrai,* it would be a most unequal match. I never aspired to wed a man of rank, or great fortune. Or to be a countess."

"Yes, I was born into a wealthy family," he said, "but I entered this world a commoner, exactly as you did. The title came to me in recent years and through an accident of genealogy. I rarely encounter other aristocrats, in town or locally. I expect to cultivate a neighborly relationship with such people as the Ducies and the Berkeleys, but nothing more."

"But what will they think if you wed a woman who has been your employee?"

"They'll never share their thoughts with us, so why worry? Your pedigree is far superior to Lady Berkeley's. Her father was a Wotton butcher, and she lived with the earl as his mistress for many a year. Of the five children she's borne, only the youngest is legitimate." With a twisted smile, he continued, "As for inequality—I'm all too aware that the niece of the Seigneur of Anneville is quite above my touch."

"That's nonsense," she protested.

"My sister values your friendship. I'm confident that you'll be an affectionate to aunt to my nephew Daniel. And you're the perfect chatelaine for Bevington Castle, for you already know my servants well and have their respect."

Sophie bowed her head, humbled by his homage.

"Does that signify acceptance? You might as well have me. If you tried escaping to Chiswick, I'd simply chase after you and implore you until you give in."

He took her hand. Instead of kissing it as she expected him to, he studied her bare fingers. She'd recently removed her husband's signet, and the pale imprint had vanished from her skin after several days of garden work.

"You used to wear a gold ring," he said softly. "I hope its absence means you feel ready to accept one of my bestowing."

Forgive me, Tobias, Sophie pleaded. I do not care to be forever alone. This man doesn't demand too much, only that I join his family and share his home. I believe my life with him will be a pleasant one.

"My lord," she began, "you do me great honor. I will be your wife."

Cass was wounded by her lack of enthusiasm—she seemed perfectly composed, apparently resigned to the inevitable. Her still face and subdued manner proved that he hadn't won her love, merely her acceptance of his name and title and worldly possessions. Had his persuasions somehow worked against him? The marriage he'd described was one of mutual convenience. To her, he realized with a pang of regret, it probably would be. For him it was so much more.

Determined to endear himself to her, he said, "You shall have whatever you want for a bride-gift, Sophie. Anything you desire is yours for the asking."

"How could I possibly ask for more?" she wondered. "As Lady Bevington I will have so very much." Her gaze shifted from his face to the castle ramparts, then moved to the surrounding arbors, and her thoughtful expression was replaced by one of longing. "But yes," she murmured. "I do have a request. There is something I should like."

"Then you shall have it," he promised rashly. He didn't expect her to demand jewels, or a financial settlement, for she wasn't acquisitive. Her lack of regard for material things was part of her charm. What could she possibly desire?

"The preservation of these gardens. No, more than that—I want your permission to restore them. I know exactly what must be done to achieve it. Never in my life was I so amazed, for in your library I found a large collection of letters and purchase accounts and even some sketches—a complete history. The original pleasaunce was set within the castle keep. The terraces were built later. A pair of stags carved from stone once stood at the entrance to the bowling-green, I know their dimensions and how many men set them in place. The canal and the pavilion were added a century ago. Topiaries were nearly always here, and knot gardens. Roses, too."

"But what about that fashionable modern landscape you designed for me?"

"I never cared for it as much as you did, *dé vrai*. If you just consider how long the castle has stood here, you'll understand that formality is more appropriate than—"

"I understand that this means a great deal to you, Sophie. That's the only consideration that weighs with me."

Her eyes sparkled, and the corners of her delectable mouth curved upward. "No arguments? No debate?"

"None," he said replied, enchanted by her teasing smile. "From this moment these grounds are yours. Do whatever you please to them."

"Chièr Cassian, *mercie bein des fais!"*

She flung herself at him, pressing her full lips against his in a hasty kiss, far too brief to suit him. But she'd given it freely, and joyously. She'd called him by his name!

"I'll find Emrys Jones and tell him."

"Right now? But we haven't chosen the day for our wedding." He was impatient to settle the matter, but already she was dancing across the grass, the sketchpad tucked under her arm.

She'd pledged to be his wife, he reminded himself. He would take comfort where he could, and disregard the abrupt desertion that marred the luster of this most shining victory of his cursed life.

Cass lowered the wick of the oil lamp on the mantel to reduce the size of the flame. After shrugging out of his coat, he unwound the constricting cravat from his neck.

It had been a long and momentous day.

That damnably uncomfortable inn at Newbury where he'd breakfasted on cold ham and scalding tea, and his tedious journey along rain-slicked roads were dim memories now. He'd won the hand of his ladylove. Only, he hadn't even laid eyes on her since she'd left him in the rose garden.

While dining with his sister, he'd given her a concise, severely edited account of his meeting with Sir Michael Tait. His failure to find Luis in Cleveland Row or at Oakes Court was a severe disappointment to Cecelia.

To cheer her, he'd revealed his marriage plans. As she dried her tears for Luis, she'd pelted him with eager questions. Did he and his future countess prefer a private license to banns? Which rooms would Sophie occupy after their marriage? He didn't like to admit it, but he doubted his bride-to-be had spent a single moment considering such things as banns and bedrooms.

Going into his dressing room, he slipped the studs from his shirt sleeves and placed them in their box. Tonight he greatly missed his valet's ministrations and distracting chatter. But he dared not think about Luis, poor fellow, or that cruel devil Tait, or he'd be awake till sunrise. Off came his shoes and stockings and breeches.

He could hear female voices coming from the adjacent chamber—Sophie and her waiting woman—then metal grating against metal as one of them stirred the fire. Then there was a long silence.

Was she in her bed? Did she lie there dreaming of him, or of rose bushes and statues of stags and crumbling walls?

The creak of a floorboard told him she was still up. He moved to the connecting door and flattened his palm against the whitened wood. "Sophie?"

He waited, heart hammering, for acknowledgement. Light was leaking through the gap between the bottom plank and the low, uneven threshold.

"Is it you, Cassian?" she called back. "Where are you?"

His fingers crept toward the iron ring. Twisting it, he swung the door open.

She wore a nightgown, long and white and edged with lace. Waves of unbound hair fell almost to her waist. One hand was clamped to her throat in a gesture of surprise, and the flame from her chamber stick shone upon a ring with a large, clear, glittering stone.

A Bristol diamond.

His pent-up breath eased in a sigh of satisfaction.

"Why are you here?" she asked.

"This is my dressing room."

"*Ma fé*," said Sophie, peering at his chest of drawers with shaving mirror on top, and the wardrobe. "And all this time you were so near."

Taking her elbow, he led her through the narrow passage to his bedchamber. "The room we'll soon be sharing."

Up came her chin. "But I like the convenience of my own entrance and stairway. I don't mean to give up my parlor and my little study where I keep my books and papers and paints."

Was she implying that she preferred separate accommodations? "You need only give up the room you've been sleeping in." He trailed her to the casement. Through the sheer fabric of the gown he could see slender legs, the graceful curve of her hips.

"Your windows must look out on the gardens."

"They do," he confirmed. "In the mornings when you wake, they'll be first thing you see—after me." He covered her shoulder with his hand, and felt her warm flesh beneath the filmy muslin. His heart shuddered at the contact.

"How long until we shall wed?" she wondered, looking up at him.

"Marriage by license is swift but might appear unusual—if not furtive—in our little hamlet. I feel a certain duty as lord of the castle to follow the rites proscribed by the church, even though we'd have to wait for the vicar to cry the banns on three consecutive Sundays."

"I don't mind. I should like to inform my family at Anneville beforehand."

"Will any of them come, do you think?"

"If I asked it," she told him. "But I won't. It's a long journey, at a time when no one can be spared from farm and orchard work."

"Patience is not a virtue I can claim," Cass confessed. "Any delay will be hard to bear. When you are near me, and we are together like this, I can think only of—" Lightheaded, he drew a sustaining breath. "Of being your husband."

Sophie, increasingly aware of her nakedness beneath her gown, caught the meaning of those husky, wistful words. And she noticed that his gaping shirt revealed a powerful chest shadowed with dark hairs, rising and falling as though from exertion.

"There's a flame inside you, Sophie, it touches me every time I kiss you. I long to discover exactly where it lies." The heat of his desire for her showed in the blue fire of his eyes.

Her own craving for physical intimacy was impossible to withstand. Before his marriage proposal, she'd often, albeit blushingly, imagined becoming his mistress. Now she was three weeks away from being his wife.

He'd aroused a passion that was overwhelming in its intensity, tempting her to test its power—and if she did, there could be no turning back. Giving herself to him would be an irrevocable act of commitment.

And a form of renunciation.

Her lingering feelings for Tobias remained pure and uncomplicated, but she received nothing in return. It was too easy to love a ghost.

She'd made a promise to this man standing beside her, who lusted for her and tormented and teased her. She was grateful to him for reviving her deadened senses. Perhaps by sharing her body and giving him the pleasure he craved, she could break free of the clinging specter of her lost husband.

"I am willing to lie with you, Cassian." Fixing her gaze on the pulse that fluttered on his neck, she added, "Tonight." Had she been too bold? "If you want me to."

"If I *want* you to? You need to ask? You know how much I—" Suddenly he swallowed. "But—you're sure?"

Oui. Oui-dgia. But the words wouldn't come, panic had closed her throat. So she reached up to frame his startled face with her hands, and drew him down to receive her answering kiss.

He gave her no outward sign of encouragement. His mouth was firm and still, his massive body unyielding. Why didn't he react? She pressed closer, until her breasts brushed against him—how full they felt, so deliciously sensitive. She wished he would touch them.

His response came in the sound that formed deep in his chest and emerged as a low moan. Unleashing some powerful force that he'd held in check, he came alive in her arms.

He returned her kisses with a fervor that thrilled her. His fingers gripped the neck of her gown, crushing the cloth and lace as if they were enemies. She heard the fabric tear, and his palms cupped her flesh, his fingertips grazed her nipples. He exposed her shoulders, then her breasts, lowering his dark head to worship each one with his lips.

Now she was the passive one, unable to move while he took away what remained of her garment. His hands slowly trailed down her bare waist, then swept across the curve of her bottom.

He knelt to draw off her stockings, and she felt his hands caressing her thighs, her knees, her ankles. He'd managed to touch every inch of her body—except the secret, hidden place where her fever ran so high, aching for his attention.

He peeled away his shirt and smalls. When he took her in his arms again, she could feel his sex straining toward her, firm and insistent. His heightened state of arousal increased her own desire until she was so weak and helpless with it she didn't know what to do next.

"Bed," he muttered, forcing her backward while at the same time holding her against him. They edged awkwardly across the floor, out of the lamplight and into the darker side of the room. He swept aside the embroidered hangings, and together they tumbled onto the mattress.

Again Sophie felt those urgent hands upon her, sweeping her long hair aside and stroking her nipples. His kiss was an act of possession, his probing tongue mated with hers. She arched her back, leaned into him, seeking relief.

His hand rested briefly upon her mound, then his fingers moved down to part the moist and heated folds of her skin. Her yearning manifested itself in soft whimpers.

"Yes, now," he whispered roughly, impaling her with his swollen length.

She gasped as she took him in. No pain, only a burning pressure and the sensation of being filled and stretched. Gripping his forearms, she felt tensed muscles as hard as stone. He was so large, so strong, and never had she seemed so small and indefensible.

He dove into her, not at all gently but with a wildness that took her breath away. His body rose and fell, again and again, and she felt his rigid flesh deep within her. Thoroughly unprepared for this assault upon her senses, she trembled, she burned.

"Ah," he cried with each stroke. "Ah."

She opened her eyes to find him staring down at her, watching her. Did he realize his power over her, or know that she reveled in all that he did? Was he even aware of her, or was he lost in his own delight?

"Sophie." He drew back, then heaved forward. "My Sophie."

Her sense of self faded as the fire at her core consumed her. She was a writhing mass of sensation. She could no longer think, or see, she could only feel, and what she felt was so strange and yet so exquisite that it couldn't be real. She was cold and hot at once, she was trembling from the inside out— and suddenly she heard her voice cry out as a shattering force rocked her entire being.

He was still there, still part of her. His motions grew more frantic. He made a guttural noise. She felt another pulsing inside her, this time it came from him. His sweat-slick body fell forward, his damp brow rested against her collar bone.

She lay beneath him, stunned by the intensity of his loving. A merging not only of bodies, but possibly even of souls.

Cass touched her cheek. "You sing out," he said. "I made you sing." He couldn't mask his relief. "I dared not hope for that so soon—the very first time. But I might have known it could be like this for us." He wished he could see her face better, his curtained bed was darker than a cave. His fingers felt for her mouth, to find out whether she smiled.

This woman, he marveled, had been fashioned for his delight, and he for hers. At last he had experienced the full force of her inner fire. With this shared passion as a foundation, their marriage would surely succeed. Whatever her reasons for accepting him as her husband, she surely recognized this bond between them. Time would strengthen it, of that he was certain.

Unless he lost her goodwill.

He rolled onto his back as the ugly events of seven years ago hurled themselves at him. His brief but harmful experiments with laudanum. His sister's sorrows. The violent rift with Tait. Their duel on Hounslow Heath. Spilled blood and shattered lives.

How would Sophie react if she found out that he'd wanted to kill a man—had very nearly done it?

He ought to tell her everything. But she lay beside him so sweetly, so trustingly, her soft cheek resting against his shoulder. This was not the moment to utter the terrible acts that burdened his conscience, of the grief and blind rage that had driven him to desperate actions. And he dared not provoke unfavorable comparisons with the worthy Tobias by reciting a sordid tale of vengeance and scandal.

But if he didn't tell her, he cautioned himself, he might endanger her. Tait was cruel and vicious, capable of great evil—heaven alone knew what harm he'd done Luis Costa. If those foul hands ever touched his unsuspecting Sophie . . . .

She stirred against him.

"I should go," she told him softly.

"Not yet." But before he could prevent her, she left the bed.

He also rose and covered himself with his shirt. The fire was fading but the lamp glowed weakly—he saw the pale outline of her body as she searched for her nightgown. She slipped it over her head and held the deep tear in the front together with one hand.

"Ruined, is it?"

"Not past mending," she answered.

"If I admitted how long it's been since I had a woman," he said ruefully, "you probably wouldn't believe me."

She had the delicacy not to question him, but her shadowed face expressed curiosity.

"I hardly remember—most definitely not since I met you. Perhaps I was saving myself for marriage. And then I let my guard down for a moment, and a pretty rogue seduced me."

He accompanied her to her bedroom. After he pulled back the flowery crewel-work coverlet, he asked, "May I stay? I'll leave before daybreak."

"It wouldn't be wise," she murmured, "to—to be together again until after the marriage." Her restraint was a marked contrast to her earlier boldness. "Suppose I presented you with a babe but eight months beyond the wedding?"

Cass hadn't considered that, and he had to respect her concerns. He only hoped she wasn't regretting what they'd done. "I'll attempt curb my amorous impulses," he told her, "but these three weeks will be the longest I've ever endured. I'm meeting with the vicar first thing tomorrow."

He returned to his chamber to sort out the tangled sheets. He felt sated, yet ever so slightly cheated, for she'd shared her body but without offering him her love. Not so long ago, he reminded himself, he'd despaired of winning either. So even if this wasn't the total triumph he dreamed of, it was hardly a defeat. Because he'd made her sing.

CHAPTER 14

And many idle phantasies,
Traverse my indolent and passive brain.

~Samuel Taylor Coleridge

The practice of religion, Andrew Searle believed, was for superstitious and gullible folk. It wasn't piety that lured him to the parish church on a breezy Easter morn, but the expectation of meeting Sophie there.

Gathered beneath St. Mary's ancient vaulted roof were people from the village and castle, the men clad in Sunday suits and the women wearing their most festive finery. Andrew didn't crack open a hymnal or join in the celebratory anthem. His focus was the cozy tableau in the box pew decorated with the earl's coat of arms.

Cass looked like a nobleman born in his dark coat and starched white neckcloth, his black hair brushed into perfect waves. His madonna-like sister was trying to quiet her son, who bounced up and down excitedly. Sophie Pinnock sat with them. While the congregation chanted responses, Cass addressed a few whispered words which left her looking pleased and uncomfortable all at once.

Envy pierced Andrew as Sophie smiled up at the handsome libertine seated next to her.

He concentrated on the vicar's sing-song voice, soaring and falling with overly dramatic effect. It struck him as a comical performance, but not enough to enliven the communion rite. Andrew rose with the congregation to recite the creed and sat again for the announcement of holy days and fasts.

The vicar settled his spectacles on his nose. Pitching his voice still higher, he read from a paper, "I publish the banns of marriage between Cassian Moreton Carysfort of St. Mary's parish, Bevington, and Sophie Elise Nicolle Pinnock of St. Nicolas parish, Chiswick."

He paused, waiting for the mild furor to subside.

"If any of you know cause or just impediment why these two persons should not be joined together in holy matrimony, ye are to declare it. This is the first time of asking."

Andrew's prayer book slipped from his hands and struck the stone floor. No one noticed. Everyone was staring at the earl and his lady landscape gardener. The parishioners murmured and bobbed their heads, ignoring the vicar as he launched into the Offertory. Miserably trapped, Andrew sank down on the pew, storm clouds breaking in his head.

Cass. Sophie. An engagement.

But she was destined to be his own wife, the mother of his sons. His salvation.

Cass fancied her, he'd been frank about it. Still, Andrew hadn't imagined he would ever offer marriage—not to a commoner, the widow of a professional man. He was an earl and was supposed to choose an aristocratic and socially prominent damsel like the ones he'd danced with and been spurned by in London all those years ago. He was an eligible catch now, he had a title as well as a fortune.

As for Sophie, she couldn't possibly be in love. Andrew had believed her too attached to her Chiswick home to exchange it for a castle. What could be her reason for agreeing to this preposterous match?

Yet again he'd been rejected even before he'd had a chance to propose. Cecelia Carysfort had always been beyond his reach, towering above him on her pedestal. But Sophie had tidied his cottage and rambled the wood with him. He sat with her while she painted; he showed her his poems. At night they met in his dreams.

He sat numbly throughout the general confession and the absolution, uncomforted by the assurances of divine redemption. He didn't want to think about sin, and refused to believe that the loss of Sophie could be a judgment upon him.

Later, when the parishioners filed to the front of the church to receive the sacrament, Andrew climbed to his feet and slipped out through the nearest door. He found himself in the churchyard, surrounded by headstones. The scent of moss and evergreens was stifling, redolent of death.

He searched his pockets for the blue glass bottle, a sure method of keeping his demons at bay. It wasn't there—had he left it at the cottage?

Plunging through a gap between the tall yews, he took the hillside path winding up to the castle. By the time he reached the gate to the deer park, his lungs burned and his legs ached. Sweat dampened his face, his fatigue all the greater because of his unanswered craving for the drug. He lurched through the woods, desperate to reach his cottage.

He was thrown into confusion by the sight of a blurred figure sitting on his favorite tree-stump. "Friend!" the man greeted him.

Andrew blinked to clear his vision. "Sam!" he replied with false joviality. "What brings you to Bevington?"

"You, of course."

After submitting to a hearty embrace, Andrew took his fellow poet inside. As he hastily rearranged furniture and cleared away books and papers, he carried out a surreptitious search for his bottle. Where the devil had he left it?

Sam accepted a glass of wine and claimed the better of the two chairs. "I've been at Bristol, where I conferred with Cottle about the new edition of my poems. He regretting not having news of you lately. I realized I hadn't either, not since you stopped with us at Nether Stowey. Too busy scribbling, eh?"

"Constantly," lied Andrew.

"I'm glad to hear you've found and embraced your muse again. You'll be surprised by my current venture—making plays. I've more time for composition now that Charles Lloyd has vanished into Dr. Erasmus Darwin's sanitarium. Mightily expensive, that place, but the poor fellow's mind is well worth saving."

Andrew opened a cupboard. No bottle.

"But I've not been lonely, for Wordsworth called on me a fortnight past. What a profoundly insightful man he is! We stayed up till the candles guttered, talking of our plays and whether we should attempt to have them produced in London. Mine is a Spanish tragedy in blank verse, which I've titled *Osorio*."

Sam Coleridge was never merely content to discuss his own projects, he had a habit of encouraging the confessions and confidences of his friends. As the visit wore on, he scented a creative crisis, Andrew could tell from his questions. To stave off an inquiry, he handed over a selection of his story ballads and encouraged Sam to read them.

He was reluctant to admit the evil of his situation to his hero, the most gifted of all his poet friends. If he did, his woes would be related to any number of others: Charles Lamb, William Wordsworth, Robert Southey. Andrew desired their admiration, not their pity. He would not be mourned over like that madman Charles Lloyd, and described by all as a poor fellow.

Failing to locate his laudanum, he concocted a fresh mixture. With trembling hands, he scraped a knife edge against the cake of crude opium to loosen the grainy powder, adding it to a glass of water. Speedily he consumed four teaspoons of the tincture.

He offered to share with his visitor, who readily accepted. "I hadn't intended to remain above a few hours," said Sam. "But you know how it is with the elixir—in a very little while I shall find it beyond my powers to rise from this chair."

"Stay the night," Andrew invited him. "You can take my bed, and I'll sleep by the fire."

They talked and drank together for the rest of that day and into the night. Under the drug's influence, Sam grew less voluble. He sat silently, mouth open, for minutes at a time. When he spoke, he acknowledged his struggles with the forthcoming edition of his poetry and expressed a flattering desire to collaborate with Andrew in future.

"However, that must wait till after my visit to Wordsworth and his sister. In the meantime, what will you be doing? Tutoring your Lord Bevington's nephew?"

"I declined the post," Andrew replied. "And in a most decided fashion, so I doubt his lordship will renew the offer. I'd intended to set up an establishment nearer to London— oh, Sam, the hopes I had! All dashed to bits, by a woman's weakness, and the selfishness of a man I regarded as a friend."

"A blighted romance?"

Regretting his bitter outburst, he muttered, "I hope not. It's not certain yet. I've nowhere to go now—I already declared to the earl that I intended to leave this place. I'm so damned feeble—at any exertion I feel as though a heavy weight is pressing down on my chest. Perhaps I'll turn out to be consumptive, like my mother." He drew a long, labored breath.

"You can make everything right again," was Sam's languid response. "Tell the earl you'll dedicate your next poem to him. That will restore you to his favor."

Darkness fell. After many hours the waking dream-state produced by the laudanum gave way to drowsiness. Sam sought the bed in the corner, and Andrew settled down on a nest of blankets before the hearth.

He slept deeply throughout the night. At dawn he woke, feverish and agitated, his body damp with perspiration. Unwrapping his sheet, which had wound itself around him like a shroud, he stumbled to the table and grasped a quill, eager to record his visions on paper. He wrote in haste, finishing his journal entry long before Sam began to stir.

Their breakfast consisted of a stale cottage loaf and fresh butter, and the weak contents of the teapot.

"I must hear about this curious dream you had," Sam said.

"No dream," Andrew replied, "a most vivid nightmare. Although it didn't seem so at the beginning, for I was a guest at a wedding feast. The bride was bright as an angel, the groom handsomer than the devil."

"Were these people known to you, did you recognize them?"

He nodded. "But I didn't share in their happiness. Sorrow rose inside me, I could not stay. Suddenly—magically—I was transported to a great ship with huge white sails, in a becalmed sea. All the passengers on board, and the crew, were dead."

"Dead?" Sam echoed in fascination.

"Skeletons, their bones visible beneath pale, transparent flesh. Except for one," he amended. "A dark youth. At first I thought he was a corpse, but he wasn't. He cursed me. Said I had done a hellish thing." His shaking hand gripped his teacup, and he drained it in a gulp.

"What then?"

"I heard a roaring wind. Thick black clouds filled the sky. To escape the gale, I leapt into the water. My limbs felt numb, I thought I was drowning. And yet I could not die. I *wanted* to die."

"Why?"

Despair, thought Andrew, and guilt. Sophie was forever lost to him. Cass, his friend, had stolen her from him. Envy burned in his heart, wrath flowed through his veins. And murderous visions rose in his mind.

"The waves cast me onto the shore," he went on. "I struggled to my feet and walked deep into a forest. It was this one, and I came to this very cottage. On the table I found pen and paper—as you see before you. I sat down and wrote out some words—*the Hermit in the Wood.* At that moment I awakened."

Sam was staring at him, lips parted. "You describe it so vividly. You should make a poem of it."

Andrew reached for his journal and ripped out the pages.

Crumpling them in his fist, he let them fall. "I don't like remembering."

His friend rescued the papers and placed them on the table, flattening out the creases with his palm. "A wedding. The skeleton ship. A curse. And a hermit in a wood." He pressed his knuckles against his prominent teeth. "These elements in combination with my vision of the great sea-bird might make an epic ballad."

"If you say so."

"May I keep your notes? They could be useful."

Andrew nodded absently. A liberal dose, he told himself, was certain to wash the ghoulish images from his mind. Leaving Sam to pore over the written account of his fearsome dream, he went searching for his bottle of liquid delight.

"Marriage settlements," Cass explained to the portly young man seated with him in the library. "When I first returned to England I consulted you about the provisions I wanted to make for my sister and the child. I'll be wed in a fortnight and must ensure my wife's financial welfare."

"With all respect, your lordship would be better served by my senior partner."

"Over the past year, Mardyke, you've handled my affairs with admirable precision."

A flush stained Mr. Mardyke's dumpling cheeks. "My lord, I'm most gratified by your good opinion."

"The castle and its lands will naturally descend to my firstborn son, who will hold the courtesy title Baron de Somery in my lifetime. My Carysfort inheritance will provide for the countess and our younger sons and any daughters. I've written down the amount I wish to settle upon each."

Mardyke took the paper and studied it. "And what does Mrs. Pinnock bring to the marriage in the way of income or real estate?"

"You need not consider that. Her property remains her own, for her sole and separate use, as ordained by her late husband's will." Moving away from his desk, Cass instructed, "You will travel to London, at my expense, to collect some documents from her brother-in-law, also an attorney. To him you must deliver this letter from Mrs. Pinnock, informing that family of the engagement."

"Yes, my lord."

"While in town, I want you to call upon Mr. Balthasar Prowdie in Arundel Street. Due to ill health and advancing age, he's retiring from practice and must surrender all deeds and documents relative to the Bevington estate. Henceforth they will be your responsibility."

His visitor's eyes popped. "My lord!" He swallowed before vowing, "I'll do my best for you."

"I've no doubt," Cass responded. "Prowdie will explain the rent structures and incomes—prepare for some long sessions, for he's slow of speech, and meticulous. He offers to house you, but I expect you'll be more comfortable at Nerot's Hotel. If you give my name there, the staff will take especial care of you."

The dazed expression had left Mardyke's face, and his voice was calm when he replied, "I shall do whatever your lordship thinks best."

"Lastly, I come to the most important of your tasks. A week from Sunday, the third reading of the banns will occur at the church of St. Nicolas in Chiswick. After the service you'll receive a signed certificate from the cleric. Bring it to me, posthaste, for I mean to be wed the following morning—the first of May."

"You may depend upon me, my lord." A spark of humor flashed in the gray eyes.

"Good man."

Before he could say anything more, Sophie surged into the room, Echo prancing in after her.

"You're here—I thought you might be," she cried breathlessly. When the attorney rose from his chair, she added, "My lord, forgive the intrusion. I thought you were alone."

"This is Mr. Mardyke, my man at law from Bristol. He is staying the night."

The young man bowed. "My felicitations, madam, on your approaching nuptials. Is there anything else your lordship requires of me?"

Cass shook his head absently. With Sophie so near, he was hopelessly distracted. He couldn't recall ever seeing her so deliciously disheveled—there was a smudge of dirt on her chin, loose strands tumbled from the thick coil of hair at her nape. And on her gown—could that be hay clinging to the fabric?

"Then I shall excuse myself to review these papers, and make ready for the journey to London. And Chiswick," Mardyke concluded, with a smile.

As the door closed behind him, Sophie asked, "Did you give him my letter for the Pinnocks?"

"I did." Cass pinched her cheek. "Have you been mucking out my horse boxes?"

"Very nearly. Cassian, I've made the most wonderful

discovery! I found a stag."

"It was bound to happen. The deer park teems with them."

"*Nânnîn*—in your stables. A stone stag. I told you of the pair made at the time of Queen Elizabeth's visit to the castle, remember? I found one beneath a horse blanket, with an old saddle on top. But its head and antlers are missing," she added forlornly.

He struggled to contain his amusement. "My sweet Sophie, I shall commission a dozen stags, if you want them. Carved from purest marble."

"How you spoil me."

How I love you, he thought, wishing her face would light up for him and not merely for his promise to adorn her gardens.

Joy and good fortune had finally found him. Like the hero of a fairy tale he would dwell here in his castle, a beauteous countess at his side. For her sake he would forget the haunting betrayals of his past, and concentrate on a happier future.

The dog nuzzled Sophie's knee, seeking her attention. Stroking the long nose, she said, "If only I could find the other stag. I mean to keep up my search."

"Have you any Jersey-bound letters? Mardyke can post them for you."

"I've been so busy I've not yet written my family." Gently tugging on Echo's ears, she said, "I shall do it tonight."

"Be sure to tell them how charming I am," he advised her. "But you should probably refrain from mentioning how eagerly I await our wedding night."

"*Dêmon!*" she cried, flouncing away from him. "Is that your only thought?"

At least his priorities were reasonable, he thought, vexed at taking second place to a headless stag.

✑

Sophie read her letter twice before folding and sealing it. Her sudden engagement to her aristocratic employer, an acquaintance of fewer than four months, would perplex the people who loved her most. She'd tried to allay any concern they might feel.

Although she hadn't pretended to be madly in love, she'd characterized the earl as generous-hearted, affectionate, a devoted brother and uncle, and a man of excellent reputation. Scattered throughout the lengthy epistle were the words "respect" and "admiration," which failed to depict his vibrant personality and gave no hint of the pent-up passions he'd released.

She'd felt all fluttery inside when Cassian had alluded to his desire for her and showed his impatience to have her in his bed again. She remembered the weight of his body against hers, how he'd murmured her name at the moment of ecstasy, and a quiver of anticipation surged through her.

This intensity of feeling, this giddiness, couldn't possibly last, she warned herself. It was spring. She'd endured a long period of celibacy. She was about to be wed. But she wasn't sixteen this time, she was twenty-one, and well aware that marriage was a serious commitment with serious consequences.

The evening silence was shattered as a shower of tiny hailstones struck the windowpanes. Sophie, fearing damage to her flowers, hurried to the casement. There was no sign of a storm, the sky was clear enough that she could see stars. She drew back again in alarm when bits of gravel rattled against the glass—a signal from someone below? She could just make out a male figure on upper step of the terrace. Cassian? Her pulse quickened at the prospect of moonlight dalliance with her intended.

Without hesitation she reached for a shawl and rushed down her spiral stair. The breezeway was cold, and she shivered. "Where are you?" she called softly.

"Over here."

It wasn't his voice.

"Didn't mean to alarm you," Andrew Searle told her, "but I had to see you. Don't want Cass to know," he mumbled. "Something I need, you must ask him for me."

"Yes, of course," she agreed. "What is it?"

"Perhaps he told you I declined to tutor the little boy. Meant to go to away—but my great plan came to nothing. My health fails, it might prevent my finding employment elsewhere. I'd like to stay on at the cottage for the time being. Until I'm better."

He did look dreadful, continually licking his cracked lips and rubbing his eyes. Sophie assured him that he needn't fear being cast out. "If you're ill, Dr. Jenner should see you."

"I need no doctor." He swept up her hand and squeezed it tightly. "Only you," he rasped. "Your kindness, your friendship."

She tried to free her hand of his convulsive grip, but he wouldn't release her. *"Oui-dgia,* I am your friend. And so is the earl."

"You are contented with your engagement?" he asked.

"Mine is no blackened betrothal, Mr. Searle." Her attempt at a jest failed to raise a smile.

"I've known Cass most of our lives," he told her gravely. "A man of many faces, many moods. In my youth I loved him as a brother. But in later years, his cruelties and callous selfishness almost made me hate him."

She stared. "You use strong language, sir."

"He means to have you, Sophie. Always he gets what he wants. You couldn't escape this marriage even if you wished it."

"But I don't," she stated firmly—truthfully.

"He'll use you. Hurt you. And lie to you, so sweetly that you believe in him and everything he says." Lowering his voice to a near-whisper, he said, "I speak from bitter experience, Sophie, when I warn you not to make the mistake of giving your heart to a Carysfort. For if you do, assuredly it will be broken."

CHAPTER 15

Every thing doth pass away;
There is danger in delay:
Come, come gather then the rose,
Gather it, or it you lose!

~Giles Fletcher

"Daniel, take pity on your aged uncle!" Cass chased the wayward ball as it rolled across the grass.

Sophie, seated at her easel, laughingly reminded him that he'd suggested the game.

"To my regret," he panted, stooping to capture the ball. "Young rascal, he doesn't understand why I must conserve my strength."

"Nor more do I."

With a wickedly suggestive grin, he confided, "I require all my stamina for the wedding night. I can't risk disappointing my bride."

"*Scélérat!*" A fiery blush spread across her face. "You scoundrel!"

"Tio Cass," called Daniel, "toss the ball!"

The third reading of the banns had taken place that morning. On the morrow they would be wed—if Mr. Mardyke returned with the necessary certificate from Sophie's parish priest in Chiswick.

Preparations continued as though the ceremony would proceed. All the tenants, villagers, and farm laborers had been summoned to the castle for a lavish wedding feast at midday. Under Bitton's supervision, the footmen had arranged long wooden tables and benches in the forecourt. Emrys Jones was already cutting flowers for decorative May garlands.

And the lord of the castle continued to jest about the wedding night to come.

Many faces, many moods. Andrew Searle's warning words haunted Sophie on this day of nervous anticipation.

During the past four months her future husband had displayed every one of his faults. He had a temper, *vraiment.* He could be imperious, *sans doute.* But because he'd never given her cause to doubt his word, or his integrity, she had nothing to fear. Poor Mr. Searle's illness had brought about his strange fancies and inexplicable mistrust of Cassian.

She swept her paintbrush across the paper, adding a violet wash to her watercolor of the irises springing up in front of the ivied wall. Carefully she fanned the tip over each petal, deepening the purple tints.

"Sophie, have a care!"

She looked up as the ball soared past her head and vanished in the tangled foliage.

"I'll find it," she promised, abandoning her camp stool.

She felt behind the clumps of irises, where she imagined it to be. Her searching hands parted the thick curtain of greenery growing up the wall. Instead of making contact with stonework, as she expected, they met no resistance.

She had uncovered an opening. Eager to explore, she crept inside.

"Sophie," Cassian called to her. Distance and the barrier of ivy made his voice indistinct.

The cavern smelled of dampness and mold. She moved warily through the darkness, one step at a time. Her foot struck the ball and she crouched down to pick it up. It was wedged against a solid object of cold stone.

"What's become of you?" Cass lifted the vines to peer inside, admitting enough light for Sophie to make out a large, pale shape.

"Ma fé," she whispered. "The other stag." Then, louder, so he could hear, she said, "Ask Emrys Jones to cut back the vines so I can see."

With eager hands she traced the animal's back, sliding slid them up the neck, feeling for the collar of roses. She studied the head—its ears and antlers were intact.

"How long have you been hiding here?" she wondered aloud, her voice echoing in the dank gloom.

Later, after Emrys Jones hacked away the ivy, the cave's vaulted shape was revealed.

"If I fitted it with a door," he commented to Sophie, "I might stow shovels and rakes and such inside."

Daniel tugged at his uncle's sleeve. "Don't let him have it, Tio," he pleaded. "I want to play here."

Cassian looked to Sophie for guidance. "Let it be for Daniel," she replied. "Mr. Jones, you can use the space at the back of the pavilion for your tools, as we discussed the other day."

"Aye, ma'am. Day after tomorrow I'll get a party of strong men to shift yon statue."

"You'll do it tomorrow." When she saw the gardener's raised brows and Cassian's black frown, she realized her error. *"Oh, las, les neuches!* Our wedding!"* In her excitement at finding the long-lost stag, her approaching marriage had flown from her mind.

Cassian turned away from her and marched across the greensward, fists tensely curled at his side.

Many faces, many moods. The words echoed as she trailed after him. Her forgetfulness had offended him, angered him.

"Where are you going?" she cried.

He did not stop. She quickened her pace and caught up with him. His jaw was clenched, his nostrils flared. Desperate to appease him, she could only repeat, "Why must you leave?"

"You don't want me hanging about, getting in your way. Go back to that creature Jones, and your wretched stag, and all those damned flowers."

"I'm sorry if I was thoughtless. But you agreed that I could restore these gardens. *Your* gardens."

"Mine? When were they ever? They belong to you and that Welshman."

"You're being absurd," she said in exasperation. "Why do you dislike Emrys Jones?" Her question had struck a nerve, she could tell. Suddenly he looked more uncomfortable than wrathful.

"Fool that I am, I gave you leave to employ whomever you pleased. I must abide by my word." He continued his interrupted progress towards the house.

Sophie picked up her skirts and hurried after him. "A brief time ago you teased me about our wedding night, and now you flee me as though I'm an enemy." Trying for a lighter note, she smiled and said, "With this demonstration of how disagreeable you can be, I'm tempted to cry off."

That stopped him in his tracks. "You can't. Not after letting me—not after we—not after that night. I'm honor-bound to give you my name."

"Untrue," she contradicted. "I was no trembling virgin, no victim of seduction. I acted of my own free will, and gave myself because I chose to. Yes, we were bound by a pledge. But should either or us, or both of us, prefer to be released from it—"

"Is that what you want? To break our engagement on the eve of our wedding?"

"I merely stated the facts."

"You needn't snap at me," he said petulantly.

"I can't help it. We've a saying at home, *'Qui éouse ou Jèrriaise, janmais vira à son aise.'* If you want to live in peace, don't wed a Jerseywoman."

"I thank you for the warning, madam." He moved swiftly to the terrace steps and vaulted up them two at a time.

His annoyance had not subsided by the time she saw him again, at dinner. He twirled the stem of his wine glass in an endless rotation. He drank a great deal but seldom touched his food. He rarely turned his face in her direction, and when he did it was bleak. No smiles, no laughter—he resembled a man doomed to attend his own funeral on the morrow rather than his bridal.

If there was to be a wedding. The solicitor hadn't yet returned with the essential document. Without it, the ceremony couldn't take place.

Insight came to her in a flash. His ill-temper earlier in the day, and this evening, were bred by his fear that their marriage would be postponed. He felt powerless, thwarted. Like his sister, he was unskilled at controlling his emotions; frayed nerves and dread of delay made him testy.

Hoping that the arrival of Bitton with a glass of choice port would smooth the creases in his brow, she accompanied Cecelia to the drawing room. But when he joined them there, he looked no more cheerful.

He listened to their discussion about the preparations for the feast—the baking of cakes and the roasting of meats—for a few minutes. Then he said, "So much effort, for an event that may not even take place."

"If not tomorrow morning," Cecelia answered brightly, "then the next. The food and drink will keep for one more day."

"What the devil detains Mardyke? Something's amiss. He met with an accident on the road. Or else that clergyman at Chiswick fell ill and failed to call the banns."

The clatter of carriage wheels broke in upon his gloomy predictions and he crossed to the window. "A chaise and four is coming along the avenue," he announced.

Sophie went over to look. The vehicle's glowing lamps marked its progress up the incline, and the horses hung their heads in fatigue, mouths foaming.

"Mardyke," Cassian told her on a triumphant note. "And the certificate." The taut muscles of his face relaxed. "Jerseywoman though you may be, pert and argumentative, I shall marry you tomorrow." He kissed her hard on the mouth.

Another transformation, thought Sophie, so sudden that it made her head spin.

He placed her hand on his arm and led her out of the room,

down the staircase to the great hall, where Bitton was relieving the attorney of his valise. All smiles and good humor, Cassian welcomed him.

"Mrs. Pinnock," Mardyke greeted her respectfully. "I bring a letter from your brother-in-law."

It was two pages, uncrossed, and contained few surprises. Writing on behalf of the family, Mr. Pinnock stated their general disapproval of her haste in contracting a marriage to the Earl of Bevington. And in the final paragraph he hoped that she wouldn't forget their goodness to her at the time of Tobias's death, and her duty to preserve his property for his eldest nephew—and rightful successor.

When she folded up the letter, Cassian asked, "Do the Pinnocks object?"

"I thought they might break the connection, out of pique. But they are wise enough to maintain it out of consideration for young Toby's future." After a brief consideration, she said, "If he shows an interest in landscape design, and an aptitude for it, he shall have my husband's books and instruments. And after he completes his apprenticeship, I'll provide a sum of money to help him set up in business."

"Generous," he commented.

"It's what Tobias would have done," Sophie asserted. "Is the certificate in order?"

"Most certainly," the attorney replied. "I had it from the cleric this morning after early communion. I made wondrous good time from Chiswick, and halted only long enough to change horses. I felt like a heathen traveling on Sunday, there were so few carriages on the road, but it meant a swifter journey."

"You must be exhausted," she said sympathetically. "I've

never heard of anyone covering such a distance in a day and a night. Let Bitton take you to the room you occupied the last time you were with us." She felt quite comfortable asserting the rights of chatelaine, even though they wouldn't be hers for a few more hours.

Cassian regarded her with transparent affection. "Yes, Mardyke, by all means go upstairs. Tell Bitton what you require in the way of refreshment."

"Your lordship is most kind. But I cannot retire until I've turned this over to you." He indicated the small leather-covered case on the trestle table. "Mr. Prowdie forgot to give it to you. Shall I open it?" At the earl's nod, he inserted the miniature key in the lock and raised the lid, revealing a jumble of jewelry.

"Grand Doue!" cried Sophie.

"I wasn't aware the Bevington collection was so impressive," said Cassian.

"There are even some diamonds," Mardyke informed them. "In the document box is an inventory detailing the provenance of significant items. Most of what you see here is a century old, or more. The earl before the last one was at odds with his countess and only gave her a marriage ring, and your lordship's predecessor never had a lady to adorn."

Sophie picked up a brooch of cabochon emeralds and dangling freshwater pearls set in heavy gold. "How quaint."

"That piece dates from Tudor times."

Sophie wondered if it had been worn by the Lady Bevington who had welcomed Queen Elizabeth to the castle, whose husband had commissioned the stone stags.

Cassian's long fingers sifted through the heap of bracelets, pendants, rings, and collars. Passing the chest to Sophie, he told her, "You should keep these. If you like them, wear them."

She studied his face, seeking clues to his state of mind. The blue eyes were as unclouded as the sky above, the mouth soft and smiling. Looking at him now, she could hardly believe this was the same tempestuous man who had berated her in the afternoon and avoided her eye throughout dinner. Now he was bestowing his ancestral jewels upon her.

In future she would try to keep her own temper in check and strive to be patient with him. They were both stubborn, equally determined to prevail in any dispute. This marriage, unlike her last, would be far from peaceful.

And yet, she reminded herself with a secret smile, it was certain to be exciting!

A lark's song broke the silence of the morning, waking Sophie from a warm, deep slumber. She lay very still, staring at the flat wooden canopy overhead, and wished the butterflies tumbling in her chest would be still.

Her wedding day.

Such a youthful bride she'd been five years ago, standing at Tobias Pinnock's side in St. Martin's church. Eager and shy, pleased to be a wife but desolate about leaving her close-knit family and island home for England.

The sun shone brightly today, as it had then. A good omen.

Last night before going to bed, she'd removed her late husband's miniature from her workroom. She'd placed it with his signet ring, inside the little box of valuables on her dressing table.

When a dying Tobias had predicted her remarriage, she'd

tearfully silenced him. She took comfort from the knowledge that he'd expected this day to come—though had not imagined she would become a countess.

Nan appeared at her usual time, carrying a fistful of lilies of the valley. "You might carry these, ma'am, or wear them in your hair."

She thanked the maidservant, touched by the offering.

Cheeks ruddy with excitement, Nan the fastenings of Sophie's cream silk bodice. The gown divided in front to reveal a coral-colored underskirt edged with a lacy flounce.

Cecelia soon arrived on the scene, arrayed in lemon taffeta. "Oh, you are charming!"

Sophie extended each of her arms in turn so Nan could button the long, tight sleeves. "I haven't the proper gloves," she mourned. "My only white ones are long, and I need short."

"Wear mine. Nan, go and look in the topmost drawer of the chest in my dressing room. Make haste, now, for his lordship has already gone down to the church."

Sophie swallowed and found one those butterflies stuck in her throat.

"Let me arrange your hair," Cecelia offered. She wielded the brush and comb, then expertly wound Sophie's thick mane into curls and secured them to her head with gold pins. "You need no longer make do with the gamekeeper's daughter, you know. One of the Bristol employment agencies can provide you with a skilled Frenchwoman."

"I'm not fashionable enough to warrant a Frenchwoman, and I prefer to keep Nan Parham. She's clean and cheerful and has proved her competence. I can ask no more than that."

"Cass might decide to cut a dash in London. Wouldn't you like that?"

"Probably not."

Tucking in a few white flowers at the back of Sophie's coiffure, Cecelia said, "There, now. You look utterly lovely, and smell divine. What about jewelry?"

"My pearl earrings."

When Nan delivered the gloves, Sophie remembered that she needed to keep her hands bare for the duration of the service. She gave them to Cecelia. "Keep these for me, till afterwards." She gathered up the remaining flowers in an informal bouquet, drew a deep, steadying breath, and announced that she was ready to proceed to the church. She made her way carefully down the spiral stair, with Nan helping to carry her skirts.

"Follow along with us," she said to her misty-eyed maid, "and mind I don't drag my hem along the grass. You may sit at the back of the church during the ceremony." She knew that this would raise Nan's status within the household hierarchy, for no other servant would be present.

The girl curtsied. "An honor to me, ma'am."

"You will continue waiting on me, as you've always done. But with my own rise in the world it's only right that I increase your wages."

Nan shook her golden curls as if dazed. "Dear me." Immediately proving her worthiness, she bent down to keep Sophie's trailing skirt from dragging across the stone-paved courtyard.

The three women followed the hillside path to the church, entering by an ancient Norman portal that never failed to remind Sophie of the similar style of architecture that prevailed on Jersey. Although the interior was chilly and poorly lit, the morning sun enriched the colored panes in the east-facing altar window. Nan smoothed Sophie's overskirt once more and fussed with the lace on her sleeves before slipping into a pew at the rear.

Sophie followed Cecelia up the broad center aisle. Cassian, pacing back and forth in front of the choir stalls, came to a sudden stop. Sophie gave him a smile and received one in return. She moved forward, but came to a sudden stop when Andrew Searle stepped out from behind a marble tomb of a recumbent Bevington in armor. His face looked as white as that of the carving.

The vicar observed, in his squeaky voice, "A bride, a groom, two witnesses. My lord, shall we begin?" Glancing down at his prayer book, he warbled, "Dearly beloved, we are gathered together here in the sight of God . . . ."

Sophie recited her vows calmly, in contrast to Cassian's swift, brusque responses. She sensed his impatience to get through the ceremony. Clasping his right hand, she promised to love and cherish him—but she stumbled over the word *obey.* A taunting gleam flickered in his blue eyes, and she wondered how soon he would make her rue that clause. And for the first time, she realized, she'd mentioned love in his presence.

He took her left hand and slid a ring over the fourth finger, a wide band of gold with a single table-cut diamond. She had no time to examine it before they knelt. The vicar prayed over them, then bestowed her hand on Cassian and declared, "Those whom God hath joined together, let no man put asunder."

A blessing followed, then a psalm, followed by various prayers and exhortations. When the service ended, the clergyman led the newlyweds and their witnesses over to the marriage register, and everyone signed it.

Cecelia, tears sliding down her alabaster cheeks, hugged her brother and kissed her new sister-in-law.

Andrew Searle hovered silently. Sophie tried not to think about the cryptic warning he'd voiced the other night. He was mistaken, her heart would not be broken. Whatever his grievance against Cassian, it hadn't spoiled their friendship—he was the groomsman.

The entire wedding party proceeded down the aisle toward the door. Cecelia returned the gloves. "Wait, let me see your ring first," she said, before Sophie could put them on. "Heavens, it's grand!"

"One of the Bevington jewels?" Sophie asked her husband.

He nodded. "I removed it from the box when you weren't looking. God knows how old it may be."

Emrys Jones waited in the churchyard. His long gray hair was unbound, hanging loose about his shoulders, and he held a flowery garland. "All happiness to your ladyship," he said. His rare smile vanished and he snatched the bouquet from her grasp. "Nay, nay," he scolded, "these bring bad luck. The flower heads hang downward, bowed in sorrow."

"Your Welsh superstitions have no meaning for me. I'm a Jerseywoman."

"Carry this instead," he insisted, pressing the garland upon her.

Bound up with white and pink ribbons, it contained an array of blossoms to match: blackthorn flowers, crab apple, snowy wood anemones, pale pink lady's smock. She thanked him, and as Cassian drew her along the stone-flagged walk, her shoes crushed the ill-fated lilies of the valley.

Daniel raced across the castle courtyard to meet the newlyweds. In his arms he carried a wriggling puppy whose pointy nose and floppy ears matched Echo's.

"Whose is it?" Sophie asked.

"Mine!" he declared blissfully. "Tio Cass gave her to me this morning. Her name is Rosa—that means 'rose' in Portuguese."

"Parham's lurcher bitch whelped again," Cassian explained. "Cecelia and I decided Daniel should have a pet of his own." Fingering the pink satin ribbon encircling Echo's slim neck, he asked, "Where is this from?"

"I dressed her up so she could come to your party." Glancing up at Sophie, the child asked, "What am I to call you? Tia Sofia?"

"Tante Sophie," she told him. "Let me kiss you, for you are my nephew now."

A cheer rose from the country folk as their lord and lady passed by long tables, and mugs of ale were lifted in toasts. Sophie smiled and nodded as Cassian presented individual farm tenants and villagers to her, greeting each by name.

A tall, fair-haired lady approached her, smiling broadly. "I'm sister to Matthew Parham, m'lord's gamekeeper. Our family are dairy-folk. I make the cheeses."

"I used to make them myself," Sophie told her, "when I lived in Jersey. Now I know where to go when I miss my cows."

"Oh, m'lady, I'd be pleased to welcome you any time," Miss Parham declared.

Cass, overhearing this exchange, marveled at his bride's ability to endear herself to others. He hoped she could show him how to make himself popular with his people. He didn't want to loom above them in his hilltop fortress, descending once a week to attend church and only addressing them in a prepared speech at the twice-yearly agricultural fair. He wanted to know them all, from the most prosperous shopkeeper to the lowliest laborer in the field.

His marriage, he believed, would add much needed shine to the thickly tarnished reputation of the Earls of Bevington. The two men who had held his title earlier in the century had never been well beloved. One was typically described as brutal and cruel, and figured in local legend as a wife-murderer. His son had been a recluse, a reputed sodomite.

When they took their seats at the head table, more toasts were drunk and the platters of food began to circulate. Determined to perform his duty as lord of the castle, he prepared himself for a long day of feasting and receiving felicitations. He partook of the dishes in front of him and sipped the vintage wine Bitton poured into his glass.

This was, he realized, his first family party.

He'd always been at school when his aunt and uncle had feted Cecelia on her birthdays. At his coming of age, shortly after he left university, he'd still been mourning his parents and there had been no celebration. His sister's Portuguese marriage—a nasty business, a necessary evil—had been finalized in secrecy.

He looked down the table at Daniel, covertly feeding pieces of bread to his pup. A splendid boy, lively and bright. Growing like a weed, too. With the excitement of the wedding, he'd stopped brooding about—

Cass felt that dreadful, insistent tug of pain and loss and guilt. He couldn't help but think of Luis, even on this happiest of days.

As the afternoon wore on, he grew more and more eager for the delights the evening held in store. He longed to escape with his bride to the privacy of his bedchamber. To remove that pretty gown and caress the soft body beneath. To bury himself deep inside her where he could find sweet relief from all his cares and fears.

Sophie was his solace, his treasure, his dearest wife. And if only he could hold her trust and earn her love, he would have every happiness a man—or an earl—could wish for.

CHAPTER 16

On me love's fiercer flames for ever prey
By night he scorches, as he burns by day.

~Alexander Pope

Cass led his bride along the shadowy corridor, bearing a flickering candelabrum. Echo, still sporting her festive pink ribbon, trotted after them as if assured of her welcome. In the bedchamber they found a fire in the grate and on a table a bottle of claret with two glasses and a plate of fruit.

"No more," Sophie said, when Cass asked if she cared for any food or drink. "My head still spins from the champagne we had at dinner." Her gaze veered away as she told him, "Nan won't be coming up to wait on me. You must—undress me."

"I can think of nothing I'd like better. Well, one thing," he amended, following her into the dressing room, "but we'll come to that."

His very first husbandly task was unfastening the back of her gown. She stepped out of the dress and hung it on a peg, then tugged at the front lacings of her boned corset. "Why do you wear it?" he wondered. "Your waist is so slender."

"To make the dress fit better." She sat down on a low wooden chest to remove her stockings, and as she leaned forward her bosom swelled over the top of her shift. She glanced up and caught him ogling her. "Wicked man."

"I'm allowed. Weren't you listening to all those prayers the vicar read this morning? Suggestive stuff. All about carnal lusts and appetites, and fornication. Man and woman becoming one flesh. There was that bit about honoring one's wife as a vessel—implying that she needs to be filled. And the part about worshiping thee with my body."

She trembled. From cold, or anticipation?

"Take this." He passed her a banyan, a rich burgundy color, and chose another for himself to wear. "We can sit before the fire, it will warm you."

They removed a pair of cushions from the window seat and arranged them on the floor. No sooner had they settled down at the fireside than Echo joined them.

"Where does she sleep?" Sophie asked.

"Lately with Daniel, although her place will likely be taken by her sister Rosa. If you object to her presence, I'll train her to lie elsewhere."

She smiled down at the brown muzzle resting against his knee. "I don't think you will succeed. If she has a jealous disposition, I can lie elsewhere."

He shook his head emphatically. "I want you beside me, Sophie. All night, every night. You've sworn to obey, remember?"

"I wondered how long it would be before you pointed it out to me." She shoved at him lightly, playfully.

Capturing her wrists, he pressed her backward against the

pillow. As her mouth parted in surprise, he kissed it, using his tongue.

"Enough," he said, pausing for air. "I must pace myself. I've never made love to a countess, and I suspect an extraordinary performance is in order. We'll have but one wedding night, it should be memorable."

He left her long enough to pour out a glass of wine. Returning to the nest of cushions, he asked if she had enjoyed their wedding day.

She nodded. "Your tenants and servants were all so glad to share in the celebration."

"Many expressed pride in having so fair a Lady Bevington. You've lived here many more weeks than I, and have already settled into the rhythm of castle and village life. I still feel an outsider here," he acknowledged.

She reached for his hand and curled her fingers around it. "I confess, I disliked Bevington the first time I saw it. I remember that day so well—the rain and the fog. The rooms seemed so vast and gloomy. And you frowned at me."

"Did I? How unhospitable of me. To be sure, I thought you very pert—and excessively pretty for a landscape gardener. I watched you from the library window while you wandered my grounds and fell in love with them."

Said Sophie, shaking her head, *"Nânnîn,* I tried not to care at all. My livelihood depended on making the alterations you wanted. All the same, I wasn't sorry to be dismissed. When I left Bevington I believed it was forever, and that I'd never see you again."

"I doubt you would've done, if that Moncrieff fellow hadn't come here right after you. The drawings he showed me were obviously your handiwork—that's when I began to regret sending you away. I couldn't put you out of my mind. So I went to Chiswick. At the time, of course, my only motive was to hire you to make improvements here. But even then, I was conscious of your many charms."

"What nonsense!" she sputtered. "You glared at me."

"Frowning. Glaring. You sketch a most sinister character, lady wife."

"You were extremely disagreeable. It wasn't till later, when I was gathering snowdrops, that you demonstrated your amorous nature."

"And what of yours?" he retorted fondly.

She stared into the flames. "There is wantonness in me, I cannot deny it." Firelight added ruddy tints to the thick coils of hair and made her eyes glow. The wine-red garment enhanced her exotic allure.

"We're well matched, Sophie."

Looking him in the face, she said fervently, "I do hope so."

"I shall prove it to you—now." He cupped her cheek in his palm, sliding his hand down the slope of her neck to rest on her shoulder. "As fetching as you are in my banyan, the moment has come to remove it."

He took great delight in exposing every inch of creamy skin and all the luscious curves. Then he began plucking the gold pins from her hair and let the rippling waves cloak her glorious nudity.

He swept his tiny bride into his arms and laid her on his bed. Her eager embrace fired his blood. Fleeting caresses sent chills along his spine. The child-like fingers brushed against the hairs on his chest, then slid across his shoulder blades. This creature he'd once regarded as so prim and proper, who had refused to be his mistress, was a wondrously uninhibited bedmate.

His mouth found her breasts, firm and full, and his tongue teased each nipple, urging it to bud for him. Her head rocked from side to side, and her chest rose and fell more rapidly. He studied her reactions, committed them to memory so he would know how best to please her.

He treated her more gently than he had during their first mating, when he'd ravished her and she had reveled in it. Now he cherished her, and was rewarded was not merely with her cooperation, but her active participation. She held him and reached for him, and at his murmured encouragement, she stroked his thickened flesh.

He placed his hands along the insides of her thighs, drawing them apart. Her maidenhair felt like silk. She liked being touched there, her gasps told him so. Slipping his fingers into her crevice, moist with readiness, he found the source of her pleasure. How many times, he wondered, could he make her sing tonight?

By the time he entered her, she was already crying out, and his swollen length was sensitive to the pressure of her inner contractions. "Ah, Sophie," he murmured. They fit together perfectly, man and woman made one.

Sophie welcomed his invasion. His strokes came slowly at first, in a mesmerizing tempo, till suddenly his body surged towards hers with greater force. She marveled at his hunger for her, and hers for him. It crested high, to break in a wave of physical release, and she caroled to him at the moment of her submersion. And she felt him heave against her as though he, too, had been cast upon the shore by the strongest of currents.

In his arms, in this bed, she felt whole-hearted and healed. Was it gratitude that brought tears to her eyes, or a kind of love, or simple relief that fate had offered her this second chance at happiness?

A low, keening sound came from the other side of the bed curtain.

"Echo," said her husband. "I forgot about her." He pulled back the hangings to look out. The dog took this as an invitation and bounded onto the mattress, tucking herself into a ball.

"It doesn't matter," said Sophie.

"If she makes a nuisance of herself, I'll order her off the bed."

She reached over to smooth the damp curls tumbling over his brow—an intimate and wifely gesture. "And if I turn out to be a nuisance, will you do the same?"

Laughing, he kissed her nose. "Never."

They shared a glass of wine, cuddling together among the sheets and pillows. Long silences were interspersed with conversation. Their dialogues centered on their very different perceptions of the prolonged and rocky courtship that had brought them to this state of mutual bliss.

"You were arrogant," she insisted.

"And you stubborn," he maintained.

But if he hadn't been arrogant, she acknowledged, she wouldn't have been so intrigued. "Besides, there was—still is—an air of mystery about you."

Giving her no chance to explain, he pressed feather-light kisses on her lips, her bosom, her belly. She giggled and writhed, and he grew more daring. The dog was speedily and ruthlessly evicted.

Again Sophie experienced that delicious loss of self as he turned her into a wild, desperate being. She opened her body to her mate, she shuddered and sang out, and afterwards slept soundly, cradled in his arms.

∽

A fortnight into her marriage, Sophie was constantly on the watch for signs that her second foray into matrimony might turn out as well as the first.

She and her husband seldom enjoyed a state of perfect harmony, yet their clashing wills had not made life intolerable. Debates and battles and teases occurred frequently, but more often than not they ended in laughter. Even though their personalities were so different—or too similar—they were fond of one another. And whenever he reached for her hand, and kissed her, and made love to her, she was certain that marrying him had been the right and best choice.

As wife, countess, and castle chatelaine, her responsibilities differed very little from those she'd known at Chiswick. Each morning she met with Mrs. Harvey and Bitton, familiarizing herself with the management of an establishment far larger than the one she'd previously presided over. She laid down rules for the conduct and duties of the staff, relying upon the upper servants to uphold them. She instigated a weekly payment of bills, reviewing all accounts herself—and was astonished by the quantities of candles and flour and sugar required. But otherwise she found no cause for interference.

Emrys Jones visited the house daily to give a report on the progress of the restoration effort. The stone stag, cleaned of grime and cobwebs, now stood at the entrance to the bowling green. Knots of herbs were being laid out within the castle keep to recreate the pleasaunce of earlier times. Sophie had given him leave to hire an apprentice, for she wasn't sure he'd be content to continue in his unpaid post indefinitely. He had also brought in a trio of under-gardeners, members of the prolific Parham family, with fair hair and brawny arms and tanned faces. Sophie outfitted them with green woolen aprons. The luxury of having so many minions to carry out her wishes could not, however, console her for the gardening time her marriage had taken away.

Husband, sister-in-law, and nephew vied for her attention, and her perusal of the garden archives suffered many an interruption. Cecelia often sought her out to learn her opinion of a fashion plate or a music selection. Daniel begged her to play with him and help him teach the puppy new tricks. And Cassian expected her to be available to him at all hours. He presented her with a small horse and elegant sidesaddle so she could ride with him. He toured her through the countryside in his phaeton. He took her on long, aimless rambles through the deer park.

"I've rarely seen my brother so content," Cecelia told her one day as they sat together sewing. "Or so calm. He's not been cross since the day of your wedding."

"Oh, but he has been." Sophie had witnessed several outbursts in the past two weeks, and she seemed to be the sole target of his dissatisfaction. She returned her attention to the piece of linen she embroidered, filling in a pattern of striped roses she'd designed and drawn herself. It would look well, she thought, covering the chaise longue she'd discovered in an unused tower chamber.

The earl charged into the morning room. "Our horses are waiting," he announced. "Change into your habit, quick as you can, so we may be off."

"Are we going somewhere?" she responded calmly.

"Didn't I tell you? I had a message from Merchant Fry

of Bristol. My shipment of wine and port is due at Parham Pill today. I'm riding over to meet the wherry and watch the unloading of the barrels."

Said Cecelia, "It sounds terribly dull for Sophie. Must she accompany you?"

"She was with me when I placed the order, and I thought—" His enthusiasm dimmed. "No matter," he said with a shrug. "If you don't care to come along, I'll not insist."

Sophie had planned to copy some notations from the old account books. But this was still their honey-month, and she felt obliged to comply with her husband's wish. "I'll meet you in the stable yard," she told him, sticking her needle into the material stretched out on the frame before her.

"Cass, don't encourage her to go dashing about the countryside on horseback," said Cecelia. "She's a countess now. Take her in the carriage, or your phaeton."

With a smile, Sophie retorted, "What good is being a countess if I can't do as I please? Eccentricity is perfectly acceptable in aristocrats. By choosing to wear country clothes and gallop about on my horse, and weed my own flower beds, I show that I'm far too grand to concern myself with convention and propriety!"

Her husband, she noticed, was pleased by her bold declaration. The thunderclouds lifted from his brow and the sun broke out in his smile. Without a thought for the garden research she'd hoped to accomplish, she hastened to her rooms to put on the crimson broadcloth jacket and matching skirt she wore for riding.

Her cream-colored horse, slightly larger than a Welsh pony, was named Cloud. Sophie, translating it into Jèrriais, called him Nouage. Before mounting she fed him a fistful of oats, and his velvety lips tickled her palm as he nibbled.

"Does Echo join us?" she asked, for the lurcher capered about the stable court expectantly.

"Not today. I want you all to myself," Cassian answered. Advising the groom to shut the dog into a box-stall until the horses were out of view, he climbed onto Saladin's back.

Along their route to the Severn they passed hayfields where men mowed and women raked, and pastures in which milk cows feasted on tender spring grasses. Cassian pointed out the various farms, naming the tenant of each one.

"Before much longer, I expect to be as knowledgeable about dairy farming as anyone in Bevington Vale," he boasted. "I started out at quite a disadvantage, for I've lived only in cities, or abroad."

"Dairying is a way of life on Jersey," commented Sophie. "We did the milking ourselves, Méthe and I, with the help of the servant girls. And when I lived at Anneville Manor, I'd go out to the fields early in the morning to visit Uncle Edouard's herd. All those years at Chiswick, I missed having cows."

"Shall I buy some?"

"Have a care," she warned, "I might just say yes."

"I'm perfectly serious. You could keep them at the home farm, and let them graze that overgrown field abutting the gardens. The old moat would keep them in place, just like a ha-ha."

She waved her riding crop at some grazing animals. "I don't want these mud-brown ones. Mine would be Jerseys," she said loyally.

"Next Gloucester market day, I'll make inquiries. You can go with me, and demonstrate another of your eccentricities to the local populace by assembling the herd yourself."

The road led them away from the gentle hills and escarpments forming the vale and into the flatter terrain regularly flooded by the Severn estuary. The constant surges of water cut ditches into the loamy soil, but the lands that had been drained were fertile enough to support a rich carpet of grass.

At Parham Pill a single farmhouse nestled between the pastures and the sandy flats along the broad waterway. Its occupant operated an occasional passenger ferry across the Severn, weather conditions permitting, and provided lodging and refreshments to travelers. The tide was partly out, and the trow that had transported the wine and port from Bristol lay anchored at a distance from the landing. The boatmen had to carry the liquor casks the rest of the way, across soggy sands and shallow pools, to the waiting wagons.

When her husband fell into conversation with one of the drivers, the farmer invited Sophie into his taproom to wait. "There's no one about at this hour," he assured her. "I'll send in the wife to wait upon you."

"If you don't mind, I'd like to look about," she told him. "Have you a dairy?"

"Aye, we've cows enough to keep us in milk and cheese. The wife raises her hens as well, fattening them for market and selling the eggs."

The farmer's lady was unprepared for the Countess of Bevington's tour of her poultry yard. Enclosed by palings, it was spacious enough to accommodate a multitude of fowls, and contained both a pond for her geese and a running stream. At first she was tongue-tied, answering Sophie's questions with nods and shakes of her head. But soon she was volunteering information, boasting about the profits of her enterprise.

"I feed my hens on curds from the dairy, and steamed potatoes," she explained. "They also get boiled wheat and a small quantity of corn each day. I let my geese graze, and they thrive on't, but they do favor lettuces and cabbages when I have 'em. Each has given me an 'undred eggs a year."

This yield impressed Sophie. "And have you a dovecot also?"

"I'm having one builded, soon's I've laid by the funds for't."

"You've got white peacocks! How lovely they are."

"My man made me a present of 'em, thinking to put me in a good humor. A more useless pair I've never known—prancing and strutting." Placing her hands upon her ample hips, the woman glared at the offending birds. "Showy, yes, and rare, but they aren't fit for table or laying. I need fowls what earn their keep." With a gleam in her eye, she turned on Sophie. "Grand enough for a castle, they are. Will your ladyship have 'em?"

"I couldn't possibly—they were your husband's present to you."

"Nay, nay," the woman answered quickly, "he'll not gainsay me."

"I'll make an offer you can't refuse, he'll have to respect that."

"My lady, I'd pay *you* to take 'em away, I'm that wishful to be rid of 'em. We'll do like the gentlemen when they talk business," said the farmer's wife, "and discuss it over drink. Let me pour out two glasses of my elderberry wine."

Matters were arranged to their mutual satisfaction by the time the earl's barrels had all been stacked on the carrier wagons.

"I hope there's room for a wicker cage," Sophie told Cassian blithely. "I've just purchased a pair of peafowl for the sum of twenty shillings. Pure white, and very beautiful."

When the farmer brought the crate over for his inspection, he acknowledged that the birds were unusual. "The dogs will almost certainly plague them to death," he warned.

"I told her ladyship, they be used to 'em," interjected the farmer's wife, determined to send the fowls away. "Cats, too."

The crate was tied to the back of a wagon. Cassian handed the woman a gold guinea, telling her the extra shilling was to cover the cost of bread and cheese and a bottle of cider. "I thought we might have a picnic," he told Sophie.

"Shouldn't you travel ahead of the carriers?" she asked when they rode away from the farm.

"It's too fine a day to spend in a cellar, and I trust Bitton to see that the wines are properly stowed. Look about for the best place to take our meal. You've the choice of high ground or low."

"High," she decided. "The views down the Vale are so pretty."

They found a suitable hillside and left their horses to crop the grass while they enjoyed their own simple repast.

When she had eaten her fill, Sophie lay on her back to study the ever-changing patterns of the clouds that scudded across the blue sky. Her sense of well-being was complete.

Glancing at her husband, she asked, "What makes you smile?"

"My bewitching countess. Is there such a thing as a Jersey witch?"

"Oui-dgia," she said lazily. "Mine is a magical island, with many legends and mysteries. We have the Cat of Carrefour, which can shrink in size until it vanishes into thin air. And there's a White Lady who follows people about but cannot be touched. I myself have seen *le Tchan du Bouole.*"

"What is that?"

"The Dog of Bouley." In a low, sepulchral voice, she said, "A large black hound with enormous eyes. He chases humans by night."

"And you survived the encounter?"

Laughing, she said, "There's no harm in him, a visitation merely foretells bad weather. I know sorcerers who can cure warts, and others who will locate a spring with a willow wand. Farmers and fisher-folk tell many a story of black magic, to explain why the cider goes sour or storms rise at sea. Cows are most commonly afflicted by charms—they cease to give milk, or the cream doesn't turn, or the butter won't come. Anyone can visit a white witch—or wizard—to find out how to undo the spell."

"You're *my* white witch." He held the bottle to his lips for a drink. "I wish you'd put a charm on my sister, and make her agree to have Daniel inoculated against the smallpox. I've tried to reason with her, and both Dr. Jenners recommend it. But she pays no heed to anything we say."

"Is it so important?"

"The disease can maim—or kill. Young children are especially vulnerable. This new procedure has proved effective for preventing it altogether, and I trust the doctors. Cecelia refuses to."

"But she worries over her son, you know how protective she is. It's not surprising she's wary of a medical experiment. You may be forward-thinking, Cassian, but your sister is not."

"I am the boy's guardian," he said implacably. "I must take all necessary steps to ensure his good health and welfare. I'd hoped that you could help me persuade her, but if you mean to take her side against me—"

"I've done no such thing," she protested. "I will not take sides at all, or involve myself in this dispute. I'm saving my energies against the day we argue over our own children."

"Will you flout my authority where they are concerned?"

She regarded him intently. "I hope I won't have to. *Dé vrai,* each of us will have strong feelings and opinions, so when we're at odds we must compromise. Shall I share my notions of child-rearing?"

"By all means."

"Our daughters' education," she began, "will be every bit as important as that of our sons. We don't want them growing up to be idle, useless young ladies."

"How could they be," he murmured, "with such a mother?"

"And we shall value our younger boys just as much as the heir. I dislike your English system of primogeniture, with the eldest son being treated as a god and the rest left to fend for themselves in the world. The Jersey laws of inheritance are more fair, with all children, male and female, inheriting a substantial portion of their family's property."

"That's why there are so few great fortunes on your island," he responded, "or intact estates. Every generation subdivides them into smaller holdings." After a brief pause, he said, "You look forward to bearing my children?"

She looked away, towards the slate-colored waters of the Severn and the rolling green hills beyond. "You require an heir, that I know. And I do long to be a mother. My first marriage was barren, and that was a great sorrow to me."

To cover her discomfiture, she began plucking wildflowers to make a chain. She couldn't let him know that abstinence was the cause of her failure to breed. Cassian, so vigorous and virile, might think the less of her late husband for his inability to engage in marital relations in his last years.

He tried to help her, inexpertly tugging entire plants out of the ground.

"Take only the part with blossoms," she said, showing him how by pulling some buttercups.

"What's this one?" he asked, handing her a stalk of blue flowers.

"Tèrrêtre. Speedwell."

"Here's clover and a moon daisy. These I know. What do you call them on Jersey?"

"P'tit têf'lye and *mèrgot."* She crawled across the grass to pick some yellow cowslips. Feeling a sharp tug on her habit, she looked over her shoulder. He held up a pink bloom. "It's a ladysmock—*Pentecôte."*

She never reached the cowslips, because he placed his hands on her waist and turned her around to receive his kiss. His mouth tasted of apples, from the cider he'd drunk, and she supposed hers did also.

"Even in the midst of a meadow, you manage to find an occupation." Taking her flowers away, he laid them on the grass. "Allow me to provide you with another."

"Cassian," she murmured against his neck as he raised her red skirt and black petticoat, "someone might see us from the road."

"They'll assume we're a pair of randy haymakers. Or," he added, his hands creeping up to caress her thigh, "eccentric aristocrats."

As the weeks passed and Cass saw no outward proof that his

bride reciprocated his love in part or in full, he grew despondent.

He'd bestowed his name and title. He lavished jewels upon her. He had sanctioned her plan to preserve his gardens. He bought her a horse to ride and was negotiating the purchase of several Jersey heifers. He had agreed to the construction of a *colombier* so she could keep doves as she had done in girlhood. He gratified her every whim. He indulged her. He adored her.

He did these things to give her pleasure, not for any personal reward. But he was unconvinced that she cared for him as deeply and profoundly as he cared for her. While waiting for the longed-for miracle, he tried to believe that half a marriage was better than none at all.

What troubled him most of all was the knowledge of how undeserving he was of the love he craved.

His life up to now was littered with mistakes and failures and lies and at least one crime. If Sophie learned about them—from him or anyone else—their tentative relationship would suffer irreparable damage.

He studied white peacock's stately progress as it marched through the rose garden. Behind tall lily spikes topped with bell-shaped blooms, the hen was seeking materials for the nest she'd begun in the sheltered niche in the wall. Greatly to Sophie's dismay, she must wait until the bird finished laying her eggs and hatched her brood before placing her bench there.

Cass strolled through the shrubbery walk to the laburnum arch. The vines were in full leaf and pendulous yellow clusters covered the length of the arbor. He approved his wife's foresight in saving it from destruction. Reaching up, he broke off a flower.

The lady he'd won, whose love was so elusive, never sought his company. She was always wandering to one of her many projects—none of which involved him directly.

Altering his tactics, he'd become a less demonstrative and more restrained lover, constantly fighting to rein in his passions. He worried that if he got her with child so soon, he would lose his small share of her attention. Siring an heir was not as important a consideration as she believed; he hadn't been born into an aristocratic family and as yet felt no dynastic compulsion to procreate.

"Rosa, Echo, come back!" Daniel shouted. "Tio, stop them!"

The dogs raced along the tunnel, twin flashes of brown.

"I'm s'posed to keep them out of the garden," said their pursuer, face flushed and black curls in disarray. "They'll chase the peacocks."

"Echo—to me!" Cass commanded.

The lurcher came to an immediate halt and trotted to his side. She lifted her pointed muzzle worshipfully, her brown eyes begging absolution for her misdeed. A pity that his wife couldn't be controlled with such ease, he thought wryly, stroking Echo's ears.

"Have you seen your Tante Sophie?"

"She's in the library," Daniel reported, struggling to lift his pup. "With Mr. Searle."

Cass shared Sophie's concern about his friend's decline, but he also feared it revived memories of her invalid husband. She'd arranged for a manservant to wait upon Drew at the cottage, and required Dr. Jenner to call on him weekly.

He wondered whether he could touch her heart by feigning illness himself. If he were sick, he thought, she could not ignore him.

Tossing the yellow cluster aside in frustration, he made his way to the stables. Today he would ride alone.

CHAPTER 17

Love and harmony combine
And around our souls intwine,
While thy branches mix with mine
And our roots together join.

~William Blake

The honey-month concluded with a blaze of sunshine and blossoms. Sophie, studying the gardens from the pavilion's broad window, felt a frisson of dejection in spite of the pleasing expanse of stone walls and flowering borders and velvety, well-tended lawns.

Her practical, efficient self was crowded out by a nervous, restless being whose heart fluttered at every encounter with her husband. Her appetite suffered. She spent her nights lying sleeplessly beside him. He seldom initiated lovemaking now, and her own boldness had deserted her. She wanted to reach out and draw him close but never dared.

How could it be possible that the fever of his passion had abated after only a few weeks of wedlock? His emotional withdrawal, after the intense and thrilling early days of their marriage, was deeply wounding.

Believing that he loved her, she'd foolishly taken his devotion for granted. Now, recognizing its value, she feared it was fading.

Her restoration scheme was no source of comfort. She had difficulty concentrating on her reference books and plant lists. Nothing could salve the wound that smarted whenever she reflected on the troubling change in Cassian. The terraces and borders and knots overflowed with bright and colorful blooms, yet they seemed paler when he was not at her side to admire them.

Turning from the window, she studied the airy, light-filled room. Ideal for a studio—quiet and secluded, with ample space for a chair and drawing table, bookcases and a desk. She could gaze out over her gardens, or paint them, or learn more about their history from the treasured folios.

Would her husband let her transform this promising chamber into something more useful? Not so long ago she could have counted on his acquiescence, after a lively and short-lived argument. This time, she decided, she wouldn't force the issue.

Making her way down the stone steps she heard his low, measured tones echo in the bathing chamber below.

She peered through the door and saw two black heads bobbing above the water, one large and one small. At the edge of the sunken bath lay two piles of clothes—Cassian's and Daniel's.

Said the boy, "But mine is so much littler than yours, Tio." He looked down and asked worriedly, "Will it ever grow?"

His uncle's booming laugh reverberated off the stone walls.

"Have no fear. By the time you reach manhood, you'll have no cause to consider yourself ill-equipped."

Sophie, unintentionally eavesdropping upon this masculine conversation, put her hand to her mouth to stifle a laugh. As a girl she'd often overheard her brothers comparing their *pinnes* and knew that size was a matter of concern—at any age.

Cassian hoisted the child's naked body high in the air. Daniel wriggled like a fish, squealing in delight. His uncle tossed him higher still, then released him, and he fell into the water with a splash.

"Again, Tio, do it again!" he begged as soon as his head broke the surface.

Observing their play, Sophie felt her heart expand until she feared it might burst. Her eyes grew moist, not from sadness but from an overflowing fount of joy.

And love.

For she was in love, she realized, and positively giddy with it. Love was the reason she couldn't focus her thoughts and energies on anything apart from her husband, and why his recent neglect made her so forlorn.

Looking up, he caught her watching. Embarrassed, she turned and ran back up the steps.

"Sophie!"

She wasn't ready to face him. This newly discovered emotion was too tender and precious, to be as zealously guarded as any seedling. A bitter blast of disdain, or the chill of misinterpretation, might shrivel it.

He burst into the room, a bathing sheet wrapped around the lower half of his body. Drops of water beaded the fine hairs of his chest, and his wet black curls stuck to his forehead.

"I wasn't spying while you bathed," she faltered.

"Then what *are* you doing up here?"

"Admiring the view. What a pleasant studio this would make—there's so much light. And space for my books and papers, and a few pieces of furniture."

He studied her for several seconds. "Then arrange it as you wish."

"You wouldn't mind?" Her fingers plucked nervously at the lavender ribbons crisscrossing her bodice.

"No." He was staring at her intently. "I don't recall seeing that gown before."

"And I've never seen you wearing only a sheet. Rather undignified," she couldn't resist adding. "For an earl."

"Jersey witch, do you mock me?" He grinned down at her. "Have a care, I might dispense with my covering."

"Go ahead," she dared him.

He was unwrapping himself when the barking startled them both—a series of frantic yaps that gave way to keening howls.

"Oh, las," cried Sophie. "The dogs have got into the gardens. Emrys Jones will wring their necks. And mine!"

She darted for the stairway and Cass followed, still clutching his drapery. The animals' cries drew them to the rose bower, and a scene of chaos and destruction.

Daniel, clad only in his shirt, was bouncing up and down on bare legs, while Echo and Rosa raced back and forth along the wall. The white peafowls had retreated to their niche, the hen clucking agitatedly as she and her mate surveyed the remains of the nest. Scattered through the debris were broken eggshells.

"A pity," mourned Sophie. "Who did this?"

"Echo," reported Daniel. "She was trying to get at the weasel. See, there he goes!"

Sophie caught sight of a slender, rust-brown creature scrambling in and out of gaps in the stonework. Echo yowled louder in frustration, and stood upright on her hind legs to scrabble at the wall with her paws.

Sophie knelt to examine the eggs, hoping some had survived. With a sorrowful head shake she observed, "Nothing left but shells—the weasel made a feast of them all. How do we get rid of it?"

"We can leave that to Echo," Cass replied. "She seems determined to do it in. The power of instinct—she was bred for coursing and seldom gets to use her skills. We'll have to take her rabbiting, you and I."

Sophie was heartened by her inclusion.

Her husband stood before her naked, but for the sheet. He was hers, every splendid inch of him. She longed for night to come so she could run her hands across those powerful limbs.

"Better find my clothes."

Sophie smiled. Her scrutiny made him self-conscious about his undressed state.

"There it is!" yelped Daniel. "The weasel—running along the top of the wall." He joined Echo and Rosa in the chase, and helped them herd the rodent out of the garden.

"A good thing Cecelia can't see him racing about without his smalls or breeches," said Sophie.

"I'm a bad influence," said Cass.

"On all of us," she retorted.

"Have a care, Lady Bevington. Your sauciness may provoke retaliation. I might just toss you into the canal, pretty gown and all."

"*Bah,* an empty threat. I'm not afraid of you."

"No?" He stalked towards her.

"You'll never do it," she said confidently. "You can't possibly catch me, pick me up, and dispose of me without uncovering yourself."

"There's logic enough in that elegant head of your to baffle lawyers," he declared. "My university debating society could've used your talents."

"Most men dislike cunning females."

"Stupid men, perhaps."

A sign, she exulted, that he wasn't indifferent. Her fear that he'd ceased to care for her dropped away as easily as the pink petals drifting down from the flowering almond.

"What are you doing this afternoon?" he asked.

"I'm bound for Gloucester to order a pair of garden seats from the stonemason."

"Is it absolutely necessary?"

"If I do it now," she told him, "tomorrow I can do other things. We've not gone riding together for many days."

"I haven't asked because I thought you so busy with all this." He flung out an arm, gesturing at the arbors of arching roses, heavy with buds.

She wished she knew how to make him cherish these gardens as she did. He was unreasonable, he was possessive—but she'd fallen in love with him despite those flaws.

"I am never too busy, Cassian, when you want me. Come with me to Gloucester, if you would not be too bored."

"I am never bored, Sophie, when you are near."

"It's raining," Cass announced, flinging back the curtains.

She was glad for the gardens, he knew, but he was concerned

about the farms. "It would be better had the hay been cut, stacked, and covered, and the turnips for winter fodder safely sown. I'd hoped to have the rape seed planted this week at the home farm, but that must wait till the end of wet weather." He looked over at his wife. She was sitting in bed drinking tea, her back propped against the wooden headboard and Echo curled up at her side. "How will you spend this indoor day?"

"Must I decide just now?" she asked lazily.

"Idle wench. You mean to remain exactly where you are."

"I would, and gladly, if you kept me company."

He shook his head at her. "Don't tempt me. I'm expecting Mardyke to come from Bristol, so I can prepare the new deeds for enclosure. I'm encouraging some of my green farm tenants to turn portions of grassland into arable land, in exchange for a reduced rent on that acreage. In the long term, it will increase the worth of the land."

"What if the tenants refuse?"

"They aren't likely to oppose me. I own the properties, I pay the land tax. I'm not promoting any radical changes," he assured her. "It's cheaper to grow corn than to buy. With a French war and fewer available markets, prices will be volatile for some time to come. I want my people to be more self-reliant."

"Your tenants are fortunate to have such an interested landlord," she commented.

"I benefit also, for I'm learning a great deal from them. I've a legal obligation to examine their houses and buildings, and instigate any necessary repairs. They maintain the hedges and stiles and fences, and keep all waterways clear. At present these Bevington leases are made at will, for an unspecified length of time. I'd prefer the term to last a minimum of seven years—or even fourteen. But I can't make such a drastic change all at once."

He liked conversing with her about agricultural affairs, it helped him to clarify his thoughts and form his plans. He valued her opinions—as she regularly pointed out to him, she was the daughter of a farmer and sister to several.

Sighing deeply, she said, "I do wish I could convince your people of the superiority of *la vaque Jèrriaise*—the Jersey cow."

"You can't expect the locals to give up their Gloucestershires, despite the success you've achieved with your little herd."

Sophie chewed her lower lip. "I must soon visit a dairy house. Nan's aunt, Miss Parham, invited me to have a look at hers."

"You'll be impressed. She's the most respected dairywoman in the Vale. Speaking of reputations . . . ." Moving to the bed, he sat down and placed his hand over her knee. "Sophie," he said gravely, "prepare for distressing news."

Setting down her cup, she leaned forward. *"Oh, las,* what is it?"

"My efforts to restore the good name of the Earls of Bevington have already failed. Your husband, I regret to say, has lost his good name altogether."

"How?"

"By making a spectacle of himself. With a female. In a meadow on the road to Parham Pill."

She sat up rigidly, an expression of horror on her face. "You cannot be serious."

"Evidently his flagrant act of disloyalty to his countess was witnessed by a regular at the Bevington Arms. Who has spoken freely, under the influence of strong ale, telling all and sundry of his contempt for such faithlessness. By his account, the sportive female wasn't even a local trollop, but a stray gypsy lass. Dressed all in red."

Gripping his shoulder, she gave him a shake. "Cassian, are you teasing me? How dreadful!"

"But amusing, don't you think?"

"Do you see me laughing? I can't bear to be regarded as the victim of an infidelity—after five weeks of matrimony!"

"You're missing the joke. Don't you think it comical that no one suspects I was seducing my own wife in that field?"

Sophie bounded out of the bed. "We must do something to scotch the rumors. But what?"

Cass thought for a moment. "I daresay the fellow noticed our horses. If we ride by his house, me on Saladin and you on Nouage—wearing that red riding habit—perhaps he'll realize his mistake."

"Chièr Cassian, you are *îngénieux!"*

"You flatter me.

He was making his way to the dressing room, when she called after him, "You haven't forgotten that Dr. and Mrs. Jenner dine with us tonight?"

"Of course not, I'm the one who asked them." Studying her face, he said, "Why so troubled?"

"Because it's my first time receiving guests formally, as your countess. And I don't know what to wear."

"You look quite fetching in that nightshift, with your hair hanging down your back."

Laughing, she dipped down in a playful curtsy. "Appearing as I am will not improve your reputation, *pon du tout*. Or impress these Jenners."

"They're the ones who should strive to make the good

impression," he pointed out. "The doctor is most genial, as you already know, and his wife is a pleasant lady. She was delivered of a child some weeks ago and is beginning to go out again. I wanted you to become acquainted before Jenner conveys her and their brood to Cheltenham to pass the summer."

"And is Mrs. Jenner an advocate of her husband's new method of inoculation against the smallpox?"

He gave her a sly smile. "I certainly hope so."

"*Dêmon.* You asked them to dine because you mean to badger your poor sister about that medical procedure."

"It's in Daniel's best interest."

Cass did expect the good doctor and his wife to assist him in persuading Cecelia. He accepted Sophie's oft-stated reluctance to enter into their dispute. This was his crusade, and he was determined to prevail.

His meeting with Mr. Mardyke took place at midday and lasted well into the afternoon. They discussed the new leases, drafted the deeds, made some revisions, and drank a goodly amount of Old Lisbon.

Before he knew it, he was dressing for dinner. He reminded Bitton that he needed gloves, and asked him to smooth out any creases at the back of his tight-fitting black tailcoat. The young man performed admirably as a butler but was less than adequate as a valet. Cass was accustomed to Luis Costa's fastidiousness, and his great delight in preparing his senhorio for dress occasions.

What the devil had become of that lad?

Although Cass might never know the answer, he hadn't relinquished hope Luis would turn up at Bevington. Complications would inevitably arise if he'd revealed all that he knew, but they could be overcome—somehow. Luis was more than a servant, he was the keeper of family secrets. His continued absence gnawed at Cass, and even in his lightest moods he was conscious of it.

If Sir Michael Tait was truly responsible for the valet's disappearance, he'd concealed his involvement with remarkable shrewdness.

Cass joined his ladies in the larger of the two reception rooms, which was decorated in shades of gold and white. Tall mirrors surmounted with the Bevington coat of arms adorned the stone walls, and all the giltwood chairs were covered in ivory damask. Cecelia, wearing a pale, diaphanous silk, matched her surroundings. Sophie, gowned in indigo, shone like a sapphire in a rich setting.

The Jenners arrived at the expected hour. The doctor presented his wife, a quiet, composed lady with a serious face, whose black mourning honored her recently deceased brother-in-law. On hearing Cecelia's son was close in age to her own firstborn, she thawed visibly.

"Two sons and a daughter," said Sophie. "They must keep you constantly occupied."

Catherine Jenner smiled. "My Robert is but an infant, no trouble at all. I am imparting proper manners and religious principles to our two older ones." In a softer voice, she continued, "I'm pleased to find another child in the neighborhood for our Edward to associate with. Lady Berkeley invites him to play with her boys, but I cannot bring myself to let him go."

"Are they so boisterous?" asked Cecelia.

"I'm sure I cannot say, for I've never met them. They are—well, not legitimate, but born when their mother was Mary Cole. Though at Lord Berkeley's whim, when she began living under his protection she called herself Miss Tudor. We heard he meant to be rid of her, when all of a sudden he took her off to London. They didn't bother to announce the marriage till several months afterwards, when the fifth son was born. I gather the earl was desperate for a lawful heir to his title and estate. Poor woman, she'll never live down her past."

"Nonetheless, I should like to meet her," said Sophie.

"The doctor has helped her through many a confinement and inoculates all her children," Mrs. Jenner revealed.

From across the room, Cass saw his sister frown. He stepped forward to say, "Do, please, explain to Cecelia that there's nothing to fear from having Daniel treated against smallpox."

"It's a simple business," the lady said earnestly. "Our Edward was treated before he was a year old."

"That was a swine-pox inoculation," her husband interjected. "I waited several years more before performing a variolation using smallpox lymph—with no ill effect. Perhaps it would be helpful, Madam, if I gave you a copy of my treatise, *An Inquiry concerning the History of the Cow Pox, Principally with a View to Supersede and Extinguish the Small Pox.*"

"It will have no effect on my opinion, sir," Cecelia replied.

She cast an imploring glance at Sophie, who rose and said with an inviting smile, "Shall we go to the dining room?"

The controversial subject was allowed to rest during dinner. The doctor entertained his host and hostess with recitations from a composition he'd written when younger, an essay on marriage.

"The most prevailing passions in the human breast," he declaimed, "are love and ambition. Marriage is undoubtedly the ultimate tribute of love—though it entails an abridgement of freedom for both parties. The choice of a wife may be dictated by affection or ambition or avarice. Some men seek a bride distinguished by high birth and good family. But we are all equal in the eyes of the divine Being who shaped us, and should follow our own hearts in this most important concern of life."

Cass held up his wineglass, acknowledging that he'd done exactly that in choosing the lady seated at the opposite end of the long table.

His Sophie was not his equal, he reflected, but his superior. He might possess greater wealth, but her bloodline was more distinguished, and she was by far a finer countess than he was an earl. She treated her guests warmly and graciously, with a natural dignity that was more ennobling than her title. But even as he gazed upon her now, so elegant and mannerly, he saw the same Sophie he'd tumbled in a meadow and sported with in their well-used bed.

His pride in her appearance and her deportment spawned a desire to take her to London and show her off to the aristocratic world, but his fierce possessiveness swiftly killed it. She was his to enjoy in private, he would not expose her to public view. His reasons for retreating to this stone-ringed fortress were as strong as ever. They were both safer here at Bevington.

After the ladies withdrew to a sitting room, Cass and the doctor imbibed a sweet, rich, ruby port. He confided, as delicately as possible, the episode at Parham Pill and the gossip making the rounds of the village and farmsteads. Jenner, he learned, had suspected the truth.

"I'll do what I can to convince my patients—and anyone else I may meet—that your lordship is a faithful husband. Though I can't conceive of anyone being foolish enough to doubt it."

"And while defending me against slander, you might also

ask if anyone is willing to relieve me of the noisiest, most troublesome pair of peafowl in the kingdom. Their shrieking is certain to start rumors that the castle is haunted. I'd have them slain and plucked and served up on a platter, in the manner of my ancestors, but Lady Bevington would never forgive me. The best I can hope for is to pawn them off on someone as gullible as she was when she bought them."

The doctor nodded his balding head, as if well acquainted with feminine foibles. "One day you must bring her ladyship to my house in Berkeley, so I can consult her about my little grotto garden."

"She'd be delighted," answered Cass, pleased that his Sophie's advice was sought by one of the most eminent of medical practitioners. "Do you grow any striped roses?"

"No, my lord."

"Be forewarned, sir. Lady Bevington will undoubtedly prevail upon you to plant them," he predicted.

CHAPTER 18

How oft in pleasant tasks we wear the day,
While summer suns roll unperceiv'd away.

~Alexander Pope

*A*ndrew Searle, reviewing the cyclical life span of the poppy, imagined distant countries with vast crimson fields of nodding flowers. The precious seed heads were harvested and pierced, the flowing juice was captured, molded, and dried, and divided into individual cakes. These were exported to England to be used and sold by apothecaries and chemists. The purchaser then sliced off tiny grains, mixed them with sugar water and alcohol to make laudanum—reconstituting the opium into juice.

Ever since Dr. Jenner had diagnosed him as consumptive, he'd taken greater quantities of the drug. No longer bothering to measure out his doses, he'd ceased to rely on his teaspoon. He sipped laudanum directly from his bottle.

The kinder weather of summer, he believed, was improving his health and his state of mind. June had brought long days and warm evenings and late sunsets.

At dusk he sometimes saw Cass and Sophie walking in the wood, the lurcher chasing after them.

The seemingly devoted bridegroom's assignations with a gypsy mistress figured prominently in local gossip. Eventually he would range farther to assuage his passions—to Bristol or Gloucester, or perhaps even London. Andrew awaited the day when a heartbroken, disillusioned Sophie would turn to him for consolation.

He opened the iron gate leading to the gardens. Her habits were familiar, he always knew where to find her.

"Mr. Searle!"

Today she surprised him. He stopped short when he saw her in the shade of the pavilion's columned porch, her arm crooked around several books and the butler at her side. With a smile, she asked if he was willing to make himself useful.

"At your service."

"Take this footstool from Bitton and carry it to the upper chamber, if you please. I'll join you presently."

Andrew had never been inside the pavilion. His steps echoed on the stone floor as he skirted the deep bathing pool. The velvet-covered stool was heavy, and by the time he reached the top of the steep stairway his lungs were laboring.

He entered a light and lofty room with pale walls and a high ceiling. In the center stood a carved oak trunk, a table, and several haphazardly arranged chairs. Andrew put down the stool and rested on a narrow day-bed with a seat of woven cane.

He was mopping his brow with his sleeve when Sophie arrived. Her snug bodice, which complemented the ivy leaves block-printed on her muslin gown, accentuated the swelling bosom and womanly hips.

Depositing her armload of books on the table, she said, "Such a beautiful day! God's weather, as we say on Jersey: *du temps du Bouon Dgieu.* You're wondering why these things are here—this is to be my studio. A place to sketch and paint, and study the letters and receipts I'm using to restore the gardens."

"Can't Cass hire someone else for that? As mistress of Bevington you must have other duties taking up your time and attention."

Her cheeks had turned bright pink. By God, she was blushing!

"Su—supervising your staff," he stammered, trying to banish his image of the newlyweds engaged in their nocturnal activities. "Receiving the local gentry. That sort of thing."

"I prefer to spend my time outdoors. Not that I've abdicated my responsibilities—*naturellement,* I continue to meet with the housekeeper and butler. I approve menus and decide which chambers want airing. It's not so tedious, for my sister-in-law has a talent for hiring efficient servants." Her chin lifted as she said, "But I've made it plain to his lordship what is most important to me."

Andrew's spirits rose at this sign of defiance. So, he thought with satisfaction, the understanding between the lord and his lady was not perfect after all. "And what does Cass say?"

She forced back her shoulders in a determined gesture. "He is learning the things I cannot change about myself."

"He never fails in having his way, you know. That is something you must accept—or else be miserable. I did warn you."

Shaking her head, she said, "You mistook my meaning. I am content, I have no regrets. Since our wedding I have known such happiness, Mr. Searle."

Why, he wondered, could she not call him by his name? In his dreams she always did.

"I've heard a terrible tale about your husband," he told her, "and another woman."

"A false report, *bein seux*. Not a word of it is accurate." She laughed, poor deluded creature.

"Cass is denying what others have seen?"

"Ask him about it yourself," she said airily. "There's an explanation but not one I care to give myself—certainly not to a man. I must go now. We're having a strawberry party in the gardens today. Daniel picked all the fruit himself. Will you join us?"

Andrew hesitated. He didn't particularly care to watch Cass dote on her. On the other hand, it was imperative that he assess the vulnerabilities of their marriage.

He accompanied her to the rose bower, where Cass and Cecelia and the boy were seated on cushions around a low table. All the silver accoutrements and utensils gleamed: tea urn, sugar bowl, creamer, basins heaped with ripe berries. Cass was filling the three silver goblets with Rhenish wine.

"Sophie and I will share," he said. "You've kept to yourself lately, Drew. Can we expect a new volume of poetry or another philosophical treatise in the near future?"

Mockery, from one who'd been his closest, dearest friend. Unkindness would be repaid, he vowed, and by deed rather than with words. Coolly he replied, "I contemplate a very different project for the summer."

Seducing the bride you were so quick to betray, he thought savagely.

"Take care not to overtax your strength, Mr. Searle,"

Cecelia cautioned him. "Dr. Jenner warned it could have fatal consequences."

"Fear not," Cass interjected. "Drew isn't reckless."

Andrew smiled thinly. "Unlike you." The ladies were amused, but he hadn't been jesting.

"Tante Sophie," said Daniel, "see how 'normous these berries are." He passed her the bowl.

She selected one and sank her white teeth into the succulent flesh. "*Pèrfection*," she declared.

It was, Andrew realized, the same exultant tone he heard in his recurring dream.

"Tio, can Luis see us from up in heaven?"

The child's piping question brought a grave expression to his uncle's face. "Luis isn't dead, Daniel."

"Maria says so."

"She's mistaken," Sophie assured him. "He will soon be back at Bevington. Your *tio* has sent a letter to Colares and placed an advertisement in the newspapers in Lisbon and London, so he'll know how much we miss him."

"I wish he'd hurry home." After this wistful comment, the boy declared that he was full. Under severe questioning, he admitted with a mischievous twinkle that he'd eaten a portion of the strawberry crop while picking it. Calling to his gangly pup, he departed for the bowling green, and the cave in the wall.

Sophie continued to sample the fruit. Andrew watched her, sipping his wine, while the Carysforts engaged in a private dialogue that rapidly disintegrated into a quarrel.

"I resent that charge, Cecelia," Cass blustered. "I'm always careful when it comes to Daniel, you know it well. In this instance, you're the one who's being careless."

"Don't cast blame on me!" his sister shot back. "There's too much uncertainty about this procedure."

Sophie murmured to Andrew, "They disagree about having Daniel inoculated against the smallpox."

"It may be dangerous," Cecelia persisted, looking to the others for support.

"It isn't," her brother declared. "At worst he'll feel unwell for a few days. If he catches the disease, he could be scarred for life, or perhaps die. To me, that seems the greater danger by far. Think on, Cecelia—do you really believe that I, of all people, would allow any harm to befall that child?"

His quiet question blocked the protest on her lips. Twisting one long black ringlet around her finger, she shook her head. "You would not."

"Well, then," he said. "If I fear nothing, why should you?"

Her inward struggle was apparent. "I live with fear night and day. This is little better than an experiment."

"One that has succeeded," he reminded her.

"Perhaps." She chewed her lip. "You'll never grant me any peace till I agree, and my nerves cannot take this constant arguing. Tell Dr. Jenner he may come, but I want to be present while he performs the inoculation."

"We'll both be there. Sophie, too."

Another victory for Cassian, thought Sophie. The force of his will was so strong that he'd overruled the boy's own mother.

He edged closer to her and murmured, "I was studying the roses before you came. My wine-colored one will bloom soon, I think."

Sophie tipped her head to one side. "It is a great mystery, *vraiment,* your interest in the Velvet rose."

"I shall explain all at the proper time." His blue eyes shone back at her. "I have a plan."

How cruel of him to tease her with soft looks and softer words when they could be observed by others. As a punishment, she jumped up and held out her hand to the poet. "Mr. Searle, let me show you the pink Scotch rose—the buds are already unfurling. If you have your penknife, you can cut some to take back to the cottage."

Andrew Searle was quick to accept her invitation, scrambling up from the ground. She laid her fingers on his arm and together they walked across the grass. Glancing back, she saw that brother and sister had resumed their private conversation. From the way their glossy black heads rose and fell, she assumed that a truce had been established.

"They're heavy things, those benches," Emrys Jones grumbled to Sophie. "Nothing for it but to shift them by cart. The turf will be spoiled with hoof and wheel marks."

She ran her hand up and down the pony's nose. "The ruts can be filled in."

"May I ride him?" asked Daniel, tugging at the gardener's green work apron.

At a nod from Sophie, he lifted the child onto the pony's broad back.

The proper siting of her new garden ornaments was of paramount importance. Surveying the wall, she said, "Mrs. Fonseca and I want the benches to go on either side of this garden, in the niches. Have you measured to see if they'll fit?"

"Aye, my lady, there's space enough."

"Then instruct the men to proceed."

The Welshman's long head moved from side to side. "Can't put a bench over here, my lady."

"Why ever not? The peafowls have roosted elsewhere."

"Soft earth. Too soft."

"But we've not had rain for days, and this spot is so sheltered." Disappointed, she pressed her forehead against the pony's cheek. "I wanted to surprise the earl—he'll be back from Lord Ducie's by midday." She considered for a minute before instructing him. "Tell the Parham boys to fetch shovels and a barrow of crushed stone. They can level the ground and fill it in to support the weight." His reluctance to endorse her command increased her impatience. "Go," she urged him. "We haven't much time—and two seats to set in place."

"My lady, if you but wait, we can make a firmer foundation with flat stones. That would be better by far."

Her nature, as Cassian so often pointed out, was a stubborn one, and he'd given her many a lesson in willfulness. She marched over to the workers and gave the orders herself, explaining exactly what she wanted done. They scattered to obtain the necessary materials.

After they left, Emrys Jones continued his attempt to dissuade her.

"You'll regret it," he told her, holding a basket while she clipped vibrantly pink Portland roses.

The men came back and began to dig, jesting and laughing as they worked.

Sensing a shift in the breeze, Sophie scanned the skies and saw dark clouds blowing in from the Severn—a sure sign of showers. Cassian would get wet, but he'd insisted on riding instead of taking the carriage. Exasperating man!

"Daniel," she called to her nephew, "best go inside. You mustn't take a chill so soon after the inoculation. And your mother says she'd like to give you another music lesson today."

The child climbed down from the pony's back unassisted. "When will you tell me the story of Geoffrey's Leap?" he asked.

"Not till you're able to play a piece for me on the pianoforte."

That response sent him hurrying away.

"What does his lordship think of the music lessons?" asked Emrys Jones.

"He suggested them. That surprises you?"

"He seems the sort to toughen yon lad with manly occupations," he said bitterly. "Teaching him to ride and shoot instead of letting him practice keyboard tunes and run about the flower beds all day."

Sophie was saved the trouble of answering his strange remark by a shout from the workers.

"Ho, there, Mr. Jones!"

"M'lady! Come and see!"

The gardener, his jaw clenched, marched across the grass. Sophie, mindful of her dignity, held herself back to a slower pace.

"Something's buried here," the eldest told them. "Ground's been dug afore, that's why 'twas so soft."

"P'raps it's treasure," said the youngest, who was Nan's brother.

"Makes no difference to you," his cousin retorted. "You'll have no share in't."

The third Parham, who had continued working diligently, suddenly dropped his shovel and backed away. "Hair," he said in a strangled voice. He turned a horrified face upon Sophie.

"Your ladyship won't want to stay. I'll swear 'tis a body layin' there."

Giving no outward show of alarm, Emrys Jones knelt down and thrust his bare hands into the loosened soil. Then he rose, removing his round hat and hanging his silvered head.

Sophie's blood ran cold. "Who can it be?" As she spoke, the memory of a swarthy face and winning smile flashed in her mind.

Non, non, non. Impossibl'ye.

He was in Portugal, where it was always warm and sunny. Not buried in the cold, damp Gloucestershire soil.

One day I go back there, see my home again...

She began to weep, silently, praying that it was not so.

Emrys Jones sent the Parham lads away to fetch more tools for digging—horse blankets—a pail of water. He turned to Sophie, saying gently, "You shouldn't be here, my lady. There are things you must do—a doctor should be sent for, to certify the death."

"Whose death?" she wondered, eyes streaming.

"We'll not be sure till they raise the body."

"If what I fear is true, how shall I tell the earl?"

She didn't have to.

Her husband heard about the grim discovery as soon as he rode into the stable yard. By then the excavation was complete and the identity of the corpse was no longer a matter of speculation.

When he entered the rose garden, Sophie ran to meet him. He caught her in his arms and held her close while she sobbed into his chest. "I know," he said. "I know."

"Emrys Jones recognized his clothes—and more. I couldn't look. They wrapped him in a blanket and laid him in the cart."

He stroked her hair. She knew it was her place to comfort him, but she felt helpless to do so. This tragedy, unlike the loss of Tobias, had come upon her unexpectedly, without warning. It was an abrupt and horrible end to the idyll she'd been enjoying, and all her hopes for a happy future now seemed as empty as Luis Costa's shallow grave.

CHAPTER 19

All nature mourns, the skies relent in show'rs,
Hush'd are the birds, and clos'd the drooping flow'rs.

~Alexander Pope

The sorrow that descended upon the lord of Bevington Castle affected his entire household.

To Sophie's astonishment, Cecelia swiftly recovered from a brief spell of hysteria and demonstrated an unimagined stoicism as Cass delivered the unhappy news to Daniel. They answered tearful questions and assured him the valet's mysterious death had been accidental.

The Portuguese nurse Maria, who had prophesied Luis Costa's tragic end, was the most vocal of his mourners. She lit candles in her personal shrine to the Holy Virgin and begged Senhorio to arrange for the Catholic priest in Bristol to say a mass for her *pobre* Luis.

Rain fell incessantly and ominously the next day. Sophie sought the peace of her pavilion workroom to immerse herself in the history of the gardens. But she couldn't evade memories of the dark youth who had admired them so much. Or the glimpse of his long-neglected body, removed to the Bevington Arms for the coroner's inquest.

Nor could she dismiss the multitude of questions raised that morning by the local justice of the peace, who was investigating the apparent murder. She'd been present when her husband gave an account of his castle visit prior to his servant's disappearance, and heard him describe his futile inquiries throughout the neighborhood. But his reserve struck Sophie as odd, and she noticed that he did not mention his London trip. When Mr. Lott asked whether Luis had been the target of any threats, Cassian had shrugged and professed ignorance.

Footsteps on the stair caught her attention. Andrew Searle, rumpled and glum, materialized in the doorway.

"I'm hiding," he told her sheepishly, "from that Lott fellow. I refuse to speak about what I know, much less all that I suspect."

"You harbor suspicions?" asked Sophie, laying down her pen. "Even if there was no mark on the body to indicate violence, I fear it to be a case of murder."

"Undoubtedly." His lids drooped, hooding his eyes.

"But Luis was so friendly, so engaging. I can't imagine anyone wishing to do him harm."

"Did you never hear Cass upbraid him? All of his dependents have suffered the effects of his hasty temper at some time or other, but he bullied the Portuguese boy more than most."

Sophie's temper surged at the charge against her husband. *"Impossibl'ye!"* she burst out angrily. "He is good to his employees—I was one of them. You're no friend to him if you can go about saying such things, accusing him of brutality.

And implying he might have committed a—a crime!"

"I've known him far longer than you," he pointed out soberly. "Have you forgotten my warning to you, after you became engaged?"

"It was nonsensical."

"Hold on to that opinion if you prefer. If it comforts you."

Fury was giving way to fear. "Cassian," she whispered. *"Nânnîn*—that is madness. He relied on Luis, he was fond of him. He regarded him as a trusted and faithful servant. He tried so desperately to find him." Driven by her chaotic thoughts, Sophie crossed from her desk to the day-bed.

Dirt all over his clothes. Sophie wished she hadn't suddenly recalled that stray detail. "From playing with Daniel," she reminded herself.

"Sorry?"

"Nothing," she said, refusing to let her mind wander farther down that treacherous road.

"Luis worked for the Carysforts at the time of Daniel's birth. All those years in Portugal, he lived with them." After a pause, Andrew went on, "I've often observed that my friend's affection for his nephew seems more paternal than avuncular. Whereas Cecelia Fonseca is the least maternal female I've ever encountered. Recollect the way Cass persuaded her to have Daniel inoculated: 'Do you really believe that I, of all people, would allow any harm to befall that child?'"

She stared at him.

"His words stuck with me. I've often pondered them. And I therefore question whether the boy is his son, not hers. And if Cass sired Daniel," he mused, "Luis would have known. He might have threatened to tell."

"A weak motive for a murder," Sophie declared shakily.

"What difference would the truth make?"

"To a prospective wife, a great difference. Would you have accepted Cass so readily had you known that another female had borne him a son?"

"Do not talk of this," she cried, "I won't allow it! Yes, my husband has many moods, his temper is uneven. He might have kept a Portuguese mistress, and Daniel might even be his son. But I refuse to accept that Cassian is capable of taking a life. If he were such a *vilain,* I'd feel it—I'm sure I would. He is not, Mr. Searle."

Her evident distress pleased Andrew. Though his plan had been less effective than he'd hoped, he'd planted a seed of doubt. She sat before him, stunned into stillness, on the day-bed that figured in his most intensely erotic dream of her.

Just last night he'd sported with a lewd and playful Sophie—spreading her creamy thighs to receive him, sighing his name as he poured his seed into her. "You, only you," she had crooned, "will give this castle its next lord."

His vision was prophetic. The next earl would spring from his loins and issue from her womb. Exactly when this conception would occur, he didn't know. Sophie wouldn't turn to him until her faith in Cass was destroyed. Observing her despair, Andrew considered the other means by which he could increase her nascent mistrust of her husband. Cass had so many filthy secrets that he could use to blacken him in his wife's eyes.

While Sophie's head was bowed, he dug into his coat pocket and removed a small box of hammered tin. With thumb and forefinger he took a pinch of the grainy substance inside and placed it on his tongue—the bittersweet cure for his pangs. Pure opium, mixed with dark West Indies sugar. When she glanced up, he pretended to brush at his nose.

"You take snuff now?" she asked in surprise.

"I began years ago," he replied, "when I lived in London. I picked up the habit from Cass. I could enlighten you about his whole history."

"Whatever I wish to know, I shall ask him myself."

"My dear Sophie," said Andrew wryly, "you would be a fool to believe anything he tells you. Only with lies can he stave off disaster."

The inquest jurors returned a verdict of murder, "by person or persons unknown." Suspicion immediately fell upon a specific person. Rumor drifted outward from the castle like thick black smoke, to the village houses and shops, and all the farms scattered along the vale. The Earl of Bevington had slain his Portuguese servant in a wild rage and buried the body in the garden.

Sophie refused to accept that her husband was responsible for the most heinous crime in Bevington since the unproven murder of Frances Charlotte, the Harlot Countess. Her commitment to him was more powerful and all-encompassing than she'd imagined possible. Even though he never referred to the accusation, she knew that it was agony for a man so proud.

Several days after the inquest the rain clouds lifted. From a desperate wish for activity, she made her long overdue inspection of the Parham dairy, the largest and most productive in the district.

The dairywoman first introduced her to the herd of red-brown Gloucestershire cows. Despite their small horned heads and elegant long necks, Sophie did not consider them as pretty as her Jerseys, but she admired the quality of the cheese they produced.

"I know all my girls by name," boasted Miss Parham before they left the pasture. "There's our Marigold, a nesh little creature. The gurt cow nearest her is Willow, one of our best milkers. We milk them in the field, after dawn and before dusk."

"For me, a most familiar task."

The dairywoman was a reminder of Sophie's own aunt, despite being so tall and strapping, with fading blonde hair tucked under her ribboned mobcap. Tante Douce Nicolle was small and round and dark-haired. Both ladies were spinsters living full and busy lives.

"I'm lucky to have kept all my maids and men," Miss Parham said. "As you know, the slightest change—a new pair of hands, for instance—affects the creatures. And their milk."

"I understand you manage the dairy yourself."

"Aye, m'lady, with my eldest niece assisting me. Come and see our dey-house." She led Sophie through an enclosure where her dairymaids washed the utensils of their trade: tin skimming dishes, butter prints, cheese knives, and milking pails. One scrubbed the inside of a barrel churn with a bristle brush. Another pegged the damp cloths and aprons to a drying line.

The dairy house was airy and well-lit, with a stone floor still damp from a recent mopping and wooden tables displaying neat rows of cream jars. Miss Parham guided Sophie to a spacious room with four large cheese presses.

"We produce double and single cheeses," she explained. "At this season we prepare as much of our Double Bevington as we can. Come July we cease making it, for cheeses don't firm up proper in summer."

"How many pounds?" asked Sophie.

"Near seventy pounds per day, I reckon, over the seven months my cows are in milk." Moving to a wooden shelf lined with cloth-covered cheeses, she lifted the gauzy material to show off the product. "Here are the pressed ones ready for their first salting. We do add color, to oblige the factor and his customers. 'Twas a time when such alteration was frowned on. Cheeses are turned once a day, and when they're firm enough we begin the monthly washing. If they sink down in the water, they're judged good. The floaters are 'hove'—hollow at the center—and sold cheap. If we go up to the cheese chamber, you can see where they dry and ripen."

They climbed a wooden stair to a lofty area filled with long shelves, all filled with cheeses.

"I thought they'd be darker," Sophie commented.

"Aging turns Gloucestershire ruddy at the surface. Other dairywomen paint the outside rind to add more color, which I confess I much dislike. Lord Bevington gave me leave to abandon that false practice. But because yellowy Gloucester cheeses are in such demand nowadays, we daren't neglect the internal coloring. These will be sorted 'cording to dryness, and wiped with a cloth once a fortnight until sold."

"And who takes them off your hands, those that you don't dispose of locally?"

"I deal with a factor from Berkeley, Mr. Hicks. In this dairy we also make whey butter for sale—it goes out to Dursley market. I've packed some of my freshest milk butter for your ladyship to take back to the castle."

When they went downstairs, she presented Sophie with a

wooden basket with a lid. Inside were half a dozen prints of firm butter, each covered with a broad green leaf.

"Butter leaves, we call 'em," said the dairywoman, "taken from the orach plant. Look underneath."

Sophie removed the covering and found that the butter was embossed with the head of a stag in a rose collar, identifying it as a product of Bevington Vale.

"'Tis the least I can do, given all the unpleasantness you've known lately. We Parhams have made it plain that none may accuse our earl of murder without getting his head broke for it," Miss Parham said fiercely. "His lordship may count on us to defend him against this foul gossip."

Sophie sighed. "It causes a great deal of harm." And pain.

"The more fools they who do the gossiping. We may ne'er discover what happened to that poor foreign lad, and 'tis useless to prate on about what we can never know."

This sensible view was not, Sophie suspected, shared by many of the locals.

"Our lads oftimes pass their evening in the village alehouse. They've heard one other person named as culprit."

Her grip on the basket handle tightened. "Who?"

"That fey Welshman. 'Tis whispered hereabouts that he fancies men. The old earl coddled him and kept him close, then left him money and a house. So long as he troubled no one else and kept to himself, naught was said 'gainst him— though no parents would send their sons to work in the castle gardens. That poor boy from Portugal was pretty, wasn't he? Well," concluded Miss Parham, shaking her head, "here I am telling tales myself, after criticizing others for't."

During her ride back to the castle, Sophie considered the account she'd heard from the otherwise scrupulous Miss

Parham. Emrys Jones, somewhat effeminate in appearance and manner, was regarded as a possible culprit. Was there any foundation for such suspicion, apart from his oddity?

Thinking back, she remembered how intrigued Luis had been by Jones.

Senhorio, he warn me no go near Senhor Shones.

This jardineiro, I no think he like me.

Perhaps, she mused, Emrys Jones had liked Luis entirely too well.

The gardener had strongly advised against setting the bench in the place where the valet's body had been buried. To prevent the discovery of his crime?

When she had delivered the butter basket to the castle kitchen, Sophie made her way to her gardens. The Welshman was thinning snapdragons in the lower terrace border.

"Nearly done," he said, looking up.

She dreaded this confrontation, but she would venture anything to save Cassian. "I must ask you some questions about Luis Costa, Mr. Jones. And—and you."

His thin lips pressed together.

"I give you my word that I'll hold whatever you say in confidence. No one else need know—you can be truthful in your answers."

"I be an honest man, my lady. From what cause do you doubt it?"

"Did you ever seek him out, or make advances towards him?" She could hardly believe she'd voiced the shameful question.

Resentment thinned his voice. "Aren't you asking whether I killed him?"

"Perhaps you feared he'd mention your—overtures. Is that

how it happened? I won't deliver you up to the authorities," she promised. "I'll find some way to get you across the sea to Ireland. Or over the Channel to Jersey. Or wherever you care to go. But I must know the truth." She placed a clenched fist upon her breast. "In my heart I believe my husband is innocent."

"But in your head, you can't be certain." His drawn face expressed pity. "I wish I might dispel your doubt, my lady, but I can't. I committed no murder. I didn't place his body in the ground, I only took it out. 'Tis hard enough living with that memory. And I'll not remain in a place where I be accused of what I never did."

"Bouon Dgieu, I don't know what to believe. Do you mean that you are not a—" A what? A lover of men? "That you don't—" She gave up, and regarded him in doubtful silence. "It's a hanging offense."

"What the villagers say behind my back, there be truth in it—but not the entire truth. I ne'er loved but one man, God rest him. I'm not one as chases young boys, howe'er engaging. Luis was safe from me. I kept my distance, as his lordship warned me to do."

"Warned you? When was that?"

"Soon after you persuaded me to be gardener again. And once more, when he came here from Bath with his servant and the little boy. Followed me like a pup, Luis did, and what could I do to stop it? He was lonely. He liked flowers. In that we were alike, and I let myself warm to him. A mistake. None would e'er believe my feelings to be fatherly. After he disappeared, the earl came back and questioned me. I said nothing of the friendliness between his valet and me, lest it be misconstrued."

That she could understand. Tortured as she was by her personal pain, she couldn't help being moved by his.

"My lady, dearly as I want to help you restore and maintain these gardens, I will not. Nor do you wish me to. Not any longer."

"Mr. Jones—Emrys, I spoke out of fear, and confusion. Don't leave me to manage everything without you." This strange and prickly specimen had become more than an associate and fellow gardener—he was very nearly a friend.

"You say that, knowing what kind of man I am?"

"I admire your skills. But not as much as I do your candor." She let that sink in before adding, "As a man who once loved deeply, you surely understand why I believe in his lordship's innocence."

His gray head bowed. "My lady, I pray he deserves your trust."

He made no attempt to conceal his doubt. Sophie was prepared to mount a staunch defense but was prevented by the woman waving at her from the upper terrace.

Her mind was playing tricks. What was Tante Douce Nicolle doing here at Bevington?

Trouble at Anneville, she feared, flying up the terrace steps.

But her aunt beamed a greeting and eagerly held out her plump little arms. "Here I am, sent by the family to meet this earl you wed so suddenly. And to see your home—*ah, ca,* it's grander than the castle at Gorey! His lordship showed me every room, and even let me peek into the kitchen and cellars."

"Miss Nicolle arrived while you were out," Cass explained to Sophie.

"Tante Douce to you, my lord," the visitor reprimanded him, her cheeks dimpling in a smile. "I startled him with my desire to see everything instead of lying down in my chamber."

He acknowledged, "I've already discovered that Nicolle

females are rarely restful."

"Give me all the home news," begged Sophie. "Is Méthe well, and Philippe's family? And Brelade and his *emigrée* bride? Will Tanmin wed his sweetheart?"

"Oui-dgia to everything."

"Come up to my sitting room," Sophie invited, "and my maid will bring some tea. You will excuse us, Cassian?"

"Oui-dgia—as you and your Tante Douce say."

When the two ladies were comfortably seated in the tapestry armchairs, the elder confessed, "When your letter informed us of this match you've made, we thought it curious. Having seen the pair of you together, I can most sincerely wish you perfect happiness."

"I believed I'd found it," Sophie confided. "In the beginning there were difficulties. Then, for a brief time, I was the most contented creature on earth. Did Cassian tell you of his servant's murder?"

Her aunt nodded.

"I'm so afraid that more trouble lies ahead. I shall be glad to have you near me. When Tobias lay dying, I longed for you—even more than for Méthe or my brothers."

"Sophie, things cannot be so bad here. *Tch'est qu'i'y'a?*"

Twisting her hands in her lap, she answered, "Everything is the matter. We hide our secrets too well, Cassian and I. His may be darker than mine, and more dangerous."

"What are you keeping from your husband, *p'tite?*"

"The heartaches of my first marriage. How shadowed it was by deceptions and self-sacrifice. He assumes Tobias and I were constantly happy."

"Then you should explain to him how it was."

"And betray Tobias? *Nou-fait!* He must be forever

remembered as the great landscape gardener. And an excellent husband—for he was that." Rising from her chair, she paced the room. "And yet, somehow I must convince Cassian how much I care for him."

"You love him."

Sophie, exhausted from emotion, sank onto the window seat. "More than he knows. I waited too long for the proper moment to tell him. The body was discovered, now cruel rumors are circulating—people here assume he killed Luis. Even his friend Mr. Searle, who has known him many years, is suspicious. That frightens me most of all. Even though I know it cannot be so."

The enfolding arms could not relieve her woes, but she was encouraged by the arrival of so firm and fond an ally.

Releasing Sophie, Tante Douce went to the gate-leg table and opened a small leather-bound trunk studded with brass nails. "Here is your bride-gift," she said, exhibiting several lengths of intricately patterned lace. "It belonged to my French grandmother, for whom you were named."

"But you gave me all your antique lace when I wed Tobias."

"So I believed," her aunt replied. "But long after you left Jersey, I came upon this *baheur* in the attic. I'm so thankful to have another heirloom to present on your second marriage. *Le Bouon Dgieu* works in mysterious ways, *non?*"

Sophie nodded, and even managed a smile.

CHAPTER 20

Read in these roses the sad story
Of my hard fate and your own glory.

~Thomas Carew

Sophie snipped a thorny stem with her secateurs and added another pale pink rose to her overflowing basket. Nymph's Thigh, the French called it, but the prim English had rechristened it Maiden's Blush. She moved on to the exquisitely scented damask Celsiana, with loose petals like crumpled shell-pink silk, and selected several of the choicest blooms. From *Rosa centifolia* she claimed blossoms like large teacups stuffed with petals, the inspiration for so many Dutch flower paintings. The miniature form, dainty *de Meaux*, provided small pink pompoms, tiny enough to make a doll's bouquet. For the sake of variety she searched out some white specimens—a moss rose and the York rose.

How splendid they would look, filling the Chinese porcelain bowl in the guest bedchamber.

Cecelia, who had been fond of her own aunt, exerted herself

to entertain Sophie's. They had remained in the drawing room to study the French fashion book Tante Douce acquired from a Jersey smuggler. Sophie, uninterested in the latest style of gowns, had retreated to the rose garden to ponder a weightier matter—her husband's amorous past.

Cassian's entanglements prior to their marriage remained a source of anxiety. Had he lied when denying that Ines Costa had been his mistress, to hide the fact that the girl who suckled Daniel had also been his mother? She couldn't decide which was worse: his unwillingness to acknowledge his own son, or his and Cecelia's pretense that Daniel was her child.

Reconsidering the Carysfort-Fonseca-Costa triangle, she reviewed Andrew Searle's observation that Cassian treated the boy as a father and the detached Cecelia behaved more like an aunt. What's more, Luis had displayed the fondness and devotion of a blood relative—an uncle.

She stared at the bare ground where his body had lain, haunted by the memory of Cassian's dirty garments at about the time Luis had vanished. But as she'd told Emrys Jones, her husband could not be capable of murder.

The Welshman's failure to come to work today was another worry. By voicing her suspicions and probing his privacy with her questions, she had apparently damaged their relationship beyond repair.

Echo, sunning herself on the lawn, lifted her elegant head, attentive to a human presence. Sophie saw Andrew Searle pass through the arched opening in the garden wall. Unwilling to hear any more of his groundless accusations against her husband, she tried to look very busy.

"I want you to have this." The object he held out was flat and square, wrapped in tattered cloth fastened with a rusty pin.

She severed one more rose stem. "Mr. Searle, I beg you to excuse me. My aunt from Jersey is here, these flowers must go into water at once, and—"

"Please." He pressed his offering upon her.

Through the material Sophie could feel a slim volume with soft covers. "A fresh volume of poems?"

He shook his head. "Read it now, alone. Take it to your chamber in the pavilion. I shall wait for you here. Signal to me from the window when you've finished, and I'll come up. You'll have questions, which I shall answer as best I can."

He looked so ill and unhappy that she hadn't the heart to refuse. She put down her basket.

Carrying the parcel to her workroom, she sat down on the chaise longue to examine it. Under the cloth she found an ordinary memorandum book with an inscription on the cover: *Extracts from the diary of A.S. 1790, 1797.*

She read the first entry.

15th April, '90. Last night Cass produced a vial of Bristol glass, assuring me that its contents would soothe my pains . . . . Laudanum, he declared, relieves his sufferings—what they might be I cannot guess. At his urging, I swallowed the dose. Its power over my mind is not easily described. Vapors of calmness suffused my hitherto busy brain, a sense of lassitude stole over my corpus. A wondrous sensation indeed. Alas, my funds are too limited to allow frequent indulgence. But Cass is a generous fellow, and has offered to supply me with the miraculous substance whenever I may require it.

2nd May, '90. Never have I seen my friend in such a state. Went in search of two w----s and brought them to my lodging, where they entertained us well. Partook of laudanum. C. imbibed more freely than I. Under its influence he grows calm. Without it—alarming wildness and unpredictability. He has abandoned sobriety and is wholly dependent upon the opiate.

15th May,'90. C. comes often, to sit and talk in his dreamy fashion. He no longer seeks polite society but prefers his solitary pleasures. Produced a cake of opium, mixed the laudanum himself.

10th June,'90. The Carysforts will leave the country, sailing for Lisbon tomorrow. I pray C. can find his peace, and break his fatal reliance upon that most dangerous dram.

Desperate to know more, Sophie continued reading.

Recent entries were repetitions of earlier ones. The poet recorded that her husband had taken laudanum regularly and in great quantities—ever since his return to England.

This record of erratic behavior and changeable moods was supported by her own experience. One minute Cassian was all laughter and smiles, outgoing and energetic. The next he would be gruff and curt, holding everyone at a distance.

His trips to London—two since the first of the year—were documented. Andrew speculated about their purpose and Cassian's activities, concluding that he went there to purchase the drug and consort with other opium eaters.

Thinking back to his January visit to her house at Chiswick, she recalled how he'd marched about her sitting room—tense, abrupt, menacing. Suddenly he'd thawed, as if by magic, and when attempting to lure her to Bevington, he'd plied his charm.

No, she protested, he hadn't taken a drug. She'd been with him all the time. Except, she recalled, when she'd left the parlor to fetch her cloak. Afterwards he had seemed so much calmer.

He'd traveled to London seeking Luis but had admitted he visited Guildford as well, offering no explanation. He returned to Bevington wan and fatigued, blaming his condition on the state of the roads. But while making love to her that night, for the first time, he'd seemed perfectly well. Had laudanum been responsible for his rapid recovery?

She forced herself to study the journal's final paragraph.

> _30th April, '97._ _Tomorrow they marry. Was I mistaken to keep silent so long? By telling everything I know, and what I fear will in time be revealed, I can save her from disaster. If C. is the boy's natural father, she deserves to know. But can I convince her, on the eve of the wedding, that C. murdered Luis Costa in a frenzy brought on by the pernicious drug? He cannot hide his sickness forever, and I grieve for his unsuspecting bride. For I am sure the poor servant is dead, and lost his life because of what he knew._

There, starkly written in Mr. Searle's legible script, was the accusation he had voiced. But this time he not only presented a motive, he documented a long history of instability.

Chièr Cassian, she mourned, why did you not confess these

things to me? They are terrible, *vraiment*. But I would not have deserted you.

Nor could she desert him now, knowing all.

She returned to the rose bower. Andrew Searle paced the bridge spanning the canal, hands folded behind his back.

"Here is your book. I will not keep it."

"I'm so sorry, Sophie."

She waved away his apology—his sympathy.

"You needed to know. I just hope I didn't wait too long."

"Please go. I cannot make sense of anything just now."

"Of course not. You are shocked. Your husband is not the man you believed him to be. He married you under false pretenses."

None of his phrases held any meaning for her. Putting a hand to her head, she said wearily, "I must think. And pray," she choked, as tears filled her eyes.

She managed to ascend the terrace steps without breaking her neck, but failed to make it all the way up the winding stair to her bedchamber. Collapsing halfway, she wept as she had not done since the day of Tobias Pinnock's funeral.

The sorrow she carried in her heart was akin to what she'd felt then. She had a living husband now, but in many ways he was a stranger. Addict, father, teller of lies, keeper of secrets. Murderer?

She faced a repetition of the pain and lies that had plagued her last years with Tobias. Once more she felt duty-bound to safeguard her beloved's health, while at the same time salvaging his reputation. This time the task ahead seemed even more formidable.

Even after shedding all her tears she sat there, slumped over in agony. Her entire body felt leaden and numb, she simply could not move.

A soft exclamation from the bottom of the stairwell roused her from her stupor. "My lady!" Nan Parham regarded her worriedly. "Did you slip?"

"No. I am well." No matter that it was untrue. "I left my basket of roses beneath one of the arbors. Would you fetch them, please, and set them in a vase of water?"

When the servant obeyed, she retreated to her room to bathe her face. Braving the ungenerous mirror, she applied a dusting of powder to her cheeks and nose to cover the redness.

"Sophie, *es-tu toute seule?*"

That was her aunt, calling up to her. *"Oui,"* she answered, "very much alone." With a doubtful glance at her reflection, she hurried down to her sitting room.

"I've had the most pleasant time with your sister-in-law while you were *au gardin*. A lovely creature, and such fine music she makes on the keyboard!" The stream of cheerful words suddenly broke off. "Sophie, *p'tite*, what is wrong?"

"My husband. *Oh, las,* he is so very ill, and needs my help. All my strength as well."

Her aunt led her to the window seat, where she sat down. While giving a brief account of Andrew Searle's diary and its revelations, she held on tightly to Tante Douce's plump fingers.

"Luis Costa's death was an accident. Cassian would not have harmed him—in his right mind."

"And he has a child," her relative said softly. "Do you believe it?"

"I love Daniel, whether Cassian is his father or not, but he's the least of my problems now. I care only about saving my husband from himself."

"How can you?"

Sophie rose. "By persuading him to go away, as he did before. His habit of taking laudanum can be broken. If he gave it up when he lived in Portugal, as it seems he did, he can do it again." With a flash of inspiration, she said, "We might take him to Jersey—to Anneville. I'll say I want to introduce him to the rest of the family. You can support me, saying how very much they want to meet him. I'll not reveal my real reason till we're safely across the Channel."

Nodding her dark head, the other lady said, "Our island in summer would cure any disorder—the healthful sea breezes, the warm sunshine. Brother Edouard would be happy to have you at the manor house again."

"Or we could take a cottage of our own."

"If the earl is so unpredictable, is it wise to be alone with him?"

"I'm in no danger," Sophie said confidently. "He cares for me. And he needs me. I cannot fail him. I will not."

"He might fail you, *p'tite*. Too many men become addicted to strong drink, and fail to break the habit. What if laudanum has too powerful a hold upon him?"

Sophie refused to give in to pessimism. "There was so little I could do for Tobias, my helplessness was unbearable. For Cassian there is a remedy. I have to believe that."

For his sake she'd salve her pain. She must forget that empty grave among the roses, or the fresh one in the churchyard where Luis was buried. For the time being she wouldn't fret over a little boy unaware that his adored uncle was his father. Or pity the tortured friend who had come forward with so many terrible truths. Nothing was as important to her as Cassian.

During dinner she struggled to maintain her composure. Covertly she studied the handsome figure seated at the opposite end of the long table, and prayed those fine blue eyes wouldn't pierce her protective armor of bravado.

At last they retired to their suite of rooms, where her masquerade of unconcern was almost impossible to sustain. Her monthly indisposition had recently subsided—Cassian had counted the days with her. After the week-long respite he assumed she shared his eagerness for marital relations to resume.

She was seated before the dressing table in her chamber, undecided about whether to spend the night in her bed or his, when he came to her.

"Leave your hair loose tonight," he said huskily, undoing her half-finished braid. "For me."

"Bein seux, if you prefer."

"Come with me—now." His need was a powerful tide surging at her, breaking through her defenses.

She did not protest but accompanied him to the room where she'd passed so many blissful nights. Dozens of glowing candles covered every surface—the mantel shelf, the mahogany chest, the window seat.

"Close your eyes," he commanded.

She searched his face for signs of intoxication, or insensibility.

"Don't look so fearful. Trust me."

His smile was irresistible. She forced her eyelids shut, then flinched at his touch. Slowly he removed her shift, leaving her vulnerable to the cool air, and when she shivered his arm circled her waist.

"I'll lead you to the bed." Slowly he guided her across the floor. "You can lie down now. But no peeking."

Her bare back pressed against the soft coolness of the sheet.

"I'll be back," he whispered.

She heard him moving about, and guessed that he was shedding his clothes. Then she sensed his approach.

"I hope you can forgive me of this my crime."

Her eyes flew open. He stood naked before her, holding a silver basin overflowing with red. She recoiled, seeing blood. Then he delved deep inside and brought up a handful of—

"Rose petals," she gasped in relief.

They drifted down upon her from above like a crimson waterfall.

As he covered her with his fragrant offering, she asked, "This is what you planned for the Velvet roses?"

"Even before we were wed," he declared, lying down with her. "I knew they would look glorious against your skin. The reality is even more provocative than the picture in my mind." His lips grazed hers.

The romantic gesture would have delighted her, if not for her fearsome new knowledge. Her beloved husband was also an opium addict and a murder suspect. The intimacy they had achieved was merely a delusion. And yet his playful fingers could stir her passion. The muscled body joined to hers provided the joyous release she craved. Her inward tremors and breathless, ecstatic sighs were the same, but at her core she felt hollow and empty and dead. Her physical connection to him remained, but was it no longer enhanced by one of the mind.

Afterwards he gently peeled away the crushed petals sticking to her breasts and abdomen and thighs. Then he plucked the ones that nestled in her maidenhair.

"Did I do wrong," he asked, "to destroy your precious flowers, all for a few fleeting moments of pleasure?"

"Not fleeting," she managed to say. "It is a shared memory."

If he expressed such regret about shredding her roses, his guilt at killing a servant so dear to him must be powerful indeed. When she considered the state of his conscience, pity choked her.

"I should've asked before stripping the flowers from the bushes—which belong to you. Do you think your roses worth the heavy price you paid?"

"What do you mean?"

"To get them, you tied yourself to a selfish, pigheaded person."

She placed her hand upon his heaving chest, in the place she supposed his heart to be. "I would rather belong to you, flawed as you are, than live without your love."

CHAPTER 21

That time is past
And all its aching joys are now no more,
And all its dizzy raptures.

~William Wordsworth

*D*aniel cowered outside the morning room, leaning against the closed door. At Sophie's approach he lifted his head to reveal streaming eyes and a tear-streaked face.

Bending down to him, she asked gently, "What's the matter?"

"You won't let the bad man hurt me, will you?"

"What bad man?" Sophie heard Cassian's raised voice, followed by his sister's hysterical tones.

"I was with Tio Cass," Daniel said, snuggling into her embrace. "Bitton brought a letter for Mama. She read it and began to cry. Then she said, 'We're found out, he's asking about Daniel.' Tio snatched it away from her. He was so angry he said 'damn' and 'hell' and threw the teapot against the wall. My mother cried even harder and then she sent me away."

Sophie tightened her hold on him, angry with the Carysforts for terrifying him with their impetuous outbursts. She didn't care whose son he might be, she only knew he was lonely and fearful and needed comfort. "Daniel, would you like to hear the tale of Geoffrey's Leap?"

"Today?"

"This very minute. My Tante Douce is taking tea in the pavilion. She knows the story far better than I."

"Does she?" Sniffing, he wiped his eyes—so brightly blue, exactly like Cassian's.

"She's the one who told it to me. I know she'll tell you, if you ask."

The brows jutted down in a frown that strengthened the resemblance. "My mother might need me."

"I'll go to her," Sophie promised him.

He scrambled to his feet. After letting her tuck in his shirt and smooth his tumbled curls, he started down the staircase. The moment he was out of view, she stormed into the morning room.

Her sister-in-law moaned, "But how do we keep him away? He might try to—oh, here's Sophie."

She noticed the scrape in the plastered wall and the fragments of floral-patterned china scattered on the floorboards. Glaring at her husband, she demanded, "What happened, to make you forget yourself in front of a child?"

He had the grace to look ashamed. "I lost my temper."

"You should control it better. You know how sensitive Daniel is."

"Cass is leaving for London," Cecelia announced.

"Personal business," he added curtly. "I'll make my apologies to your aunt."

He wouldn't escape her vigilance so easily. She must prevent him from hurting himself, for Andrew Searle's writings indicated that his consumption of laudanum was dangerously excessive.

"I'm traveling with you." Bravely she met his forbidding stare. "We'll stay at my Chiswick house. It's convenient to town and quite comfortable. And William and Mary are there to wait upon us."

"I can't let you accompany me. Not this time."

What foul, unmentionable errand was taking him away? Better not to ask, she thought, unless she wanted to hear more evasions—or outright lies.

"I've neglected my household for many months, *dé vrai*. And this is a chance to see my roses at the peak of bloom. Never fear, I'll be packed and ready to depart in no time at all. Before you are, I daresay." Satisfied that she had scored a point, she turned and left the room.

Her abrupt exit was followed by the sound of shattering porcelain. A teacup had suffered the same dire fate as the pot.

His unruliness was disturbing but couldn't deter her. She had resolved to take him away from the castle, from his clinging, needy sister and impressionable nephew—or son.

At Chiswick she could refine her strategy. If necessary, she would take him even farther from the castle, all the way to Jersey. Once there, she'd confront him about his dependence on opium. By encouraging him to talk about his valet's death, she could relieve him of the burden of his guilt. She was strong, she'd been tested before, and she intended to help him battle all his demons.

Her aunt supported her decision, offering to serve as Cecelia's companion and to keep Daniel amused. "Your place," she insisted, "is with the earl. Stay close, and give him whatever comfort you can. But be careful, Sophie."

Since taking up residence at Bevington, in the midst of winter, she hadn't left Gloucestershire. The hills and meadows along the road to London were mantled with green, leaves covered the trees and the tall, lacy heads of cow parsley bloomed profusely in the roadside verges. During their long hours in the carriage, she alternately studied the view and dozed against her husband's shoulder.

Where the highway was smooth enough to permit reading, he studied a treatise on modern agricultural techniques. Whenever they crossed rougher terrain, he closed his book and commented on the promising advances that would, he hoped, improve the yield of his tenants' farmstead. At Littleworth they broke their journey, passing an uneventful night at an inn.

During the final stages of their drive Sophie noticed that Cassian had become tense and preoccupied, and increasingly uncommunicative.

They arrived at her villa in the afternoon. The drive was laid with fresh pea-gravel. The front lawn was neatly scythed, and she was welcomed by the heady, familiar scent of cut grass. The servants, caught by surprise, greeted her with smiles and tears. Unaccustomed to her elevated status, they failed to address her properly and she dismissed their apologies with a laugh.

Her pleasure in this homecoming faded when her husband announced his need to stretch his legs after the long hours in the carriage. Watching him march down the lane leading to the village, she prayed he wasn't headed for the apothecary's shop.

"All the bedding was recently aired, ma'am," Mary assured

her. "M'lady, I should've said. The parlor furniture is wrapped in holland cloth, which I'll remove at once. Ah, but it does my heart good to have you back here, ma'am—m'lady. A countess now—though you look exactly as you've always done, not a jot of difference that I can see."

Sophie's lips twitched. "You didn't expect me to return wearing a coronet and velvet robes?"

"Nay, but I little thought you'd be wearing that same green traveling habit neither," the housekeeper told her with all the frankness of a longtime employee.

While Mary whisked covers off the parlor chairs, Sophie stepped out onto the terrace. Her planters contained brightly-hued pelargoniums; a passion flower vine twined up a trellis, filtering the afternoon sun.

She followed the path down to the river, pausing in the shade of the willows to watch the swans glide upon the water. The scene she loved and had often painted was unaltered. In this setting she could refute Mary's assertion: she was greatly changed. Outwardly she might look the same, but inwardly she bore no resemblance to the forlorn widow who had trod this Thames-side path last summer.

Her statue garden, with its smooth lawn and shaved hedges, was as appealing as she remembered, carefully maintained by William and the under-gardener. The flowering border along the outside of the kitchen garden was a jumble of roses, delphiniums, columbines, and poppies, exactly as she'd described it to Cassian last January.

She found William pruning the espaliers and nailing the remaining branches to the brick wall to support the fruits just forming. He showed her the progress of his second sowings of carrots and broccoli and lettuce. Complaining much of snails, he demonstrated the various methods he used to combat the pernicious creatures.

While she had inspected her grounds, her housekeeper had restored the parlor to its usual state and thoughtfully placed a vase of roses on a table. Tobias smiled mildly down from his frame on the wall. Sophie's fond gaze moved from the portrait of the man she'd loved dearly and faithfully, to the tall bookcase filled with blue leather volumes.

The last of their kind. She would make no more Blue Books.

When Mary came in to consult her about dinner arrangements, Sophie suggested a simple meal of fish and garden vegetables, to be served on the terrace.

"I've a summery pudding," said the housekeeper. "And I could manage a gooseberry fool, for a choice."

"That will suit us very well. Plain china will do—the Wedgwood creamware."

"Yes, m'lady."

Sophie visited her former bedchamber to sort through the garments she'd left behind in her wardrobe. She found a round gown of white linen printed with multi-colored floral sprays, the first she'd ordered from the dressmaker after setting aside her mourning attire. She plaited some cherry-colored ribbons into her thick braid before coiling it at the back of her head in a chignon. Pleased with the effect, she went to the parlor to wait for Cassian.

She opened a botanical magazine but it failed to divert her. He'd been away for quite a long time. Had he become lost, or was he wandering the countryside in a drugged stupor?

Nothing so dreadful could happen here in peaceful Chiswick, she chided herself.

She concealed the extent of her relief when Cassian returned to the house looking thoroughly rustic. A trace of sunburn bloomed along his high cheekbones, and wisps of straw clung to his black hair.

"What were you doing all this while?" she wondered.

"Exploring. I visited the shops in the high street, and ordered up a pint at a tavern. I made the acquaintance of several sheep—neither friendly nor good conversationalists. When my legs gave out, I rested against a hay-rick."

"You must be exhausted—and hungry." There was strangeness about him, and she couldn't quite define it. "We'll dine *al fresco,* on the terrace."

"Something you and Mr. Pinnock used to do?"

"Occasionally," she answered, "when the weather was this warm. If you'd rather not—"

"It sounds most delightful," he responded, but his smile never quite reached his eyes.

As it turned out, there was nothing at all delightful about their meal. Cassian was meticulously civil, but his quietude made Sophie wary and nervous. He approved the fish and its accompaniments, complimented her choice of wine, and sampled both the summer pudding and the gooseberry fool. But otherwise he said very little.

The air was heavy, the scent of flowers wafted up from the border.

This evening could have been so romantic, thought Sophie wistfully. If he weren't in the sourest of moods, and I hadn't a headache.

Rubbing her temples, she asked whether he carried any laudanum in his traveling case.

"Get some from your woman," he advised her.

"I doubt Mary keeps it," she murmured, trying to decide if

her question had made him self-conscious.

They removed to the candlelit parlor. Cassian hid his face behind the *Times*. Sophie took up her magazine and resumed her reading. Turning a page, she said, *"Ma fé,* here's a surprise! Mr. Curtis engraved and printed my hyacinth illustration. Do you remember, I'd just finished it when you called upon me in the winter. How long ago it seems."

"More than six months," he said, regarding her over the top of his newspaper. "Since that night much has happened. I lured you to Gloucestershire. You created a garden at Summit House. Cecelia and Daniel and I moved from Clifton to Bevington. You and I became engaged. And married."

He'd left out Luis Costa's unsolved murder. Sophie could think of one reason for the omission, and it added to her wretchedness.

"How long have we been wed?" he mused. "Nine weeks, ten? The proposal was a great mistake. In my defense, I never guessed wedlock would be such a hell for you."

She couldn't think what she'd said or done to provoke that bitter remark. "Cassian, what makes you so strange?"

He cast his paper aside impatiently. "I've too much on my mind as it is, without venturing upon the unpleasant subject of our mutual disappointment."

Hurt by the implication that their marriage was failing, she tried not to show it. "Then tell me what business brought you here."

"I can't talk about that, either."

"Now? Or never?"

"I'm not sure." He left the sofa to march about the room, keeping just within the bounds of her Turkish rug.

"I'm your wife. Let me help you."

He paused at the framed portrait. "You're more his wife than mine. You love him—and his house, where you are so much at home."

"I lived and gardened here for five years," she defended herself. "Of course I'm glad to be back. But it's a brief visit. I don't intend to remain."

"Why not? You'll be happier here with your precious flowers and your fawning servants. And all these bloody Blue Books." He flung open the glass doors of the bookcase and removed an armful of leather bound volumes.

He tossed them onto the floor.

"*Nânnîn!*" she shrieked.

He paid no heed, but reached for more, stripping the shelves.

This act of violence was personal. And deliberate—he knew how to inflict the worst sort of pain. She would rather he'd knocked over the vase of roses, or broken the porcelain potpourri dish on the mantel, or thrown his glass of port onto the rug.

"You've no cause to be jealous, Cassian. Listen to me," she pleaded. "I cannot pluck the past out of my heart, but I don't dwell upon it. Neither should you. If I met Tobias now, I mightn't feel what I did for him at sixteen. And if I'd met you then, I couldn't possibly have cared for you in the way I do now."

"You didn't marry me because you loved me."

She couldn't honestly deny the charge. "You rushed me. I hadn't time to fall in love—beforehand."

"You found a set of musty old account books and kept quiet about them while you formed your secret scheme. Your acceptance of my proposal was conditional. You wanted to preserve the Bevington gardens."

"They played no part in my decision—*pon du tout!* Cassian, I'm not so heartless!"

"Oh, you were willing to share my bed, and I rejoiced that it was so. But in this house, Sophie, the bed is yours. And *his.* I cannot forget that."

His tirade had come full circle, back around to Tobias.

His bizarre behavior had nothing to do with laudanum or guilt about Luis Costa. It was an outgrowth of his resentment of her first husband, and for that malady she had no cure. Her marriage was disintegrating before her eyes, and she didn't know how to hold it together.

"I'll take the guest chamber, which your servant so thoughtfully prepared for me."

"For both of us," she insisted, as he stalked out of the room. She'd made the arrangement on his behalf, out of regard for his sensibilities. Much good it had done.

She gathered up the scattered Blue Books and replaced them, not bothering to put them in the proper chronological order. She extinguished all the candles save one, and used it to light her way up the staircase.

Evidently her husband intended to sleep alone tonight. By shutting himself away, he'd also cut off access to her *baheur* and its contents. Going to the other bedchamber, she searched the drawers for an old nightgown. After removing her flowery dress, she went to the mirror to unplait her hair. The cherry ribbons had not enchanted Cassian after all. Another wasted effort.

Gazing at the bed, she rebelled at the prospect of occupying it. Her unreasonable husband would not, she vowed, consign her to an unwelcome, undesired solitude. She did not deserve it. But how could she possibly soften him?

When inspiration arrived, it brought renewed hopefulness. Taking up her chamber stick, she slipped out of the room.

∽

Cass stretched out on the tented bed and studied the shadows thrown against the wall by the oil lamp he'd left on the nightstand. His agricultural book lay neglected. Despite his emotional and physical exhaustion, his interest in sleep was negligible.

He tried to concentrate on his plans for tomorrow. But his quarrel with his wife crowded out all thoughts of stalking Sir Michael Tait.

Cursing his idiocy, he regretted his angry outburst. Sophie had offered him a semblance of the love he'd sought for so long. Why hadn't he accepted it humbly and with gratitude, instead of blustering at her and mistreating her books? If not for his explosive jealousy of a dead man, she would lie trembling beneath him this very minute, singing out her pleasure.

The night was uncomfortably warm and still. He left the bed to raise the sash window higher, tying back the curtains to admit the breeze.

A faint knock on the door told him that his Sophie had come—to make peace, he hoped.

She stood in the unlit corridor, her nightshift hitched up with clenched fists. The bowl of her skirt was filled with rose petals, and when she stepped into the room he saw they were vividly striped, red upon white.

"These are for you." Moving to the bed, she scattered them over his sheets.

When she let the final fistful of petals drop, he spied red

scratches all over her hands and wrists. "You're hurt."

"It's dark outside, and the canes are thorny," she told him matter-of-factly.

Cass seized a linen towel and moistened it with water from the washbasin. Wiping her wounds, he said gently, "I'm not worth a single rose, much less a drop of your blood."

When he placed his hands upon her shoulders, he saw fear flash across her face. Releasing her, he backed away.

He could confess everything, right now. Explain to her the cause of his duel with Tait, and all that had occurred afterwards.

Should he? Shouldn't he?

Better to wait, he decided. Let's have one last night of tranquility before chaos descends upon us both.

"Come to bed," he said quietly.

Sophie crawled beneath the covers, facing outward—away from him. Cass yearned to reach out to draw her near. He'd grown all too accustomed to falling asleep with that smooth head pressed against his shoulder.

After a long period of wakefulness, he slept.

On waking, he found himself alone.

He washed and dressed and descended to the dining room. Sophie sat at the circular pedestal table, filling her cup from a silver tea urn.

"Why didn't you rouse me?" he asked.

"You needed your rest." Her voice was remote, her manner reserved.

"Sophie—" He hardly knew how to begin his apology. "Last night—"

"You're going to London?" she broke in. "Let William know at what hour you want your carriage. Shall I ring for your coffee?"

She played the part of hostess, treating him as a guest. Last night he would have been infuriated. This morning it increased his despondency.

"I'm delivering an invitation to a gentleman living near St. James's. When I return—before he comes here—I'll share with you some matters I was previously unable to disclose."

"Do it now," she suggested.

He shook his head. "No time. The tale I mean to tell is lengthy and complicated. And unsavory. Be patient a little while longer."

The look she gave him was one of disappointment, and her great brown eyes were deep wells of pain. "I'll have Mary lay an extra place for dinner."

It wouldn't be needed. In too great a hurry to linger over his breakfast, Cass downed his coffee in haste.

Within the hour he reached the gates of St. James's Palace. When a crossing sweep hurried to assist him, he extended a silver coin. "I want you to perform a different service than your usual one."

"Aye, sir, anythin' fer that shillin'."

Cass displayed the letter he'd brought—his composition, penned by Cecelia. "Take this to Sir Michael Tait's lodging in Cleveland Row."

"Aisy enough," the youth replied, eyes fixed on the coin.

"I'll show you the house."

At the conclusion of his business, Cass began the six-mile journey to the Chiswick villa to prepare Sophie for what promised to be a volatile—and final—confrontation. Before the day was out she would see the scarred face of his enemy and learn the worst details of her husband's past.

His arrival startled the housekeeper.

"Returned already, m'lord? You've missed her ladyship, she's just gone."

"Gone?" he repeated. "Where to?"

"She bade me give you her note." From her apron pocket she withdrew a folded square.

He carried it to the parlor. Avoiding Tobias Pinnock's painted stare, he broke the seal and scanned the lines Sophie had penned.

My lord, I have taken a post coach to Bevington, where I truly belong. I cannot stay where I am not wanted—or needed. Your devoted—and loving—wife, Sophie Carysfort.

The surname was doubly underlined, for emphasis.

With an oath, he balled the paper in his fist.

"Mary!" he shouted.

Promptly she appeared in the doorway. "M'lord?"

"The nearest posting house, where is it?"

"Turnham Green, m'lord, the Old Pack Horse. 'Fore my mistress went off, she said as how your lordship was having company to dine. Ought I to prepare any special dishes?"

"I doubt the gentleman will stay more than half an hour, if that. But a bottle of your late master's excellent port wouldn't go amiss."

"Very good, m'lord." She bobbed a curtsy. "If 'tis not too bold of me to say it, my William and I wish your lordship and Mrs. Pin—and her ladyship," she corrected herself, "all happiness."

"Thank you, Mary. My thanks to William, also."

"Now we've 'customed ourselves to the change, we agree 'tis a good thing. Eh, but she was a sad little mite afore she went off to live in Gloucestershire, so lonesome-like in this empty house."

Cass battled a fierce desire to chase after Sophie—impossible, when Tait was already making his way to Chiswick. He didn't doubt that the impact of Cecelia's letter been profound, or that it would bring about the intended result.

The Blue Books had been returned to their shelves. On the wall beside the bookcase hung a small picture in a frame, Sophie's profile drawn in charcoal. With a few simple but effective strokes, the artist had captured the sitter's strength of character as well as her almond eyes and perfect nose and sloping cheek. It was a portrait created by a loving, appreciative hand.

Cass hurried out of the room—out of the house.

Wandering the grounds, he traced his wife's influence—the statuary, the clipped evergreens, the profusely colorful borders. In her willow grove he sat on the bench, watching the swans feed and mulling over the housekeeper's words.

He thought long and hard about Tobias Pinnock.

And Sophie.

The sound of an approaching carriage broke off his reverie. Heart thudding, he marched across the lawn.

The baronet had descended from the vehicle. The muscles of his scarred face contracted in a frown. "Bevington! You're also here?"

"This house belongs to my wife. I was recently married."

"I saw the notice in the paper—which informed me of your place of residence. I directed a letter to Bevington Castle, and I conclude that it reached Cecelia. I daresay you never delivered the one I entrusted one to you many months ago. Where is she?"

"Not here."

"But I had a message, begging me to meet her. She wanted to tell me—" Tait's shoulders sagged. "One of your tricks, was it? I might have guessed. Will you never cease to torture me? Seven years ago you struck me in public, at social gathering. You issued a challenge and shot me in cold blood, leaving me with this broken face. You've hidden Cecelia from me. You destroyed a valuable and irreplaceable violin."

"And you killed Luis Costa. Or had him killed. You discarded his carcass and left it to rot, practically under my nose."

"You *are* a demented bastard. I know nothing, and I'm not responsible."

"You deny he was your spy?"

"I do. How many times must I tell you?"

Cass, a master of prevarication, was impressed by Tait's false sincerity. "From whom, then, did you obtain information about Daniel Fonseca?"

"I called upon nearly every ship owner in London. I studied the passenger lists of all vessels sailing from Lisbon in recent years." Tait paused. "That's how I learned Cecelia was with you when you came back from Portugal to claim your title and estate. So was Daniel Fonseca. I haven't yet discovered who he might be, but I've got my suspicions."

"Keep them to yourself," Cass retorted. "I'm more concerned with solving a murder." He turned his back on the baronet and retraced the path to the waterway.

Tait followed him. "Your Luis Costa knew all about the mysterious Daniel. Is he a man? Or a boy? Answer me! If you don't, you'll regret it."

"Are you threatening me, Tait?"

"What good would that do? I haven't your taste for violence, or your talent for fisticuffs. Are you planning to rough me up and toss me into the river to drown? Well, get on with it, if you must. I've got nothing to live for."

Cass gave a harsh laugh. "God knows how you can make yourself out to be the tragic hero, when we both know you're the villain of this sordid piece. For lack of evidence I suppose I must acquit you of murder. But you were an adulterer. And you seduced my sister."

"I fell in love. As she did."

"That's no justification. You were married, and she was quite young."

"My wife was flagrantly unfaithful, you knew that. Virtually a whore—you must've been the only man in London who never bedded her. I could have initiated a divorce, only it wasn't worth the trouble and expense and scandal. Until I met Cecelia."

"Spare me," Cass muttered. "I've heard all this before."

"I love her still. And I'm free. She is widowed—a grieving widow. Or so you've said."

Cass clenched his jaw.

"How I used to admire your honesty—your integrity. In the political and social realm, those qualities are rare indeed. Are you still so honorable, Cass? Do you deal in truth, or falsehoods?"

"I don't deal with you at all," he growled. "Neither will Cecelia."

"You challenged me to a duel. Your reasons were known only to us. You wounded me but not fatally. You punished me for seducing Cecelia, as I probably deserved. And then you exiled yourselves for many years in a distant country. Where she married the conveniently dead Fonseca. Was that a fiction, concocted out of necessity?"

Cass maintained his silence. He stared impassively down at his interrogator, certain of the question that was coming.

"But what could be the motive for such a deception? I can think of only one. And it solves the riddle of Daniel." Narrowing his eyes, the baronet said, "You call me adulterer and seducer, and rightly so. But there's one thing you are most reluctant to name me."

"And what might that be?"

"Father of your sister's son."

CHAPTER 22

Then rose the Seed of Chaos...

~William Blake

$\mathcal{S}$ ipping tea in the parlor of the Crown Inn at Faringdon, Sophie hoped she hadn't made a grave error. To prove she loved Cassian above all, she'd turned her back upon her former home and all the symbols of her past life. And she had left him alone. If he did something harmful to himself, she would be responsible.

During the sleepless hours she had lain at her husband's side, she'd faced the bitter truth that she could do nothing to save him. Until he acknowledged his troubles and turned to her for help and comfort, her interference would be a source of contention. She'd learned the futility of imposing her will upon a man so willful. And she loved him too much to make him hate her.

Separating herself from him made her feel as though she'd reached into her body and ripped out her heart. How long could she endure this constant ache of longing and worry, and the hollowness in her breast?

She must look to others for support. And Tante Douce, a sturdy prop and a fount of Jersiaise wisdom, waited for her at the castle. Cecelia and Daniel, Emrys Jones and Andrew Searle were also there.

A serving maid delivered her food. She'd never felt less like eating but made the effort. The cheese compared unfavorably to Double Bevington. Her partisanship made her smile. *Ouidgia,* she did belong in Gloucestershire.

A gentleman traveler with a valise and portfolio intruded on her privacy and took possession of a corner table. He ignored her, bowing his rusty head over the bill of fare.

"Fingal Moncrieff," she cried in belated recognition.

He looked up. "Sophia Pinnock? Forgive me—Lady Bevington. What are you doing here?"

"Awaiting a change of horses. I've been at Chiswick and now return to the castle. And you?"

"I come from Corsham Court, where I was called in by John Nash—my employer. We met through his association with Repton. I stopped here to deliver a set of plans to a Mr. Hadlett at Faringdon House."

"Join me," she invited him. "We can't converse easily from such a distance."

Her cordiality evidently caught him off guard, but he transferred his belongings to her table and took the chair across from hers. "How much have heard about my rift with Repton?"

"Not a thing. What caused it?"

"A difference of opinion. 'Twas your fault. You infected him with your ridiculous theories about formal garden styles. I don't mean to say he's completely rejected the naturalistic landscape. But he displays a new reluctance to knock down balustraded terraces and garden walls. He even says there may be a place for arbors and statuary—in certain instances."

Sophie was more flattered than angry to hear that her former professional rival had appropriated her philosophies. In fact, she'd be delighted to have Repton actively promoting and popularizing them.

"I think it's an absurdity," he went on. "But as you pointed out that day at Clifton, fashion is fickle. Who's to say these notions won't catch on? He and Nash are both enamored of Gothic embellishment, all the rage now. For the planned extension to the north facade of Corsham, they've concocted the most elaborate mix of turrets and battlements and oriels. It puts your Bevington Castle to shame. Here, have a look."

He opened his portfolio to show her the architectural renderings.

When she failed to make any comment, he said, "You may be perfectly frank, it's not my design. Have you ever seen such a pastiche?"

"So many elements vying for attention," she responded. "Will this stylish house require a modern garden?"

"That's for Repton to decree." He tucked away the Corsham plans, and removed the ones he'd produced for Faringdon House. "A simple structural alteration. The house isn't yet two decades old, not important enough to warrant the attention my illustrious employer."

His interaction with more prominent architects had taught him humility, and Sophie liked him the better for it. She felt an inexplicable sense of comradeship. They had never been friends but had worked closely together, exchanging ideas and arguing over concepts. And he was a lasting link with Tobias.

The servant reappeared and announced that her post chaise was ready.

She rose, gathering up her reticule. "I must be on my way, to reach Cirencester by nightfall."

"The Royal Oak?" he quizzed her, and she nodded. "'Twas there we had our parting of the ways. I heartily wish your ladyship Godspeed. And should you ever require a garden folly, or something similar, do keep me in mind."

"I will," she said, and meant it.

She climbed into her conveyance feeling refreshed and rather more optimistic. She even dared to hope that Cassian might have abandoned his mysterious unnamed visitor to follow her.

Her night at Cirencester was peaceful. In the morning she darted into a toyshop to purchase a present for Daniel before continuing her journey deep into Gloucestershire. From several miles away she caught her first glimpse of the castle, its distant towers highlighted by a blazing midday sun.

Her hired coach missed the turning, rolling past the long avenue of oaks straight into the village. The driver's mistake convinced Sophie that an entrance lodge, or a pair of them, was needed to mark the drive. Each earl had left his stamp on the property, why shouldn't Cassian? His immediate predecessor had added the cottage *ornée* in the wood—picturesque, though hardly a healthy dwelling for a consumptive. As tenant of the smart lodge she now envisioned, Andrew Searle would be far more comfortable than he was living in the wood.

Fingal Moncrieff could draw up the plans. A compact building of Bevington stone, with crenellations around the roof and arched gothic windows to mimic the castle's architecture.

After paying her coachman and post-boys, she deposited

her *baheur* under the gatehouse arch and crossed the courtyard. Home—as she'd informed Cassian in her note, the place she truly belonged.

In the great hall she found Cecelia seated at the long trestle table, waving off Mrs. Harvey and a steaming cup of tea. She struggled to her feet, crying, "Sophie—thank goodness, I never needed you more! Where's my brother?"

"He stayed behind." She wasn't greatly surprised by this frantic greeting—Cecelia was a magnet for crisis. With calm deliberation, she untied the ribbons of her bonnet and took it off. "Is there trouble here?"

"Daniel has gone missing. We've looked all over—in the cellars and the garrets, the keep tower. Even the dungeon. Your aunt is wonderful, she—"

"When did you last see him?"

"At breakfast," Cecelia replied. "At least three hours ago."

"My lady," the housekeeper interjected, "perhaps you should drink this?"

"Not now, Mrs. Harvey. You may leave us," Sophie told her, reasserting her habit of command.

After the woman retreated, Cecelia continued, "The grooms and gardeners have scoured the grounds, to no avail. Sophie, I fear he's been abducted."

She couldn't help but laugh at this most absurd of possibilities. "By whom?"

"His father."

Her head jerked up. Cecelia couldn't be referring to Cassian. "I don't understand. He has no father."

Cecelia drooped onto a wooden seat and gripped the table edge. "How we've deceived you, Cass and I. He was desperate to tell you the whole truth, but I wouldn't allow it. I trusted no one—not even you. And now you're such a sister to me, I wish I had done."

"I wish it, too," said Sophie. "Who is Daniel's father?"

"His name is Michael. He's a baronet. Years ago he was our great friend. We began as social acquaintances and became lovers. Shameful, I know. And he had a wife. When I realized there was going to be a child, I told my brother. You can imagine his reaction."

Fury and outrage, thought Sophie. And he must have been terribly concerned about his sister's reputation, and her state of mind.

"There was a duel. The very next day we sailed for Portugal."

When Cecelia paused, Sophie said, "And there you created the myth of Senhor Fonseca."

"We didn't need to, we really knew him. He sold his *palácio* to Cass and emigrated to Brazil to live off the proceeds. Halfway across the ocean, his ship went down. It was my brother's idea to declare we'd been wed before his departure, to conceal my child's illegitimacy if ever we returned to England. I was sick, heartbroken—I agreed to everything."

"Naturellement," said Sophie.

"It was a difficult birth. I thought I was dying, and my son was so tiny I didn't expect him to live. We had him christened right away, and recorded his surname as Fonseca. The wet-nurse and Luis Costa were witnesses—godparents. That was February of '91."

"Luis knew your marriage was a falsehood?"

Cecelia nodded. "It's why he was murdered, either by Sir Michael Tait or a hired assassin. We've no idea how the baronet learned about Daniel's existence, or exactly what he knows.

That's why Cass is meeting with him—to prevent blackmail."

"You mean to say the man who visited Cassian at my house yesterday is a murderer, who once tried to kill him in a duel? *Sécours dé grace,* I was mad to leave him." Sophie put her fist to her mouth, gnawing the skin stretched taut over her knuckles. "His temper—he's such a hot-head. *Oh, las,* I cannot let myself think such a thing. I won't."

Somehow she had to stifle her alarm. "I'll look for Daniel," she decided. "He wandered away, there's no doubt of it. Did anyone search the deer park? This terrible man you accuse of abducting your son is far away."

With Cassian.

"He sent someone here," Cecelia insisted. "Very likely the same person who killed Luis. Oh, Sophie, what shall I do?"

She gripped the weeping woman's hunched shoulders. "Don't give in to despair, you'll make yourself ill. Go to the pianoforte and choose which piece of music you'll teach Daniel next. Tell the cook to make up a batch of those little cakes he likes. He'll be ravenous after his long ramble."

Cecelia blotted her watery blue eyes with a lace handkerchief. "Someday I hope to be as strong as you. I'm weak, and always have been. A slave to my emotions."

Sophie pressed her lips together to hold back a sharp reply. She was also under siege from emotion, her feelings were beyond description. Her husband could be dead, or dying. Out of ignorance, she had abandoned him to his fate.

Guilt about his deception, not a murder, must have prompted his reliance on opium. All this time he'd kept her in the dark, thwarting her efforts to understand him.

Bein seux, she reminded herself, she'd kept a secret from him. And if it had also contributed to his dependence on the drug, the damage she'd done could be irreparable.

"I'll return soon," she said, freeing her hand from Cecelia's grateful clasp. "With your son."

The only living creatures she spied in the woodland were the shy deer and the cheeky red squirrels darting from tree to tree. She heard the birds singing high above, and saw the iridescent blue flash as the kingfisher dove for his choice fishing place along the stream.

"Daniel!" she called, at every twist in the path.

She stopped at Andrew Searle's cottage to find out whether he'd noticed the child passing by. The door was hanging open, and she peeked inside.

The tattered curtains were drawn, shutting out the light, but not enough to hide the disarray. A blanket lay on the floor, and the bed sheets were rumpled. A jumble of scattered papers and stacks of books covered the table. Sophie spied the snuffbox amidst the clutter.

Thinking the poet might be in the loft above, she went inside and called up the stairway, "Mr. Searle, are you there?"

There was no reply. Again her gaze swept across the table. A small blue bottle anchored several loose papers.

Into her head popped the words Andrew Searle had written: *Last night Cass produced a vial of Bristol glass, assuring me that its contents would soothe my pains . . . .* Did he also rely on laudanum to relieve the symptoms of consumption?

She attempted to restore order to the scattered pages. Drafts of poems, mostly, produced by a gloomy mind. None of them were familiar to her, or finished. She spotted the memorandum book filled with extracts from his diary. Beside it was a similar volume. It might present a more complete picture of her husband's malady.

The initial entry described a woman who visited Searle by night. She lived in the castle, and had chestnut hair and brown eyes. She came to his bed, naked and willing. He felt alive only when his rigid flesh entered her welcoming body—

She was breaching his privacy—but she'd read enough to understand that he had written about her. Curiosity won out over her scruples, and she read on. Beneath the last paragraph he'd scrawled a notation: *This dream followed a dose of two hundred grains of opium.*

Turning the page, she found an account of another imagined lustful encounter, with an identical footnote. This, she realized, was his dream diary. Even more alarming than the poet's passionate obsession with her was the discovery of his regular and extravagant use of opium.

Sophie sorted through the other books on the table. Some she recognized—his well-thumbed edition of Milton, his philosophical essay, *Sonnets by Various Authors*, with Andrew Searle included. With a trembling hand she seized a calf-bound volume that turned out to be exactly what she wanted, and dreaded: a genuine diary.

Luis had disappeared late in March. Swiftly she scanned the entries for that month, turning the pages so carelessly she nearly tore them.

An accident. It shouldn't have happened. At dusk, on my way back from the village apothecary, I found him among the roses. The cake of opium was in my pocket. He babbled to me about Cass, frightened about some act of disobedience connected to that grim Welshman. In my eagerness to pursue the experiment, I offered to share my treasure. I repeated what Cass used to say, that it soothes all suffering. With my penknife I divided the sublime morsel. I licked away the grains clinging to the metal, and fed him a sizeable lump.

He remained sensible for a time. After he collapsed, his breathing slowed. He felt no pain. His pulse stilled.

I dared not leave the corpse there to be discovered. I took a shovel from the stables, unseen, and chose a place where the ground was soft enough to dig deep. It took me half the night. I laid him in the ditch and filled it in.

When I sat down to write this, I was drenched in sweat.

And still I know not exactly how much pure opium can safely be consumed.

Sophie read on, hoping to learn precisely when Searle had decided to fabricate evidence against the earl to deflect suspicion from himself.

"Sophie! You've come back to me."

She looked up. The man responsible for Luis Costa's death was standing in the doorway, watching her. Relief at obtaining proof of her husband's innocence was crowded out by panic.

"This castle of yours lies at a most inconvenient distance from town."

Cass transferred his gaze from the carriage window to the scarred face across from him. "I do not find it so. One hundred and fifteen miles is as close to London as I care to live."

Sir Michael Tait raised his brows. "Unfathomable. And

what is Cecelia's opinion?"

"You must ask. For her, country living is a novelty. I suspect she misses the Clifton shops."

"You saw Oakes Court once. Will she like it? Guildford has shops. Of course, she'd be near enough to town that she could take the carriage to Piccadilly whenever she pleased."

Cass frowned. "You forget, to Cecelia you're the enemy."

At the outset of their journey, Cass had doubted that their old friendship could ever be revived. But after a long night on the road, and part of another day, they'd made progress. Together they attacked and solved the problem of when and how to inform Daniel that his father was living. He was too young, they agreed, to comprehend his parents' tormented history. That disclosure must wait until he was older.

Tait's anticipation of his impending introduction to his six-year old son was almost endearing. Throughout the final leg of the trip he pelted Cass with questions that he'd answered at the outset: how tall was Daniel, was he really so clever, did he resemble his mother?

"I told you. He's got her black hair and blue eyes. But he's cursed with your nose and jaw."

"Cursed with—you are a hardhearted devil." But he smiled, as if aware that the teasing was proof that a particle of affection had survived years of hatred and mistrust.

On their arrival at the castle, they learned of Daniel's lengthy absence—and the curious circumstances surrounding his return. Leading them through the warren of upstairs rooms, Bitton explained that Emrys Jones had discovered the missing child.

"All curled up inside that cave in the wall, he was," the butler said. "Jones thought to look for him there, and a good thing. Dr. Jenner is examining the boy now."

"Is he injured?" asked Cass.

"He's not in his right mind. The doctor will tell your lordship what's amiss."

Cass entered the sickroom, followed by the baronet. His wife's aunt bathed the patient's legs with a damp cloth. The doctor, spectacles perched on his nose, consulted a reference book.

Cecelia sat at the head of the small bed, gripping her son's hand. The puppy lay curled in her lap, sleeping. Her expression changed from worry to amazement to fear, and she whispered, "Michael."

"Be easy," Cass said soothingly. "He comes in friendship, to see the child."

Dr. Jenner came forward. "Lord Bevington, although this case is serious I do not despair of pulling him through. If only he could tell us what brought on this strange and sudden illness."

Daniel's black head moved back and forth on the pillow, and he mumbled incoherently.

"All we can get out of him is that he drank something given him by Mr. Searle."

Cass went to the bed and gazed down at his nephew. "Laudanum."

The doctor looked up, frowning. "An opiate? But why would Searle dispense it?"

"I mean to find out, you may be sure."

"Laudanum, you say?"

"Drew has been taking it for years."

The physician addressed the butler, hovering outside, "My good man, tell the kitchen maid to brew a pot of strong coffee, and fetch it here as quick as you can."

Without replying, Bitton hurried away.

"I gather it's meant for Daniel. I could use a cup myself," Cass said.

"This child needs a dose of nettle tea," Tante Douce insisted. "On Jersey, *thé d'orti* is the sovereign remedy for purifying the blood."

Sir Michael Tait was pensively eyeing Daniel's rocking horse. He pressed down on the painted head, setting it in motion.

Cecelia deposited the pup on her son's bed and moved to her former lover. "Your face," she said softly. "Cass told me you were changed."

"Only my looks, Cecelia. Not my heart."

"Oh, Michael. Don't—not now. If my son should die—"

"He won't," Dr. Jenner declared, bending over the small figure.

"So precious to me," Cecelia said through her tears.

"I'm glad," Tait murmured. "Precious to me also. Both of you."

Cass averted his gaze from this affecting reunion.

He puzzled over why the crowded room seemed so very empty. When he found the answer, he jumped to his feet, startling everyone.

"Where is Sophie?"

She shut the diary.

"You came back to me," Andrew Searle repeated. "I knew you would. How long I've waited for this day—dreamed of it."

He slurred his words.

"I'm looking for Daniel."

"Isn't here. Took him away."

"*You* took him? Where?"

He shook his head. "Not the heir. He can't be. Got rid of him—to make sure."

She couldn't reason with him, the drug had addled his senses. "Please take me to Daniel. I want to see him."

"No. All is as it should be. You returned to me. I shall pour my seed into you, to swell and grow. My son will be a lord, he will inherit the castle. I've seen him in my visions."

"Mr. Searle," she said as calmly as she could, "you are unwell. Let me fetch Dr. Jenner from Berkeley."

When she inched toward the door he darted forward, seizing her arm. "We must lie together *now,* Sophie. Me on top and you beneath." As she struggled against him, he continued, "You will kiss and touch me, as you do in the night, every night. I'll make you see—I can give you a dream." He reached for the blue bottle.

"*Nânnîn!*" she cried, realizing what he meant to do. "I won't drink it!"

"You must," he insisted. "Receive it from my lips." He poured the laudanum into his mouth, and bent his head to bestow a kiss

CHAPTER 23

To regions where, in spite of sin and woe,
Traces of Eden are still seen below.

~William Cowper

*F*ailing to find Sophie in her rooms, or any sign that she'd recently been there, Cass rushed down the spiral stair of the gatehouse. Her little leather trunk lay outside on the cobbles. With rising anxiety, he trod every inch of the long terraces.

Emrys Jones was the only person in the gardens. He stood on his ladder, applying mortar to a gap in the wall. "To keep that weasel out," he explained. "How fares the little lad?"

"The doctor is confident of a recovery." As ever, Cass felt as awkward in the man's presence but gratitude outweighed prejudice. "I thank you, Jones. If you hadn't found my nephew—" He let his silence convey his meaning. After describing how Andrew Searle had drugged Daniel, he asked, "Have you seen her ladyship?"

"Nay, my lord." The Welshman's thin lips stretched in a

smile. "Ne'er say she's gone missing too."

"So it appears. She's not in the house. She must be searching for Daniel still. Can I enlist your aid? You know these grounds better than I. We ought to find her—immediately."

The gardener promptly descended from his perch. "Shall we begin by looking in the place where I found the boy?"

They hurried along the laburnum arch, and passed the stone stag Sophie had rescued, standing at the entrance to the bowling green. Cass waited impatiently outside the cavern while the nimble Welshman climbed inside.

"Empty," Jones reported as he emerged, wiping his soiled hands on his breeches.

Together they returned to the shrubbery walk and sped through the rose garden, where the long-tailed white peacock paraded across the grass, pausing occasionally to preen.

If I can locate my wife, Cass thought, I'll let her keep those aggravating birds, and all their damned chicks.

Jones was the first to reach the iron gate at the rear of the pavilion. Opening it, he let Cass could precede him into the wilderness.

Sophie twisted frantically in her effort to avoid Andrew Searle's lips. Liquid coursed down her cheek and neck.

He held the bottle to her mouth. "Drink—you will. For me!"

She knocked it out of his hand. His attention stayed with the bottle, which shattered against the floorboards. Sophie slipped from his slackened embrace and raced for the door.

Several narrow tracks wound through the wood, and she chose the one leading to the garden gate. Her long skirts were troublesome and the ground was uneven—she must be careful, lest she trip and fall. Searle was close behind, she heard him gasping and stumbling as he pursued her.

"Sophie, come back to me!"

Miraculously, the gate stood open. She looked back—Searle's face was contorted by his exertion. She prayed he lacked the strength for a protracted chase.

Briefly she paused beneath the pavilion's porch, uncertain whether it might serve as a sanctuary—or become a trap.

She plunged past the knot gardens and flew through her rose bower, frightening the white peafowl. Searle was gaining on her—and she hadn't yet reached the terrace steps.

She halted behind the shielding hedges of the shrubbery walk to gather her wits.

Perhaps, she thought wildly, the intricate landscape I preserved will be my salvation.

Spying a ladder against the wall, she scrambled up. The ledge at the top was a foot wide, narrower where the stones had fallen away. She crouched down and moved slowly forward, impeded by the gaps and her voluminous skirts. She hadn't enough breath to shout for help. The only sound she produced was a whimper of pain when a protruding flint cut her palm.

Why hadn't anyone noticed her? Emrys Jones must be about. Or the Parham boys. Or any servant gazing out of a window.

"Sophie!"

He was searching for her among the topiaries. Because of the tall hedge, she couldn't see him.

Awkwardly she climbed to her feet.

"Sophie, be careful! Don't fall!"

That warning came from Cassian—safely home again!

Searle was scrambling up the ladder.

From below, her husband tugged his legs, pulling him down, prying away the hands that clenched the rungs.

"Damn you, she's mine!" raved Searle. "You stole her from me!"

"Drew, you know that's not true."

With a surge of strength, the poet freed himself. Hobbling across the bridge, he called out, "If I cannot have her, I do not want to live." He leaped into the canal.

Sophie held her breath as the tawny head sank beneath the surface.

Cass removed his coat and dove in after his friend.

"Step you down, my lady."

The Welshman's quiet, insistent voice momentarily pulled her attention from the violent struggle taking place in the water. Holding the ladder steady, he helped her to descend.

"Daniel," she gasped, "was drugged."

"The lad is being tended to," he assured her. "The doctor says he'll recover."

Her heart skipped as she watched Cassian's struggle to rescue his treacherous friend, risking his life for the one who had killed his valet, drugged his nephew, and schemed to ravish his wife.

Searle flailed his arms, sputtering curses. "Damn you, let me go! I wish to die!"

"We'll both drown if you keep fighting me."

Suddenly Searle cease his struggle. His face fell slack and his mad expression faded. His eyelids drooped.

Sophie stood out of the way while Cassian and Emrys Jones hoisted the limp body out of the water and laid it on the grass. She knelt down to test Searle's breathing and pulse. "He's unconscious," she reported. "Emrys, give me your apron to wrap him in, for we must keep him warm. Find the doctor, tell him bring Mrs. Fonseca's smelling salts."

Cassian, dripping water, helped her cover his friend's inert body with the green woolen fabric. Then he held out his arms to her.

Sophie pressed her cheek against his soaked shirt. "He killed Luis, by accident. But he intended to murder Daniel." She looked into his face. "He persuaded me that you were addicted to laudanum. And worse, that you disposed of Luis so I wouldn't find out Daniel was your son."

"Good God." He stared at her blankly. "You believed him?"

"Until today."

"You believed him," he repeated. "Yet you stayed with me, and shared my bed. Here and at Chiswick. And all the while you thought me guilty of murder?"

"I was determined to cure you. I meant to take you away to Jersey, to make you abandon that cursed drug. It was to bring you to senses that I came back to Bevington."

The lips that touched hers were so cold. Worried, she said, "Cassian, you must get out of these clothes."

Andrew Searle twitched. He coughed repeatedly.

"Water in his lungs," said Cassian, kneeling down.

When the physician arrived on the scene, he waved a vial beneath the poet's nose. "This gentleman is dangerous to himself, my lord, if opium has turned him mad."

"Place him in the Bristol asylum. A fearsome place, but better than hanging."

"Indeed. Iron bars and a straight-waistcoat are preferable to the noose."

A crowd had gathered—gardeners, grooms, and servants.

Dr. Jenner sent one of them to the house to fetch scissors and a sheet, which he cut into long strips.

"Must you tie him?" asked Cassian.

"It will calm him. While we wait for my nephew Henry to arrive, we'll sit him down by the kitchen fire. And he'll need dry clothes."

Sophie gripped her husband's hand while Dr. Jenner wound the bands of linen around the poet's body.

"Should've let me die," Searle wailed as he was taken away.

Looking down at Sophie, Cassian said gently, "Don't cry, my handkerchief is as soaked as the rest of me. We've done all we can for Drew, but later we shall do more. I can't save him from the asylum, but I'll see that he's not mistreated."

Leading her to the house, he described Cecelia's meeting with Daniel's father.

"Tait cares for her still. Her hatred, I gather, was love soured by circumstances. He means to sweeten it again."

In the seclusion of their dressing room Sophie helped him remove his soggy garments. She struggled to unfasten the buckles at the knees of his breeches and slipped them off. His small clothes posed no difficulty at all.

He handed her his silver watch. "Ruined. No matter, it has no sentimental value."

"I'll give you another," she offered. "A gold one."

"With your miniature fitted into the cover, so I can keep you by me always. After you fled Chiswick yesterday, I cast away my stupid jealousy. Sophie, I honor your Tobias for being a fine husband. If he'd made you miserable, you wouldn't have contemplated a second marriage. I'm therefore in his debt."

"Cassian." She perched on the low chest, nervously threading his watch-chain through her fingers. "Now that your secrets have all come out, it's time you knew mine. If I don't share them, they'll forever impair true intimacy between us."

Cass very nearly asked her to wait till after an immediate bout of intimacy—desire for her was heating his blood. But confession, he perceived, was of greater importance to her.

"My life with Tobias was no paradise. For him I had to become an Englishwoman, to leave off my Jèrriais expressions and island habits. That was hardly a difficulty, for I was young and adaptable and eager to please him. We knew much happiness together. But when he sickened, we learned the condition of his heart. During his last years we could not—" She halted. "His doctor warned us never to—" Again she paused. "He advised against what husband and wife naturally do. We both suffered. He felt less of a man, and I was prevented from bearing his child. I had my painting and my designs and a house to manage, but it was no consolation for what I lacked. And to spare his feelings, and his pride, I feigned contentment."

"That was a generous pretense, Sophie."

"As well, I concealed my true opinions of his work. *Our* work. The plans I made for rolling parks and serpentine rivers and clumps of trees required the destruction of many fine gardens. I couldn't admit my regret, or reveal to anyone the misery it caused. I answered your summons because I needed the commission. And from the start, I dreaded ruining a landscape that to was well worth saving."

"That's no great secret. After you accepted my proposal, with your very next breath you asked permission to preserve these castle gardens." He smiled. "Your sins are not so great. Not in the eyes of a man who fought a duel, and made his sister out to be a widow when she'd never been a wife."

Lifting her head, she said, "I'm not finished. A number of the creations attributed to Tobias Pinnock are mine. To some extent we had always collaborated. As he grew weaker, I took on all his design work. He signed his name to my drawings. Together—with Fingal Moncrieff's compliance—we deceived our clients."

He sat down beside her. "I'm not shocked by that, either. You acted out of loyalty."

"Cassian, I am no less loyal to you. My love for you is unique, unaffected by what I felt for another man at a different time in my life. There are aspects of my character that you understand far better than Tobias. And qualities that he appreciated more than you ever will."

"Such as?" he probed, quite certain that he appreciated everything about her.

"My ability to apply sepia wash over pen and ink."

Well, he would concede that point. "You're correct. I can only admire your artistry as an observer, not a practitioner. But Sophie, it's not your gift for pen and ink drawing that interests me at this precise moment."

"No?"

"Not much. I crave a display of your other talents. Kiss me, Lady Bevington."

"Do you command it?"

Ah, there was the saucy smile he adored!

"Oui-dgia, as you might say yourself. Remember, you vowed to obey."

"I shall do it, then," she said with spirit, "but only because I want to." Framing his face with her hands, she pulled it down to meet her smiling mouth.

He did not resist. Her lips were soft and warm. He felt the

fullness of her breasts rising and falling against his bare chest, more and more erratically. When he could no longer bear the delicious torture, he swept her up in his arms and carried her to their bed.

EPILOGUE

'Tis she that to these gardens gave
That wondrous beauty which they have.

~Andrew Marvell

Her hands protected by thick leather gloves, Sophie set the thorn-covered shrub into the open ground. She spaded some dirt over the roots and pressed it down firmly to cover them. Reaching for the watering can, she added moisture to the hole. As she filled it in with more earth, she envisioned the arching canes that would fill the gap and spread outward along the wall—a living memorial to Luis Costa.

Echo and Rosa, ever interested in digging, came over to investigate. Sophie warned them not to disturb her newly planted rose.

Her task completed, she watched Cecelia and Sir Michael stroll through the arbors with their son. The baronet plucked a pink rose for his lady—*Quatre Saisons*, the fragrant damask rose famous for its repeated bloom. Now reconciled, the couple would soon marry.

Daniel ran to Sophie with a rose and presented it with a bow. "Put this in your hair."

"You must to do it." She held up her gloved hands helplessly.

"Permit me," her husband offered.

The child darted off as quickly as he'd come and rejoined his parents in the knot garden. The dogs, bored and neglected, chased after him.

Cassian tucked the flower in among Sophie's braids. "Did I tell you what Daniel said when told he's getting a cousin next spring?"

She shook her head.

"He expressed his hope Parham's lurcher bitch will whelp again, so the babe might have one of the pups."

"Another dog!" Sophie laughed. *"Bein seux,* that will keep that weasel away."

"What sort of rose have you planted here?"

"Rosa moschata plena. A late blooming musk, a vigorous climber, and very ancient. Luis once told me of his fondness for white roses." She removed her gloves and tossed them aside. As Cassian helped her to her feet she added wistfully, "I wish he could see the gardens as they look now."

"As always, you've achieved much in a brief time. How will you occupy yourself when this restoration is complete?"

Sophie shook her head at him. "We've a great deal more to do here, Emrys and I. Gardens are never really finished."

Cassian laughed. "So I'm discovering. Well, I once demanded that you make Bevington a show place, and that's precisely what you've done. Lady Bevington, you could set a fashion."

"Nânnîn, nobody has ever of me. I never achieved the fame of Humphry Repton or Capability Brown. Or Tobias."

"Wherever a countess leads, society must follow. If we open our gardens to visitors, you could prevail upon other landowners to preserve the formal grandeur of the past."

"You think I could?"

"My dearest Sophie," he answered tenderly, "I am confident that you can accomplish anything."

She rose on tiptoe to press a loving and grateful kiss upon his cheek.

"A paltry reward for my great faith in you," he teased. "Though we are married folk, with a child on the way, but we must demonstrate to my sister and her betrothed the proper mode of courtship in a rose bower. It was in this spot, you know, that you pledged to become my wife. Sophie?"

Lost in reverie, she asked, "Wouldn't this vista be improved if I added a garden seat to each of the arbors?"

"Yes, yes, you may have as many of them as you wish. And stone stags. And statues. And rose bushes." He took her into his arms. "Just remember you have a husband now, not a client, standing with you in this glorious garden."

"Tréjous," she assured him. "Always." Casting aside vague plans about benches and arbors, she concentrate all her talents on returning his kisses.

ACKNOWLEDGMENTS AND
HISTORICAL NOTE

Creating a novel is never a solitary effort, certainly not for this author. I must therefore acknowledge the people who assisted in the development of *The Proposal*.

First and foremost, I am grateful to my husband, with whom I discovered the splendid rooms and magical gardens of the Gloucestershire castle on which I modeled my fictional one. If he wearied of repeatedly exploring Berkeley and its environs, and so many other historic gardens, he was kind enough not to say so.

Abundant thanks to our friends Margot and Robert, for suggesting that first castle visit and companionship on subsequent ones. I'm forever grateful to them for generously sharing the many delights of Clifton village, truly a home away from home.

I'm grateful to my mother, a tireless gardener and rosarian, and to my father for demonstrating all the patience necessary in a gardener's spouse. With thanks to all those grandparents whose legacy to me was their passion for plants.

When writing *The Proposal* I became acquainted, through my research, with a famous Romantic poet, a celebrated landscape gardener, and a renowned Gloucestershire physician.

It is quite true that Samuel Taylor Coleridge was inspired to write his epic poem "The Rime of the Ancient Mariner" after a friend shared with him a disturbing nightmare. During his "honeymoon period" with laudanum he produced some of his finest verses, but in later years addiction wrecked his marriage and his health.

Debates about garden styles raged throughout the final decade of the 18th century, when painters, essayists, and poets publicized rival theories. Others did share my heroine's prejudice against Humphry Repton, though they were in the minority. Various accounts of his life and his own writings indicate that he was well-intentioned and not deliberately controversial. His transition from naturalistic to more formal designs did indeed occur in the late 1790's.

Dr. Edward Jenner's experiments and eventual success with his cowpox vaccine eventually eradicated the dreaded smallpox. Visitors to his residence at Berkeley, now the Jenner Museum, will learn how actively and selflessly he worked to develop and promote his procedure.

The experts assisting my research include Susan, a respected garden historian and landscape consultant, who provided helpful information in the earliest stages of this book. And I greatly appreciate the attentive staff at Westbury Court Gardens in Gloucestershire, Mottisfont Abbey Gardens in Hampshire, and London's Museum of Garden History in Lambeth.

I should add that many of the historic roses in the story thrive in my own garden—tending them was my favorite type of "research." The varieties known and preferred by my heroine—and by me—are unsurpassed in beauty, color, fragrance, and hardiness.

ABOUT MARGARET EVANS PORTER

Margaret Evans Porter is the award-winning author of eleven highly acclaimed historical and Regency novels, and publishes historical fiction as Margaret Porter. *A Pledge of Better Times,* her novel of England's royal court in the late 17th century, was released in 2015.

She studied British history in the U.K., returned to the U.S. to complete her theatre training, and subsequently worked in film and television. Margaret returns annually to Great Britain to research her books. She and her husband share their book-filled New England home with two lively dogs.

More information about her background and travels is available on her website, www.margaretevansporter.com.

CPSIA information can be obtained
at www.ICGtesting.com
Printed in the USA
LVHW04s2332160818
587183LV00003B/177/P